JAMES KOCHALKA

THE GLORKIAN WARRIOR EATS ADVENTURE PIE

:01

First Second

New York

FOR ELI & OLIVER
AND DECLAN & MARIPOSA!
(YOU CAN HEAR THEIR VOICES IN THE
GLORKIAN WARRIOR VIDEO GAME.)

VISIT GLORKIANWARRIOR.COM

:01
First Second
Copyright © 2015 by James Kochalka

Published by First Second
First Second is an imprint of Roaring Brook Press,
a division of Holtzbrinck Publishing Holdings Limited Partnership
175 Fifth Avenue, New York, New York 10010
All rights reserved

"Attract Mode" originally appeared in *The Devastator* №4

Cataloging-in-Publication Data is on file at the Library of Congress.

Paperback ISBN 978-1-62672-021-3
Hardcover ISBN 978-1-62672-133-3

First Second books may be purchased for business or promotional use. For information
on bulk purchases please contact Macmillan Corporate and Premium Sales
Department at (800) 221-7945 x5442 or by email at specialmarkets@macmillan.com.

First edition 2015
Book design by Colleen AF Venable

Printed in China by Macmillan Production (Asia) Ltd.,
Kowloon Bay, Hong Kong (supplier code 10)

Paperback: 10 9 8 7 6 5 4 3 2 1
Hardcover: 10 9 8 7 6 5 4 3 2 1

BY ART
WE LIVE

CHAPTER ONE

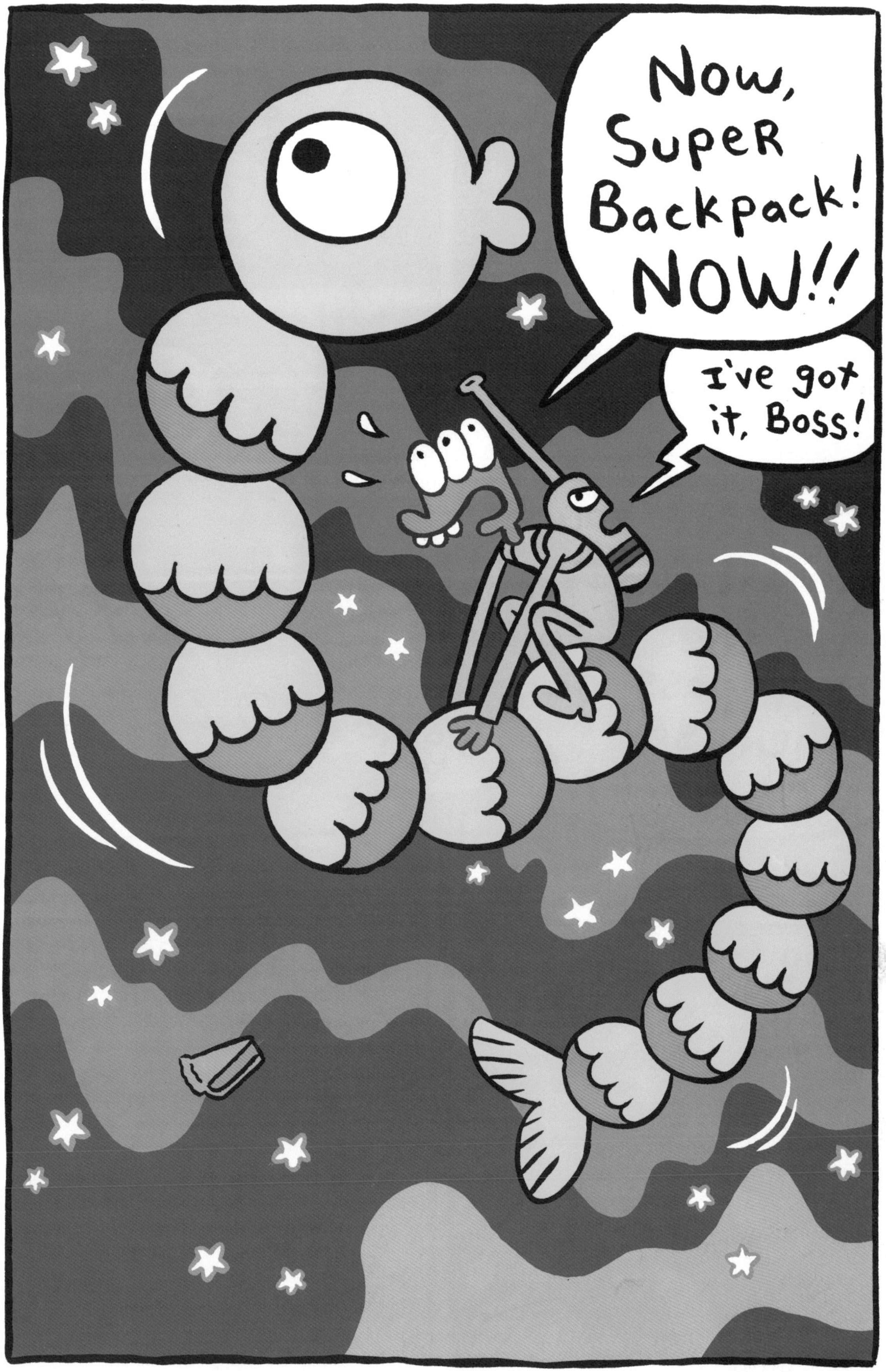
Now, Super Backpack! NOW!!
I've got it, Boss!

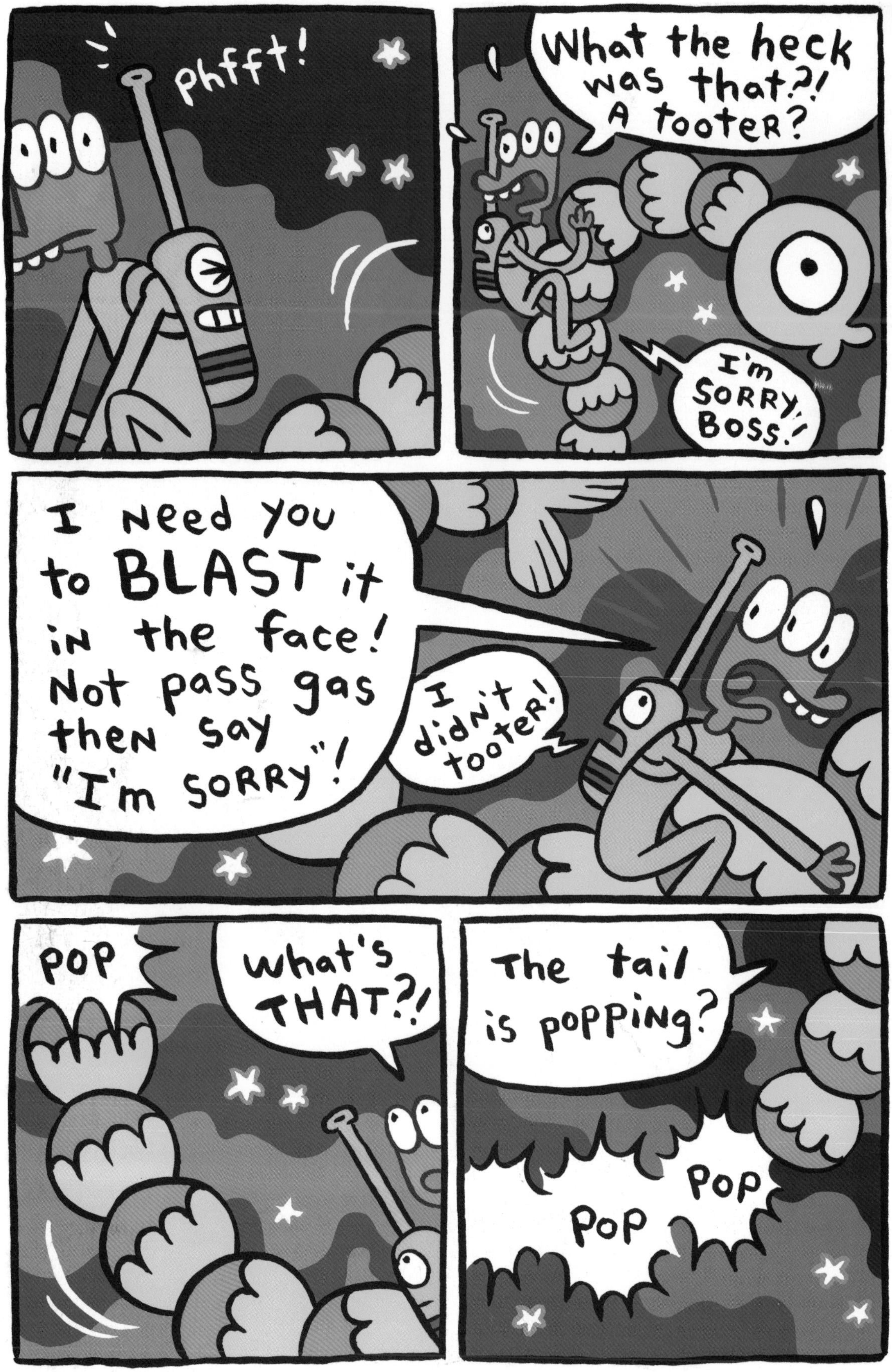
phfft!
What the heck was that?! A tooter?
I'm SORRY, BOSS.
I need you to BLAST it in the face! Not pass gas then say "I'm SORRY"!
I didn't tooter!
POP
What's THAT?!
The tail is popping?
POP
POP

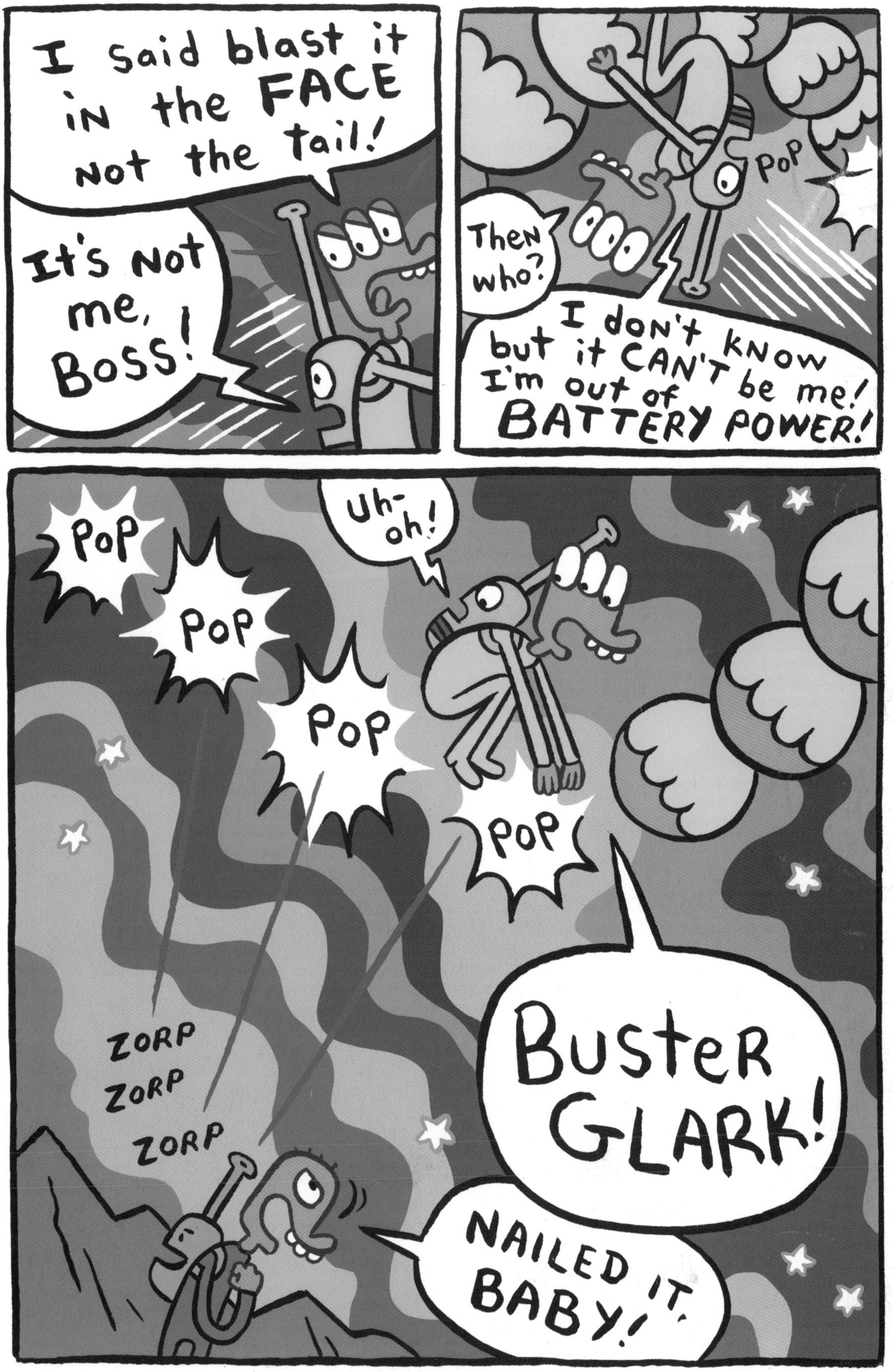

I said blast it in the FACE not the tail!
It's Not me, Boss!
PoP
Then who?
I don't know but it CAN'T be me! I'm out of BATTERY POWER!
Pop
Uh-oh!
PoP
PoP
PoP
ZORP
ZORP
ZORP
Buster GLARK!
NAILED IT, BABY!

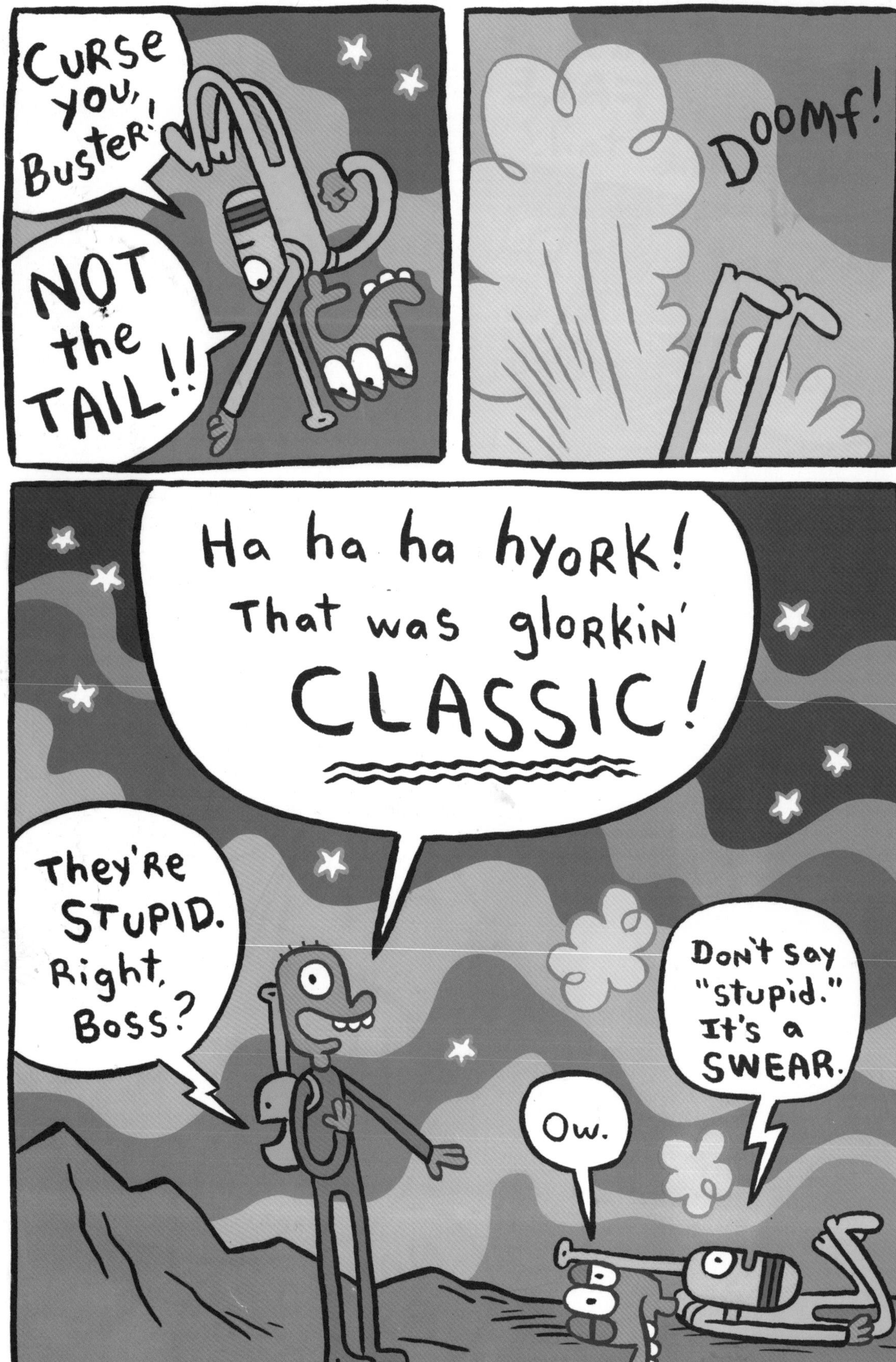
CURSE YOU, BUSTER!
NOT the TAIL!!
DOOMF!
Ha ha ha hyORK! That was glorkin' CLASSIC!
They're STUPID. Right, Boss?
Ow.
Don't say "stupid." It's a SWEAR.

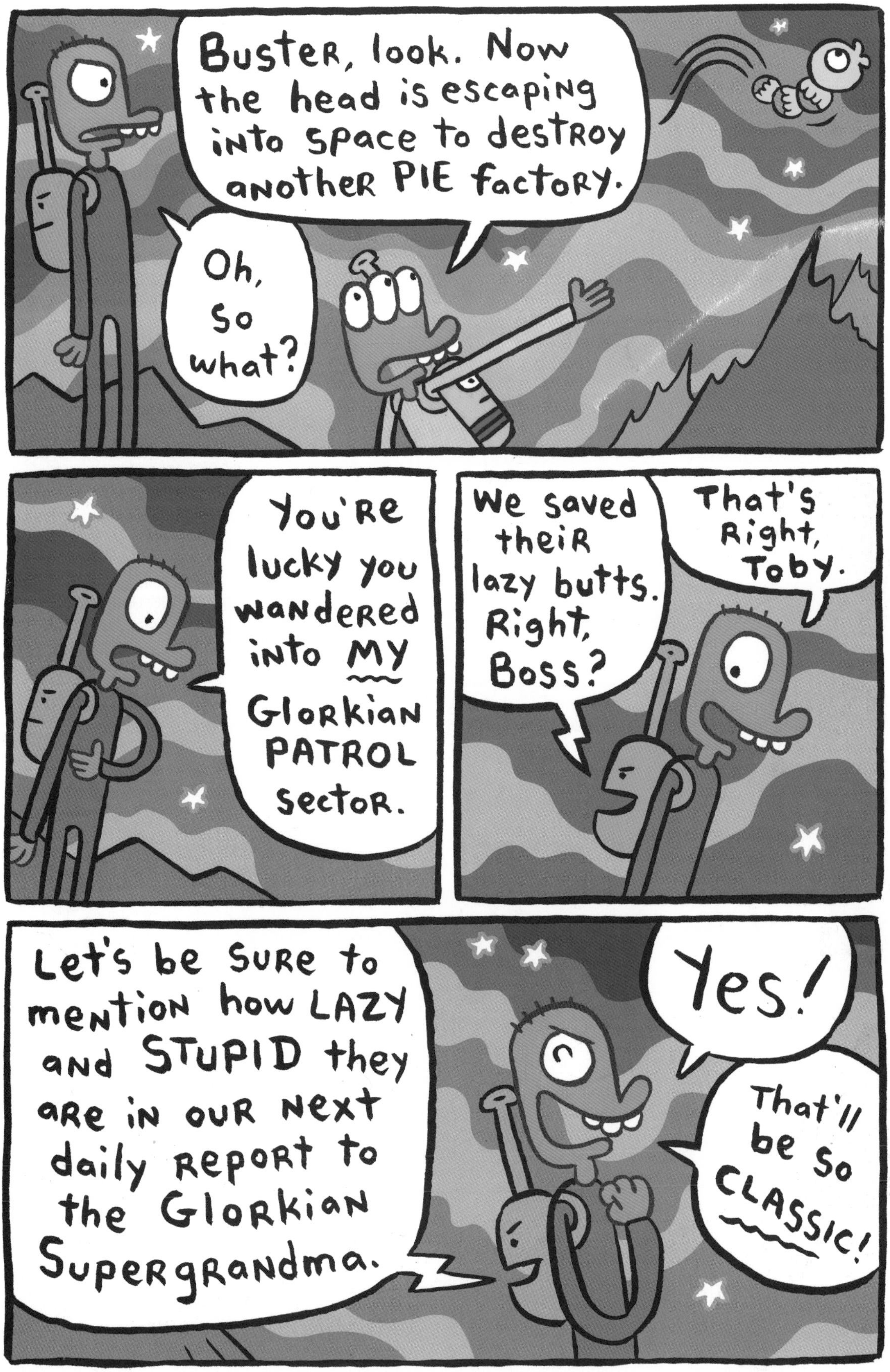
Buster, look. Now the head is escaping into space to destroy another PIE factory.
Oh, so what?
You're lucky you wandered into MY Glorkian PATROL sector.
We saved their lazy butts. Right, Boss?
That's Right, Toby.
Let's be sure to mention how LAZY and STUPID they are in our next daily report to the Glorkian Supergrandma.
Yes!
That'll be so CLASSIC!

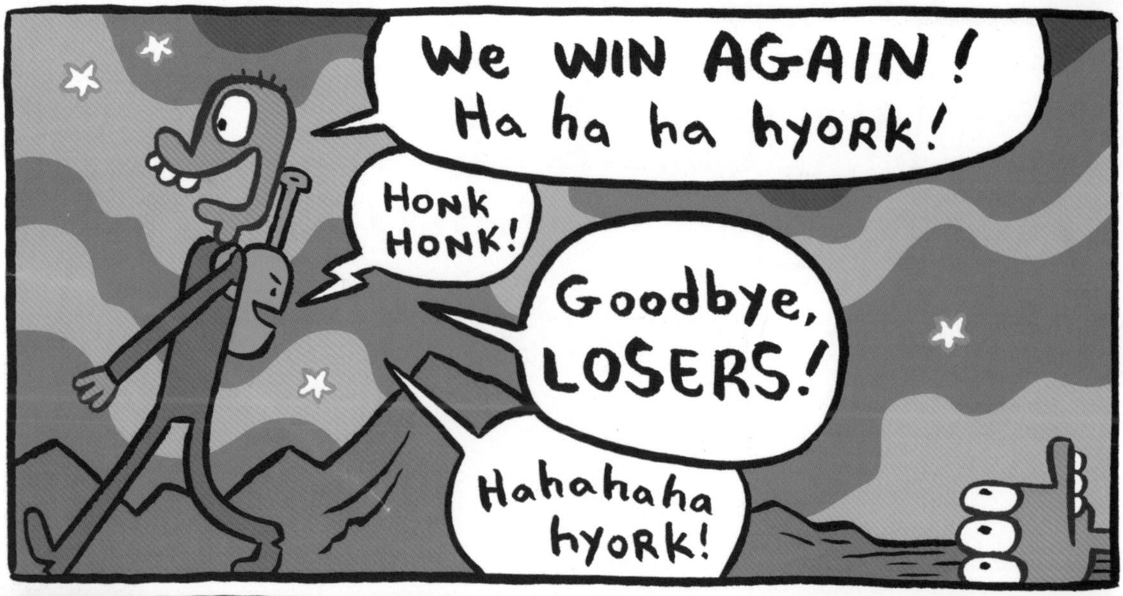
We WIN AGAIN! Ha ha ha hyork!
HONK HONK!
Goodbye, LOSERS!
Hahahaha hyork!

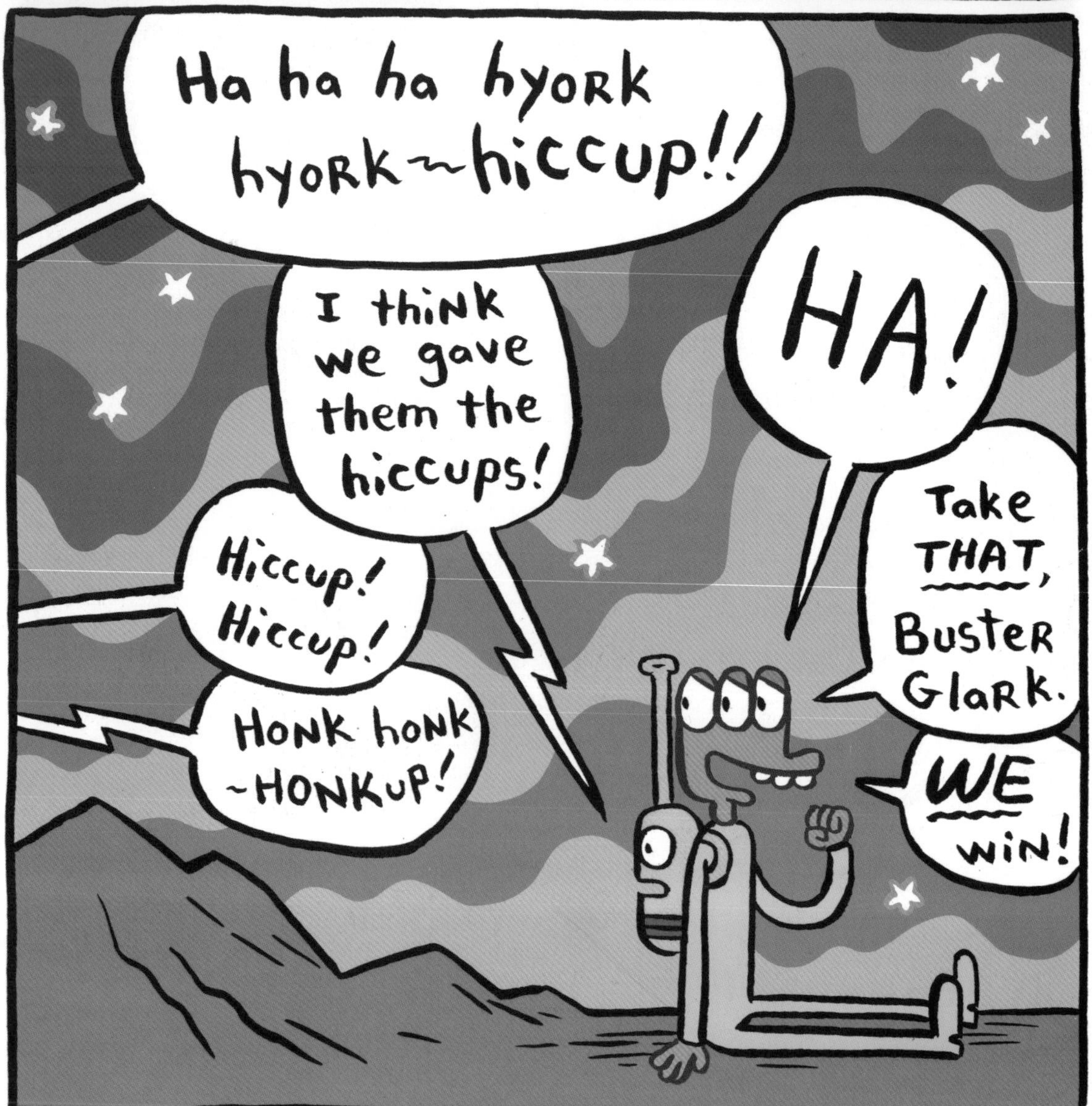
Ha ha ha hyork hyork~hiccup!!
I think we gave them the hiccups!
HA!
Hiccup! Hiccup!
HONK honk ~HONKUP!
Take THAT, Buster Glark.
WE win!

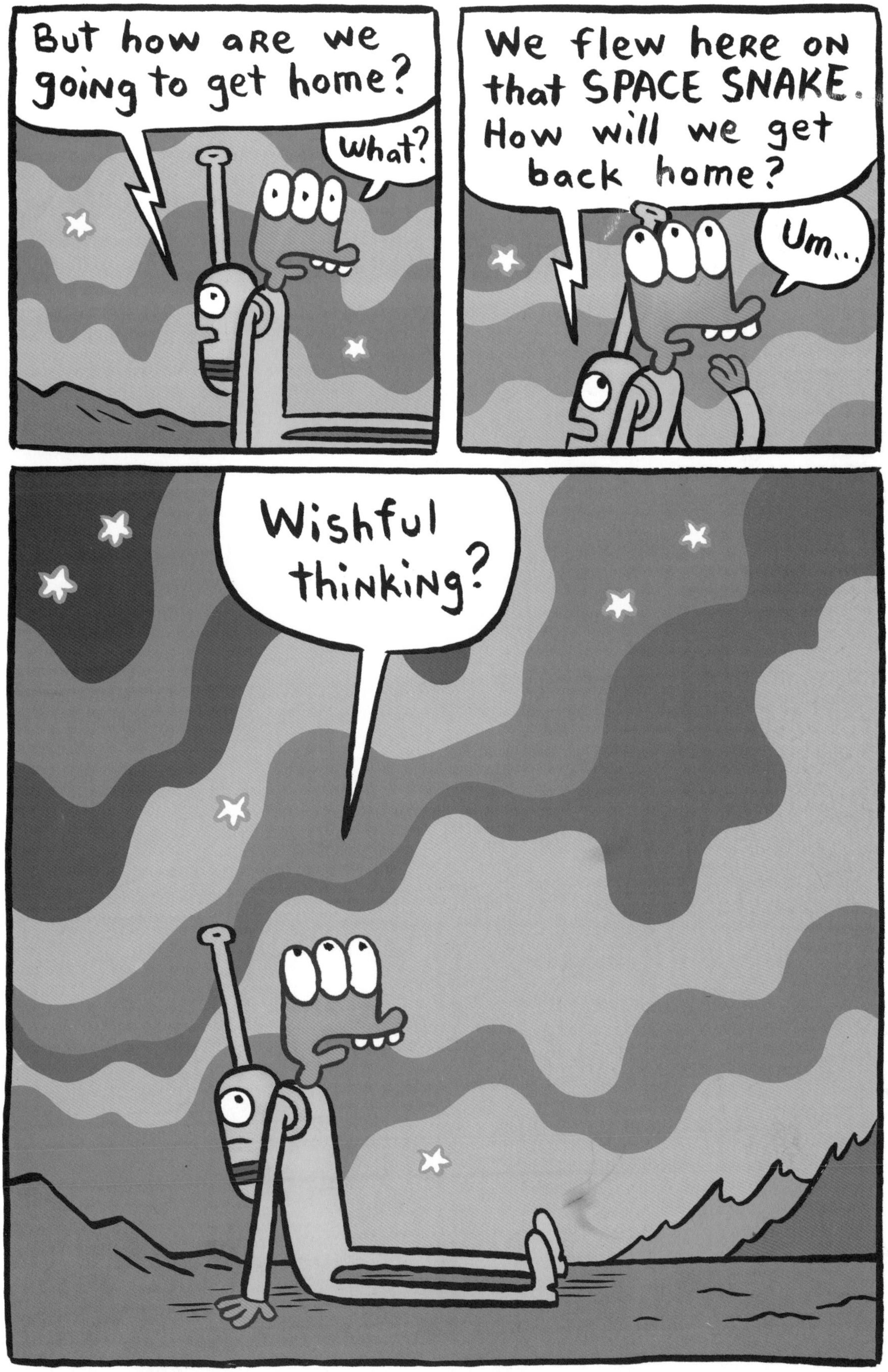

But how are we going to get home?
What?
We flew here on that SPACE SNAKE. How will we get back home?
Um...
Wishful thinking?

CHAPTER TWO

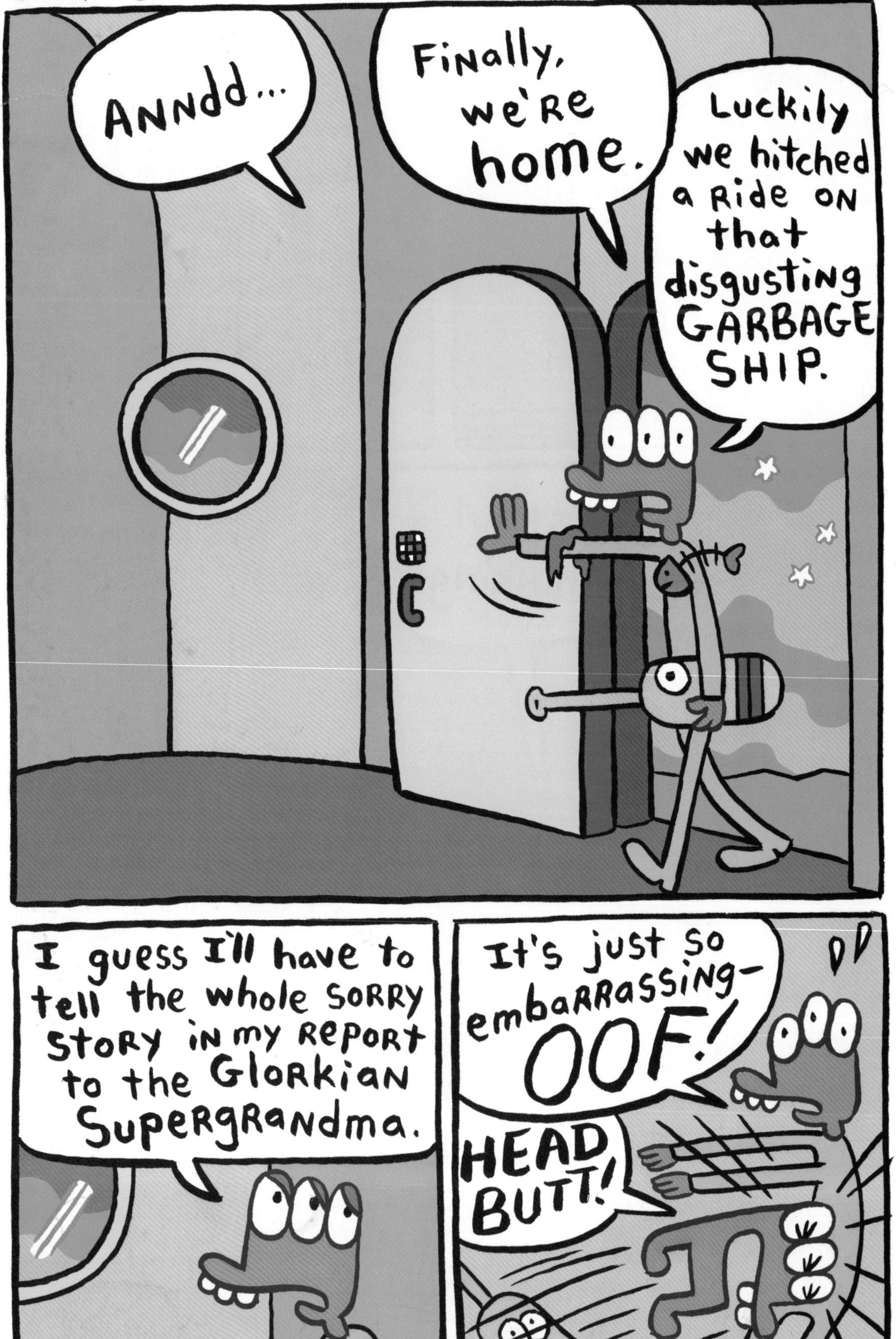

ANNdd...
Finally, we're home.
Luckily we hitched a Ride on that disgusting GARBAGE SHIP.
I guess I'll have to tell the whole SORRY STORY in my Report to the GlORkian SupergRandma.
It's just so embaRRASSiNg-
OOF!
HEAD BUTT!

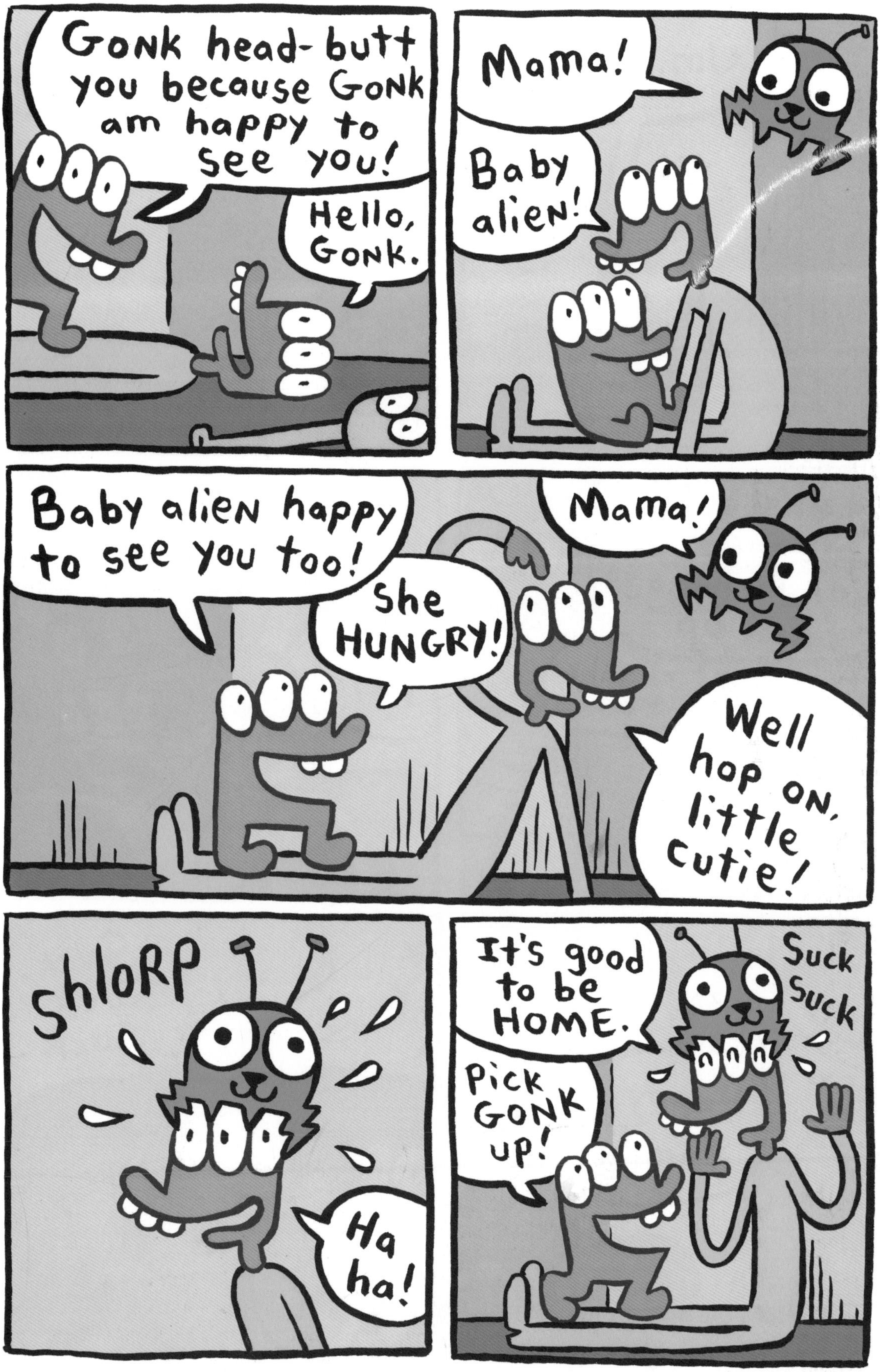
Gonk head-butt you because Gonk am happy to see you!
Hello, Gonk.
Mama!
Baby alien!
Baby alien happy to see you too!
She HUNGRY!
Mama!
Well hop on, little cutie!
SHLORP
Ha ha!
It's good to be HOME.
Suck Suck
Pick GONK up!

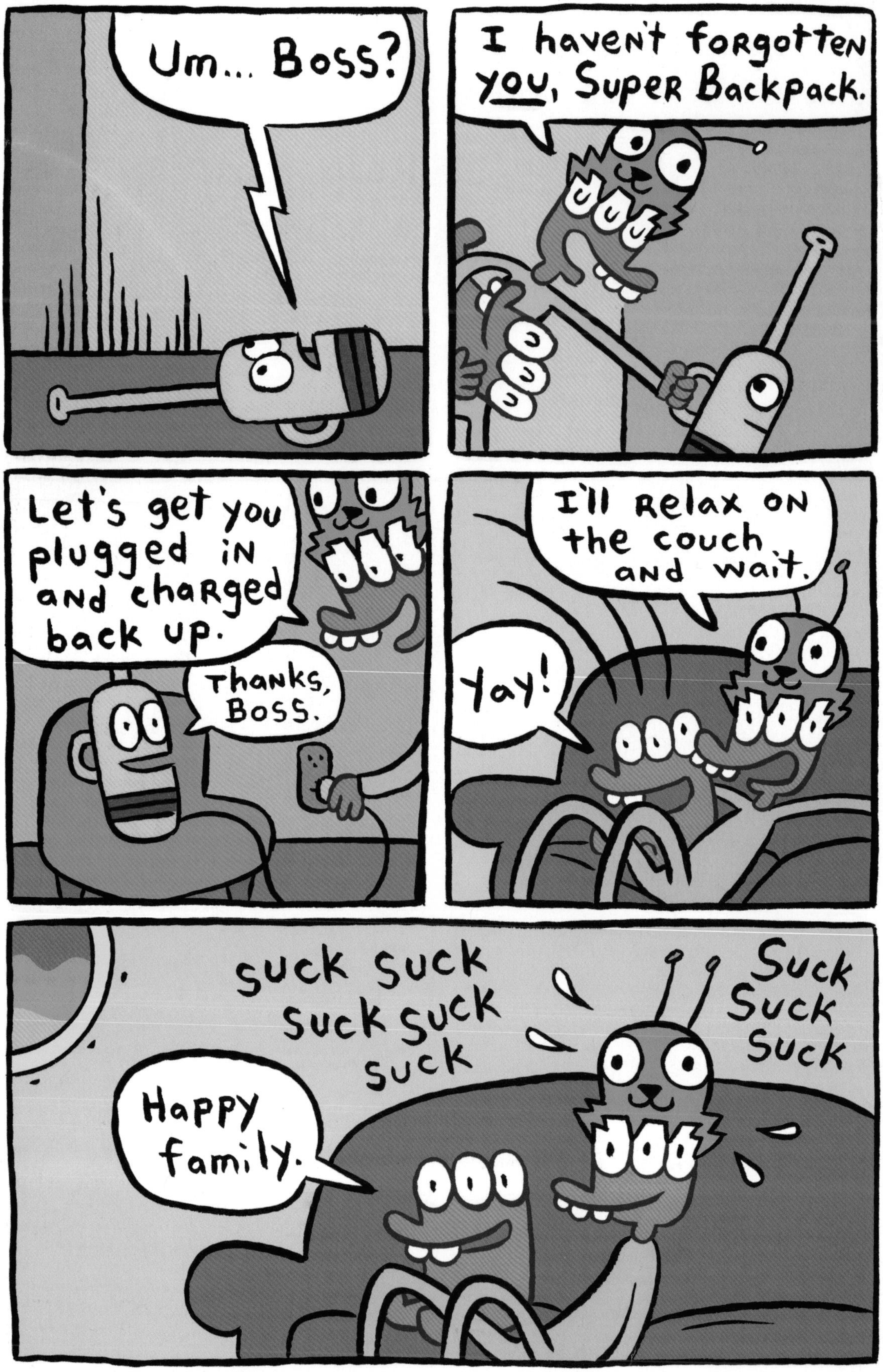
Um... Boss?
I haven't forgotten you, Super Backpack.
Let's get you plugged in and charged back up.
Thanks, Boss.
I'll relax on the couch and wait.
Yay!
suck suck suck suck suck
Suck Suck Suck
Happy family.

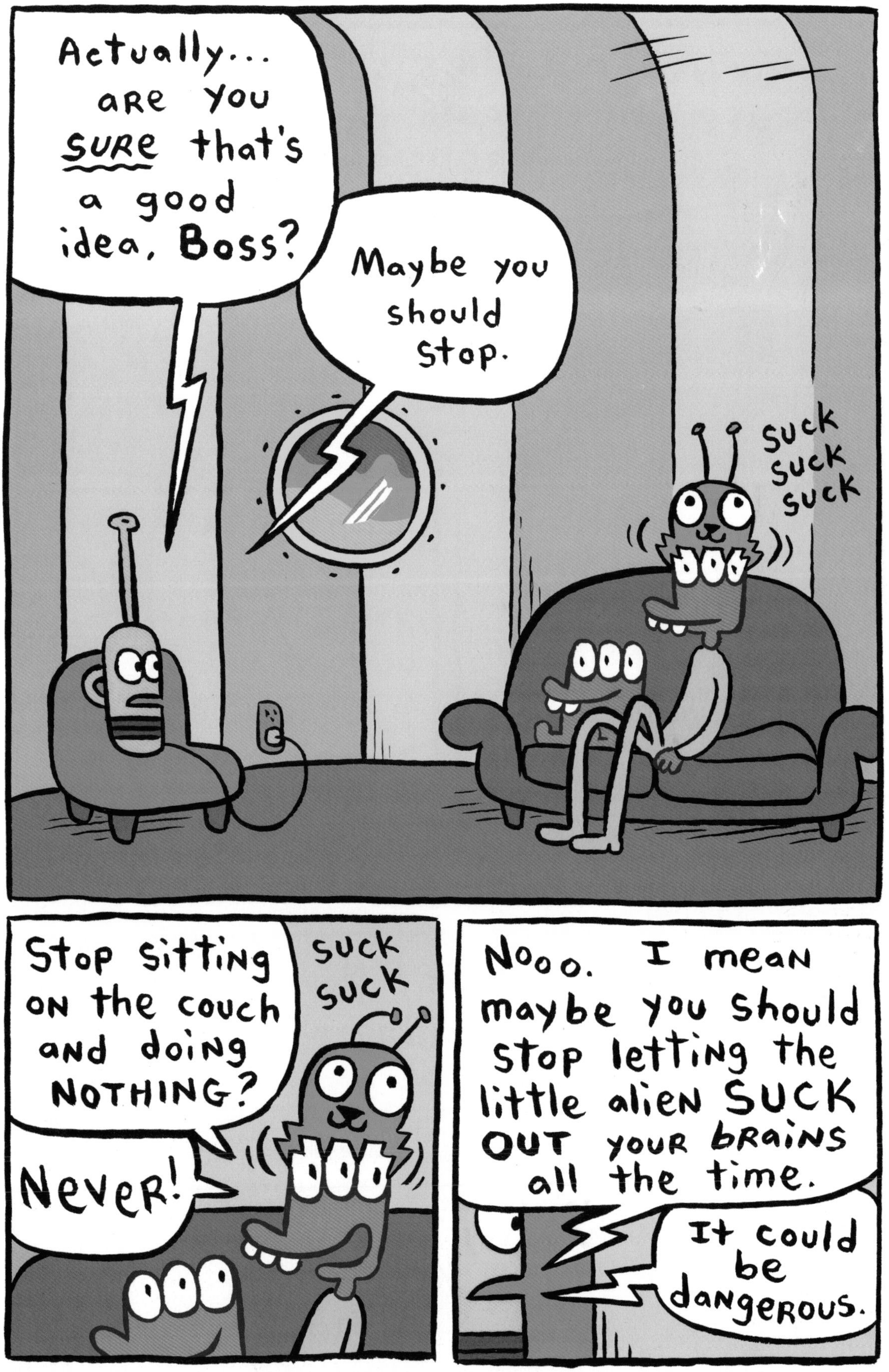
Actually... are you SURE that's a good idea, Boss?
Maybe you should stop.
SUCK SUCK SUCK
Stop sitting on the couch and doing NOTHING?
SUCK SUCK
Never!
Nooo. I mean maybe you should stop letting the little alien SUCK OUT your BRAINS all the time.
It could be dangerous.

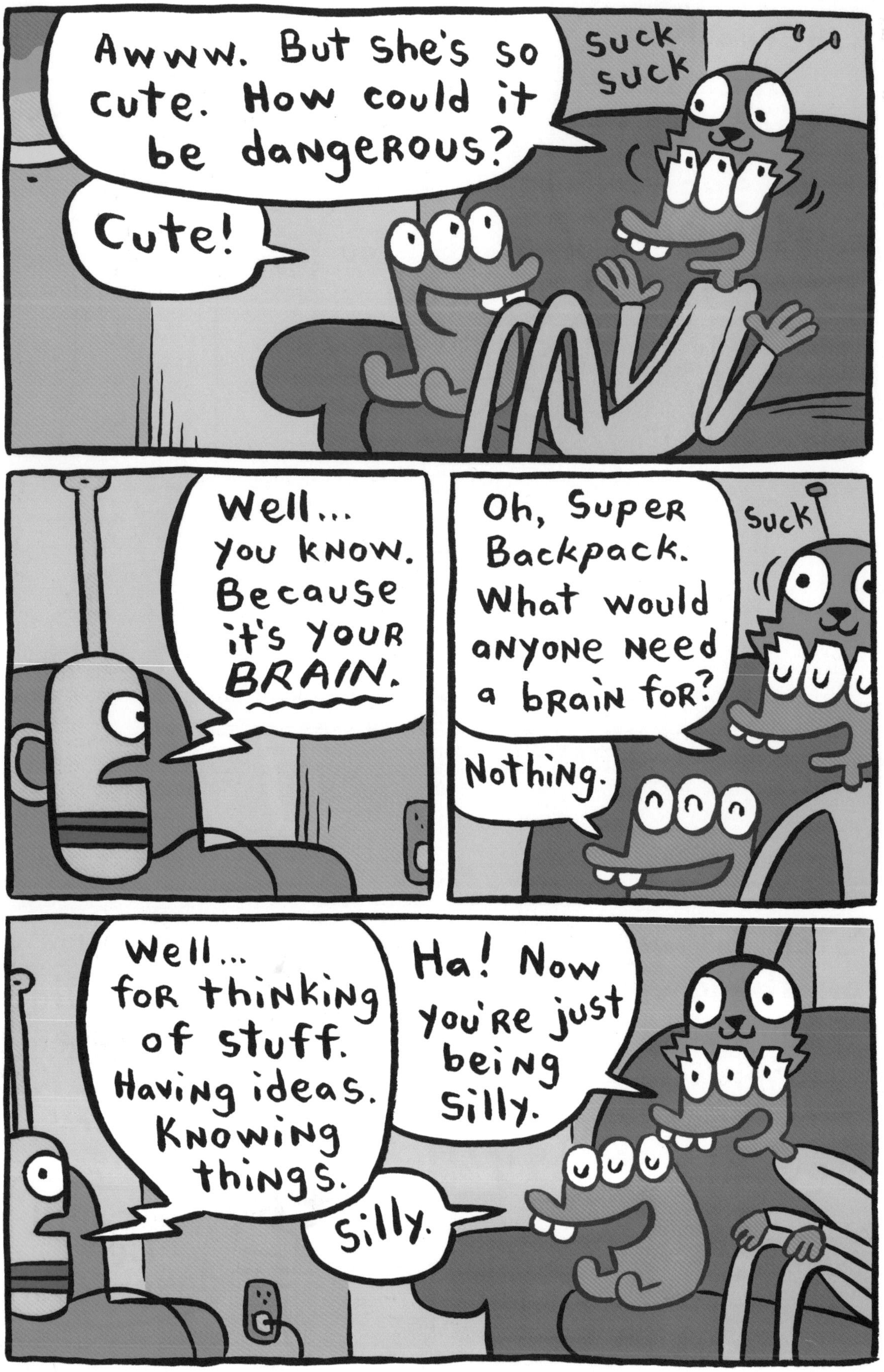
Awww. But she's so cute. How could it be dangerous?
suck suck
Cute!
Well... you know. Because it's your BRAIN.
Oh, Super Backpack. What would anyone need a brain for?
suck
Nothing.
Well... for thinking of stuff. Having ideas. Knowing things.
Ha! Now you're just being silly.
Silly.

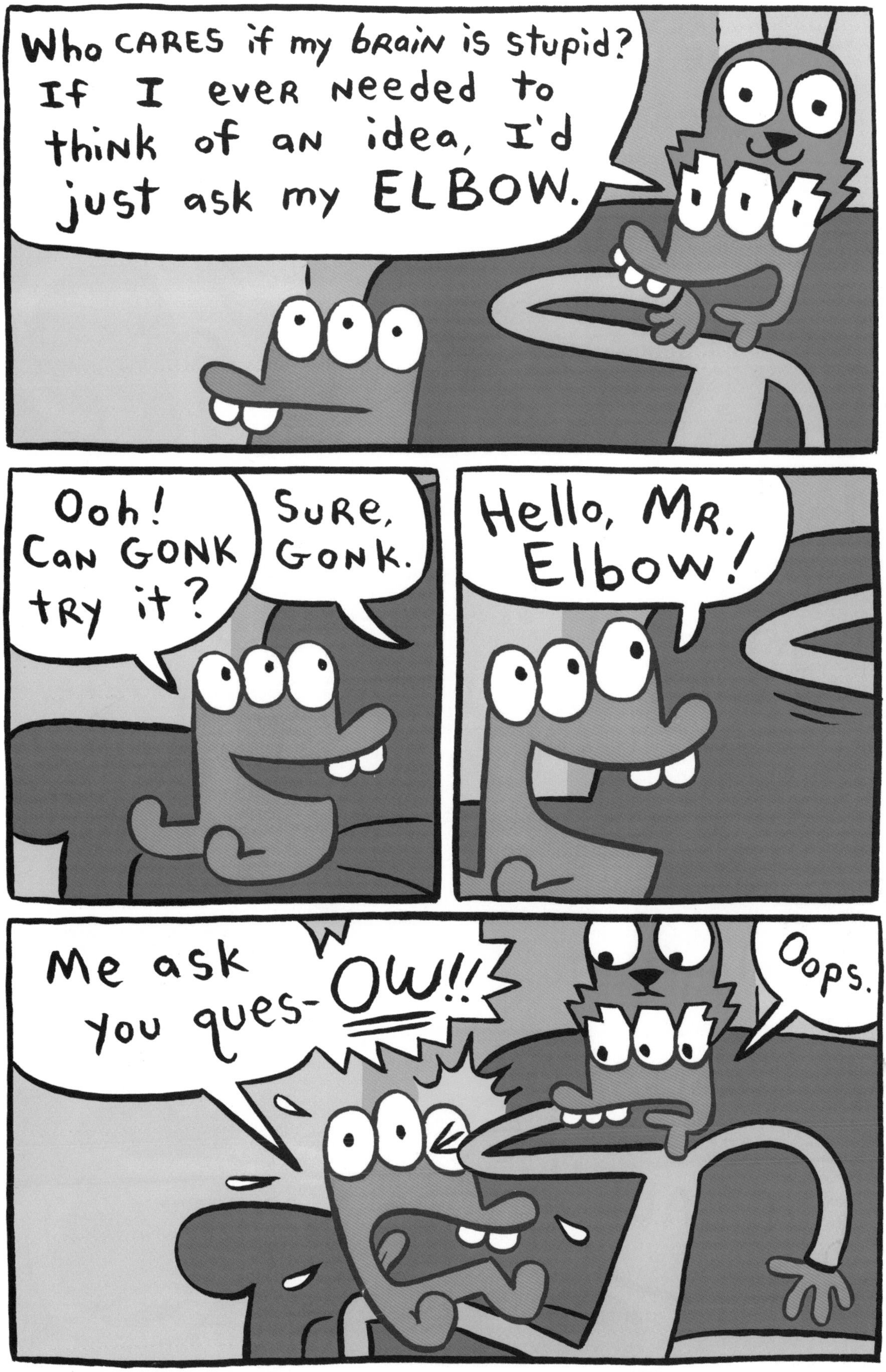
Who CARES if my BRAIN is stupid? If I ever needed to think of an idea, I'd just ask my ELBOW.
Ooh! Can GONK try it?
Sure, Gonk.
Hello, Mr. Elbow!
Me ask you ques-OW!!
Oops.

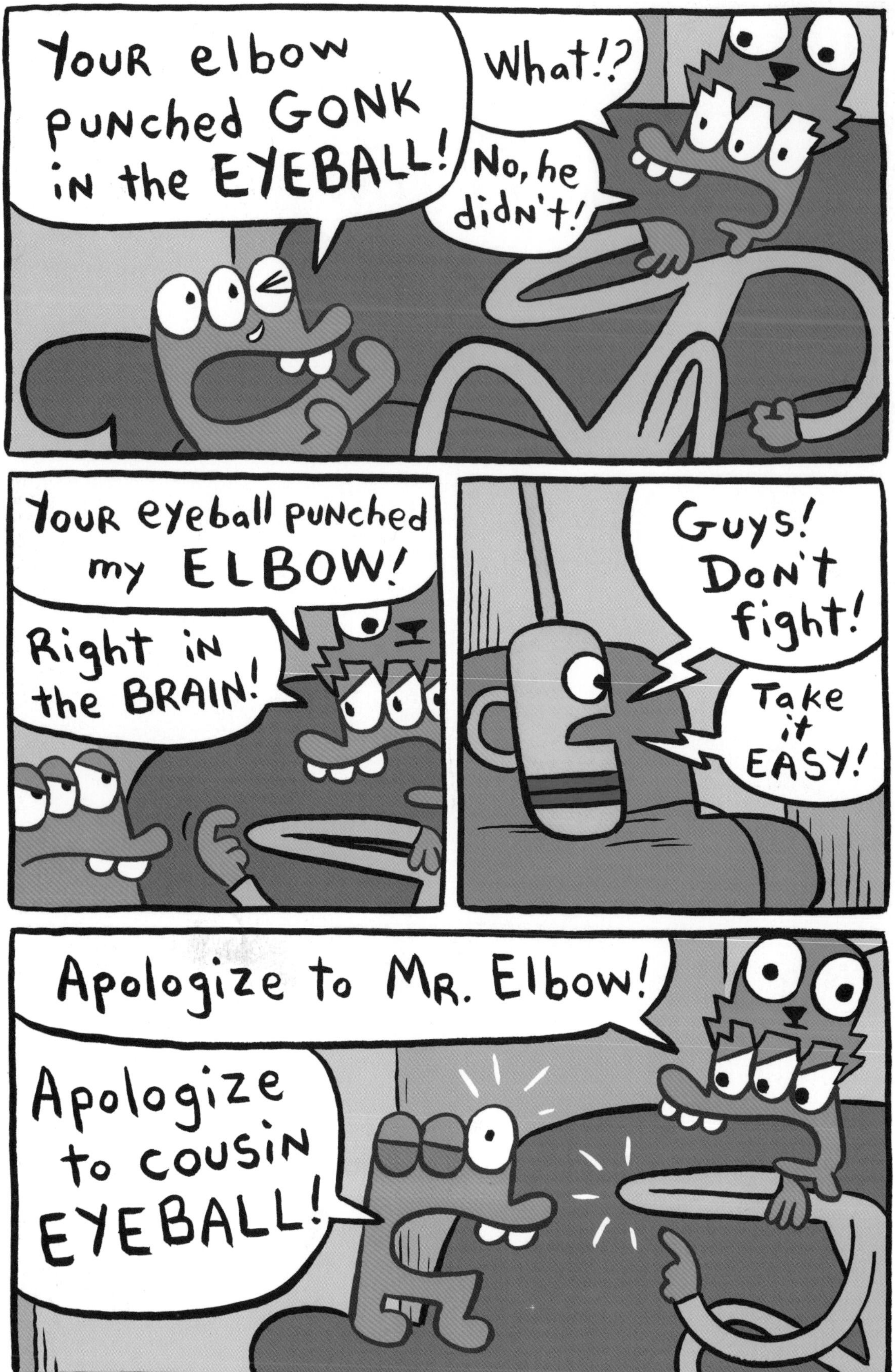
Your elbow punched GONK in the EYEBALL!
What!?
No, he didn't!
Your eyeball punched my ELBOW!
Right in the BRAIN!
Guys! Don't fight!
Take it EASY!
Apologize to Mr. Elbow!
Apologize to cousin EYEBALL!

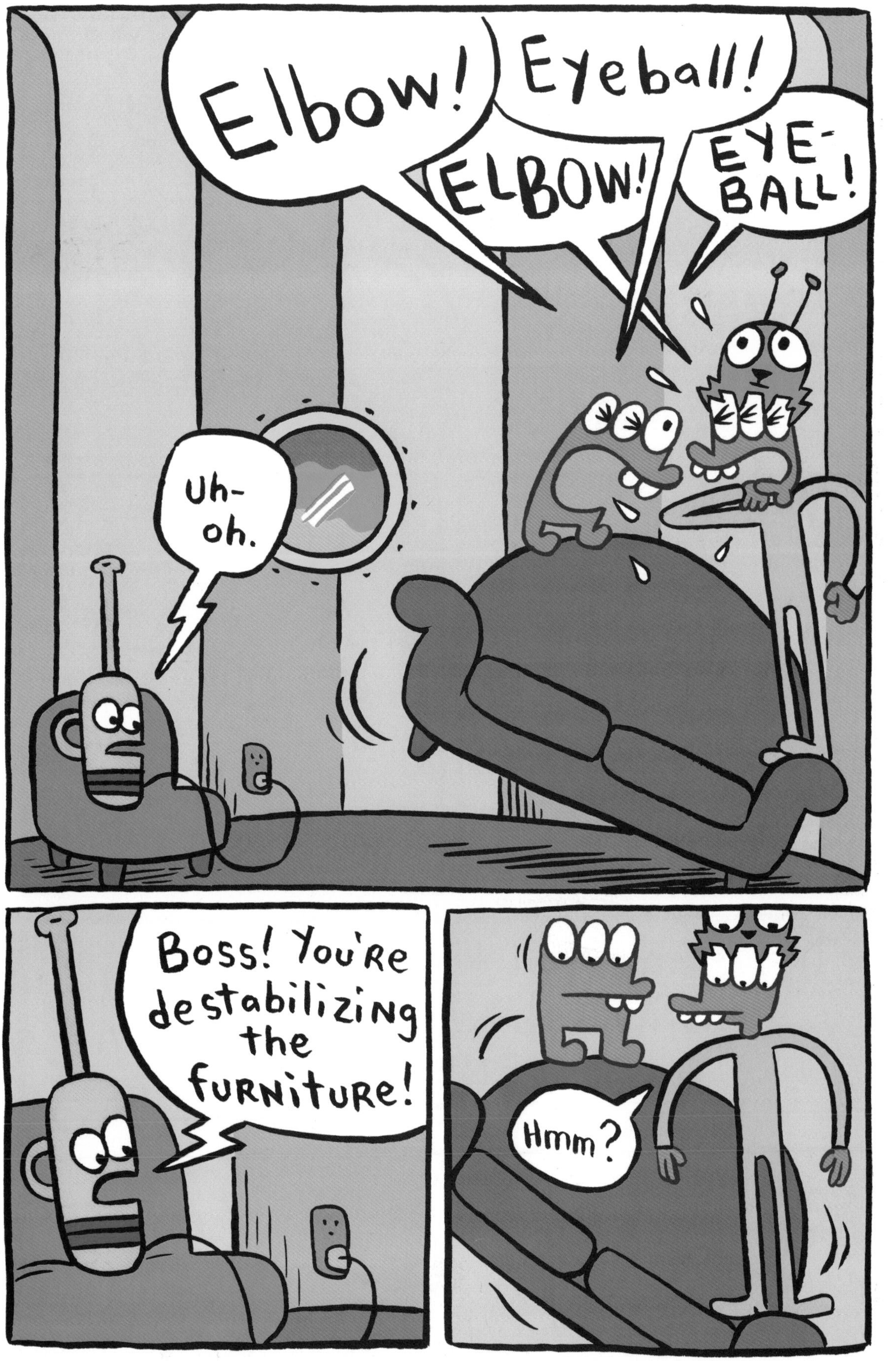
Elbow!
Eyeball!
ELBOW!
EYE-BALL!
Uh-oh.
Boss! You're destabilizing the furniture!
Hmm?

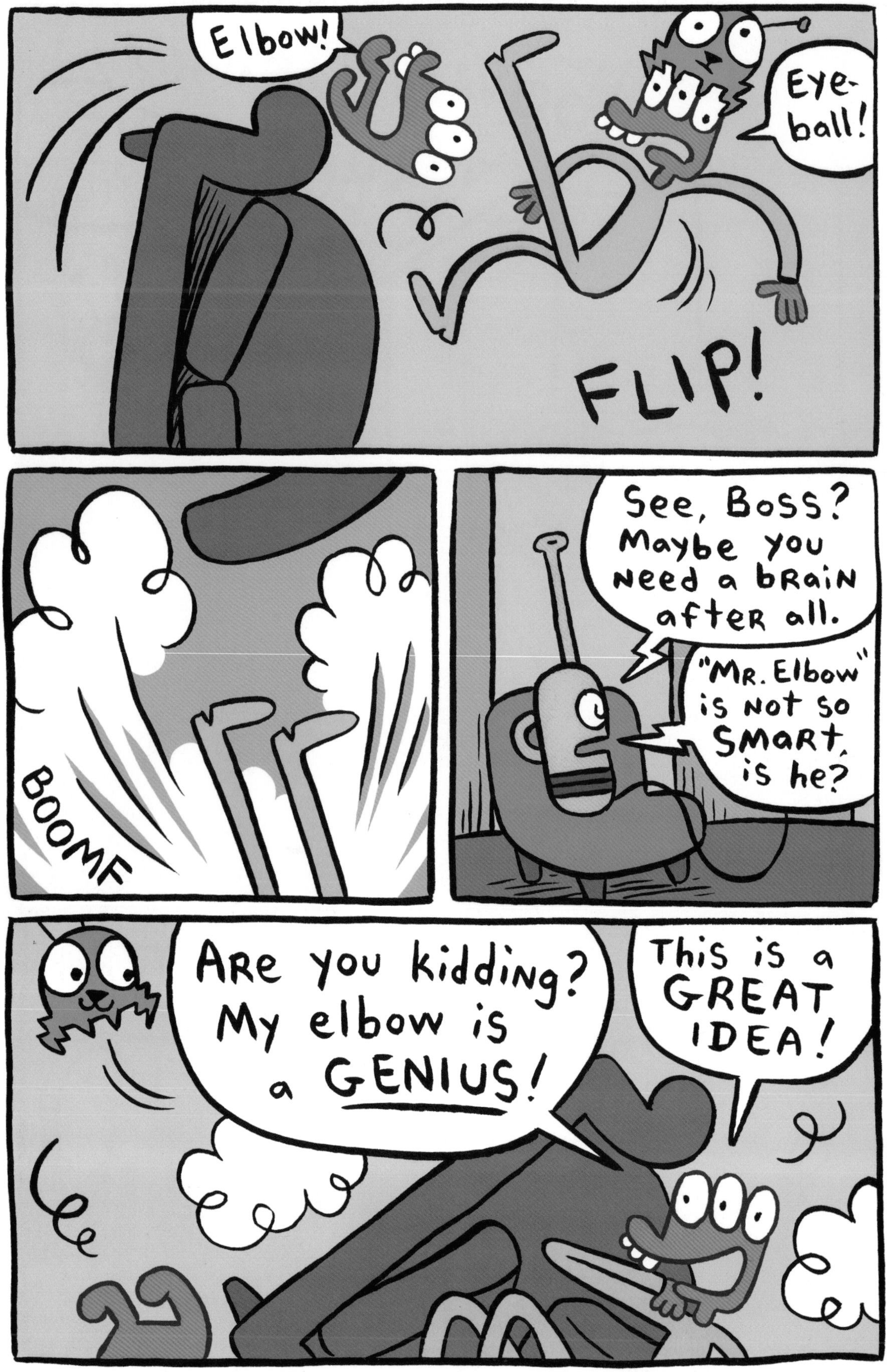
Elbow!
Eye-ball!
FLIP!
BOOMF
See, Boss? Maybe you need a brain after all.
"Mr. Elbow" is not so smart, is he?
Are you kidding? My elbow is a GENIUS!
This is a GREAT IDEA!

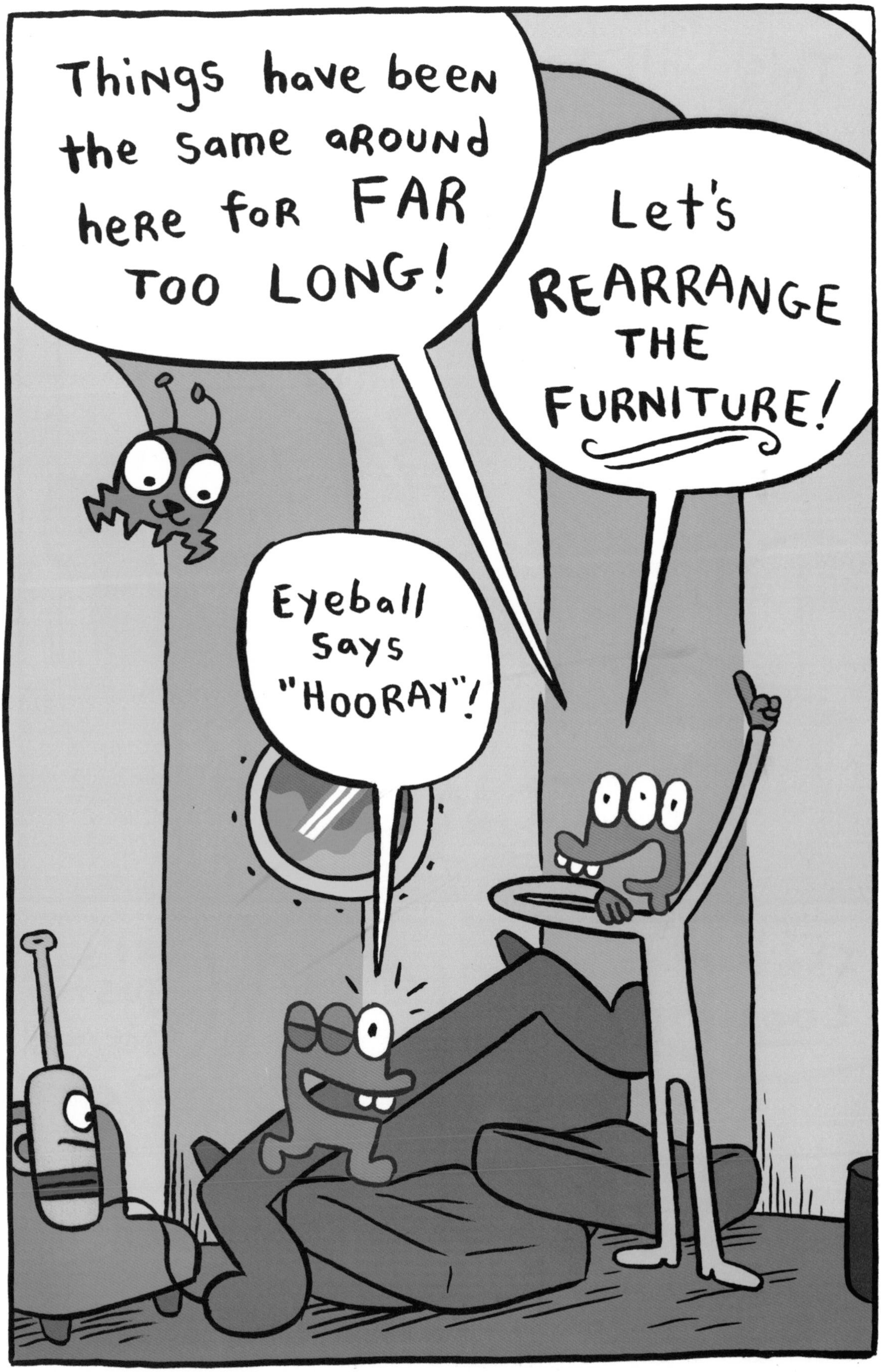
Things have been the same around here for FAR TOO LONG!
Let's REARRANGE THE FURNITURE!
Eyeball says "HOORAY"!

CHAPTER THREE

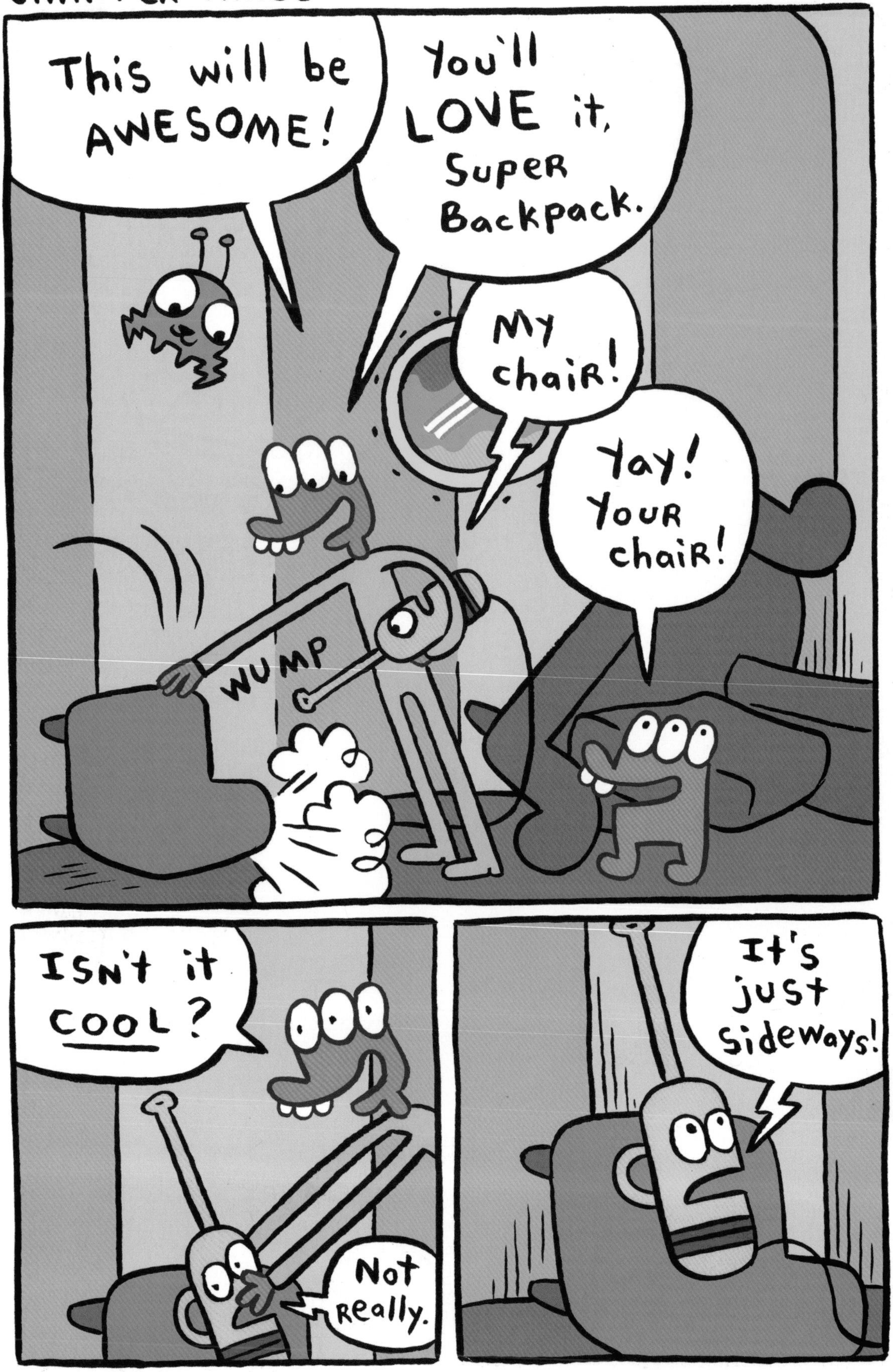
This will be AWESOME!
You'll LOVE it, Super Backpack.
My chair!
Yay! Your chair!
WUMP
Isn't it COOL?
Not really.
It's just sideways!

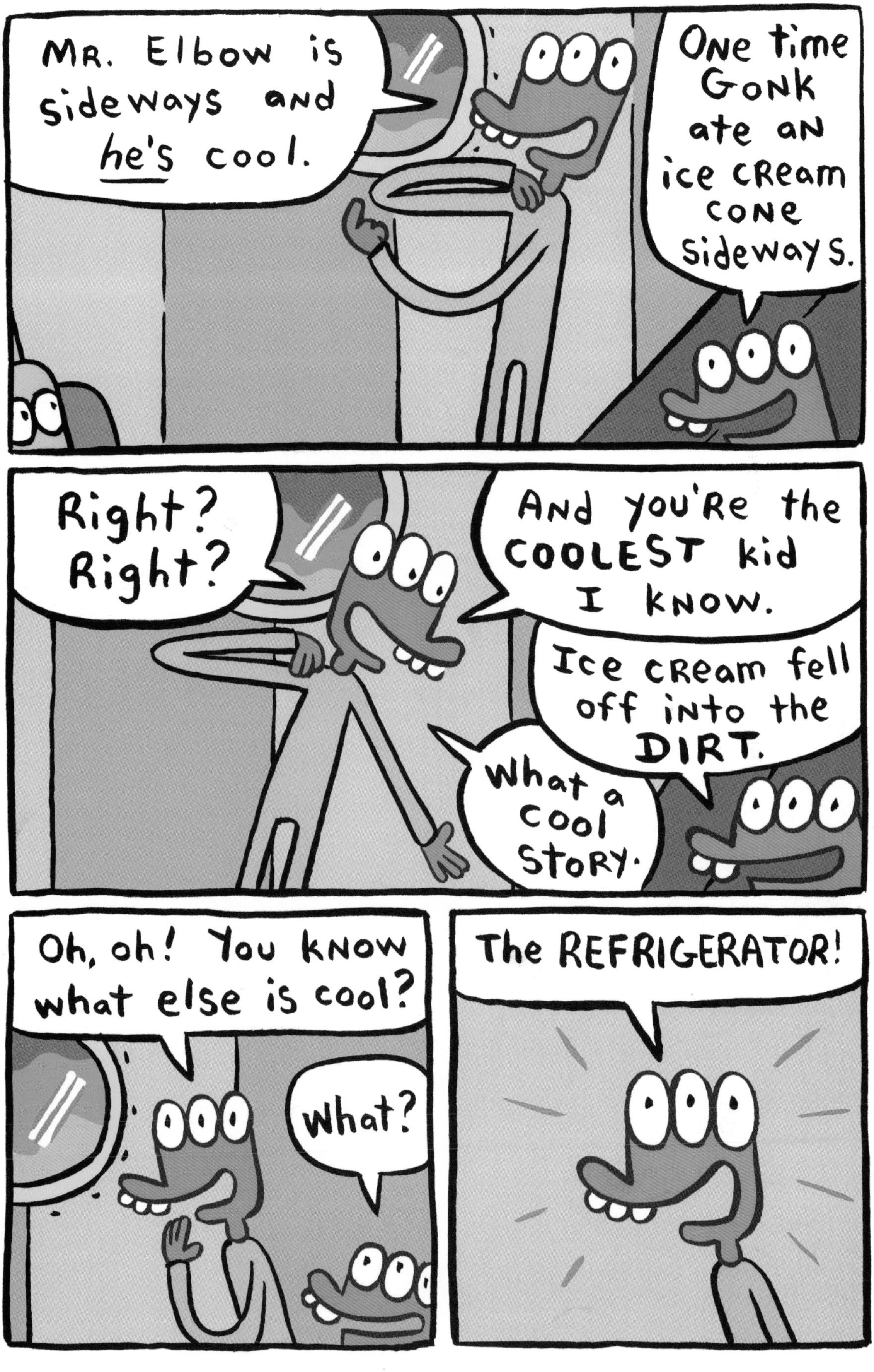

MR. Elbow is sideways and he's cool.
One time GONK ate an ice cream cone sideways.
Right? Right?
And you're the COOLEST kid I know.
Ice cream fell off into the DIRT.
What a cool story.
Oh, oh! You know what else is cool?
What?
The REFRIGERATOR!

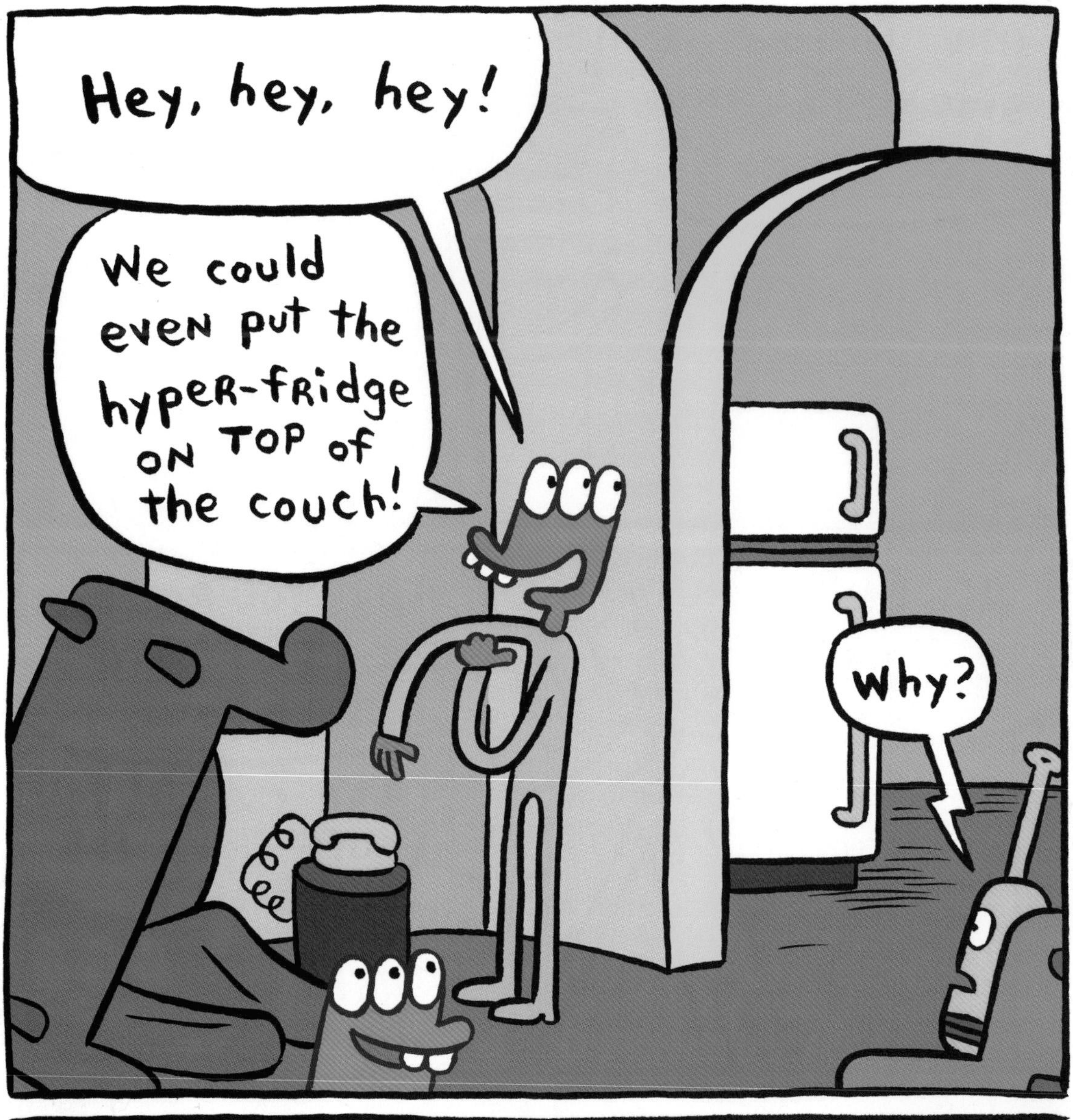
Hey, hey, hey!
We could even put the hyper-fridge on TOP of the couch!
Why?

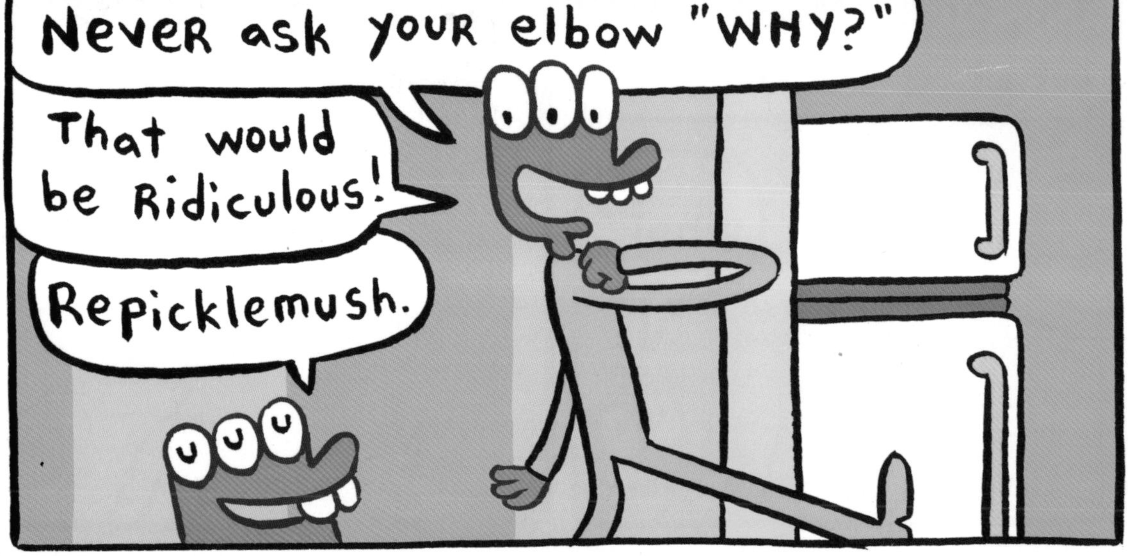
Never ask your elbow "WHY?"
That would be Ridiculous!
Repicklemush.

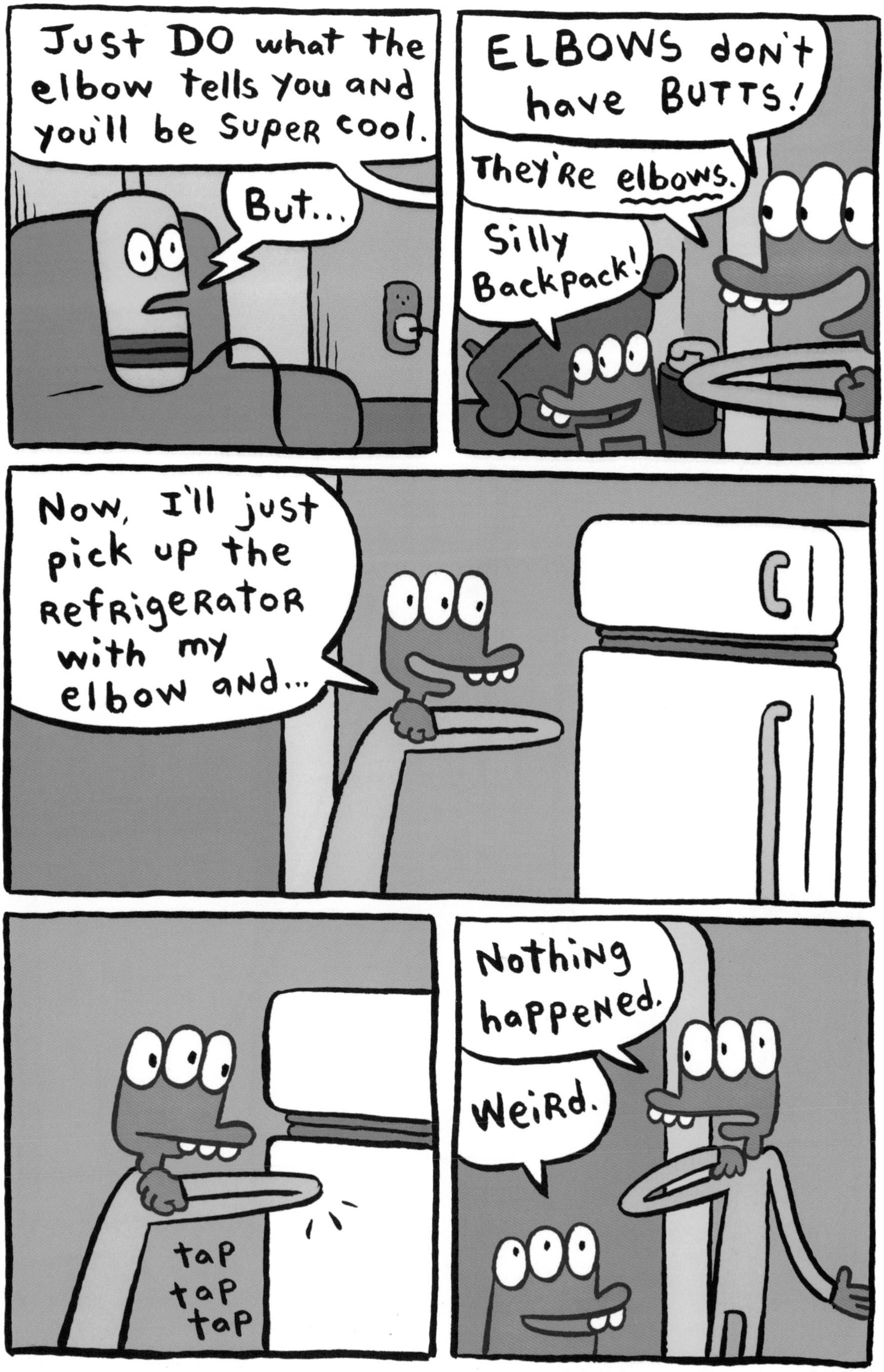
Just DO what the elbow tells you and you'll be super cool.
But...
ELBOWS don't have BUTTS!
They're elbows.
Silly Backpack!
Now, I'll just pick up the refrigerator with my elbow and...
tap tap tap
Nothing happened.
Weird.

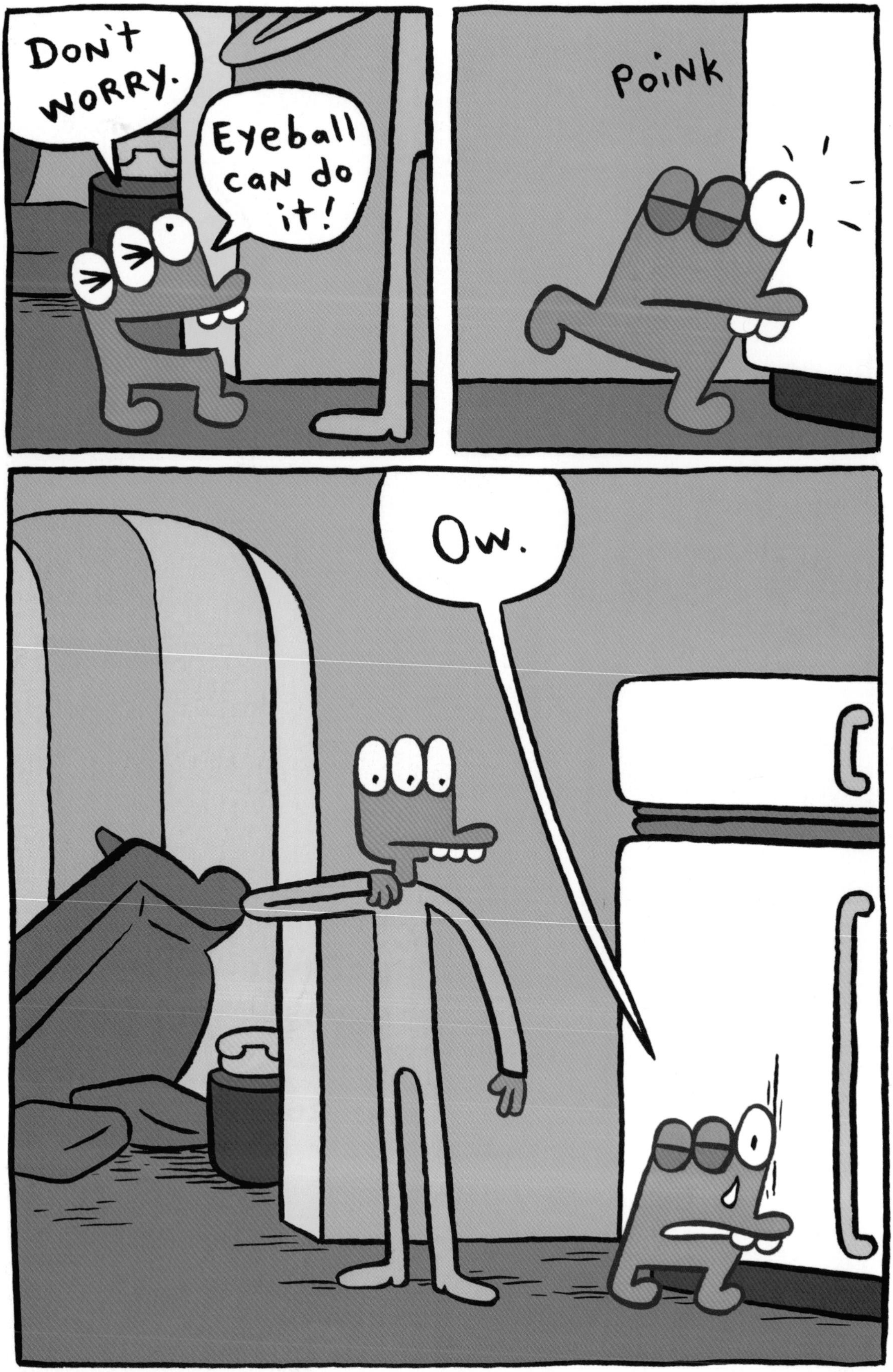
Don't WORRY.
Eyeball can do it!
POINK
Ow.

CHAPTER FOUR

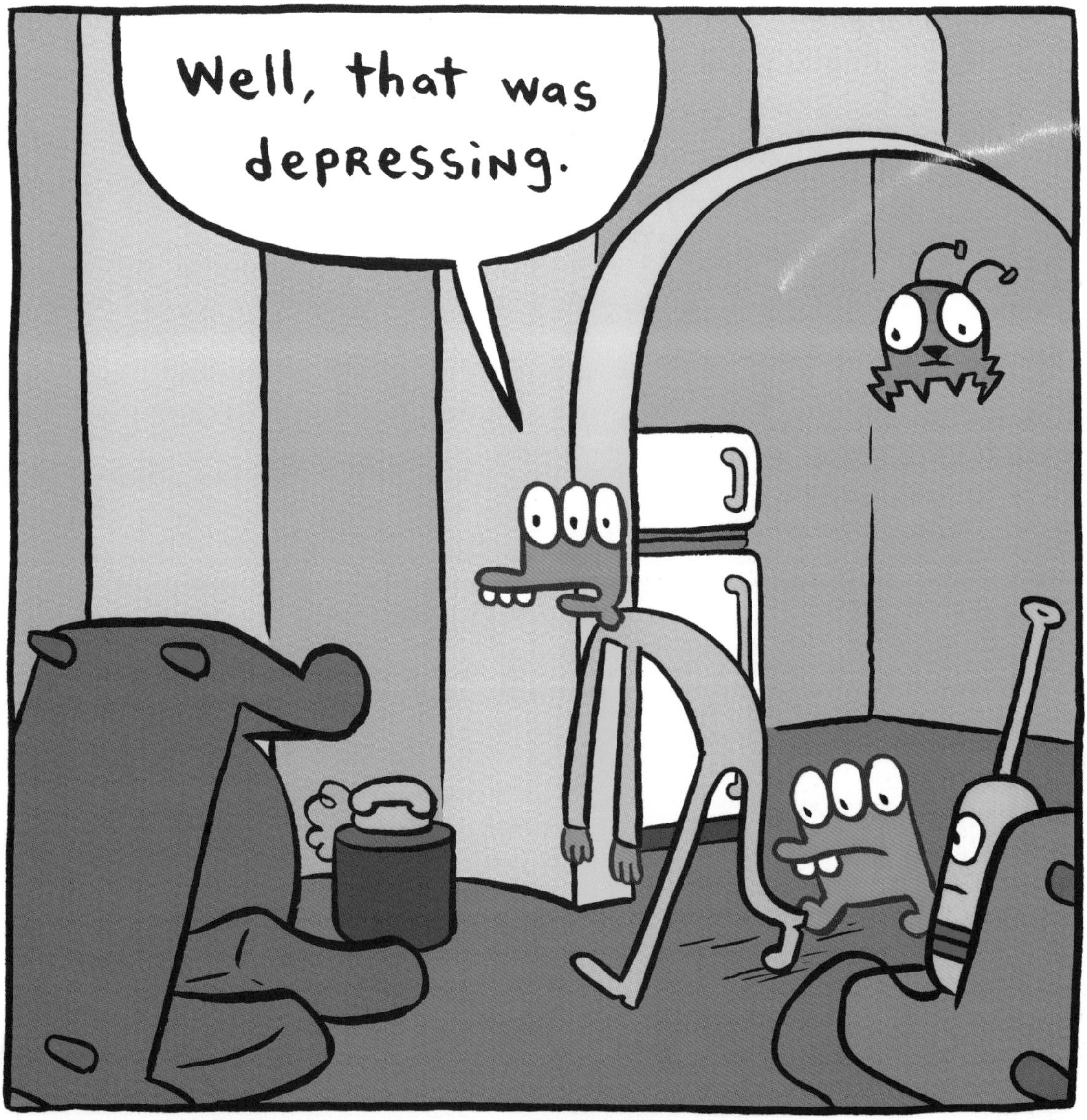
Well, that was depressing.

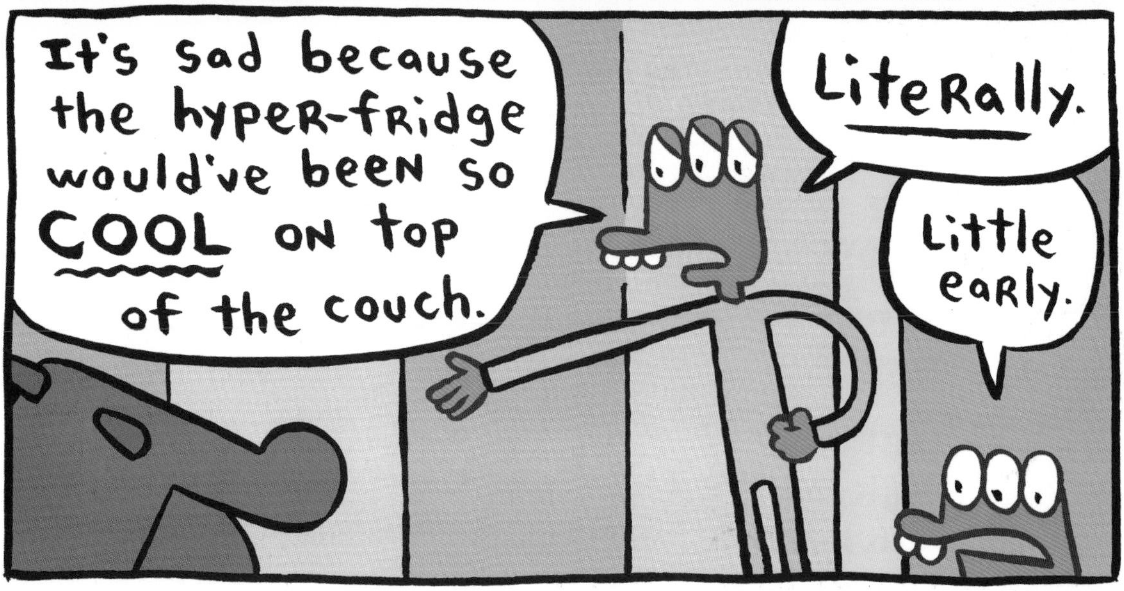
It's sad because the hyper-fridge would've been so COOL on top of the couch.
Literally.
Little early.

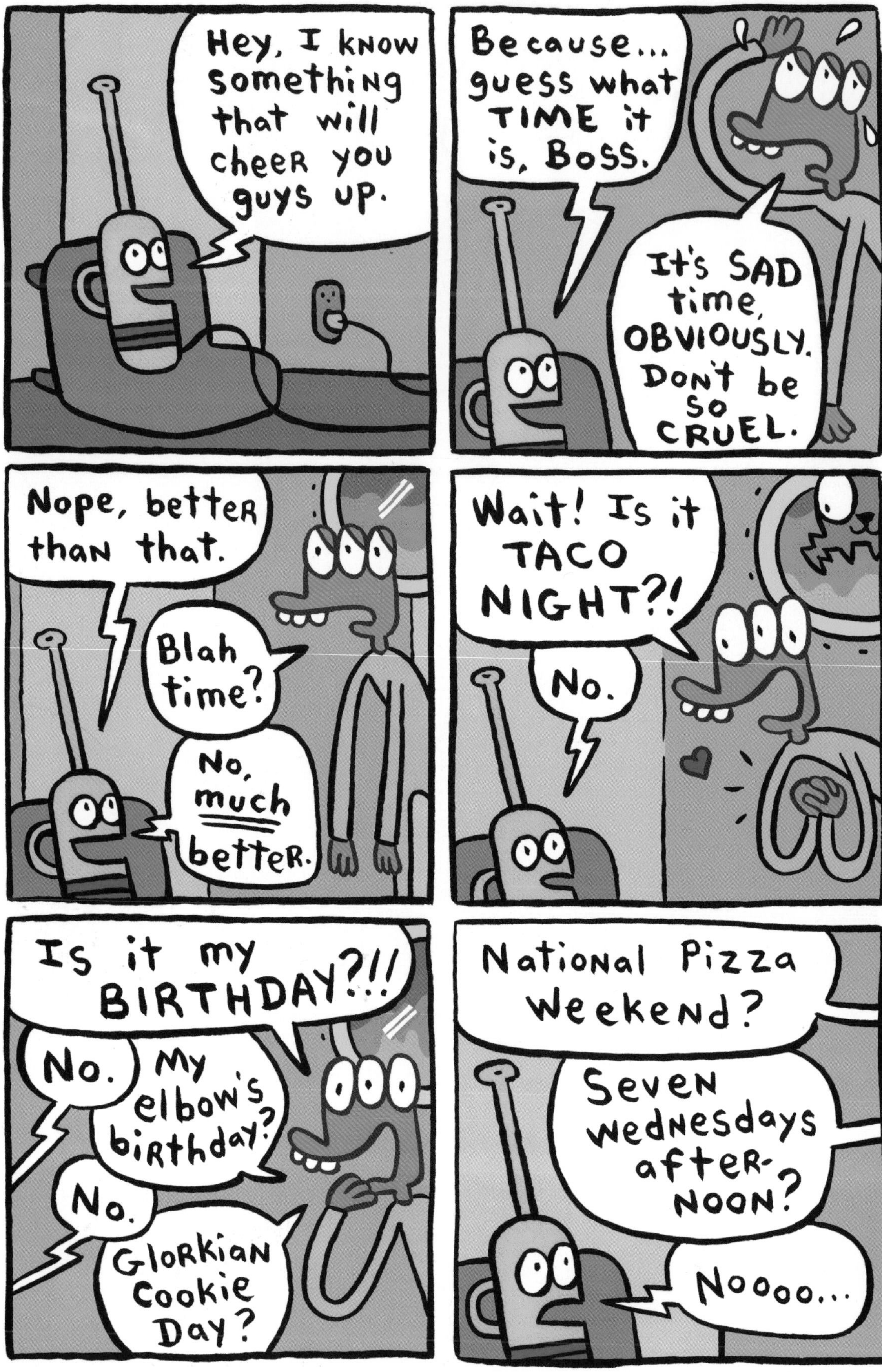
Hey, I know something that will cheer you guys up.
Because... guess what TIME it is, Boss.
It's SAD time, OBVIOUSLY. Don't be so CRUEL.
Nope, better than that.
Blah time?
No, much better.
Wait! Is it TACO NIGHT?!
No.
Is it my BIRTHDAY?!!
No.
My elbow's birthday?
No.
GlorKian Cookie Day?
National Pizza Weekend?
Seven wednesdays after-noon?
Noooo...

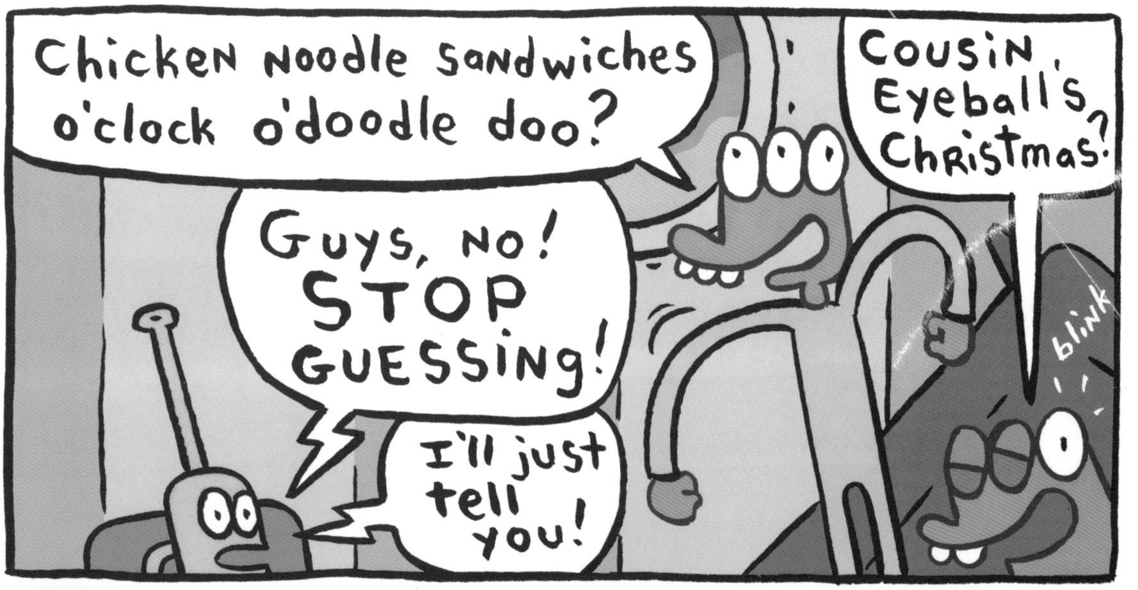
Chicken noodle sandwiches o'clock o'doodle doo?
Cousin Eyeball's Christmas?
Guys, no! STOP GUESSING!
I'll just tell you!
blink

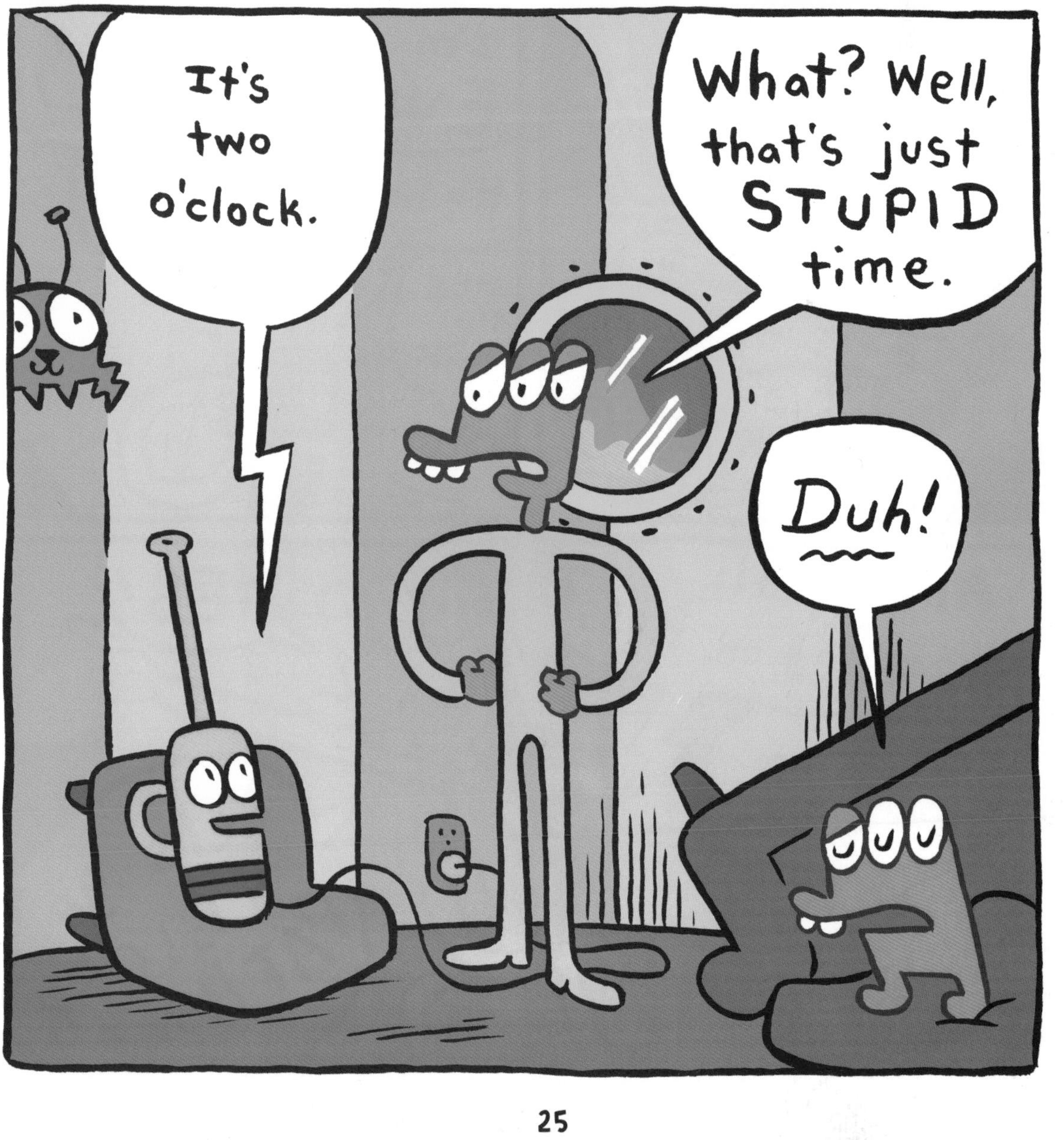
It's two o'clock.
What? Well, that's just STUPID time.
Duh!

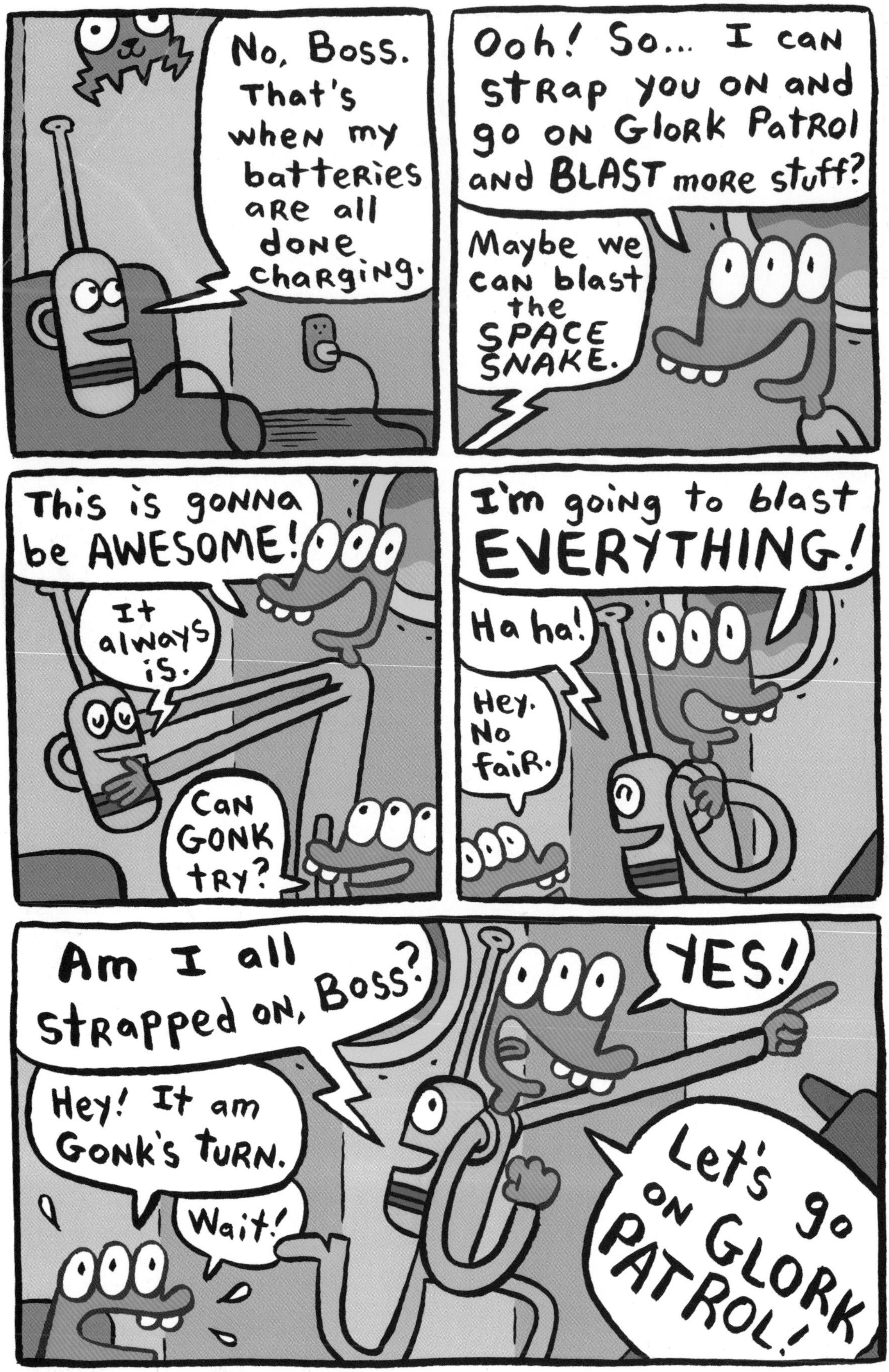
No, Boss. That's when my batteries are all done charging.
Ooh! So... I can strap you on and go on Glork Patrol and BLAST more stuff?
Maybe we can blast the SPACE SNAKE.
This is gonna be AWESOME!
It always is.
Can GONK try?
I'm going to blast EVERYTHING!
Ha ha!
Hey. No fair.
Am I all strapped on, Boss?
YES!
Hey! It am Gonk's turn.
Wait!
Let's go on GLORK PATROL!

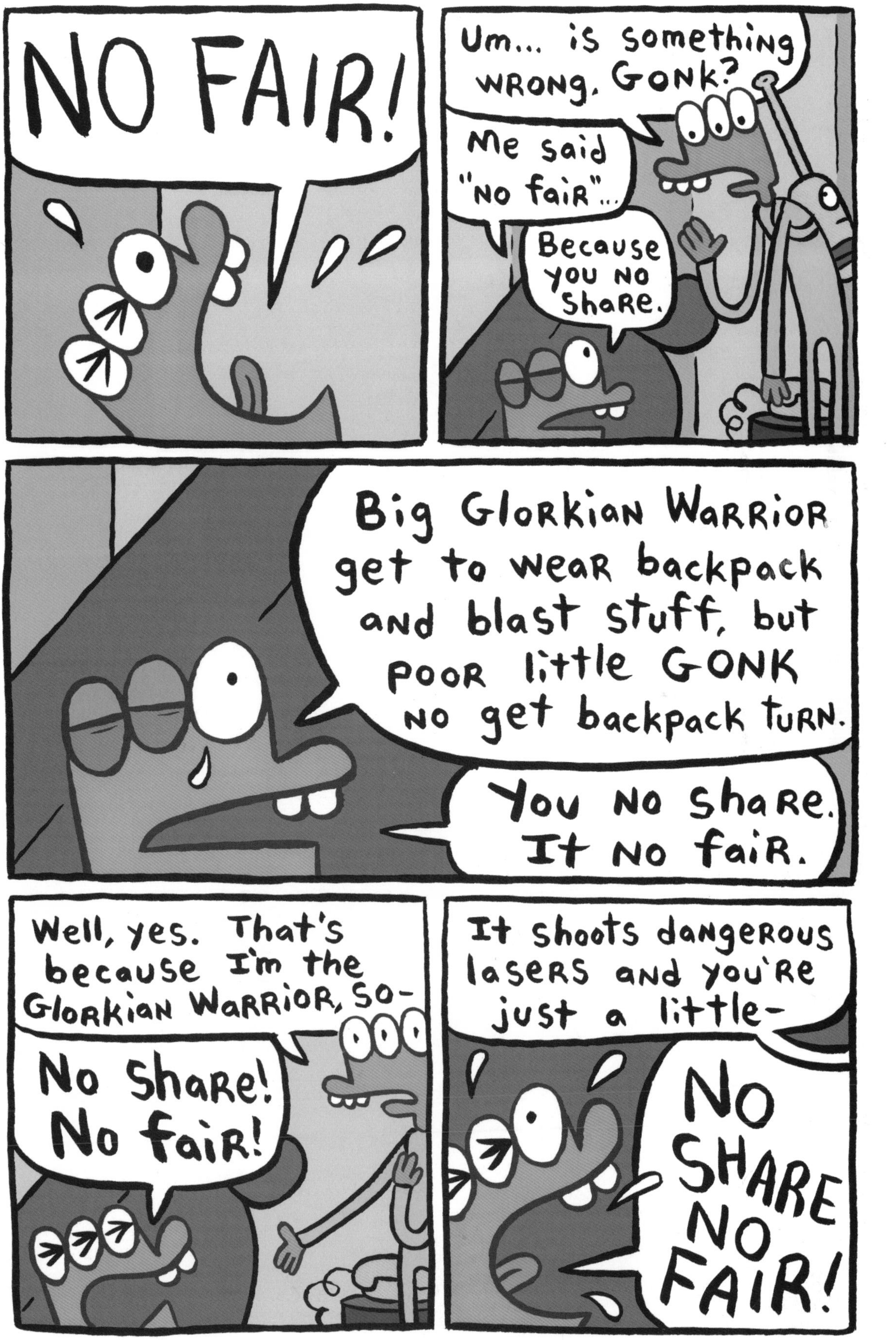
NO FAIR!
Um... is something WRONG, GONK?
Me said "no fair"...
Because you no share.
Big Glorkian Warrior get to wear backpack and blast stuff, but poor little GONK no get backpack turn.
You no share. It no fair.
Well, yes. That's because I'm the Glorkian Warrior, so-
No share! No fair!
It shoots dangerous lasers and you're just a little-
NO SHARE NO FAIR!

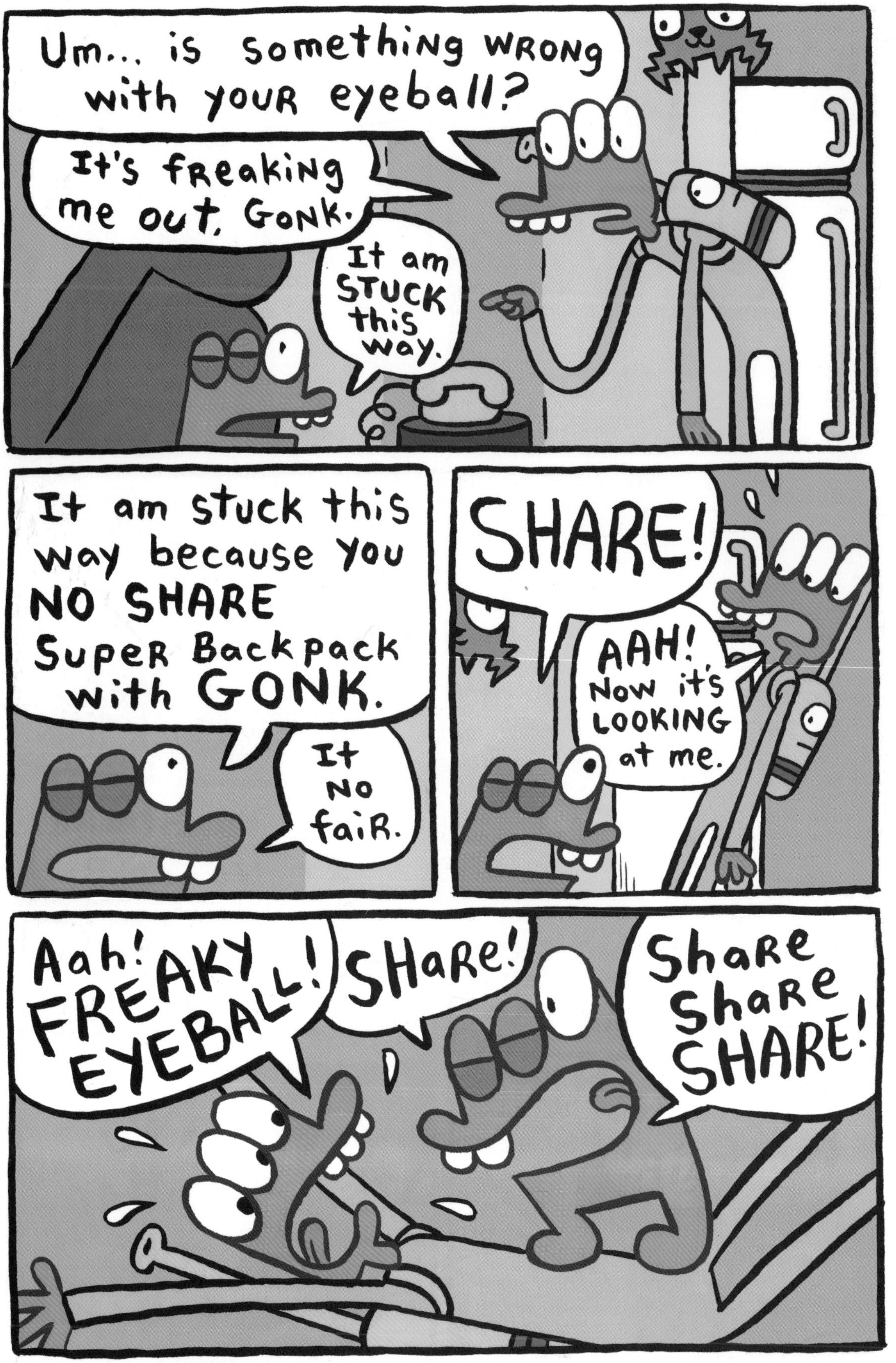
Um... is something WRONG with your eyeball?
It's freaking me out, GONK.
It am STUCK this way.
It am stuck this way because you NO SHARE Super Backpack with GONK.
It No fair.
SHARE!
AAH! Now it's LOOKING at me.
Aah! FREAKY EYEBALL!
SHare!
Share Share SHARE!

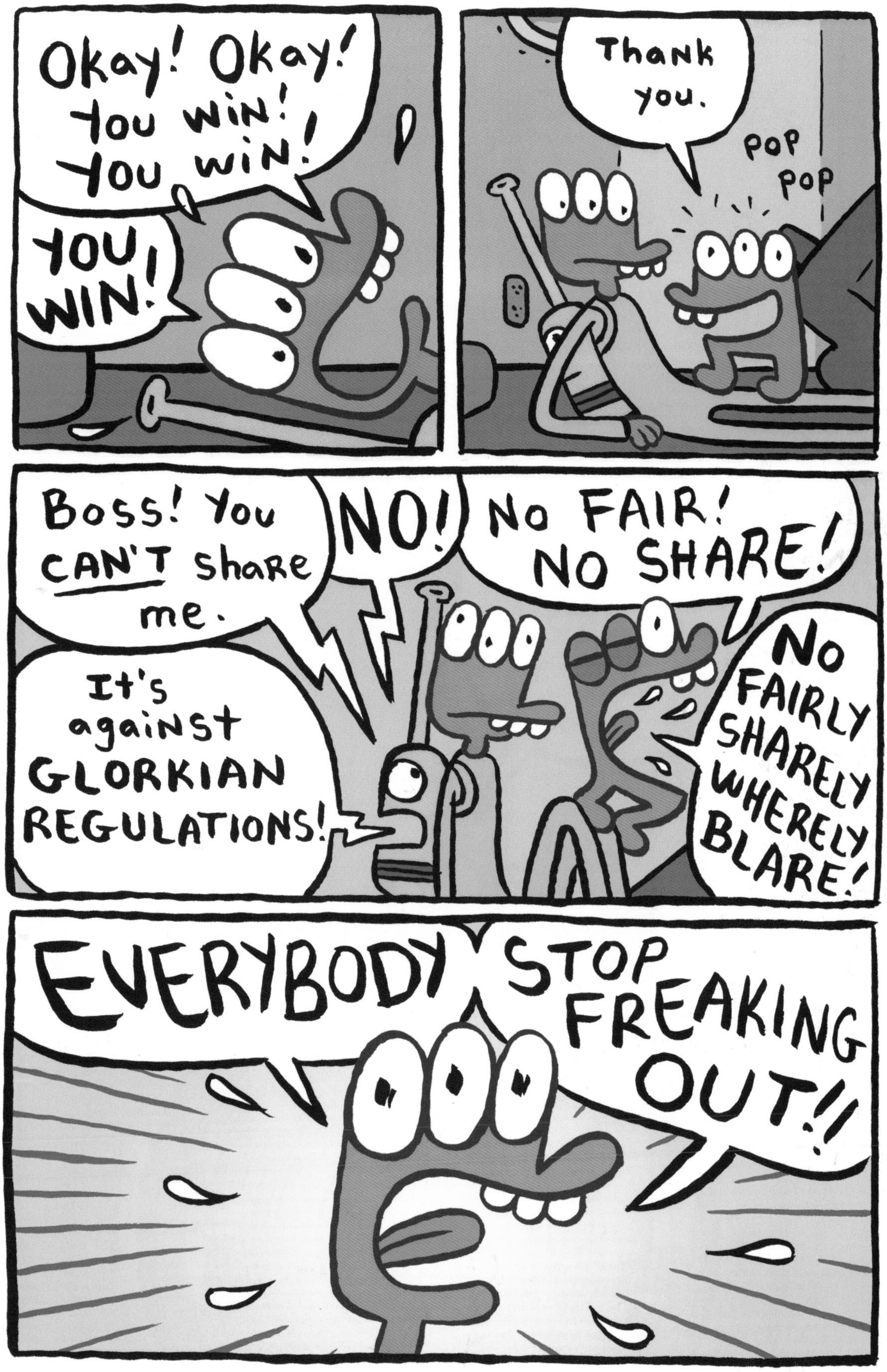
Okay! Okay! You win! You win!
YOU WIN!
Thank you.
POP POP
Boss! You CAN'T share me.
NO!
No FAIR! NO SHARE!
It's against GLORKIAN REGULATIONS!
NO FAIRLY SHARELY WHERELY BLARE!
EVERYBODY
STOP FREAKING OUT!!

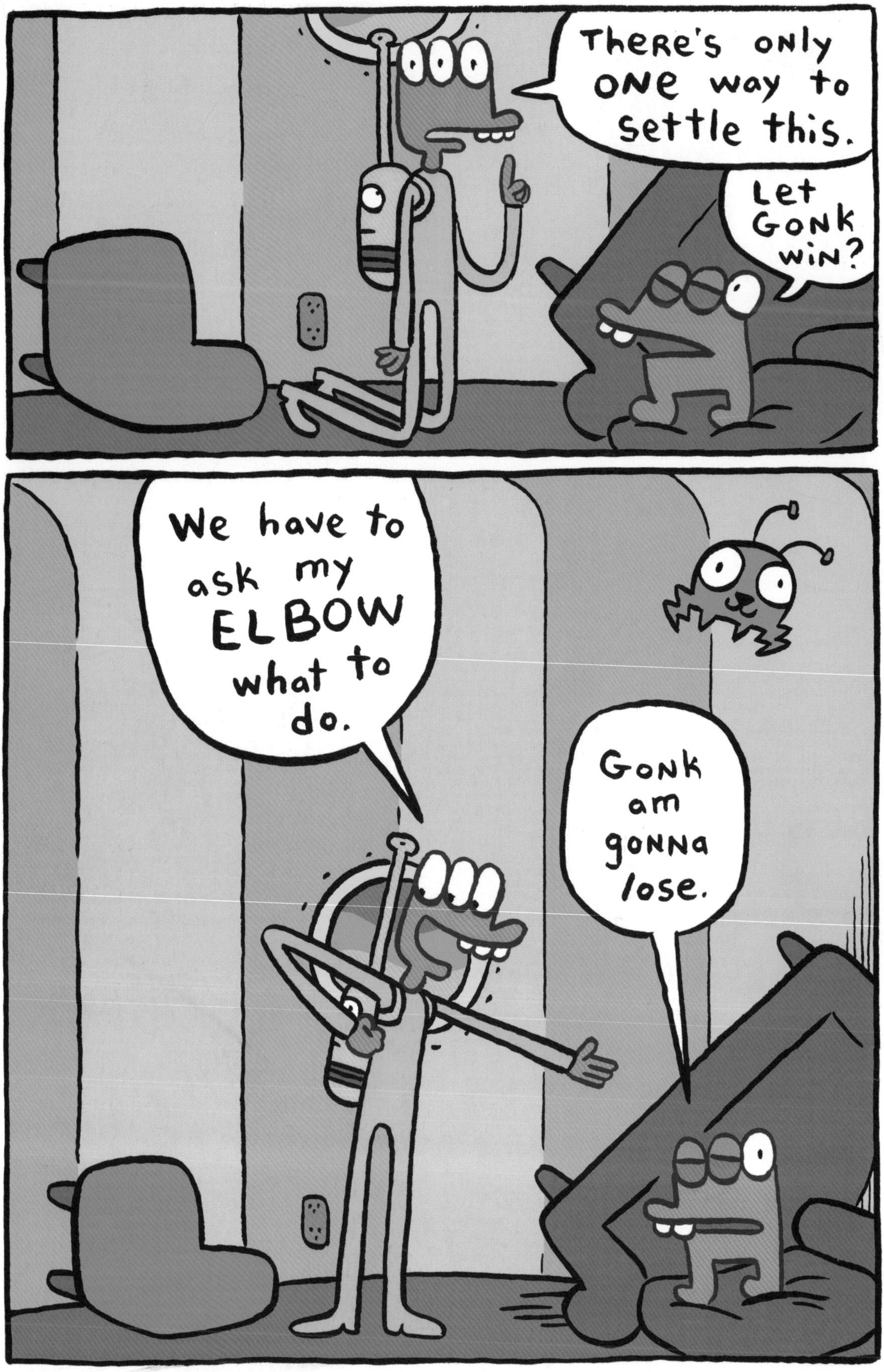
There's only ONE way to settle this.
Let GONK win?
We have to ask my ELBOW what to do.
Gonk am gonna lose.

CHAPTER FIVE

So, MR. Elbow.
What should we do?
Um... Boss?
Shhhh.
Listen.
Gonk's eyeball doesn't HEAR anything.

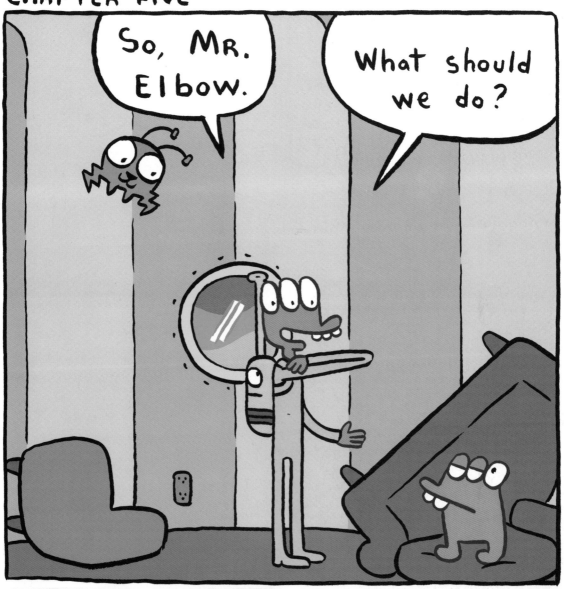

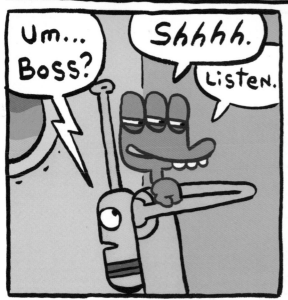

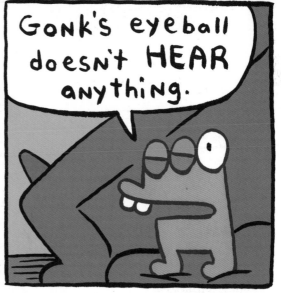

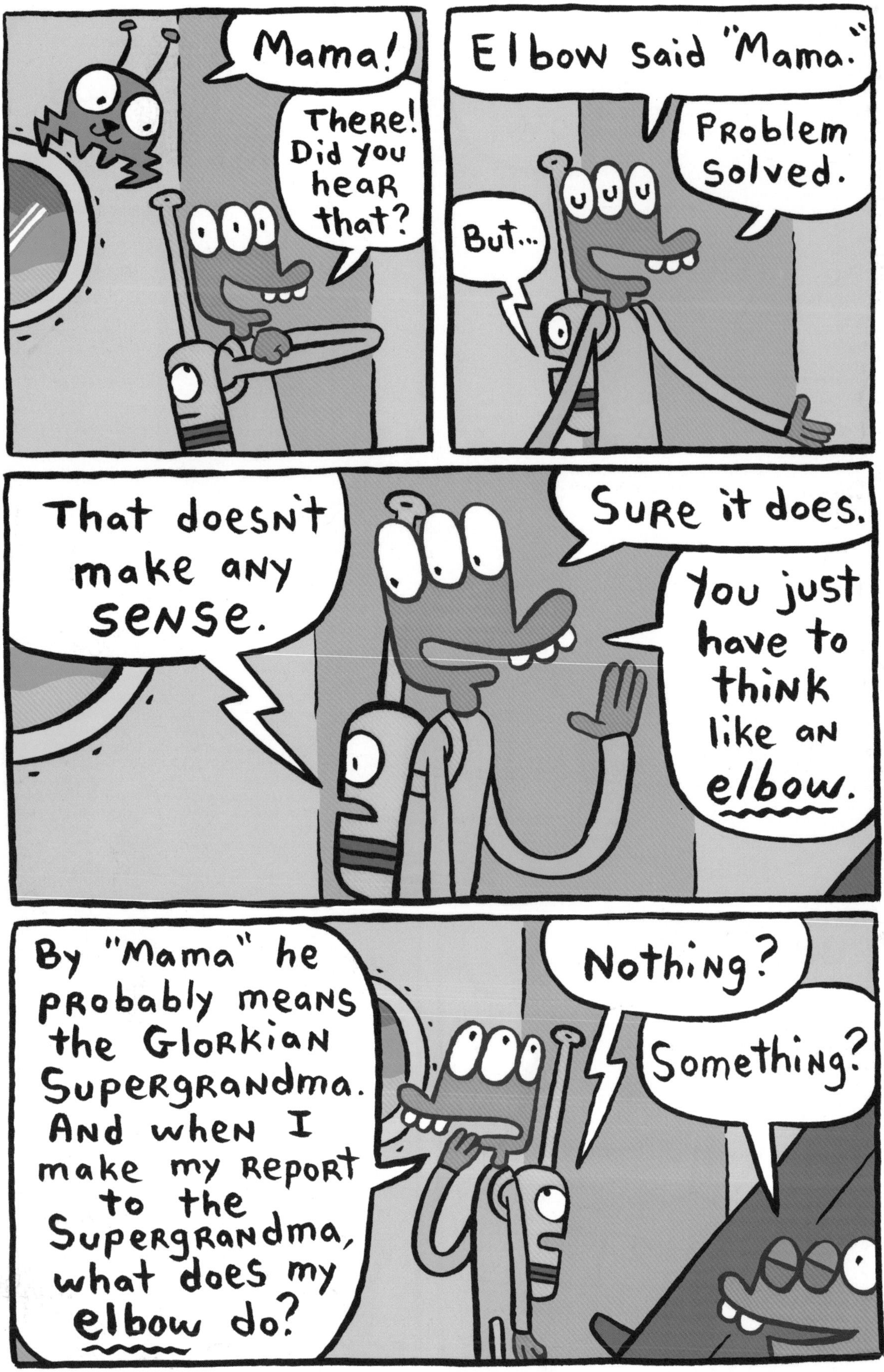

Mama!
There! Did you hear that?
Elbow said "Mama."
Problem solved.
But...
That doesn't make any sense.
Sure it does.
You just have to think like an elbow.
By "Mama" he probably means the Glorkian Supergrandma. And when I make my report to the Supergrandma, what does my elbow do?
Nothing?
Something?

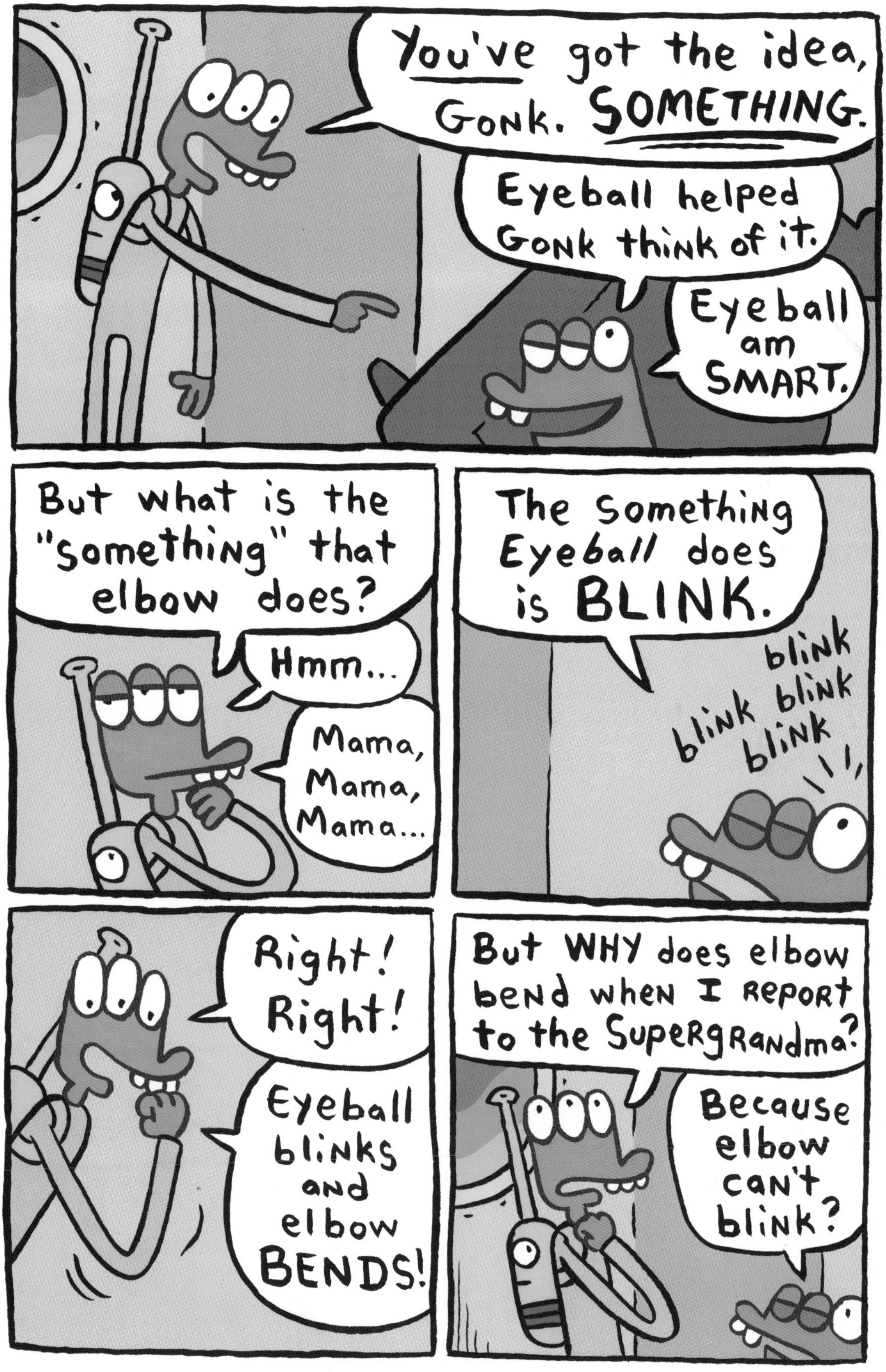

You've got the idea, Gonk. SOMETHING.
Eyeball helped Gonk think of it.
Eyeball am SMART.
But what is the "something" that elbow does?
Hmm...
Mama, Mama, Mama...
The something Eyeball does is BLINK.
blink blink blink blink
Right! Right!
Eyeball blinks and elbow BENDS!
But WHY does elbow bend when I report to the Supergrandma?
Because elbow can't blink?

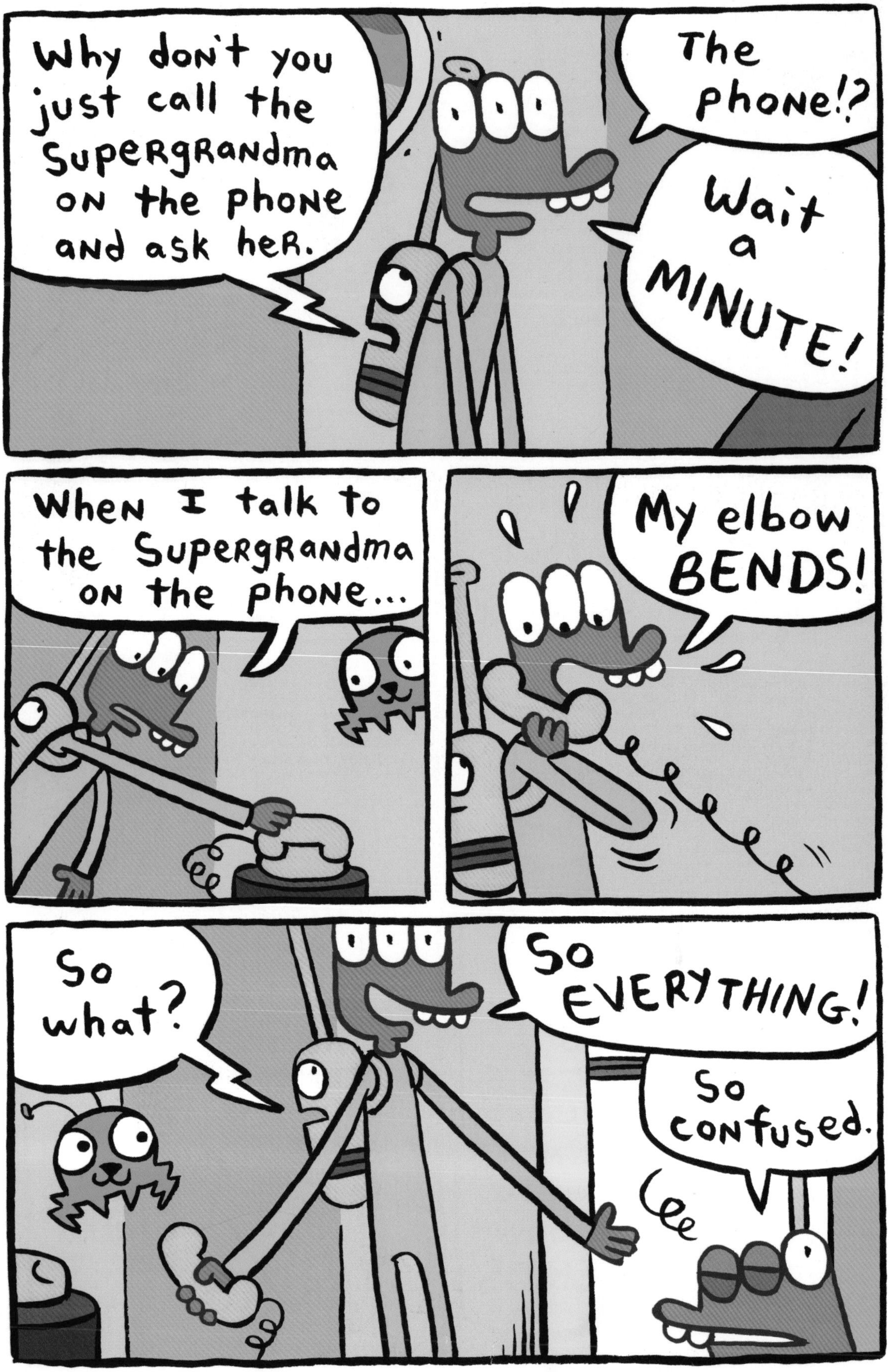
Why don't you just call the Supergrandma on the phone and ask her.
The phone!?
Wait a MINUTE!
When I talk to the Supergrandma on the phone...
My elbow BENDS!
So what?
So EVERYTHING!
So confused.

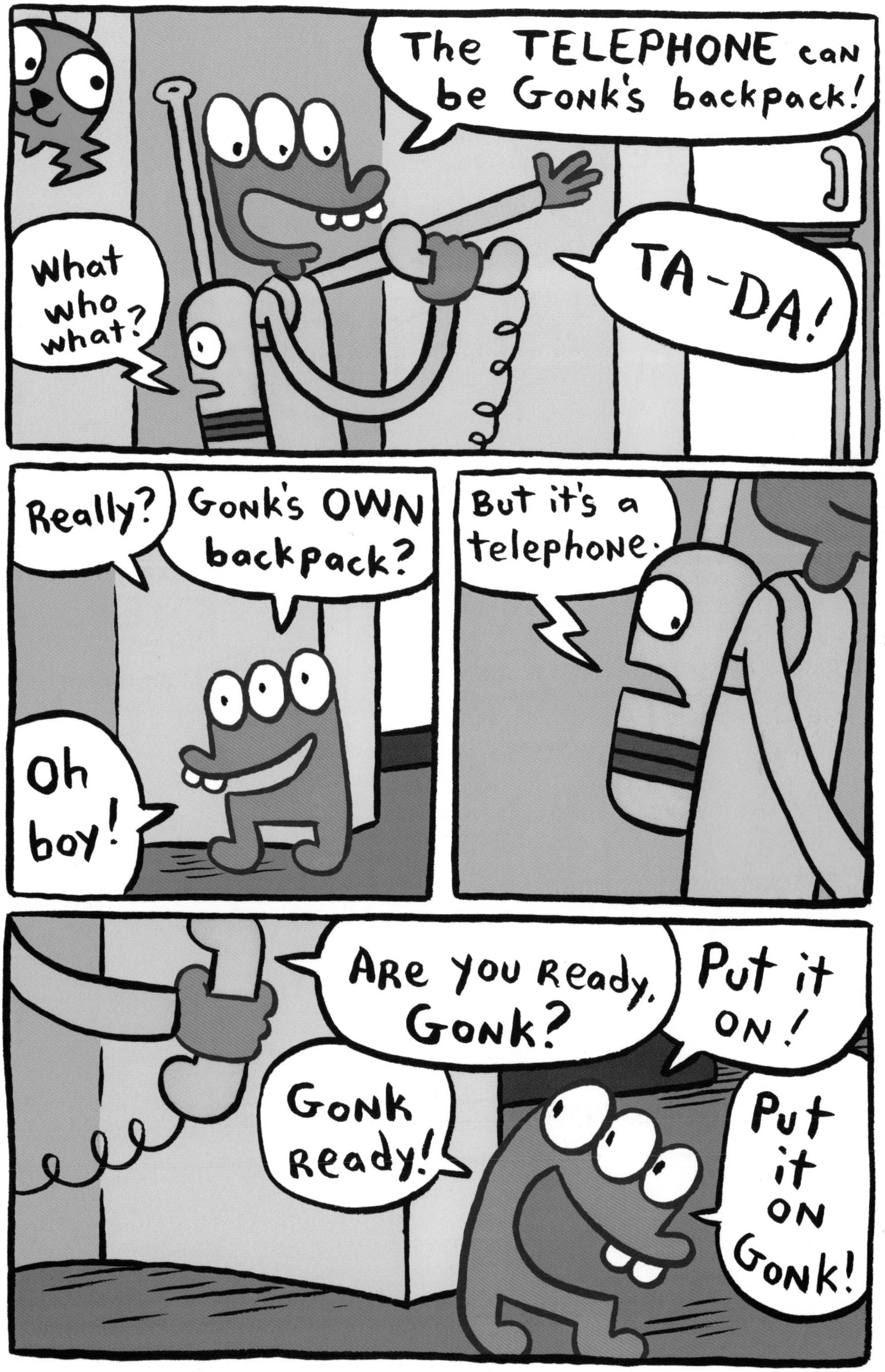
The TELEPHONE can be Gonk's backpack!
What who what?
TA-DA!
Really?
Gonk's OWN backpack?
Oh boy!
But it's a telephone.
Are you ready, Gonk?
Put it ON!
Gonk ready!
Put it ON Gonk!

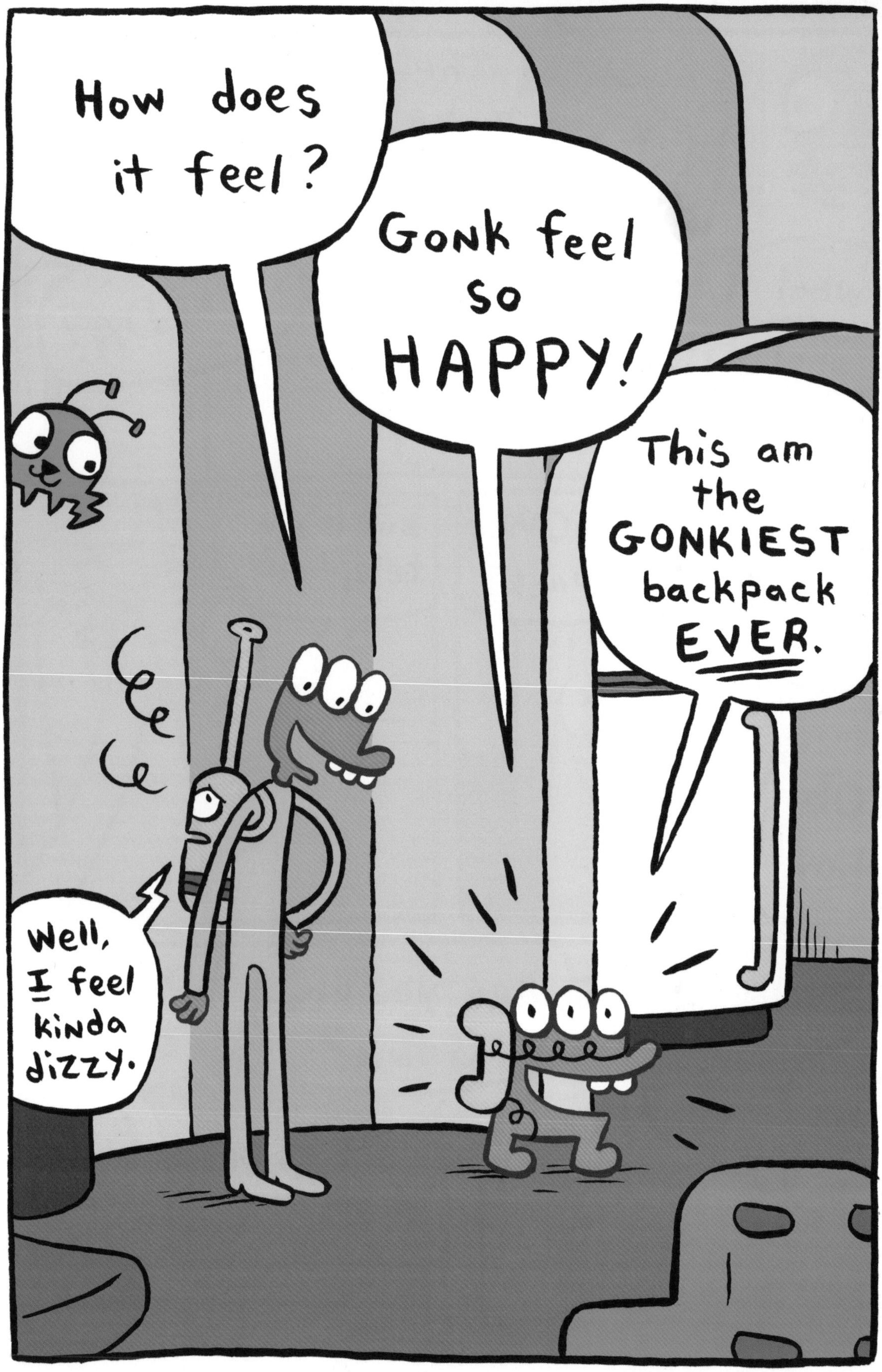
How does it feel?
Gonk feel so HAPPY!
This am the GONKIEST backpack EVER.
Well, I feel kinda dizzy.

CHAPTER SIX

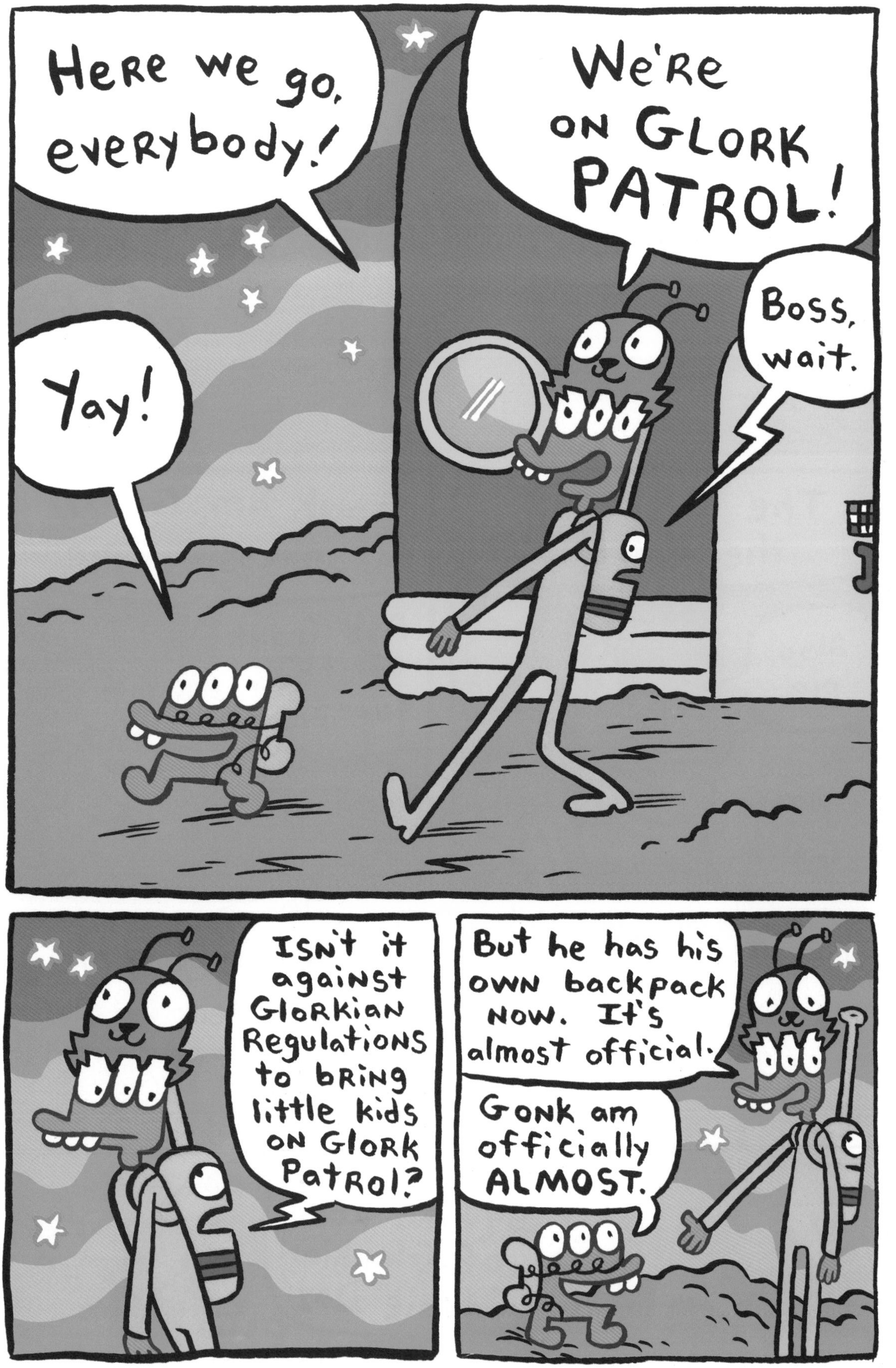
Here we go, everybody!
We're on GLORK PATROL!
Yay!
Boss, wait.
Isn't it against Glorkian Regulations to bring little kids on Glork Patrol?
But he has his own backpack now. It's almost official.
Gonk am officially ALMOST.

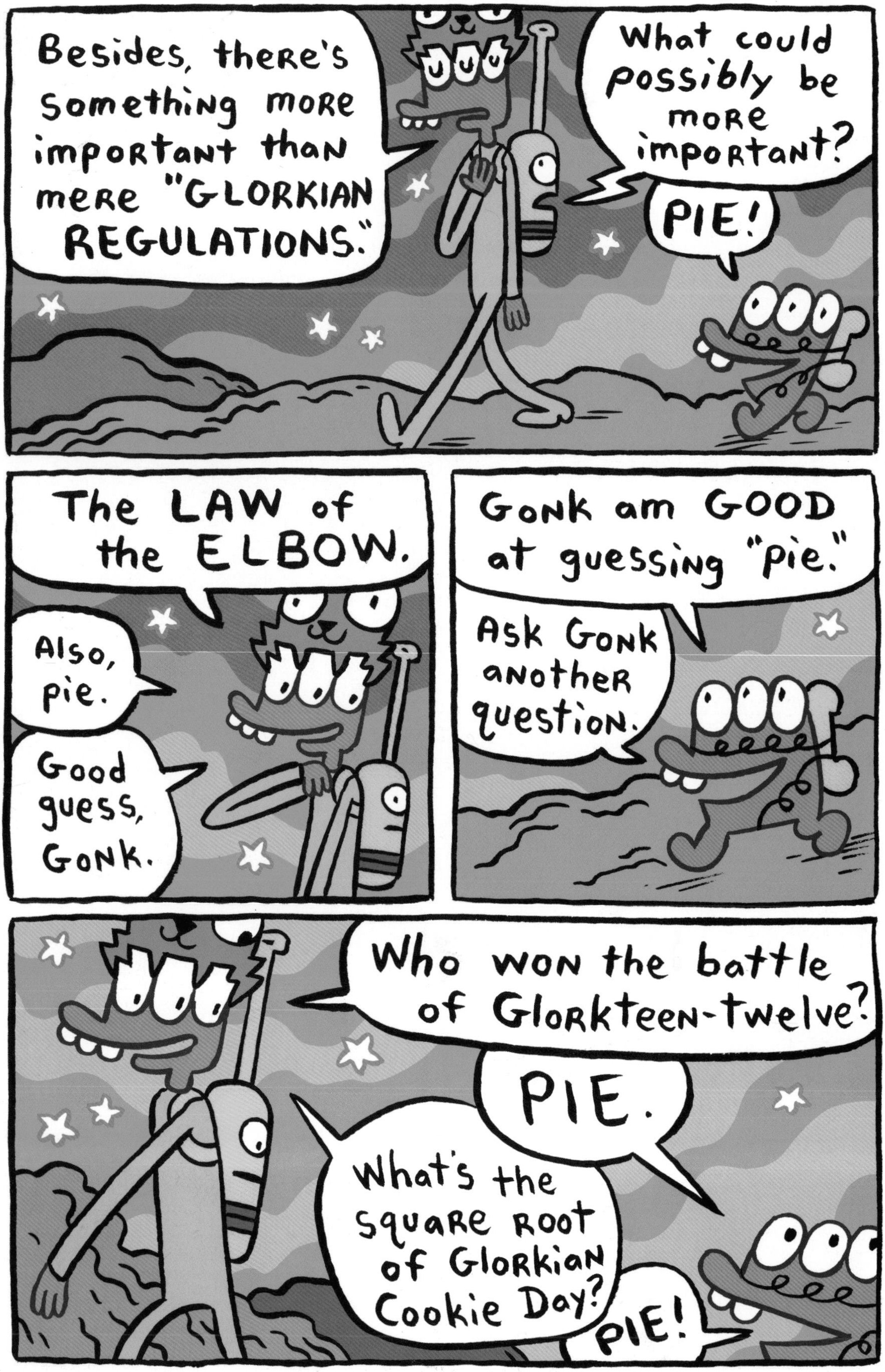
Besides, there's something more important than mere "GLORKIAN REGULATIONS."
What could possibly be more important?
PIE!
The LAW of the ELBOW.
Also, pie.
Good guess, Gonk.
Gonk am GOOD at guessing "pie."
Ask Gonk another question.
Who won the battle of Glorkteen-twelve?
PIE.
What's the square root of Glorkian Cookie Day?
PIE!

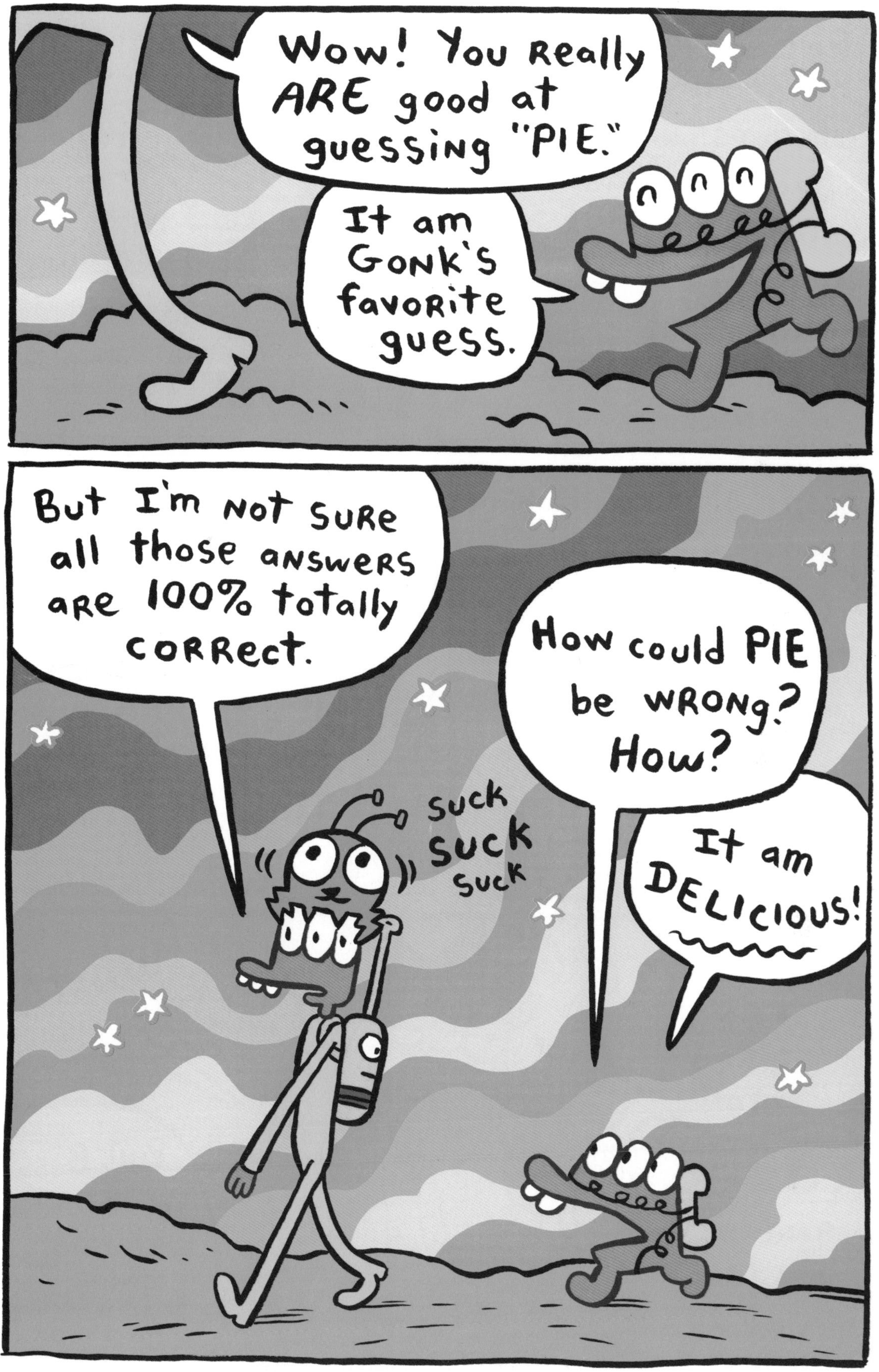

Wow! You really ARE good at guessing "PIE."
It am Gonk's favorite guess.
But I'm not sure all those answers are 100% totally correct.
How could PIE be wrong? How?
It am DELICIOUS!
suck
SUCK
suck

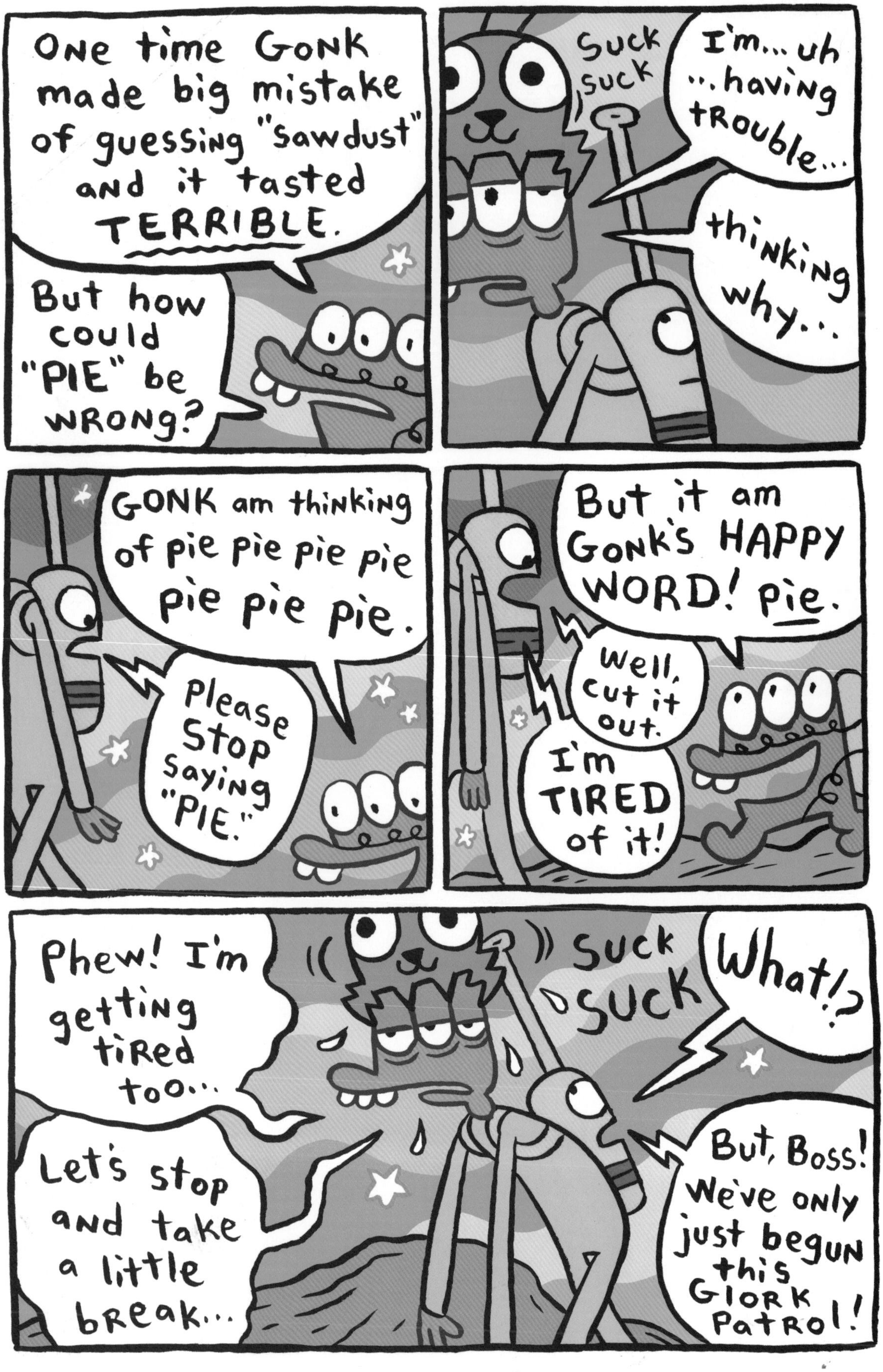

One time GONK made big mistake of guessing "sawdust" and it tasted TERRIBLE.
But how could "PIE" be WRONG?
Suck suck
I'm... uh ...having trouble...
thinking why...
GONK am thinking of pie pie pie pie pie pie pie.
Please Stop saying "PIE."
But it am GONK'S HAPPY WORD! pie.
Well, cut it out.
I'm TIRED of it!
Phew! I'm getting tired too...
Let's stop and take a little break...
Suck SUCK
What!?
But, Boss! We've only just begun this GLORK PATROL!

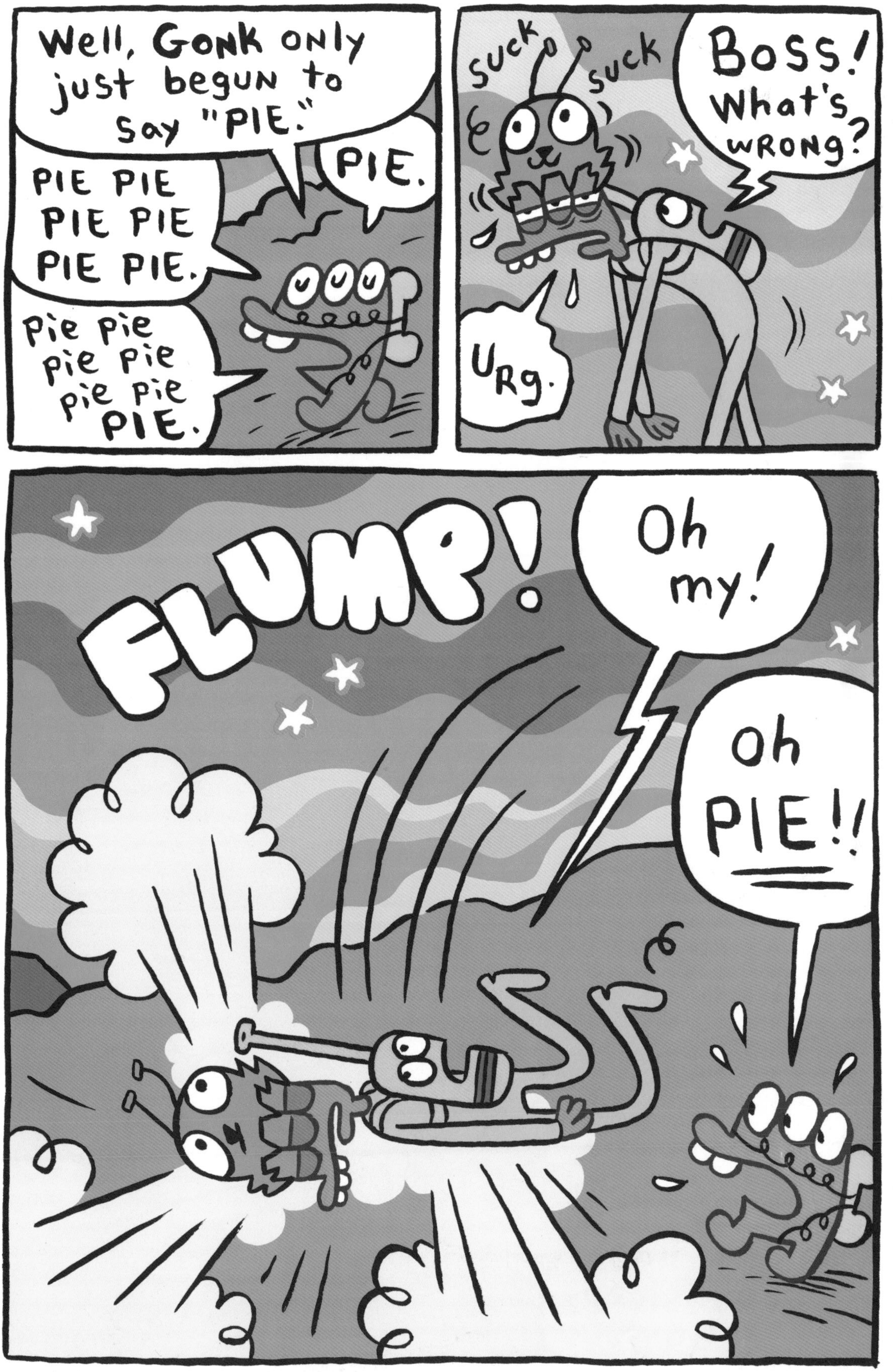
Well, GONK only just begun to say "PIE."
PIE.
PIE PIE PIE PIE PIE PIE.
pie pie pie pie pie pie PIE.
SUCK SUCK
BOSS! What's WRONG?
URG.
FLUMP!
Oh my!
Oh PIE!!

CHAPTER SEVEN

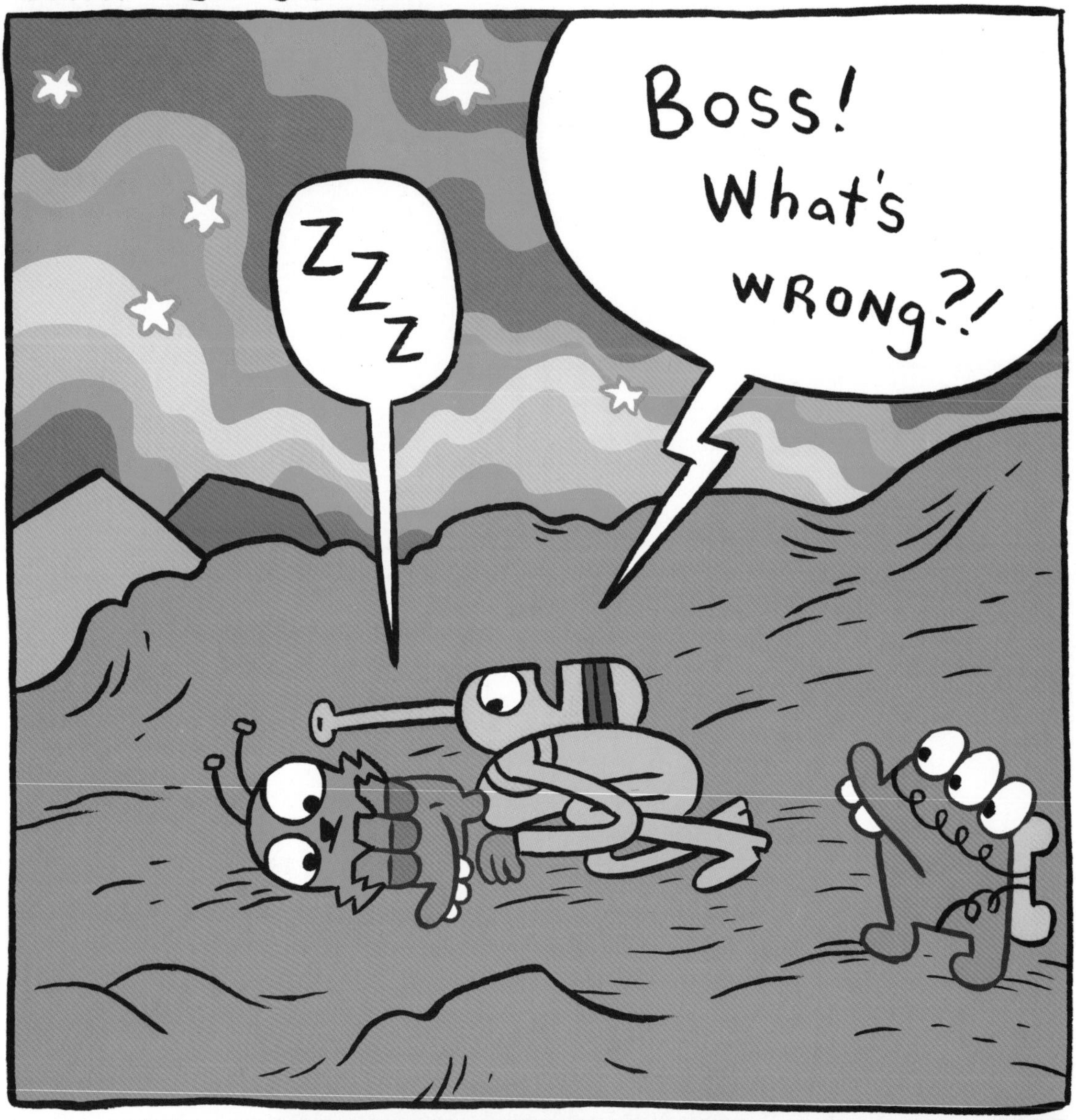
ZZZ
Boss! What's WRONG?!

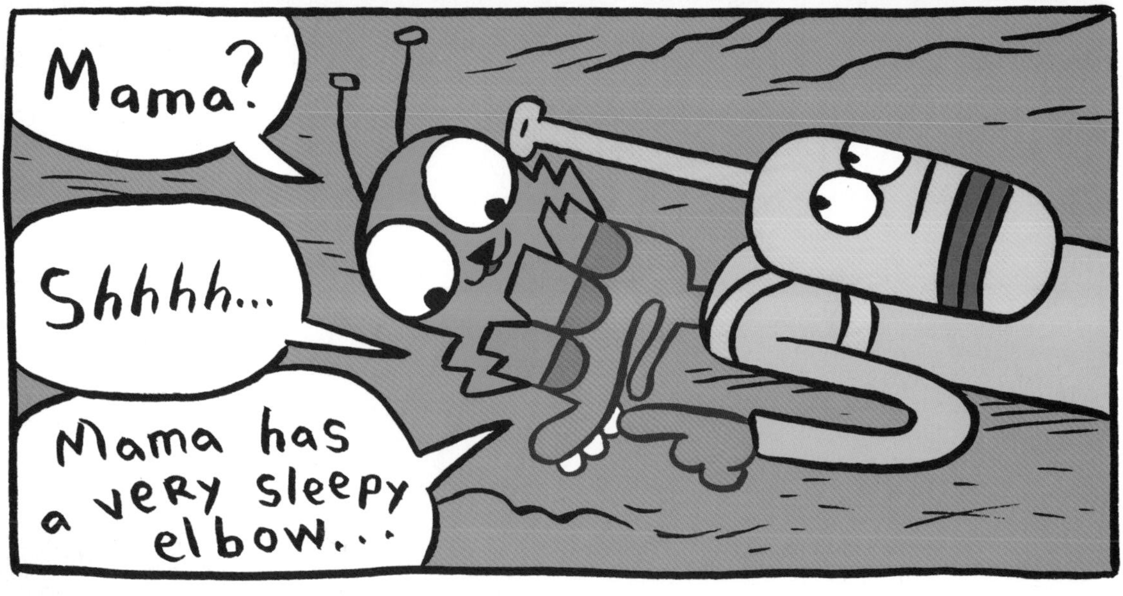
Mama?
Shhhh...
Mama has a very sleepy elbow...

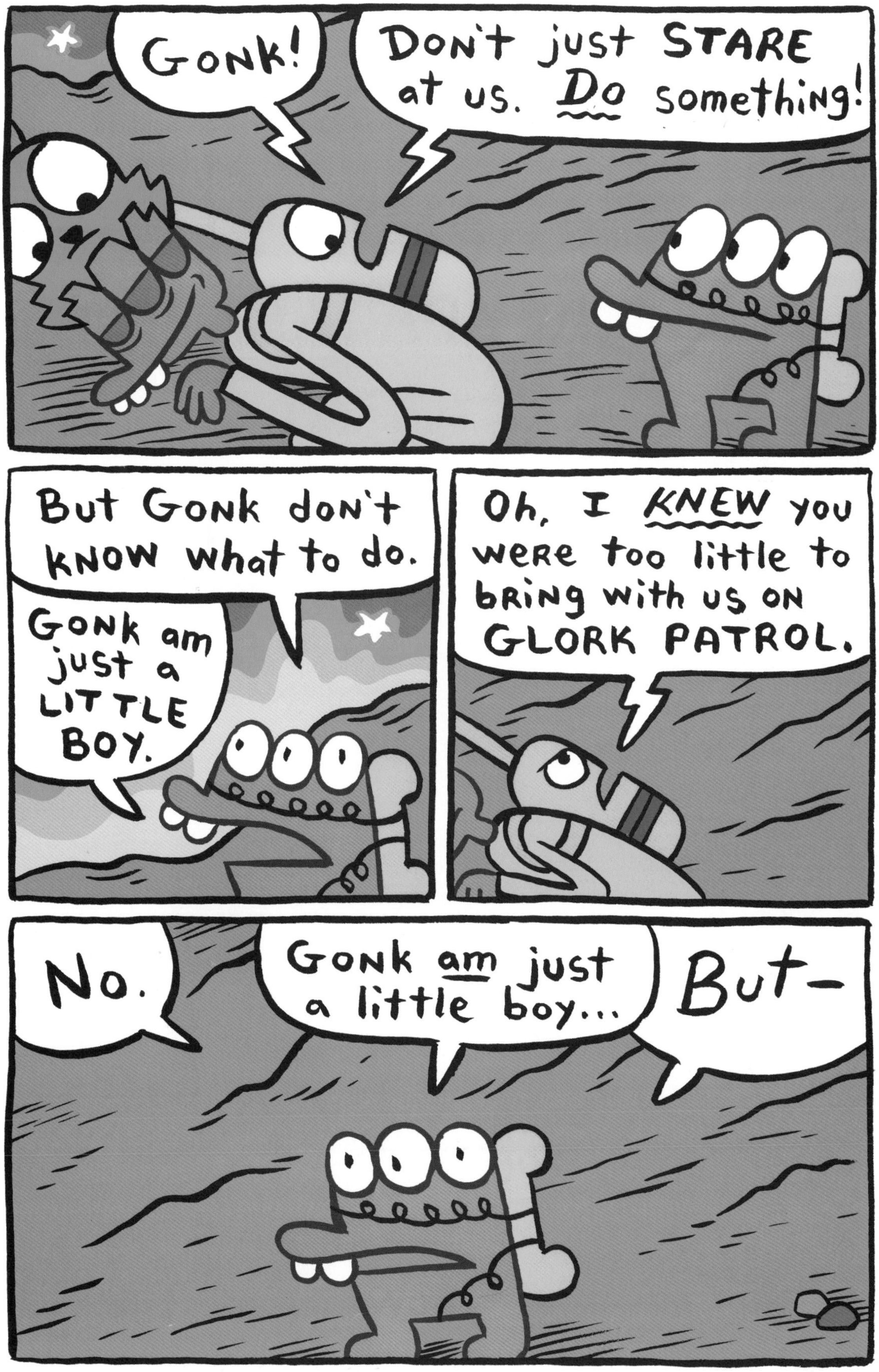
GONK!
Don't just STARE at us. DO something!
But Gonk don't KNOW what to do.
Gonk am just a LITTLE BOY.
Oh, I KNEW you were too little to bring with us on GLORK PATROL.
No.
Gonk am just a little boy...
But-

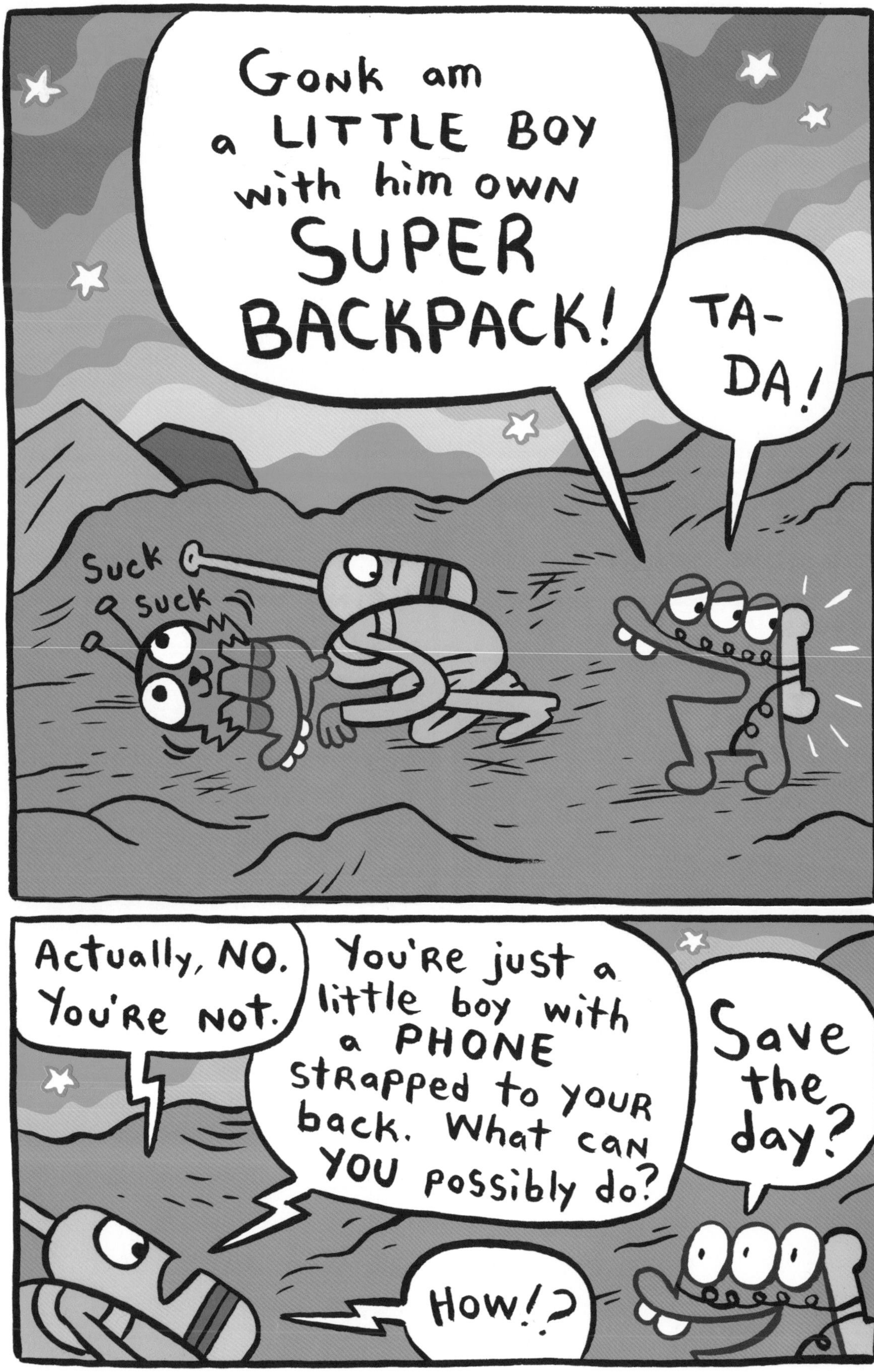
Gonk am a LITTLE BOY with him own SUPER BACKPACK!
TA-DA!
Suck suck
Actually, NO. You're not.
You're just a little boy with a PHONE strapped to your back. What can YOU possibly do?
Save the day?
How!?

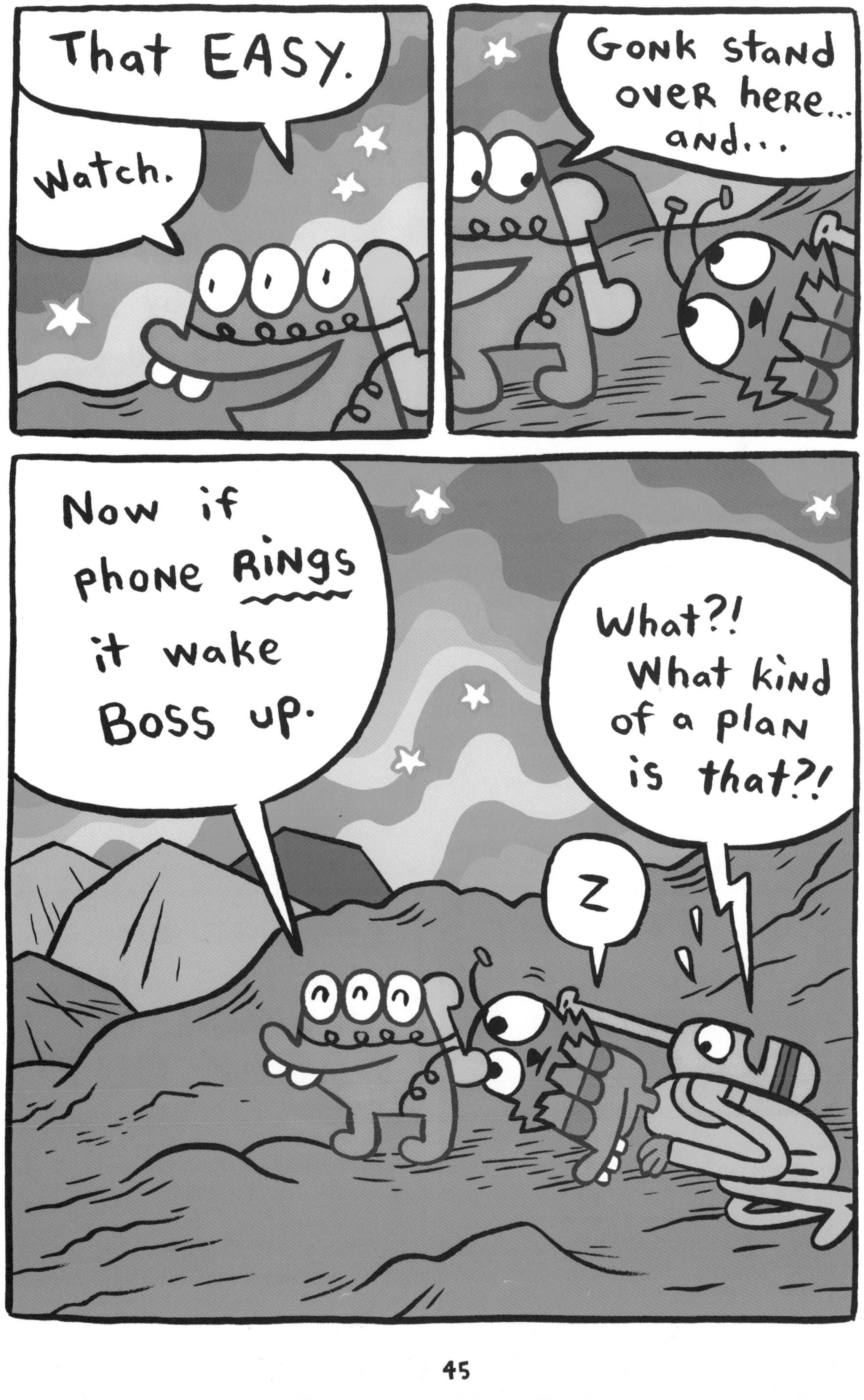
That EASY.
Watch.
Gonk stand over here... and...
Now if phone RINGS it wake Boss up.
What?! What kind of a plan is that?!
Z

CHAPTER EIGHT

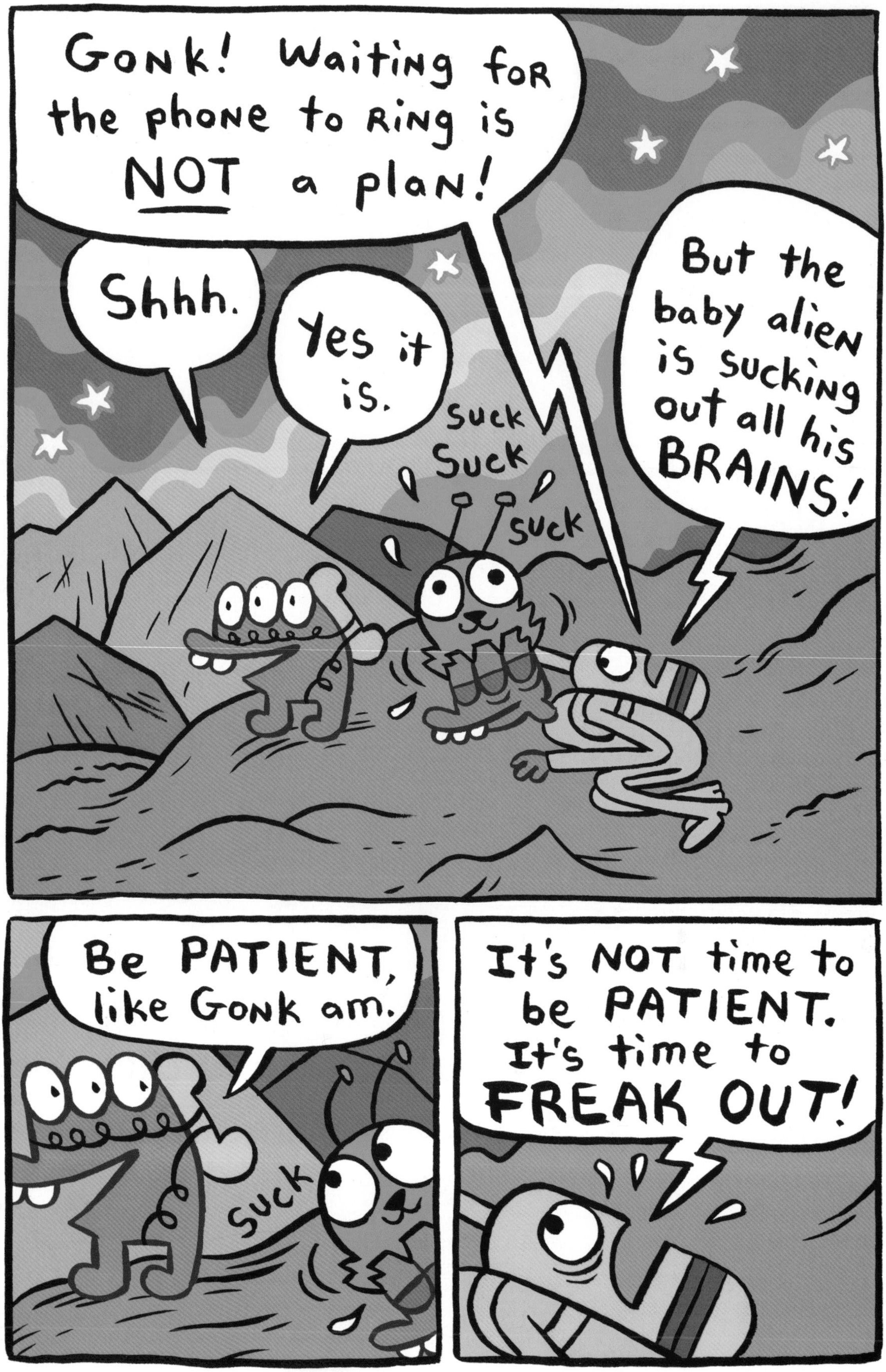
GONK! WAITING FOR the phone to RING is NOT a plan!
Shhh.
Yes it is.
SUCK
SUCK
SUCK
But the baby alien is sucking out all his BRAINS!
Be PATIENT, like GONK am.
SUCK
It's NOT time to be PATIENT. It's time to FREAK OUT!

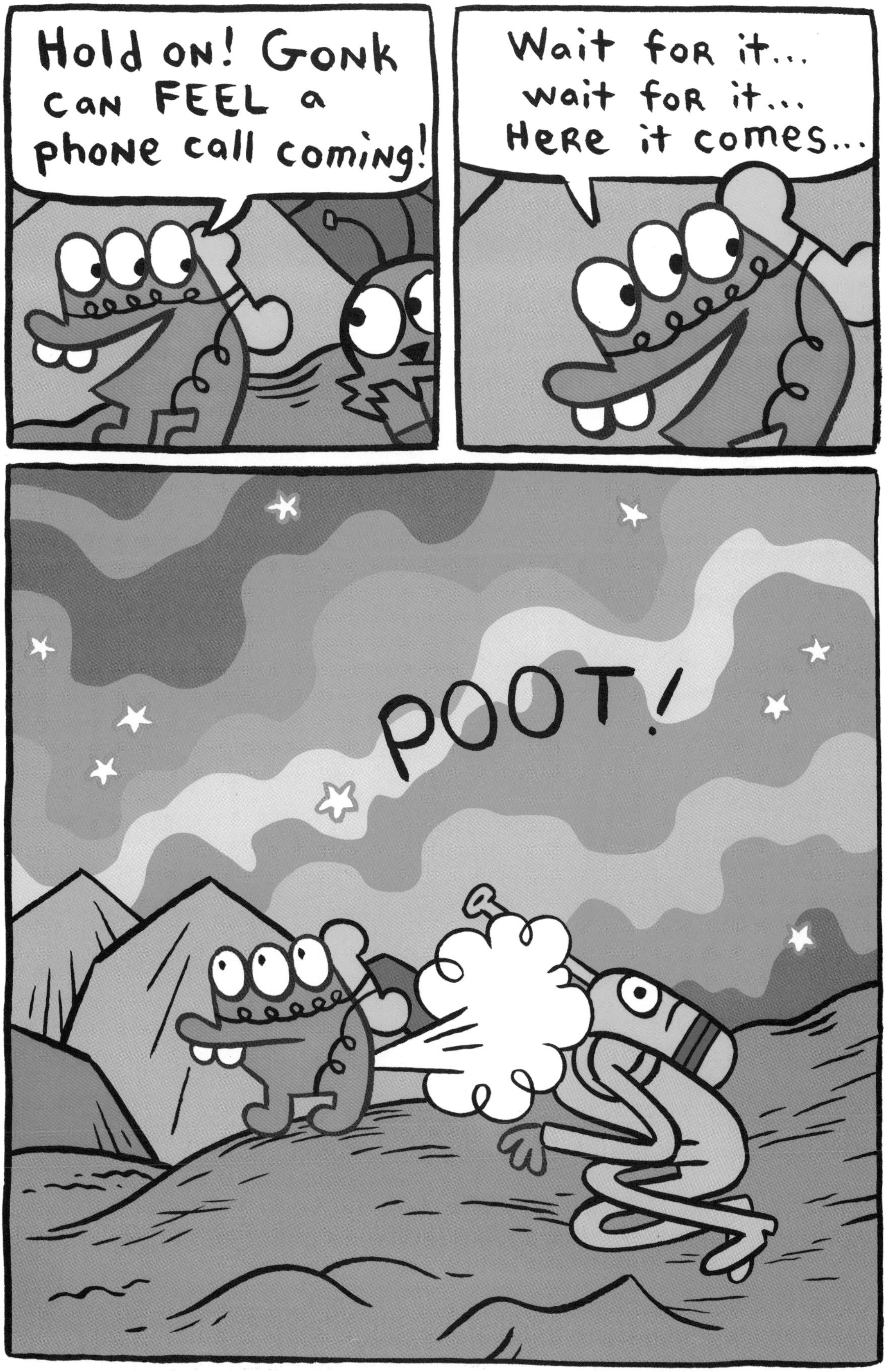
Hold on! Gonk can FEEL a phone call coming!
Wait for it... wait for it... Here it comes...
POOT!

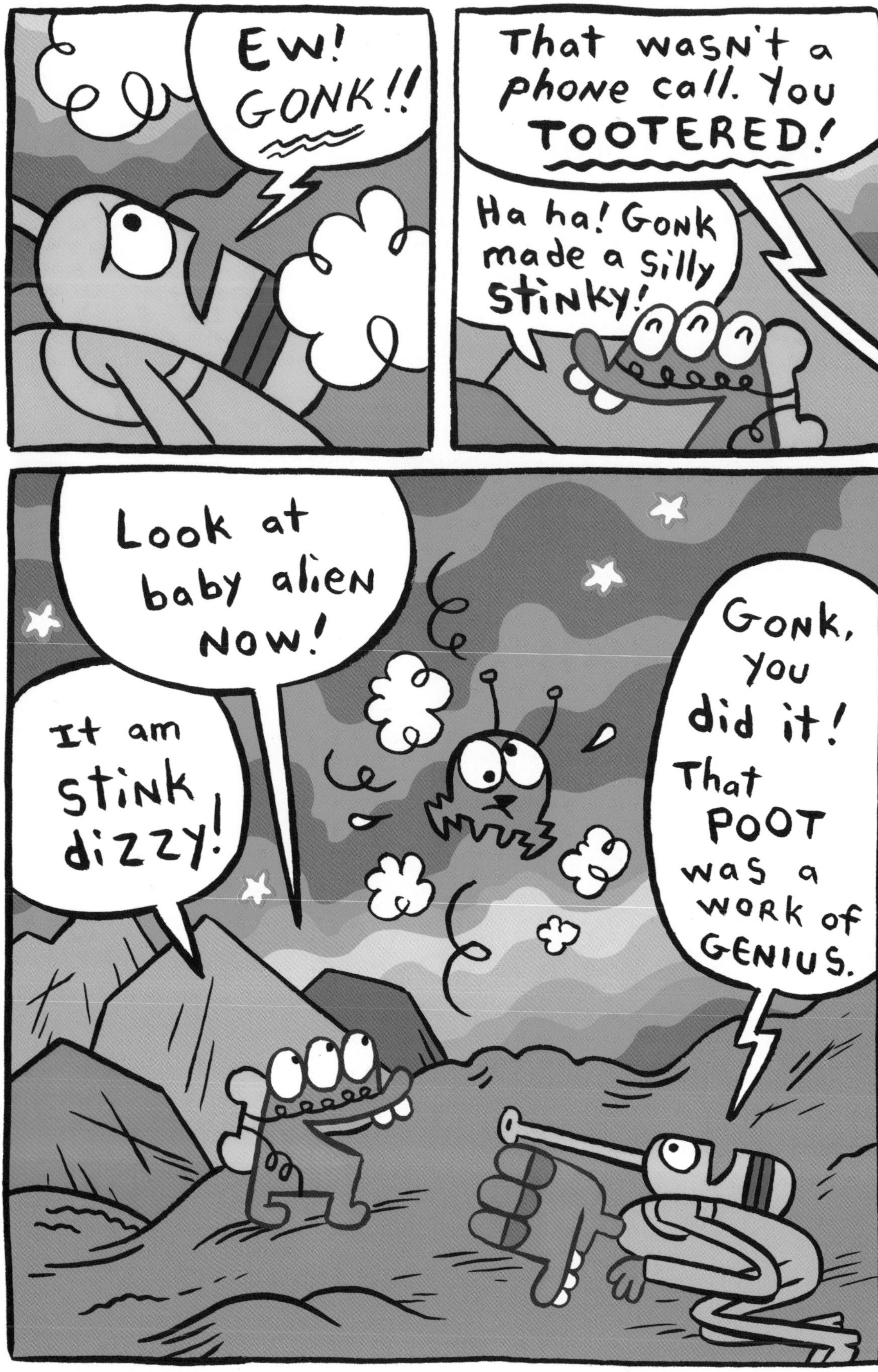
EW! GONK!!
That wasn't a phone call. You TOOTERED!
Ha ha! Gonk made a silly stinky!
Look at baby alien now!
It am stink dizzy!
Gonk, you did it! That POOT was a work of GENIUS.

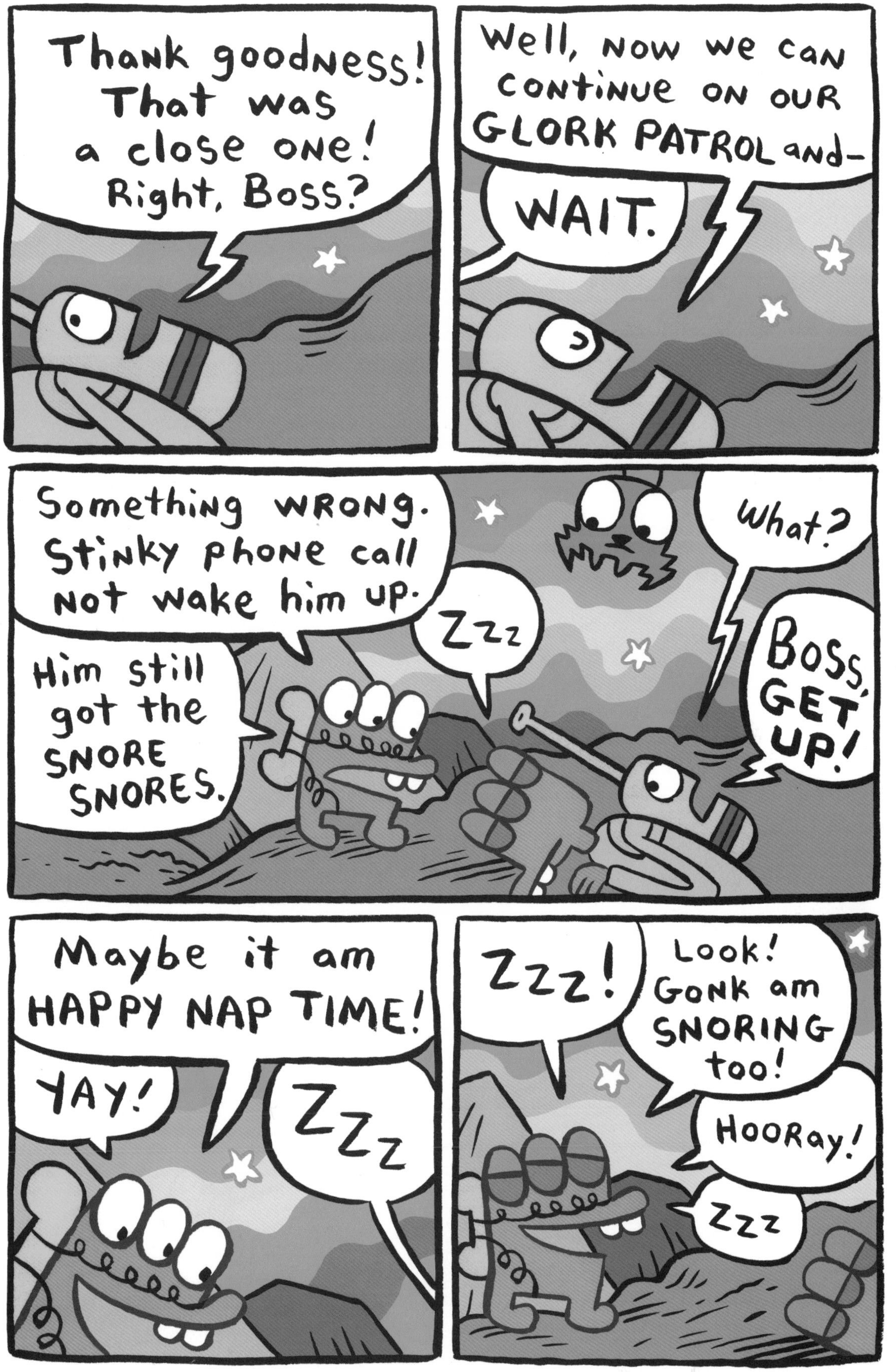
Thank goodness! That was a close one! Right, Boss?
Well, now we can continue on our GLORK PATROL and-
WAIT.
Something WRONG. Stinky phone call not wake him up.
Him still got the SNORE SNORES.
Zzz
What?
BOSS, GET UP!
Maybe it am HAPPY NAP TIME!
YAY!
ZZZ
ZZZ!
Look! Gonk am SNORING too!
HOORay!
Zzz

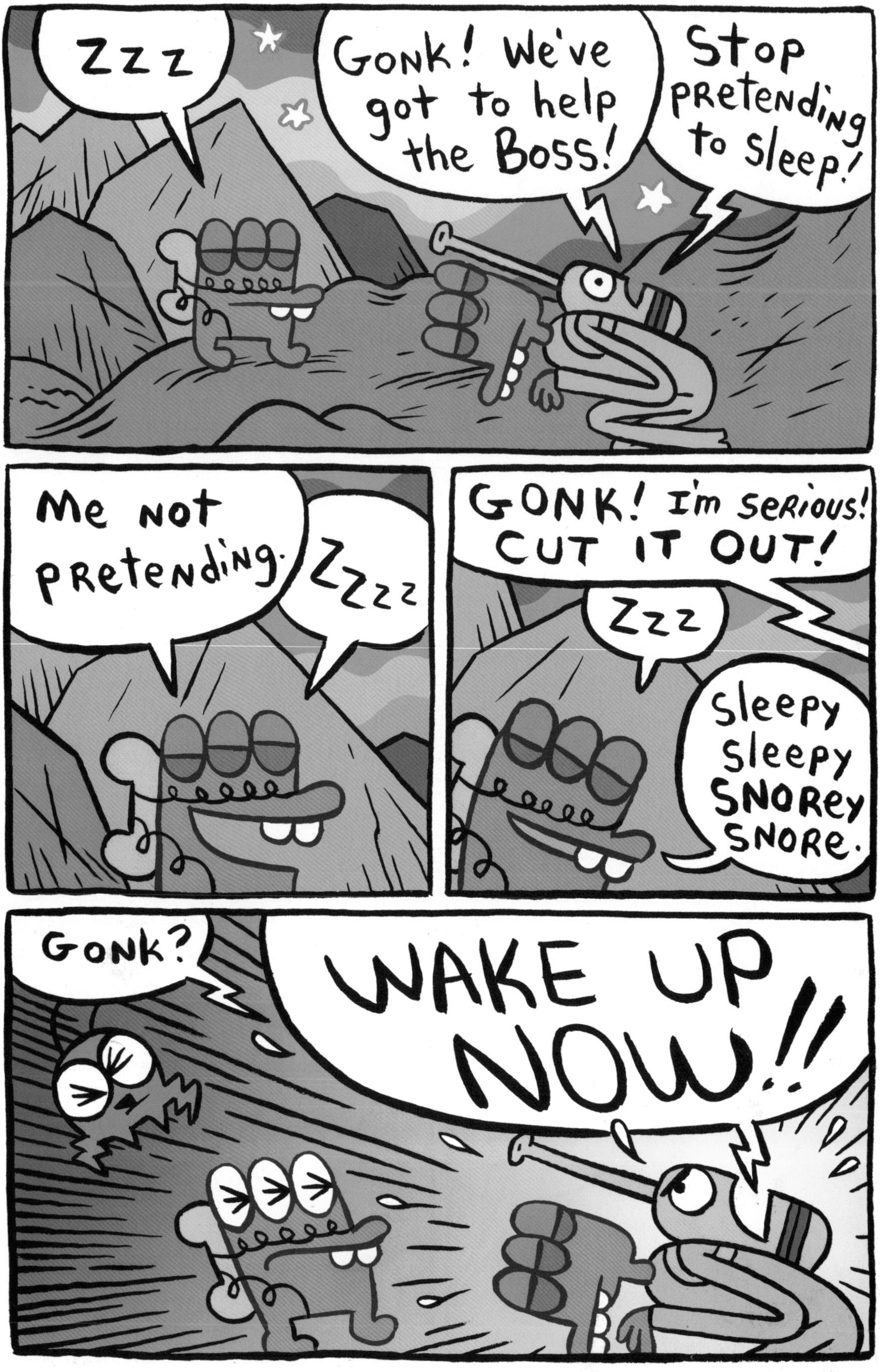
ZZZ
Gonk! We've got to help the Boss!
Stop pretending to sleep!
Me not pretending.
ZZZZ
GONK! I'm SERIOUS! CUT IT OUT!
ZZZ
Sleepy sleepy SNOREY SNORE.
GONK?
WAKE UP NOW!!

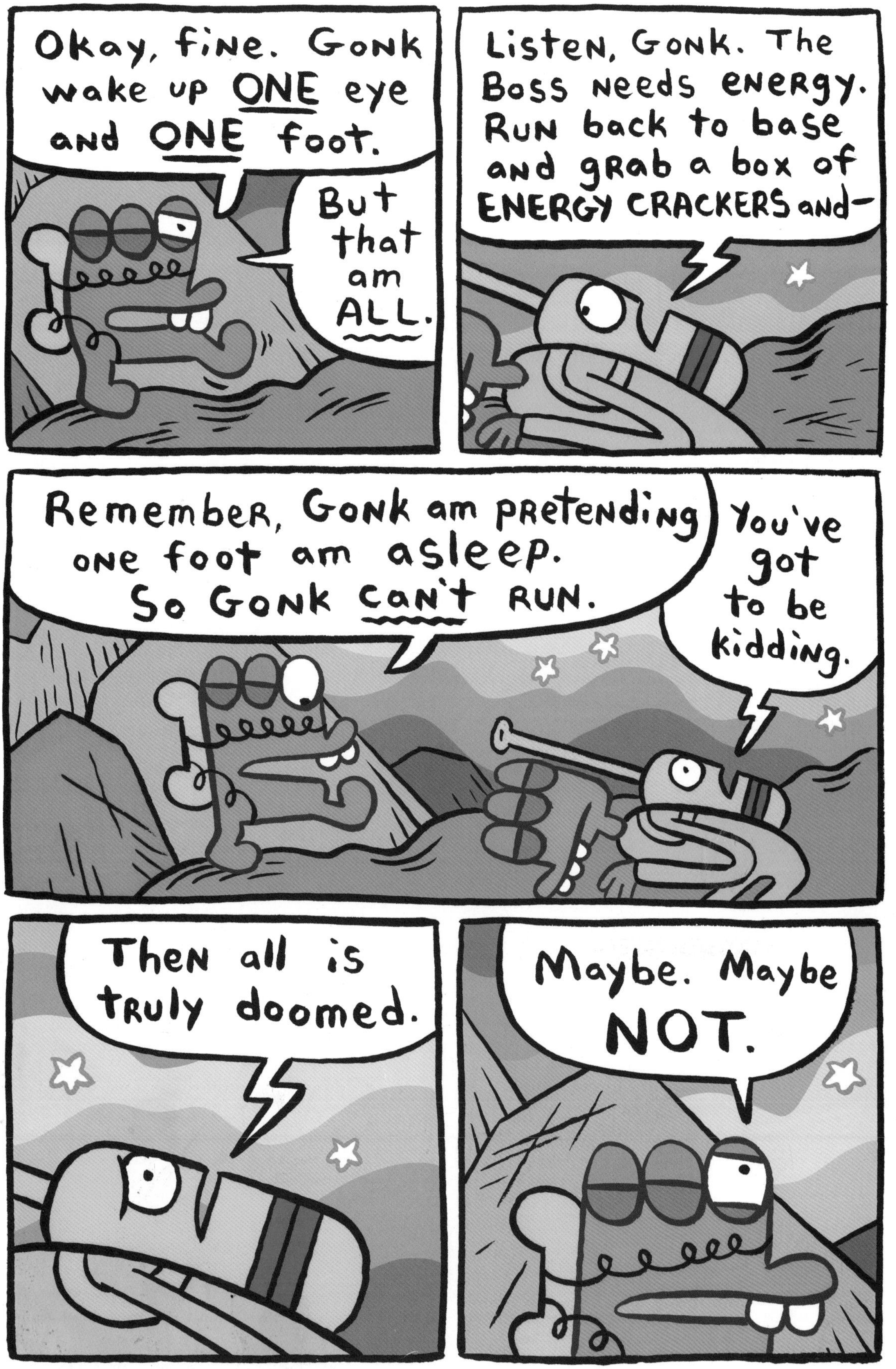

Okay, fine. Gonk wake up ONE eye and ONE foot.
But that am ALL.
Listen, Gonk. The Boss needs energy. Run back to base and grab a box of ENERGY CRACKERS and–
Remember, Gonk am pretending one foot am asleep. So Gonk can't run.
You've got to be kidding.
Then all is truly doomed.
Maybe. Maybe NOT.

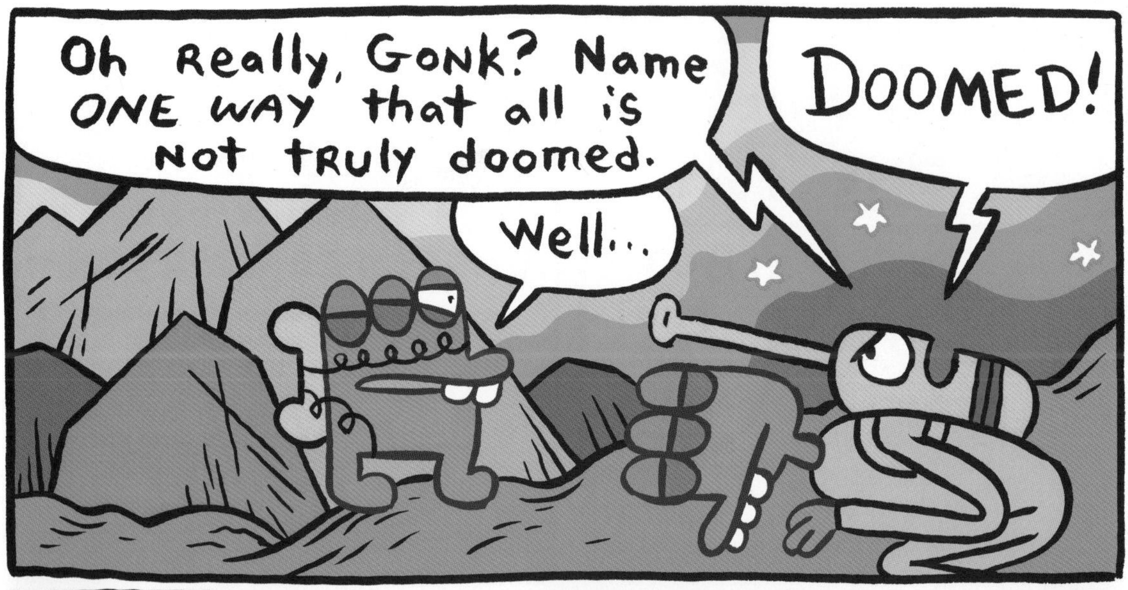
Oh Really, Gonk? Name ONE WAY that all is not truly doomed.
DOOMED!
Well...

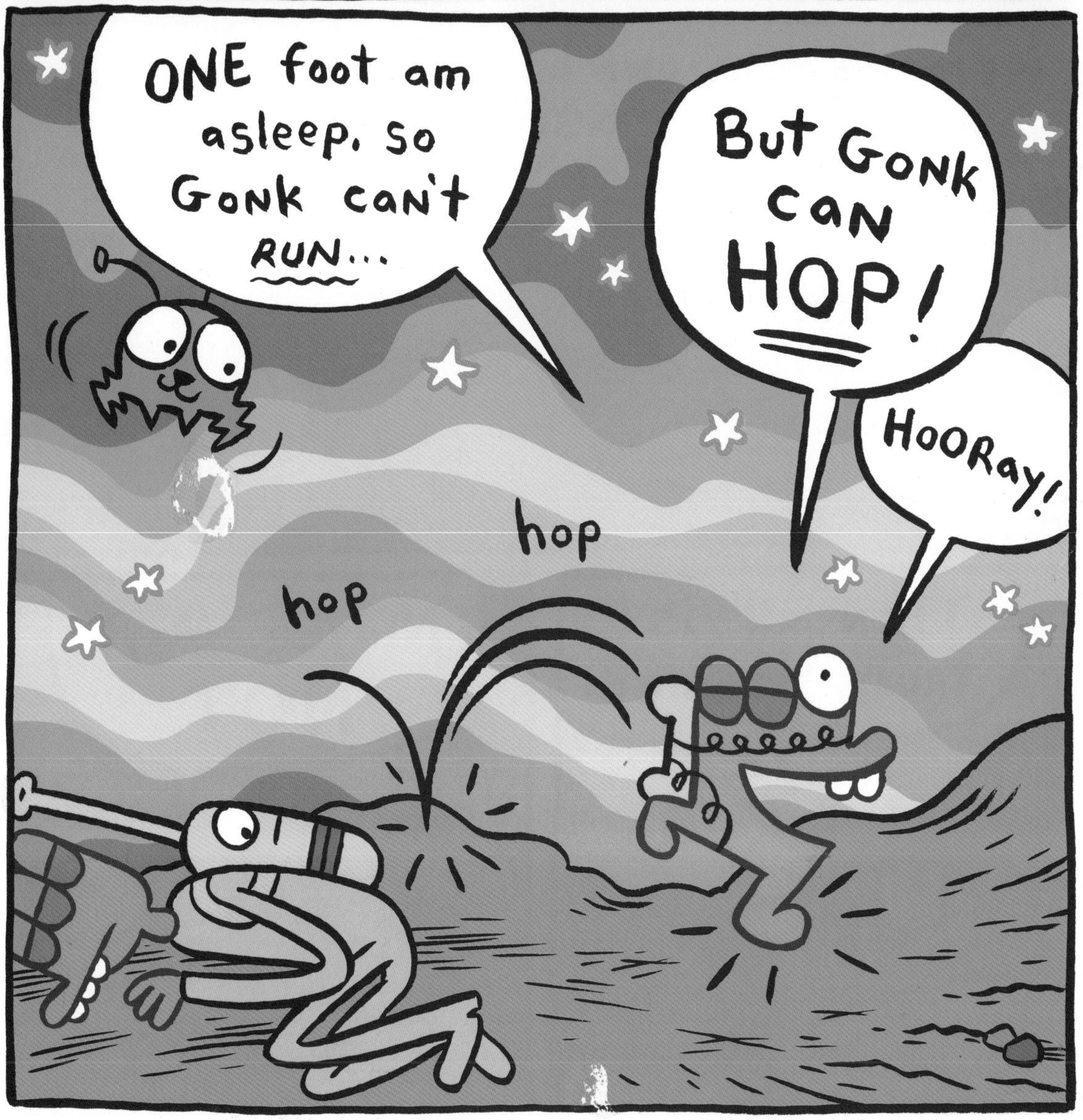
ONE foot am asleep, so Gonk can't RUN...
But Gonk can HOP!
HOORay!
hop
hop

CHAPTER NINE

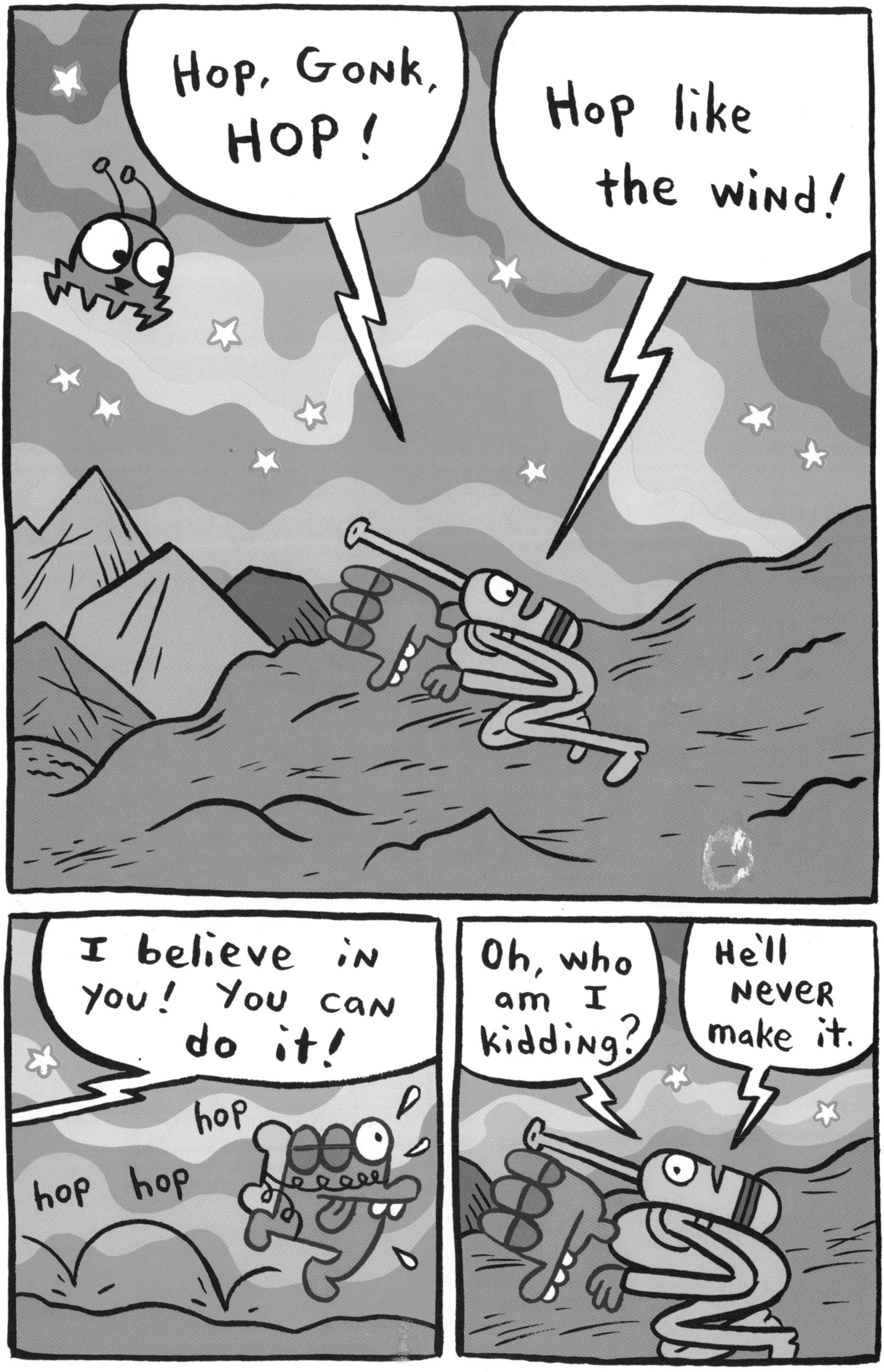

Hop, Gonk, HOP!
Hop like the wind!
I believe in you! You can do it!
hop
hop hop
Oh, who am I kidding?
He'll never make it.

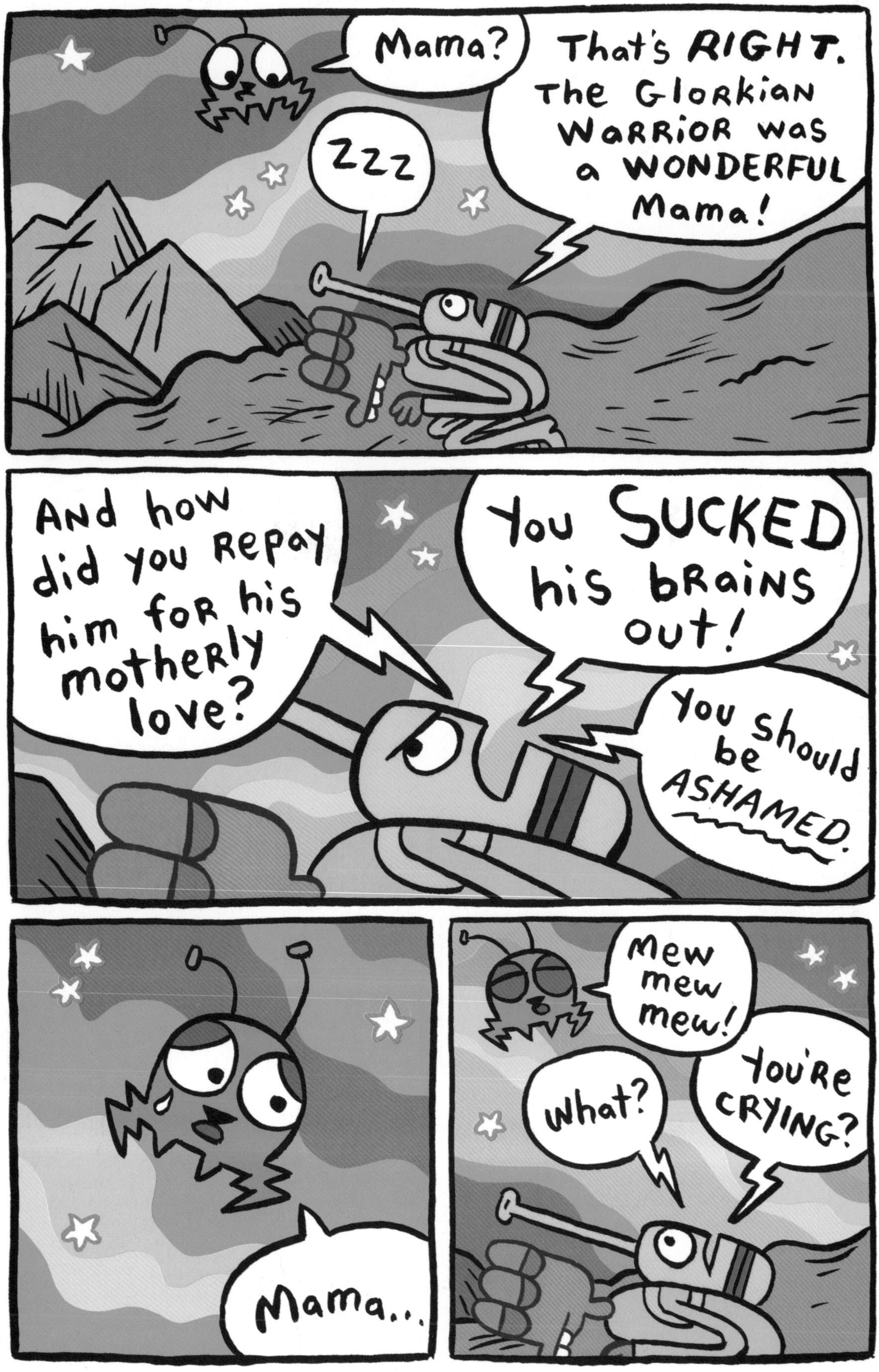

Mama?
That's RIGHT. The Glorkian Warrior was a WONDERFUL Mama!
ZZZ
And how did you repay him for his motherly love?
You SUCKED his brains out!
You should be ASHAMED.
Mama...
Mew mew mew!
What?
You're CRYING?

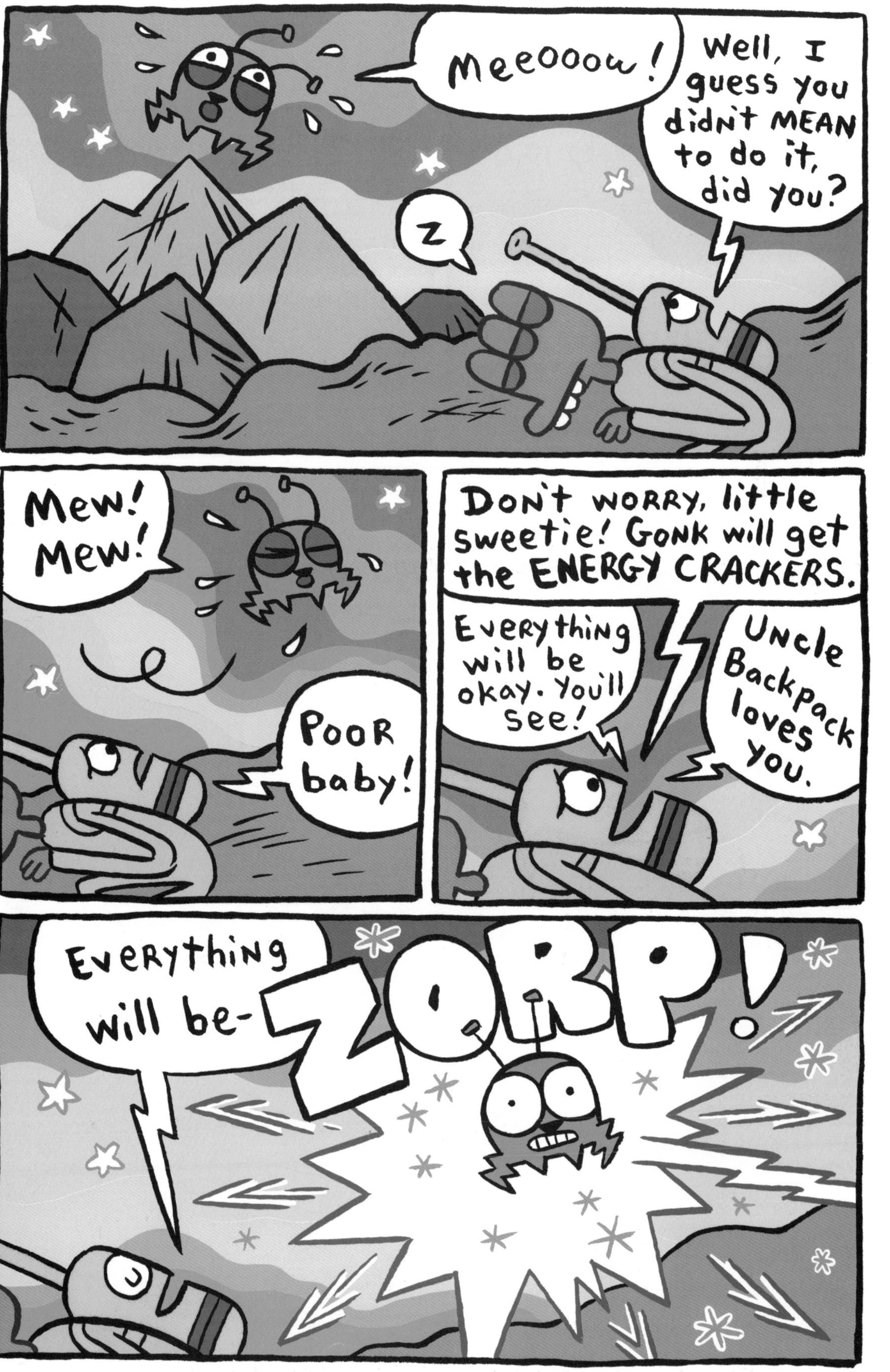
Meeooow!
Well, I guess you didn't MEAN to do it, did you?
Z
Mew! Mew!
POOR baby!
Don't worry, little sweetie! GONK will get the ENERGY CRACKERS.
Everything will be okay. You'll see!
Uncle Backpack loves you.
Everything will be-
ZORP!

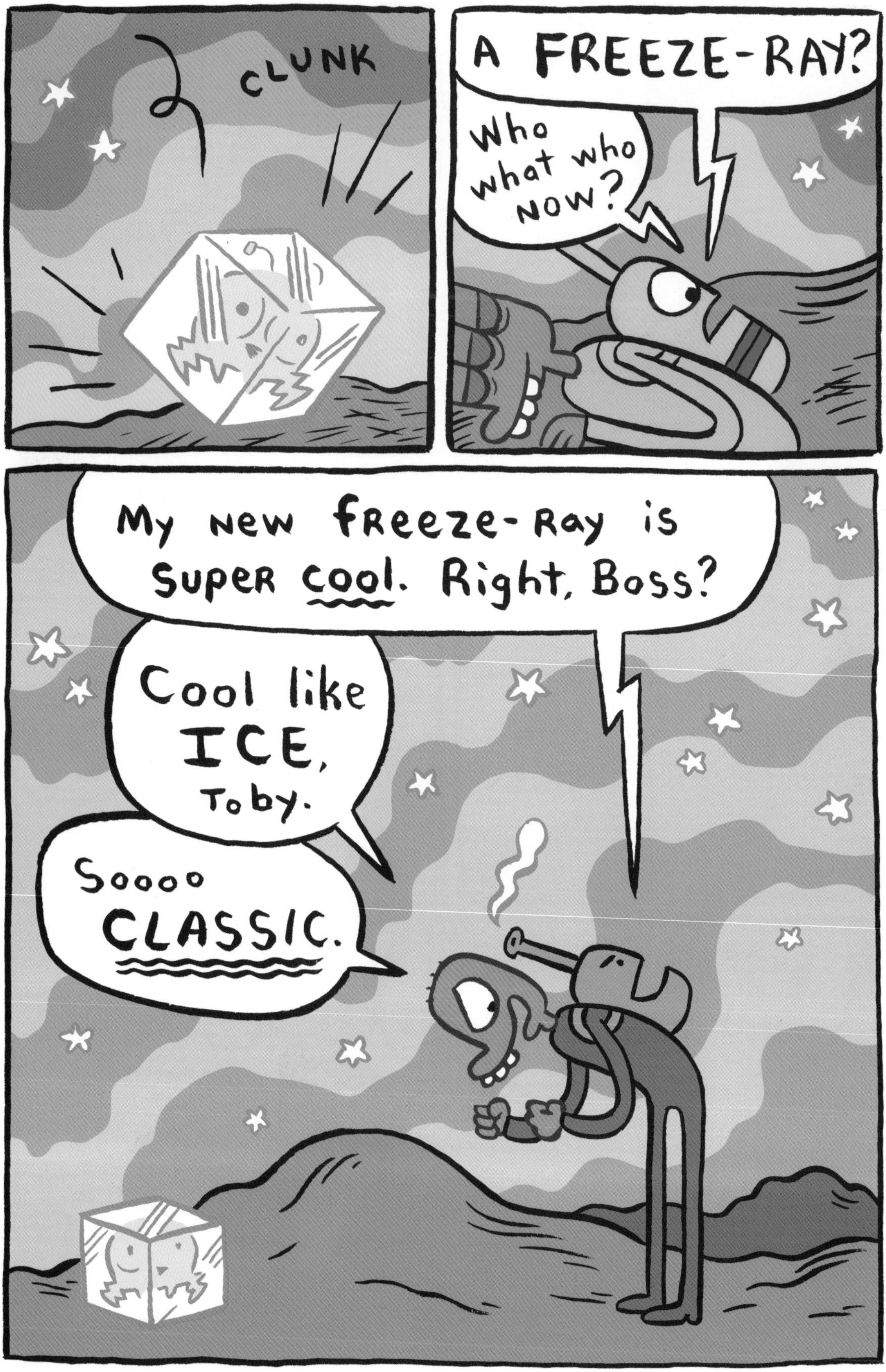
CLUNK
A FREEZE-RAY?
Who what who NOW?
My new freeze-Ray is super cool. Right, Boss?
Cool like ICE, Toby.
Soooo CLASSIC.

CHAPTER TEN

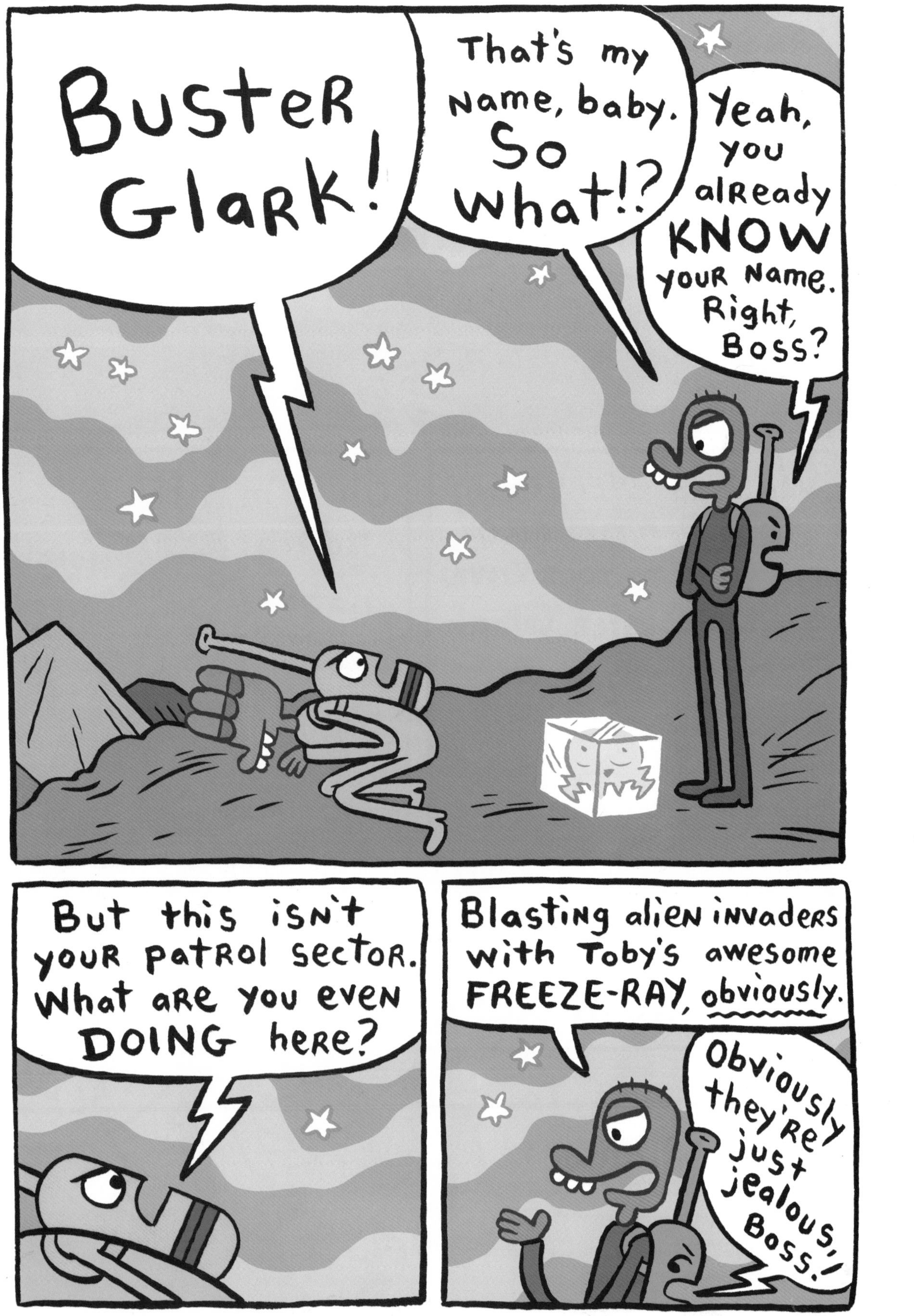

Buster Glark!
That's my Name, baby. So what!?
Yeah, you already KNOW your Name. Right, Boss?
But this isn't your patrol sector. What are you even DOING here?
Blasting alien invaders with Toby's awesome FREEZE-RAY, obviously.
Obviously they're just jealous, Boss.!

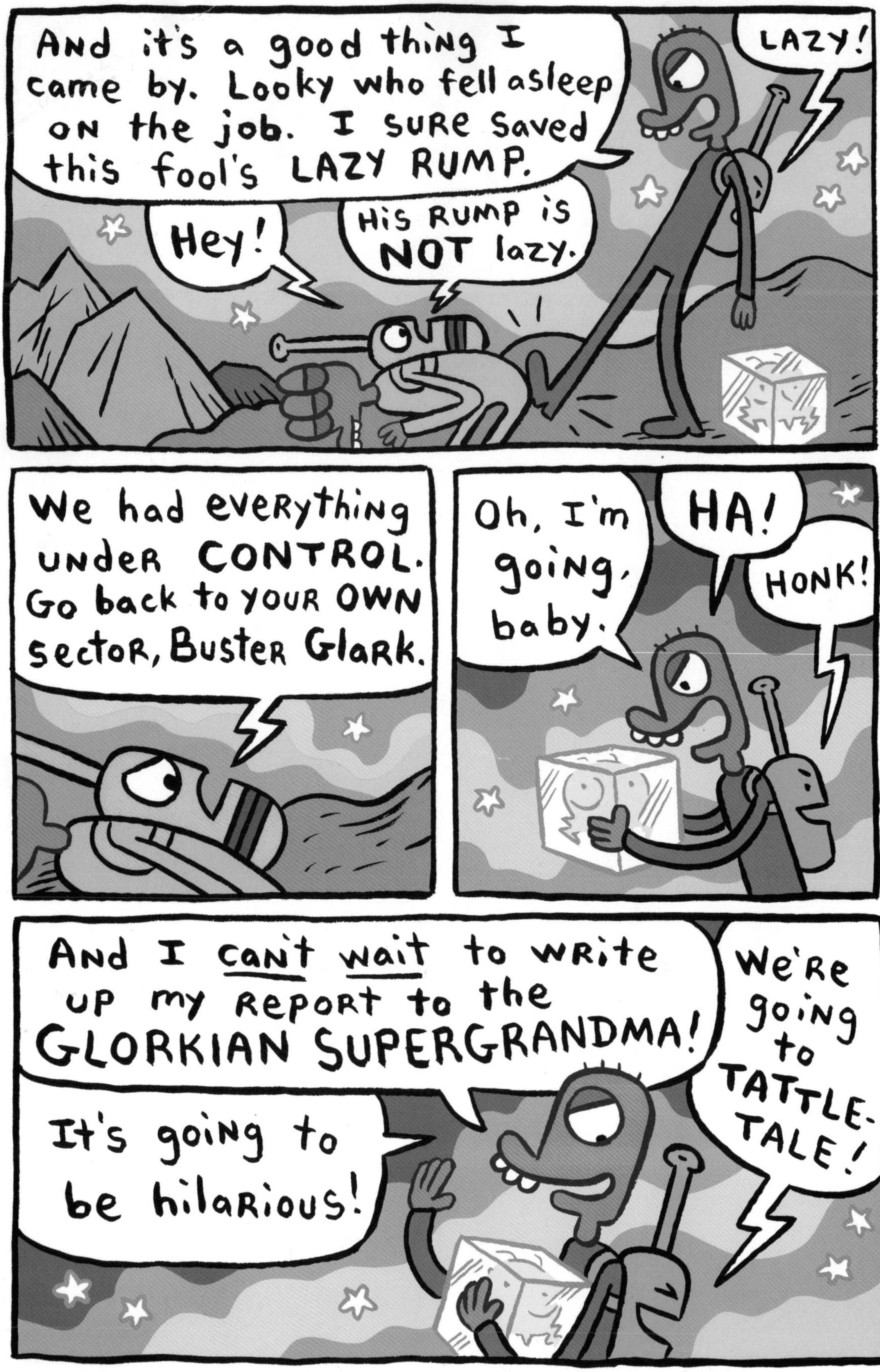
And it's a good thing I came by. Looky who fell asleep on the job. I sure saved this fool's LAZY RUMP.
LAZY!
Hey!
His RUMP is NOT lazy.
We had everything under CONTROL. Go back to your OWN sector, Buster Glark.
Oh, I'm going, baby.
HA!
HONK!
And I can't wait to write up my report to the GLORKIAN SUPERGRANDMA!
It's going to be hilarious!
We're going to TATTLE-TALE!

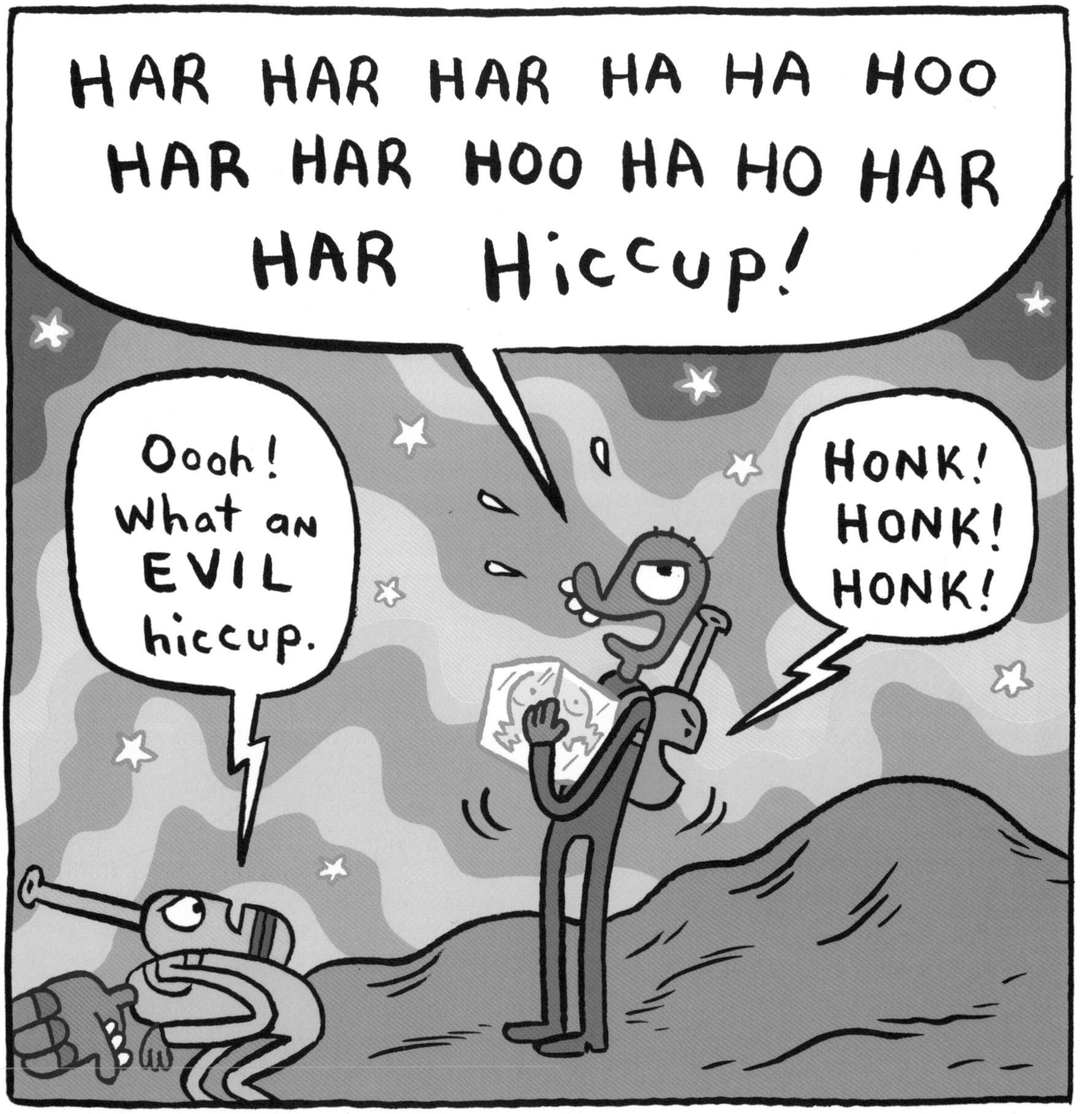
HAR HAR HAR HA HA HOO HAR HAR HOO HA HO HAR HAR Hiccup!
Oooh! What an EVIL hiccup.
HONK! HONK! HONK!

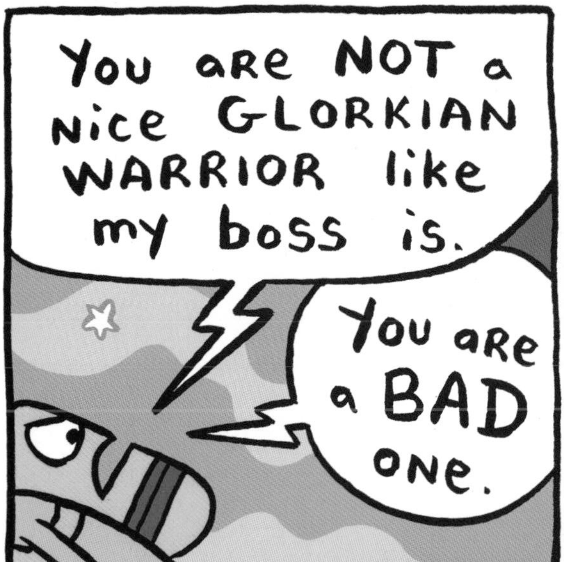
You are NOT a nice GLORKIAN WARRIOR like my boss is.
You are a BAD one.

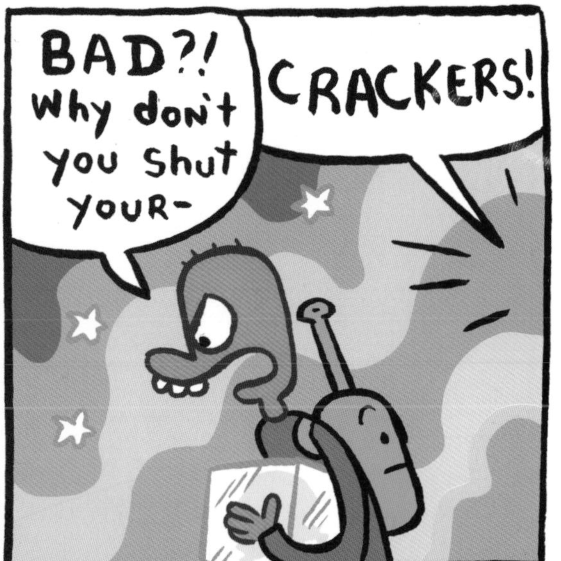
BAD?! Why don't you shut your-
CRACKERS!

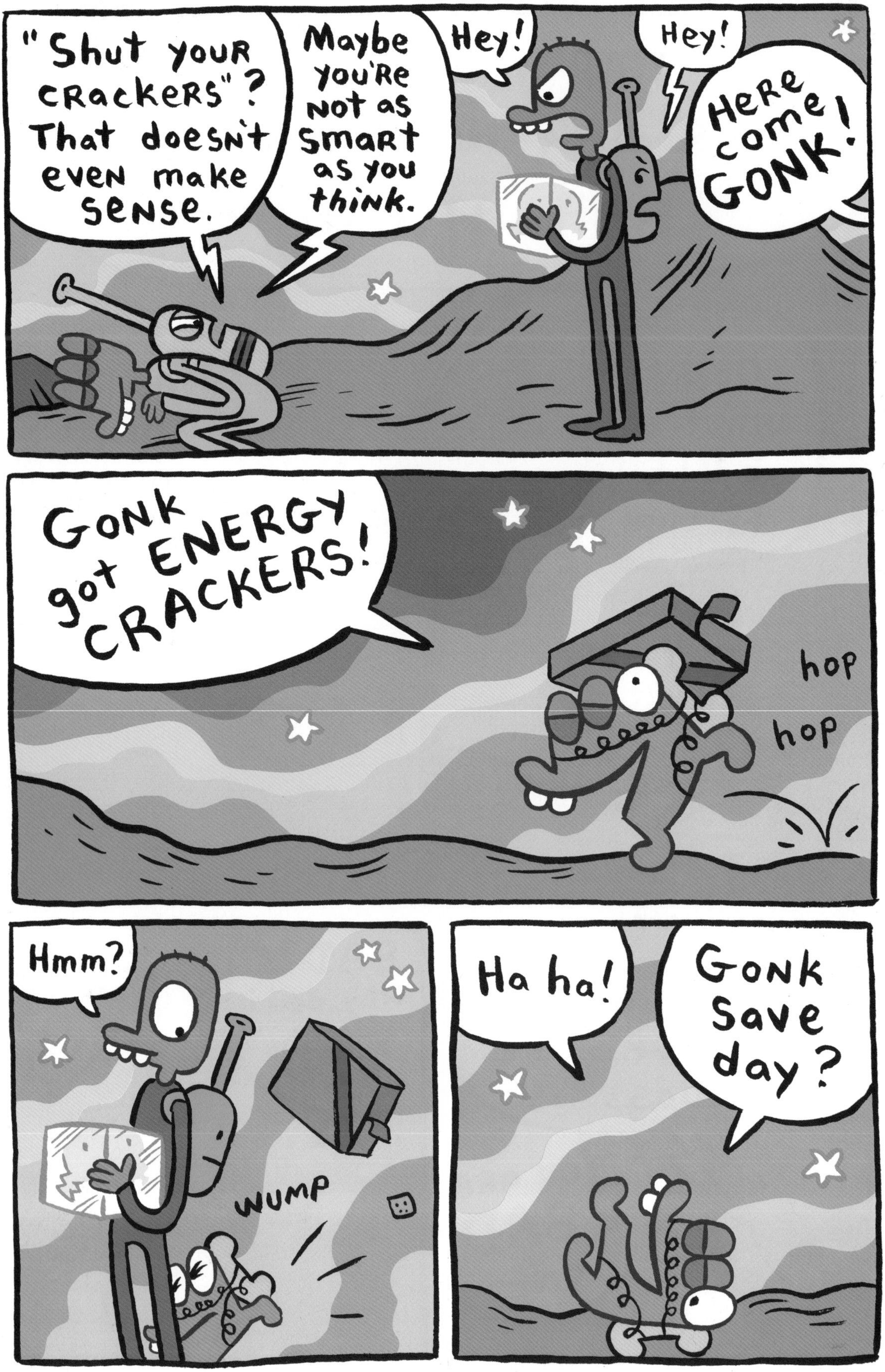
"Shut your crackers"? That doesn't even make sense.
Maybe you're not as smart as you think.
Hey!
Hey!
Here come! GONK!
Gonk got ENERGY CRACKERS!
hop
hop
Hmm?
WUMP
Ha ha!
Gonk save day?

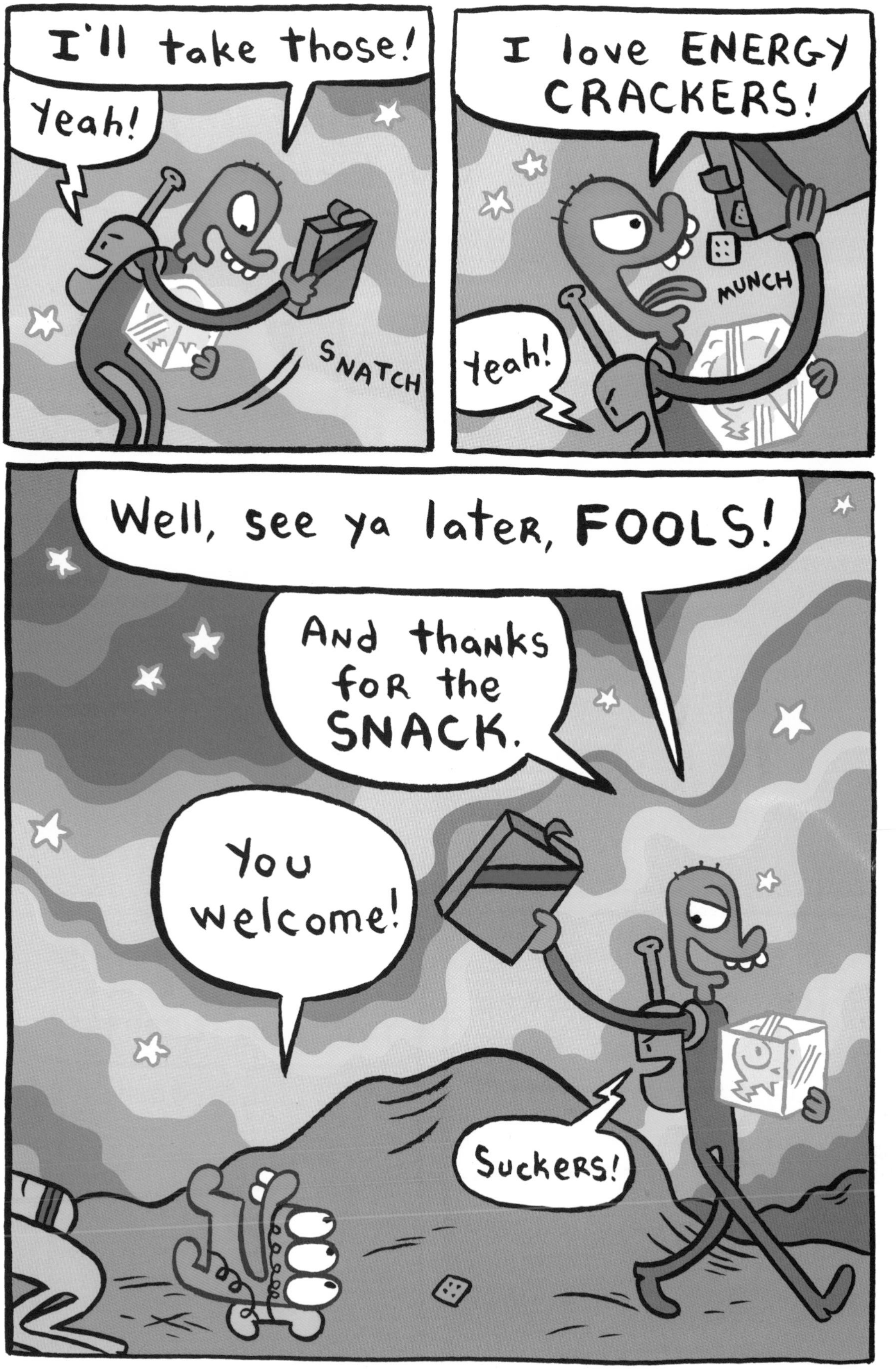
I'll take those!
Yeah!
SNATCH
I love ENERGY CRACKERS!
MUNCH
Yeah!
Well, see ya later, FOOLS!
And thanks for the SNACK.
You welcome!
Suckers!

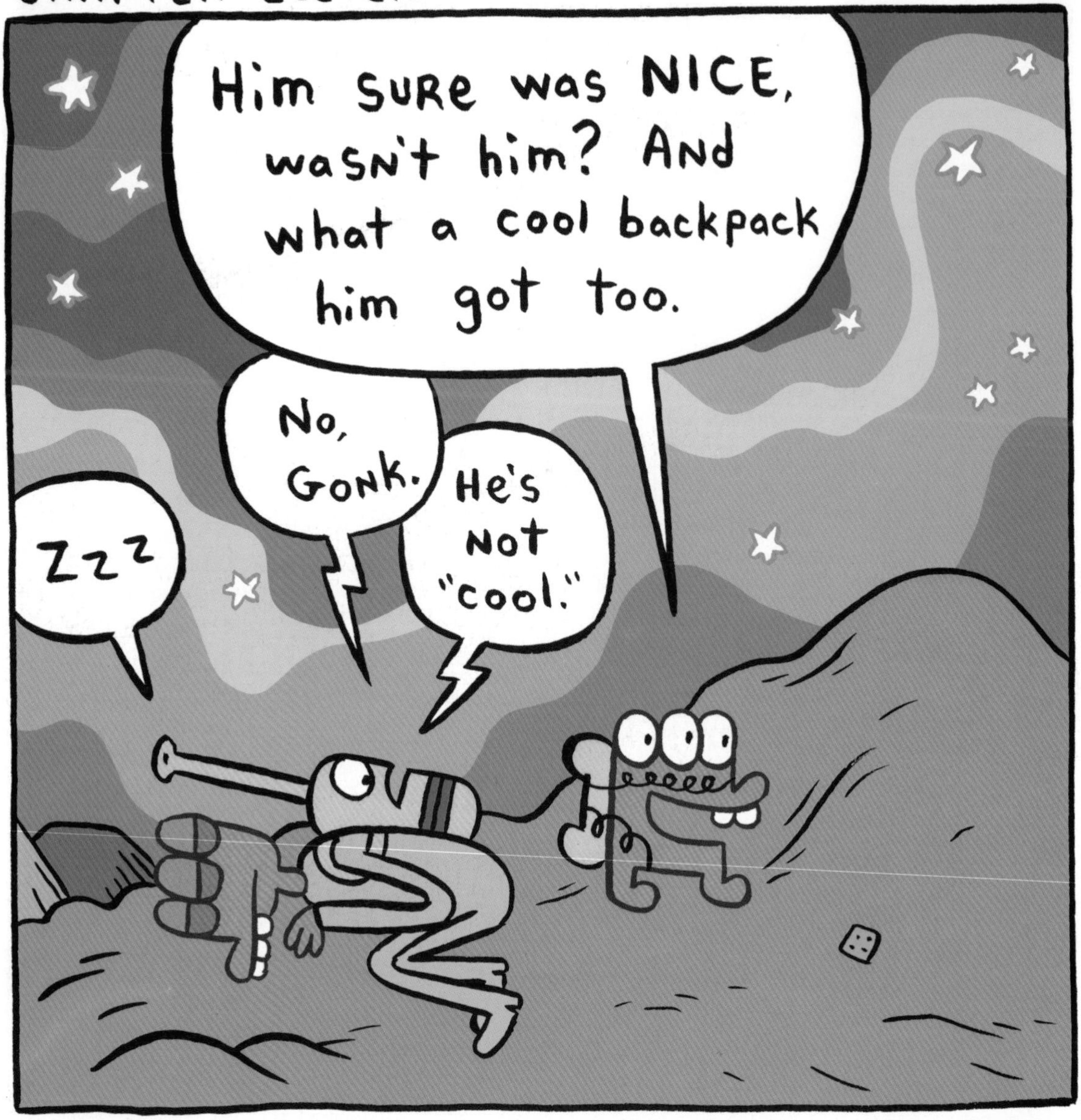
Him sure was NICE, wasn't him? And what a cool backpack him got too.
No, Gonk.
He's not "cool."
Zzz

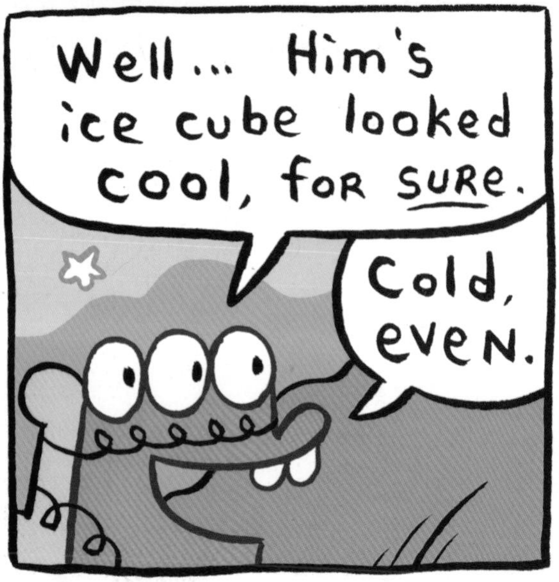
Well... Him's ice cube looked cool, for sure.
Cold, even.

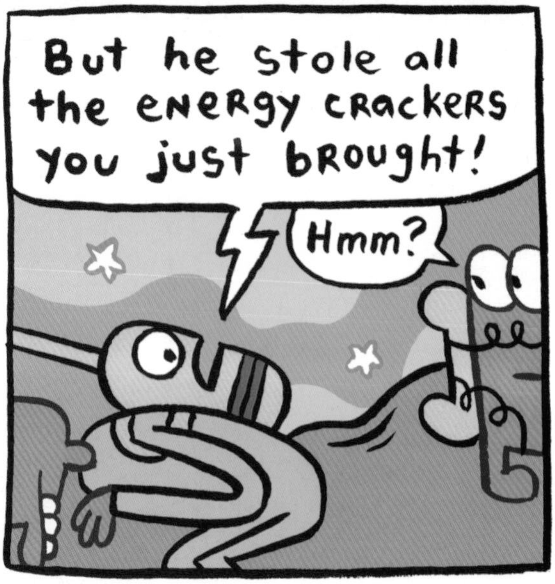
But he stole all the energy crackers you just brought!
Hmm?

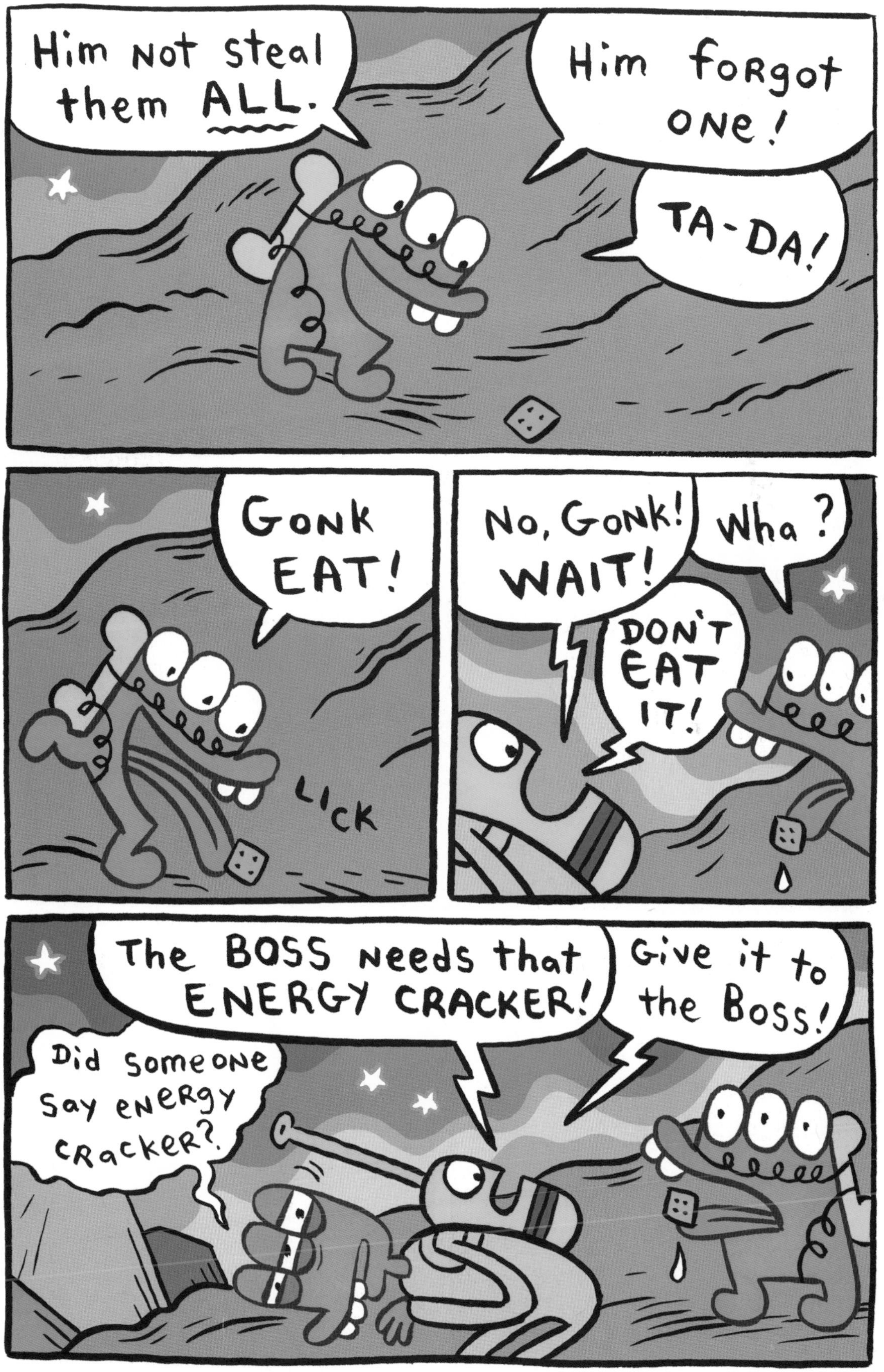
Him not steal them ALL.
Him forgot one!
TA-DA!
Gonk EAT!
LICK
No, Gonk! WAIT!
Wha?
DON'T EAT IT!
The BOSS needs that ENERGY CRACKER!
Give it to the Boss!
Did someone say energy cracker?

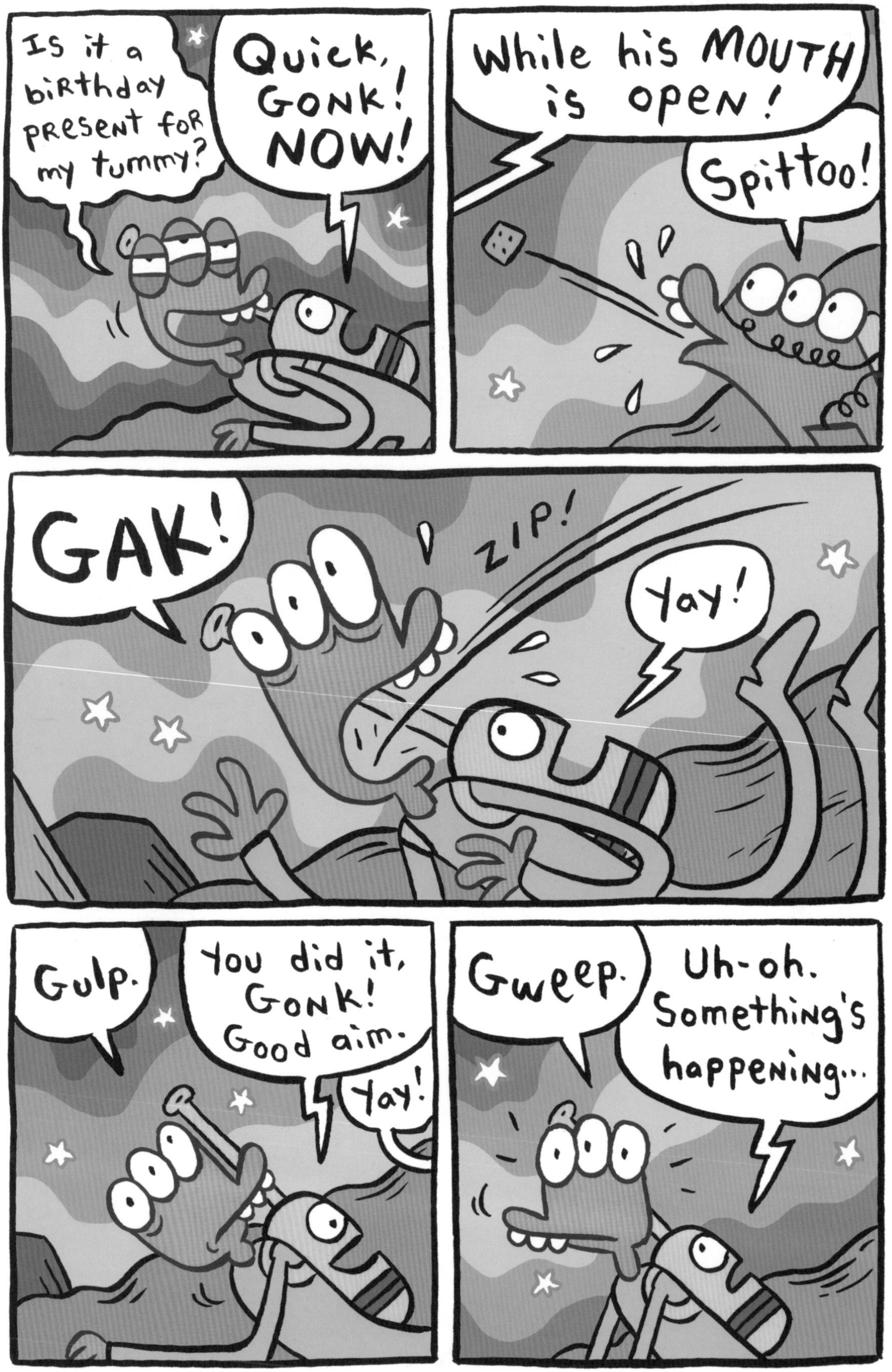

Is it a birthday present for my tummy?
Quick, GONK! NOW!
While his MOUTH is open!
Spittoo!
GAK!
ZIP!
Yay!
Gulp.
You did it, GONK! Good aim.
Yay!
Gweep.
Uh-oh. Something's happening...

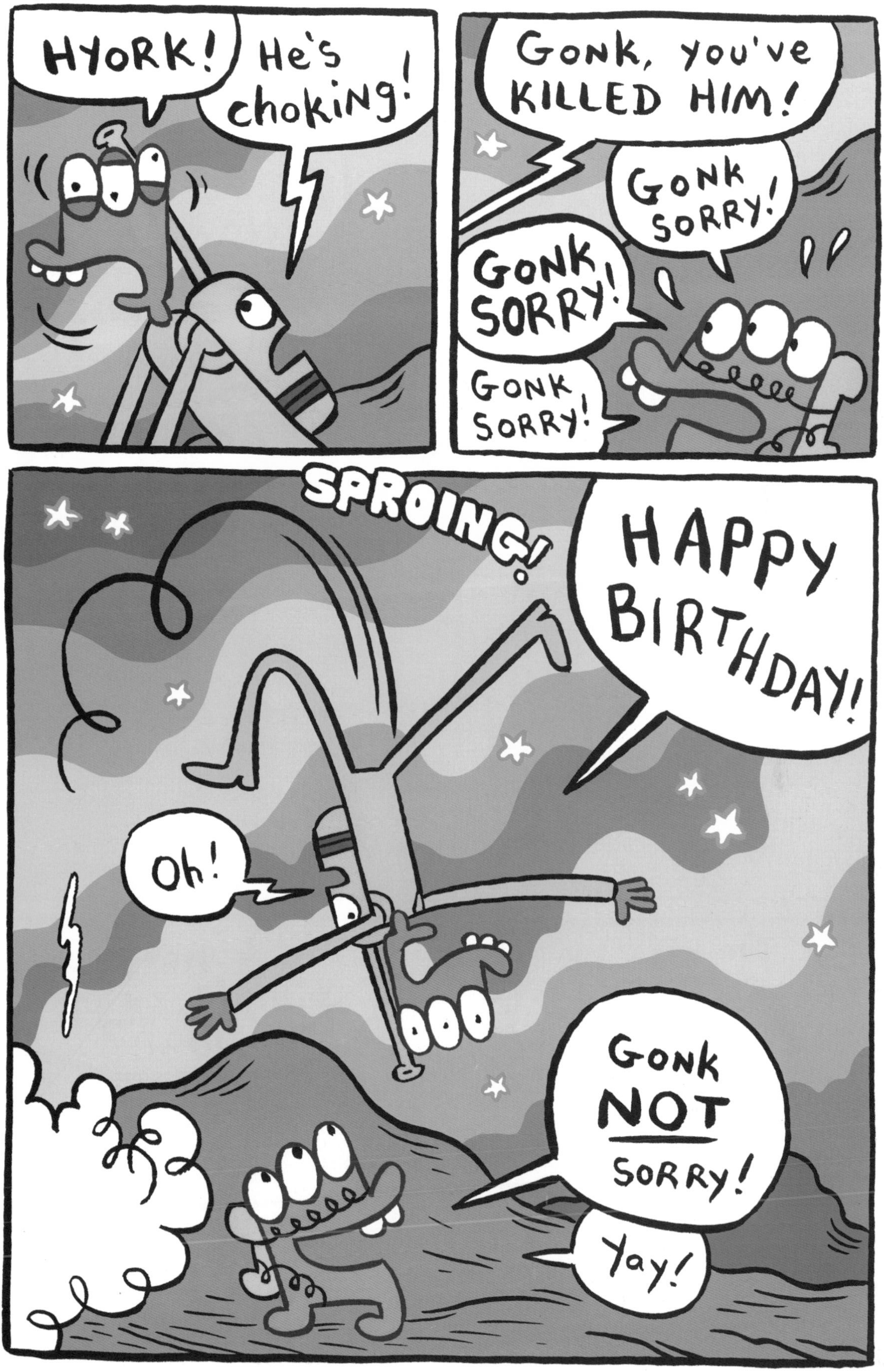
HYORK!
He's choking!
Gonk, you've KILLED HIM!
GONK SORRY!
GONK SORRY!
GONK SORRY!
SPROING!
HAPPY BIRTHDAY!
Oh!
Gonk NOT SORRY!
Yay!

CHAPTER TWELVE

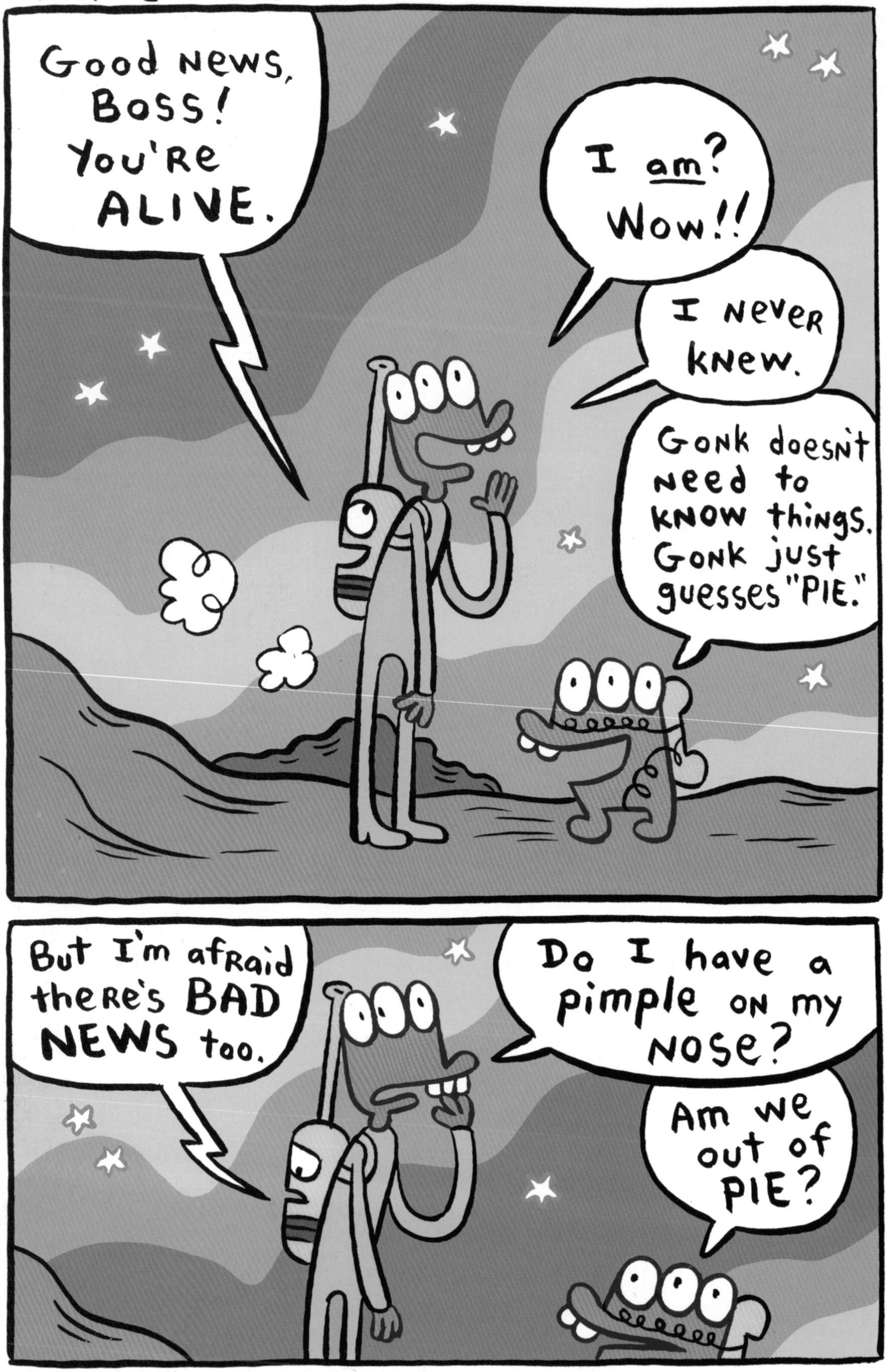
Good news, Boss! You're ALIVE.
I am? Wow!!
I never knew.
Gonk doesn't need to know things. Gonk just guesses "PIE."
But I'm afraid there's BAD NEWS too.
Do I have a pimple on my nose?
Am we out of PIE?

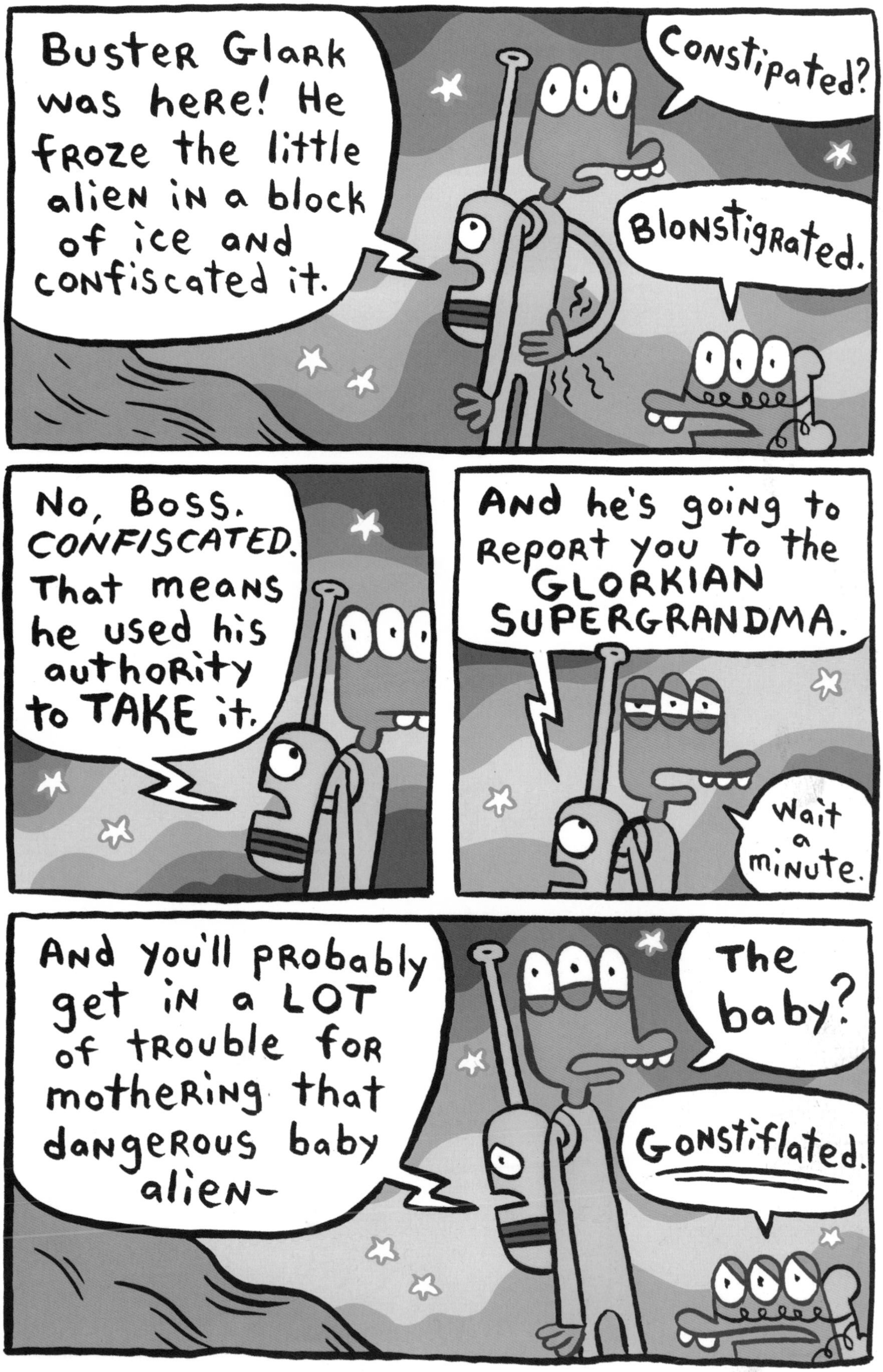
Buster Glark was here! He froze the little alien in a block of ice and confiscated it.
Constipated?
Blonstigrated.
No, Boss. CONFISCATED. That means he used his authority to TAKE it.
And he's going to report you to the GLORKIAN SUPERGRANDMA.
Wait a minute.
And you'll probably get in a LOT of trouble for mothering that dangerous baby alien-
The baby?
Gonstiflated.

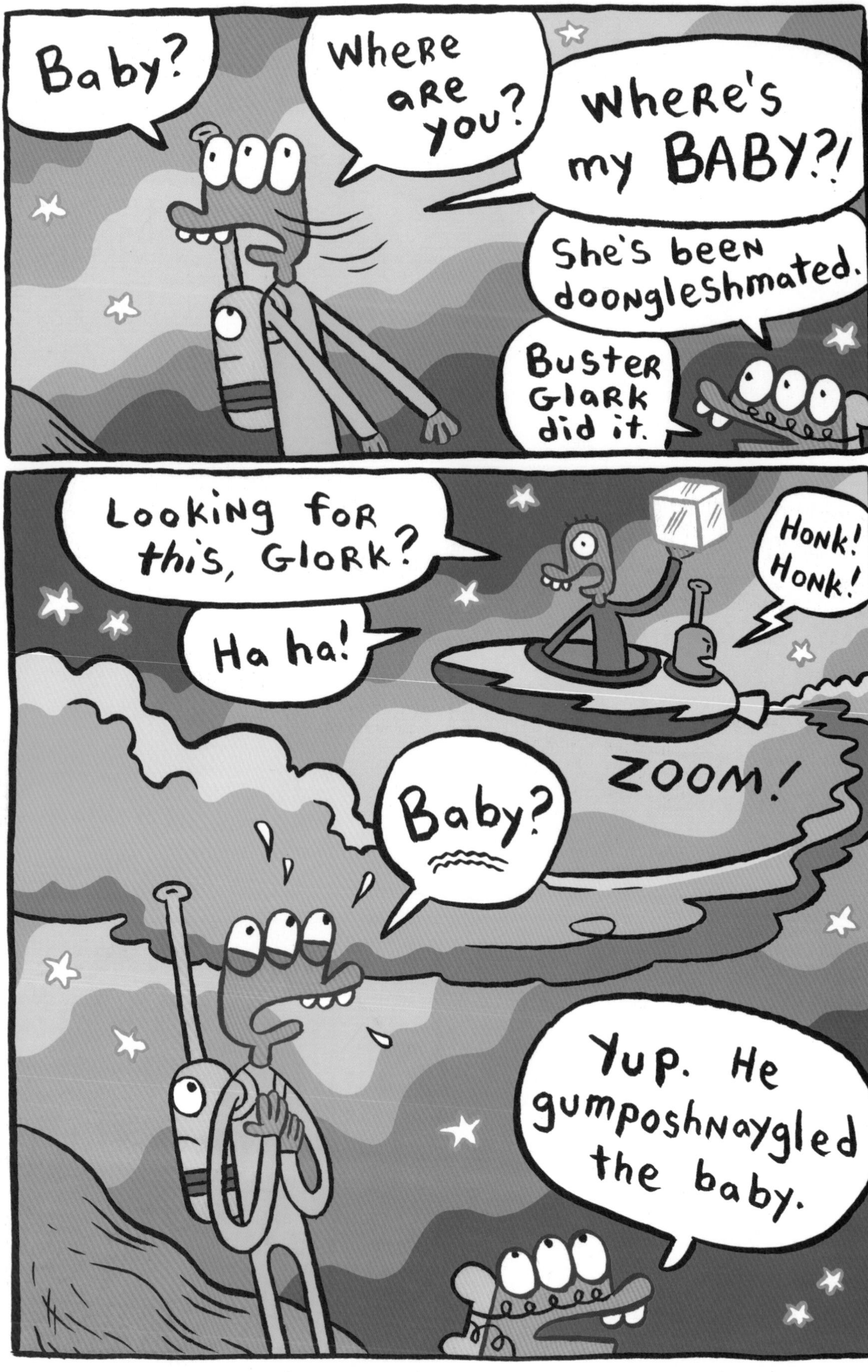
Baby?
Where are you?
Where's my BABY?!
She's been doongleshmated.
Buster Glark did it.
Looking for this, Glork?
Ha ha!
HONK! HONK!
ZOOM!
Baby?
Yup. He gumposhnaygled the baby.

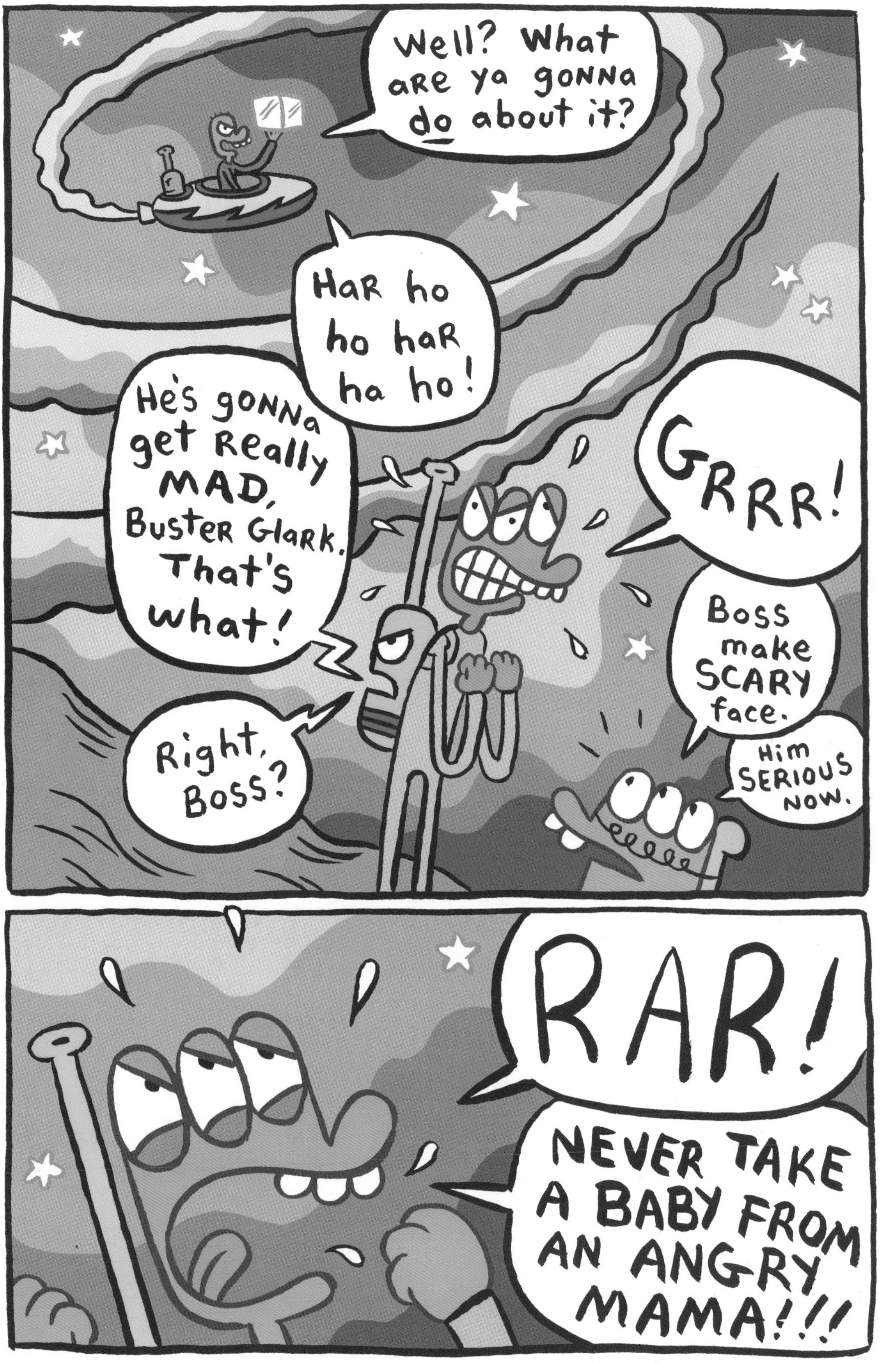
Well? What are ya gonna do about it?
Har ho ho har ha ho!
He's gonna get really MAD, Buster Glark. That's what!
Right, Boss?
GRRRR!
Boss make SCARY face.
Him SERIOUS now.
RAR!
NEVER TAKE A BABY FROM AN ANGRY MAMA!!!

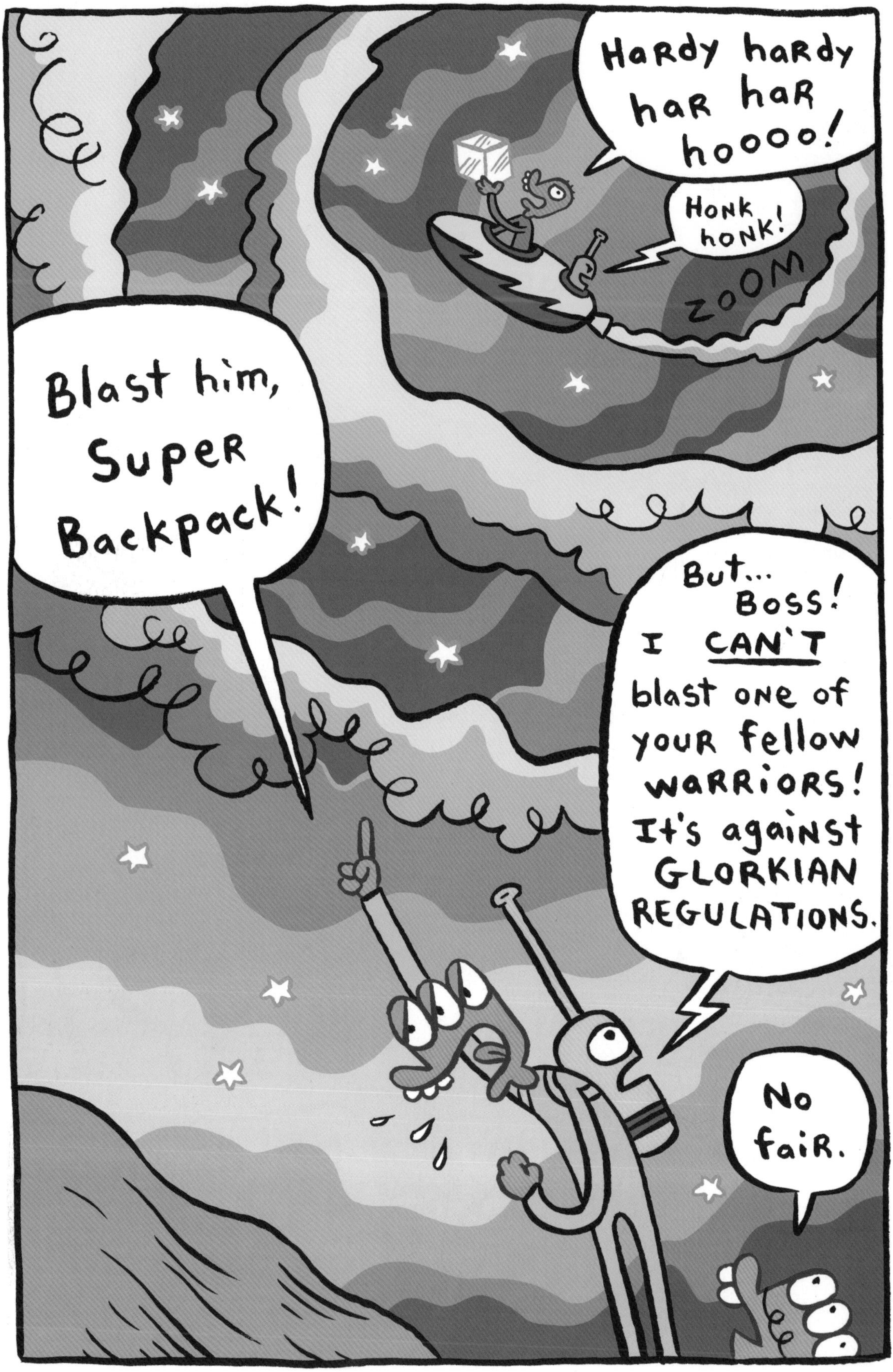
Hardy hardy har har hoooo!
HONK honk!
ZOOM
Blast him, Super Backpack!
But... Boss! I CAN'T blast one of your fellow warriors! It's against GLORKIAN REGULATIONS.
No fair.

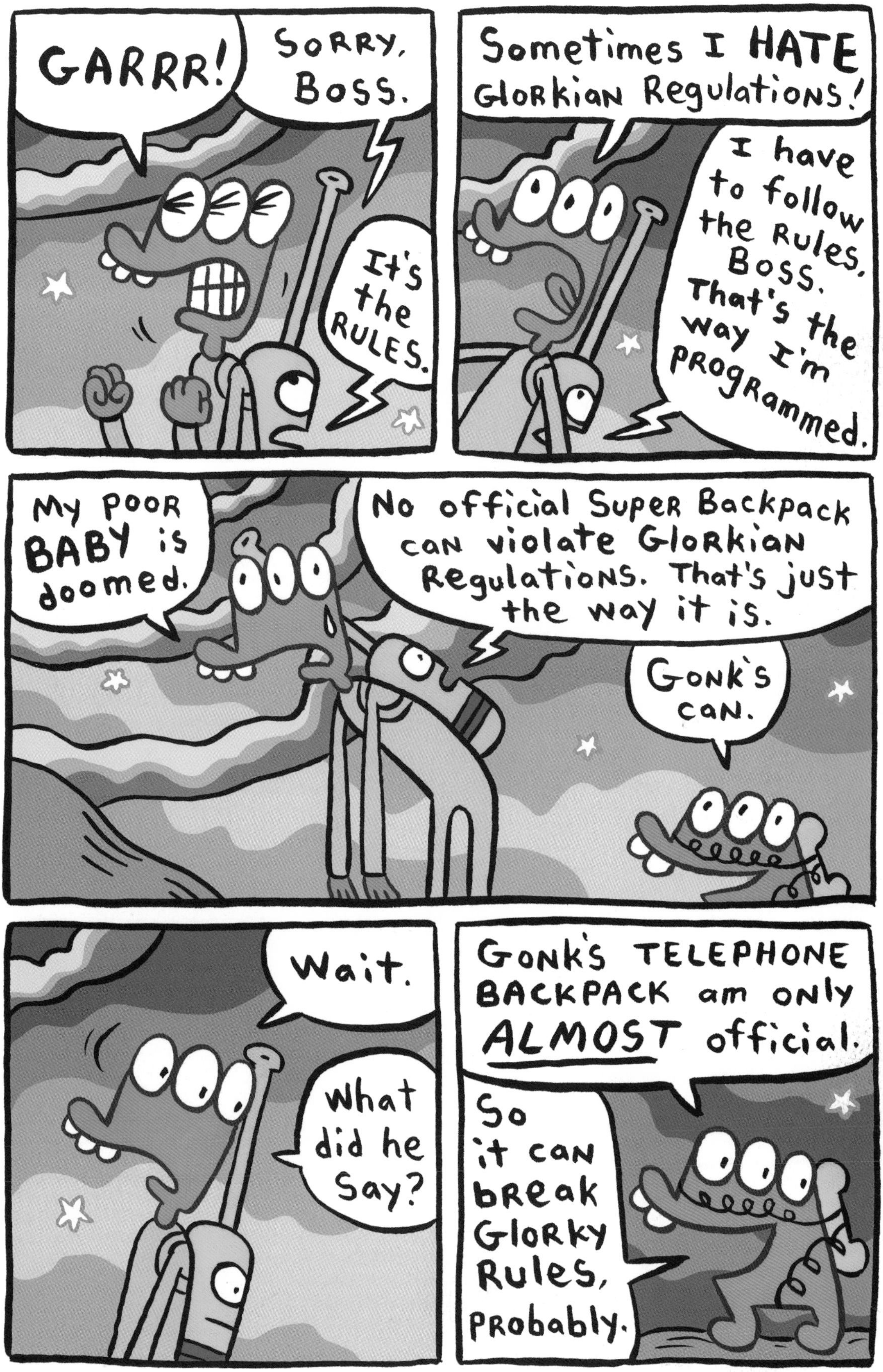
GARRR!
SORRY, BOSS.
It's the RULES.
Sometimes I HATE Glorkian Regulations!
I have to follow the Rules, Boss. That's the way I'm programmed.
My poor BABY is doomed.
No official Super Backpack can violate Glorkian Regulations. That's just the way it is.
Gonk's can.
Wait.
What did he say?
Gonk's TELEPHONE BACKPACK am only ALMOST official.
So it can break Glorky Rules, probably.

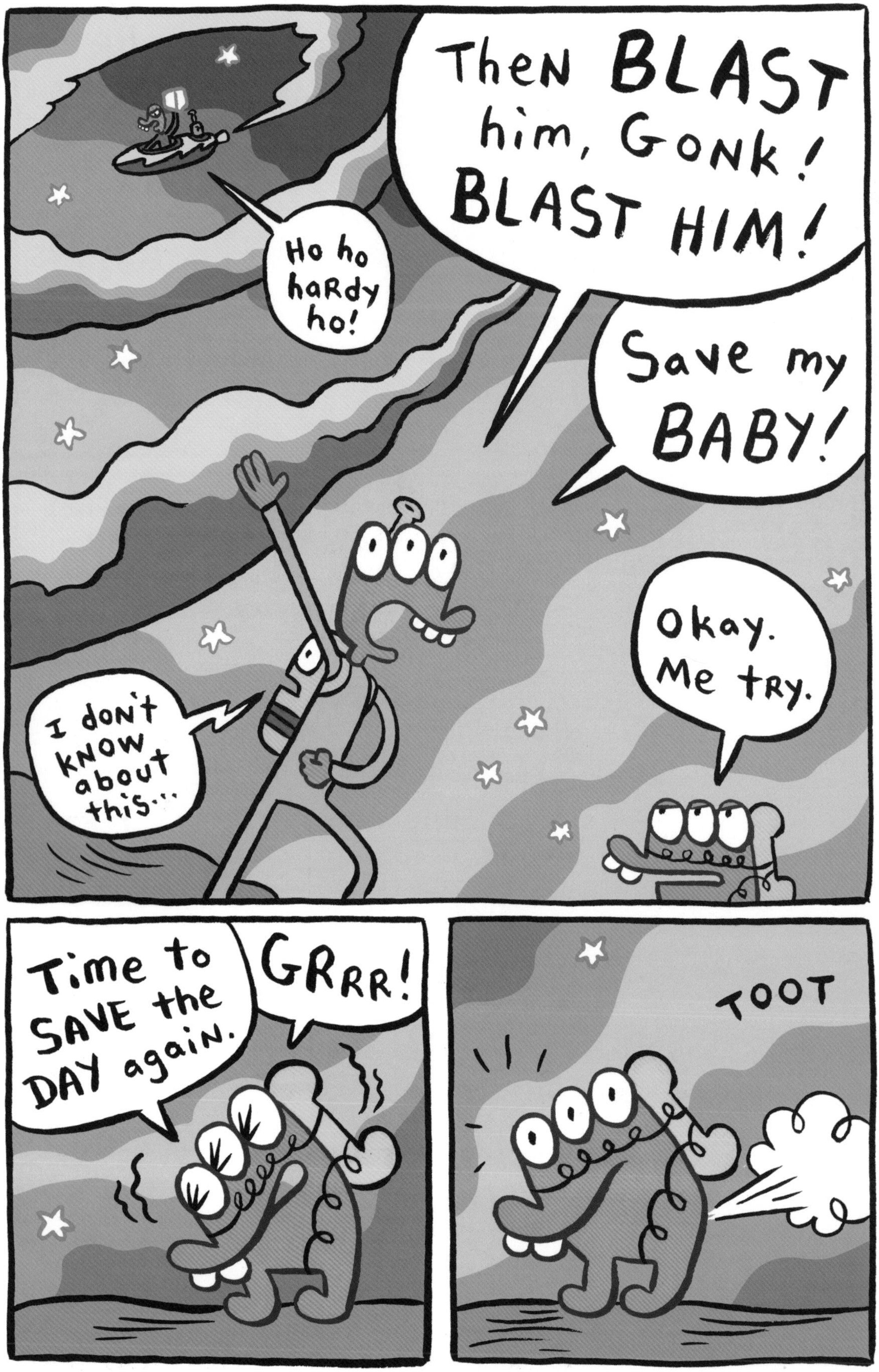
Then BLAST him, Gonk! BLAST HIM!
Ho ho hardy ho!
Save my BABY!
Okay. Me try.
I don't know about this...
Time to SAVE the DAY again.
GRRRR!
TOOT

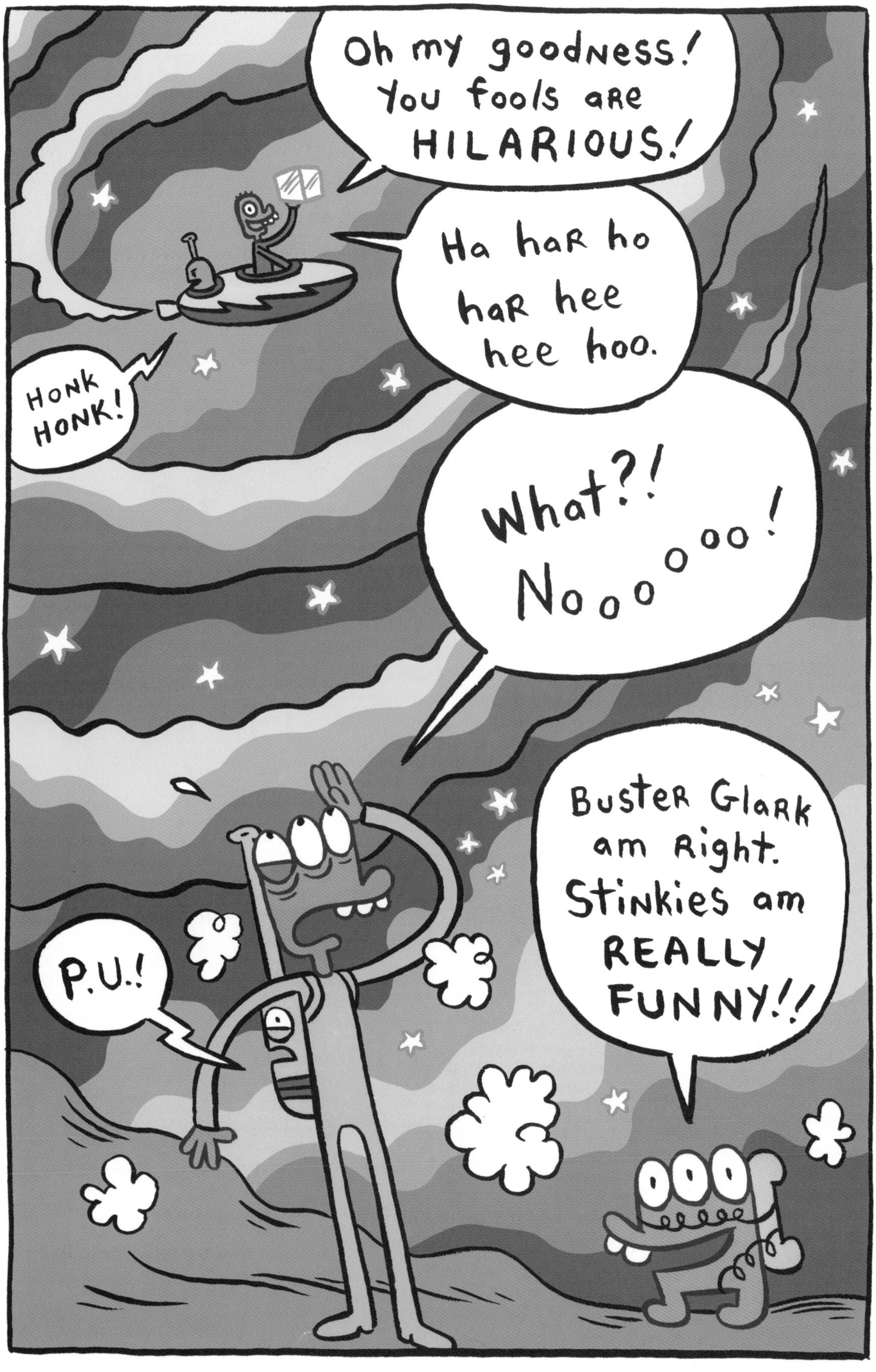
Oh my goodness! You fools are HILARIOUS!
Ha har ho har hee hee hoo.
HONK HONK!
What?! Noooooo!
Buster Glark am right. Stinkies am REALLY FUNNY!!
P.U.!

CHAPTER THIRTEEN

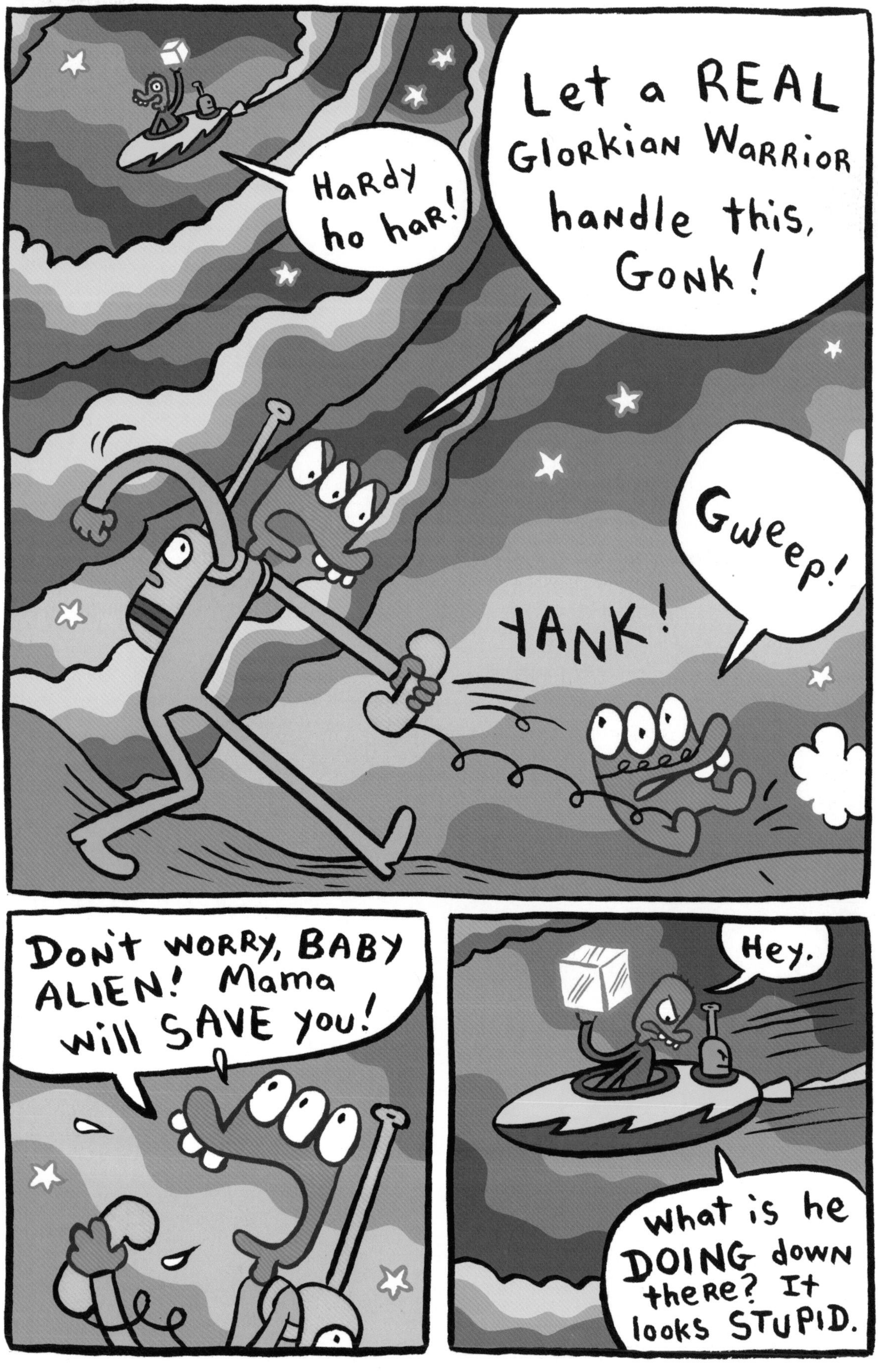
Hardy ho har!
Let a REAL Glorkian Warrior handle this, Gonk!
YANK!
Gweep!
Don't worry, BABY ALIEN! Mama will SAVE you!
Hey.
What is he DOING down there? It looks STUPID.

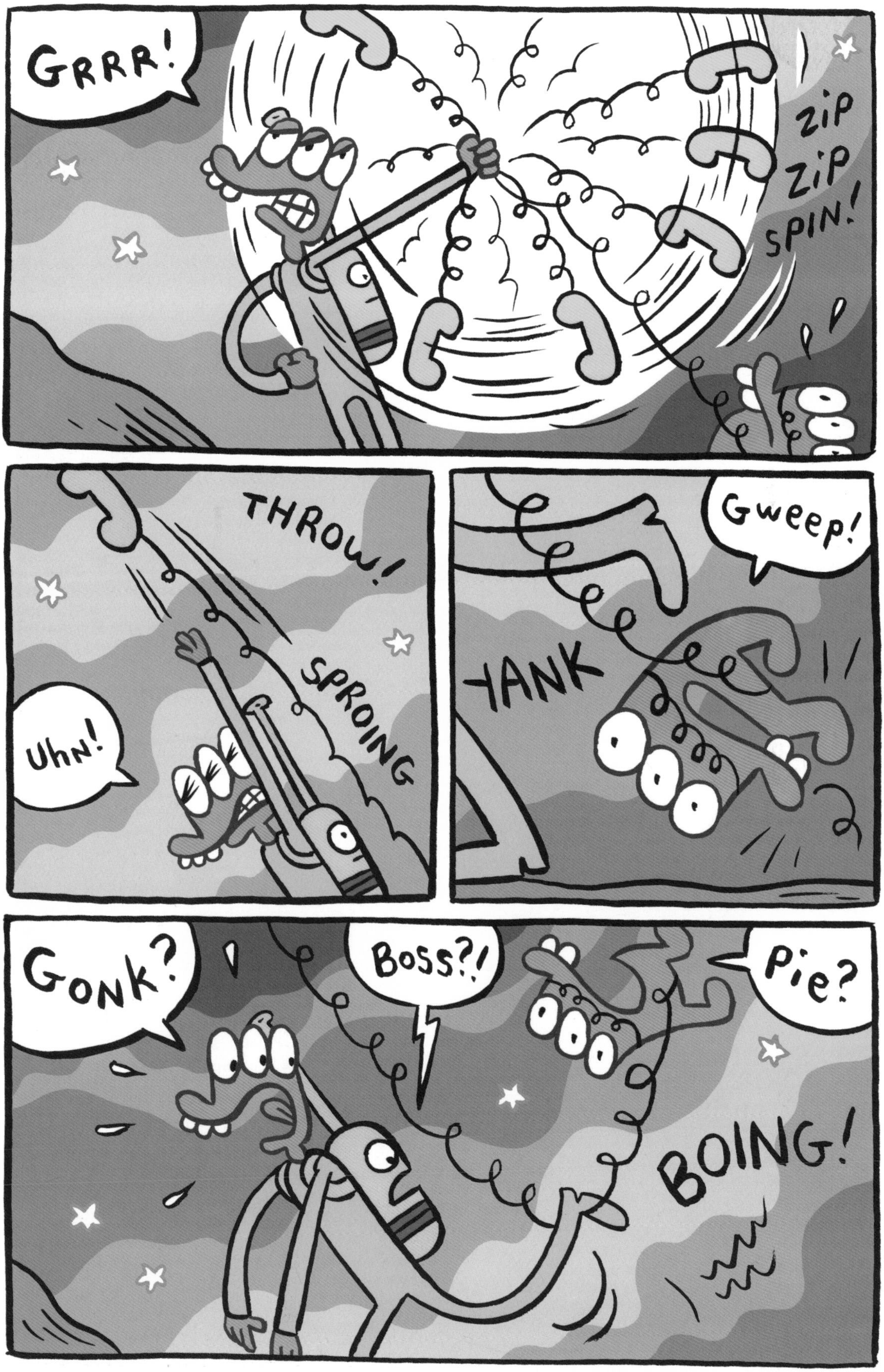
GRRR!
ZIP
ZIP
SPIN!
THROW!
SPROING
Uhn!
Gweep!
YANK
Gonk?
Boss?!
Pie?
BOING!

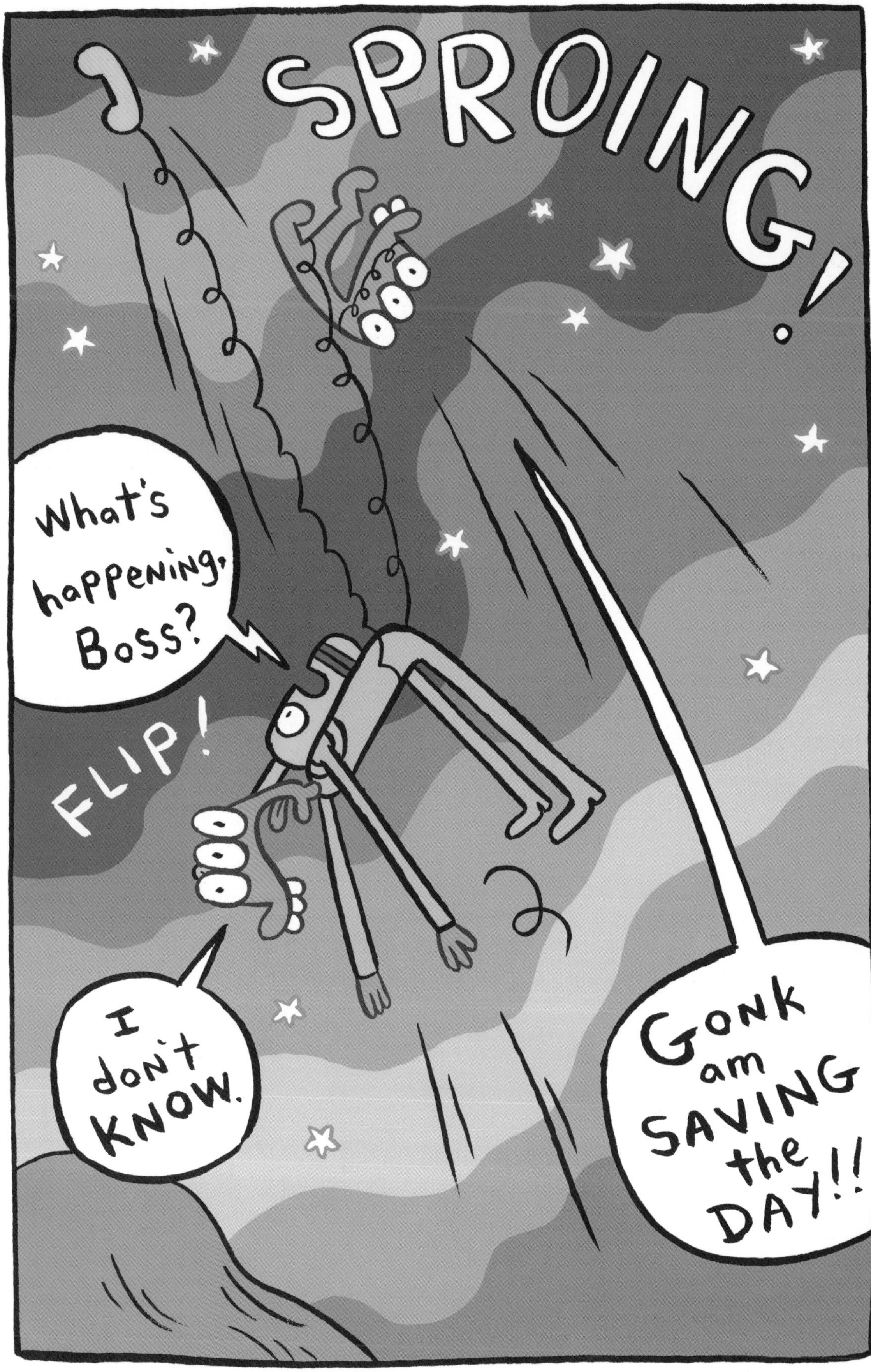
SPROING!
What's happening, Boss?
FLIP!
I don't KNOW.
Gonk am SAVING the DAY!!

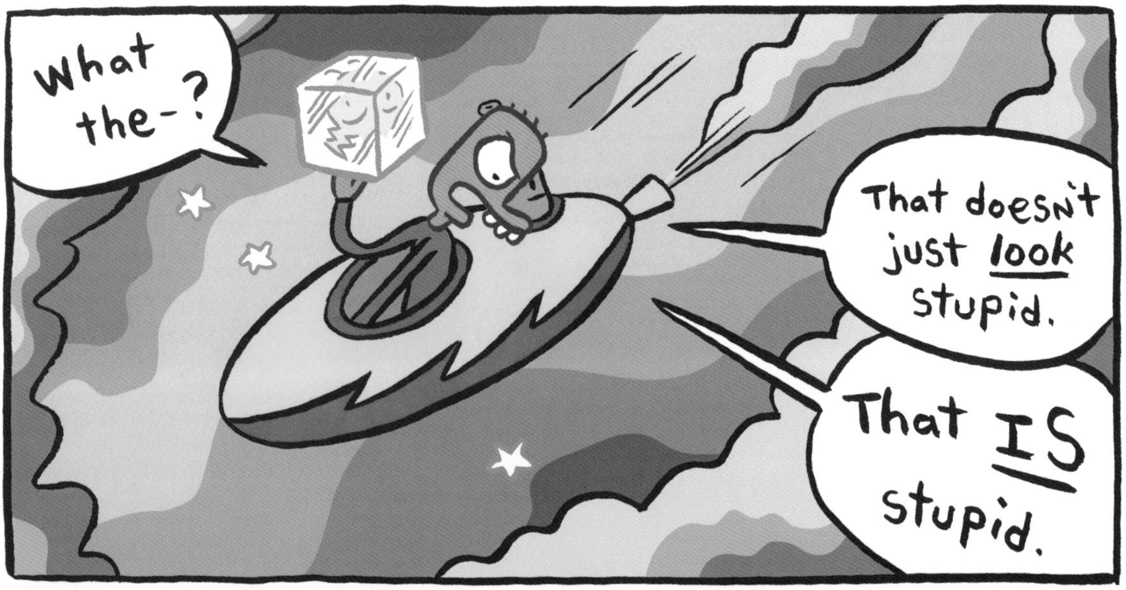
What the-?
That doesn't just look stupid.
That IS stupid.

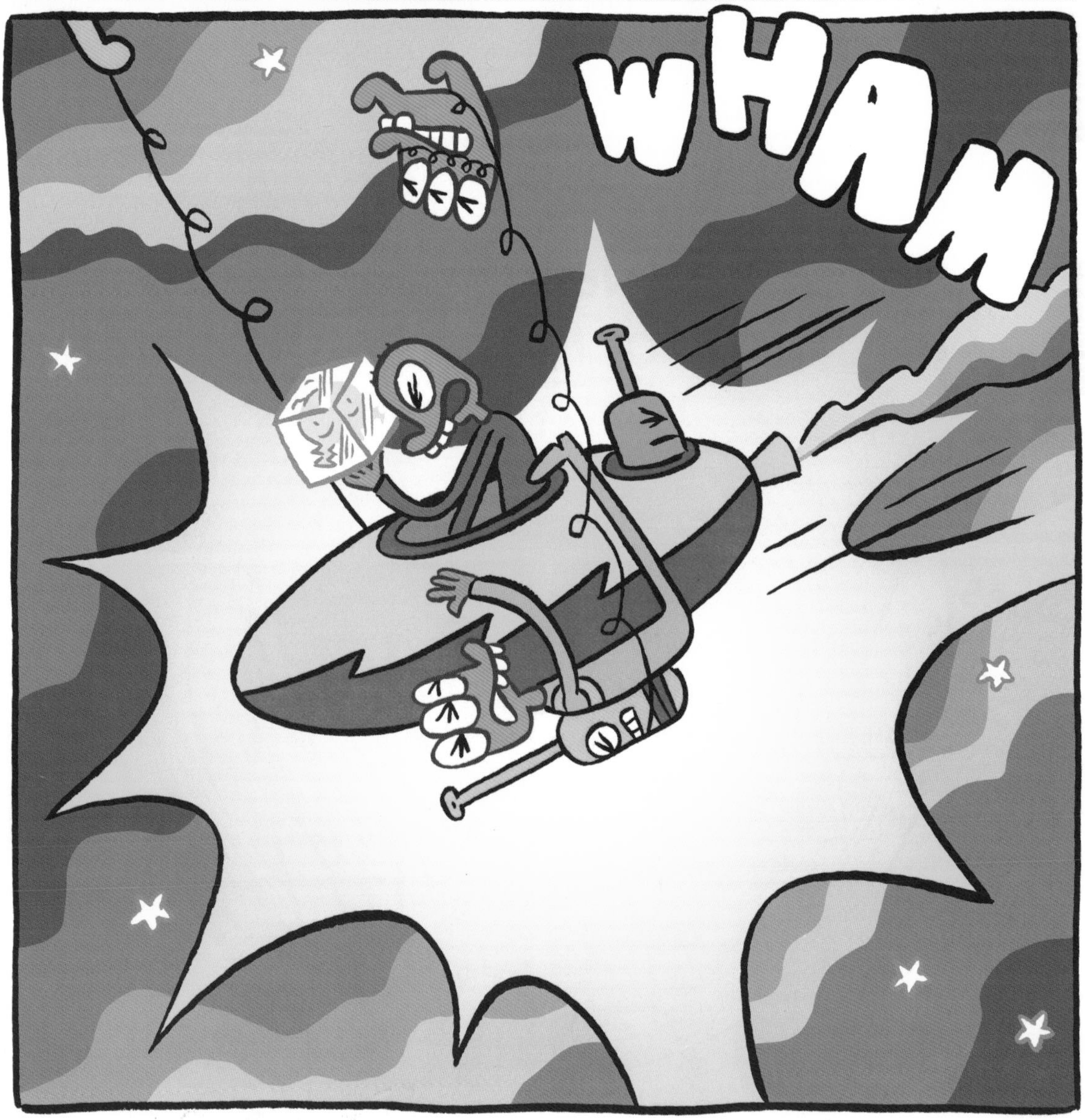
WHAM

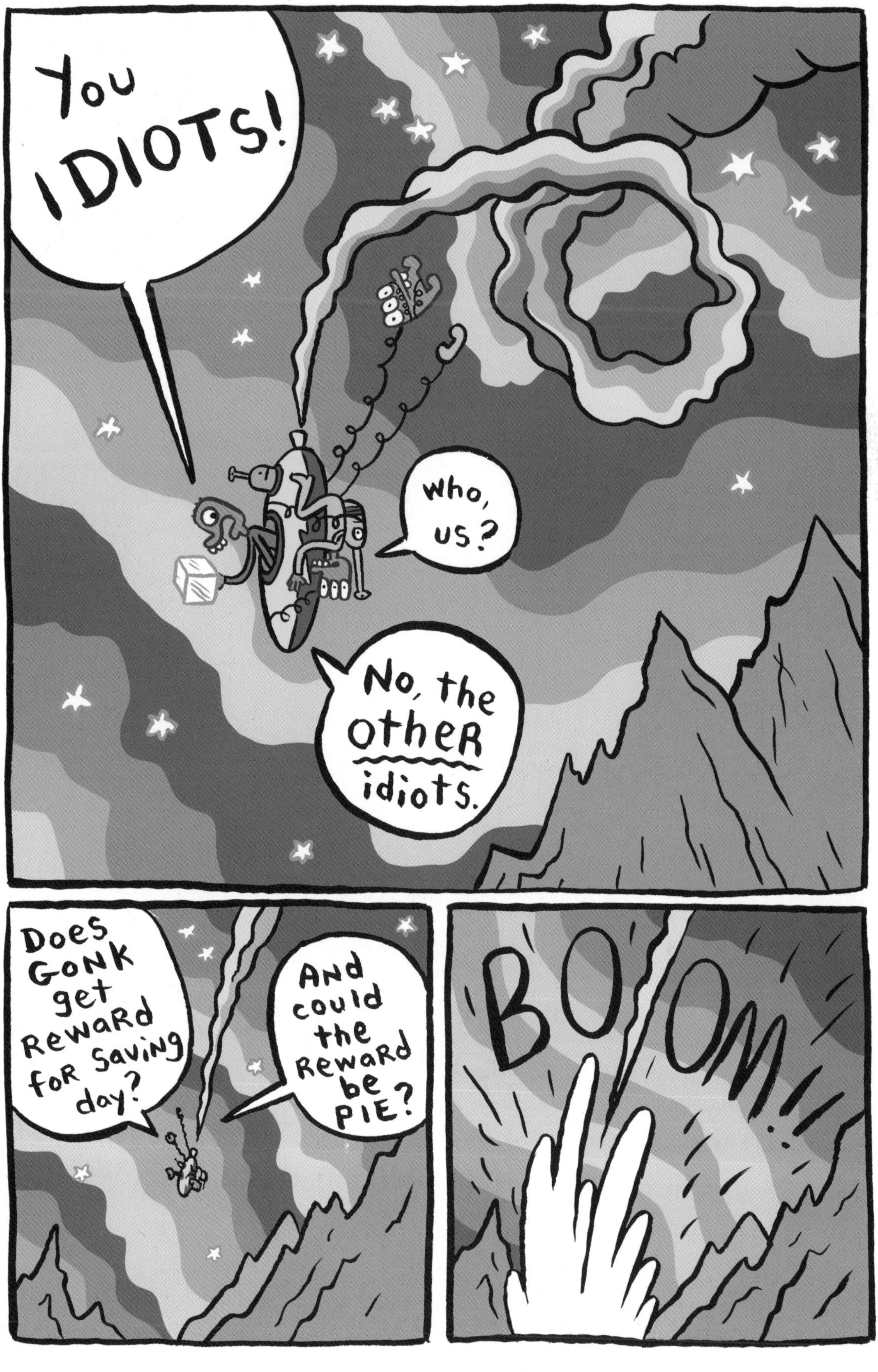
You IDIOTS!
Who, us?
No, the OTHER idiots.
Does GONK get Reward for saving day?
AND could the Reward be PIE?
BOOM!!!

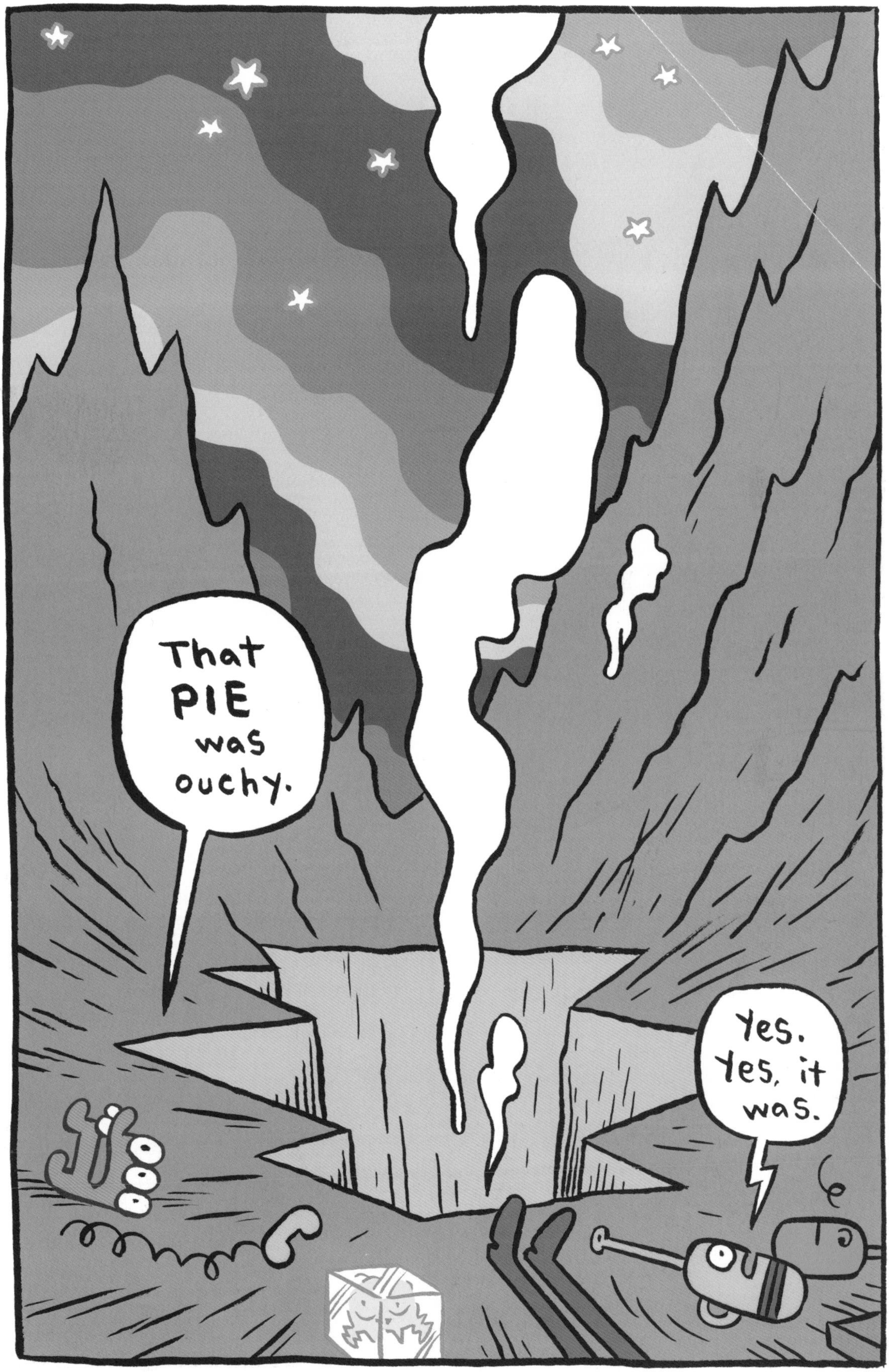
That PIE was ouchy.
Yes. Yes, it was.

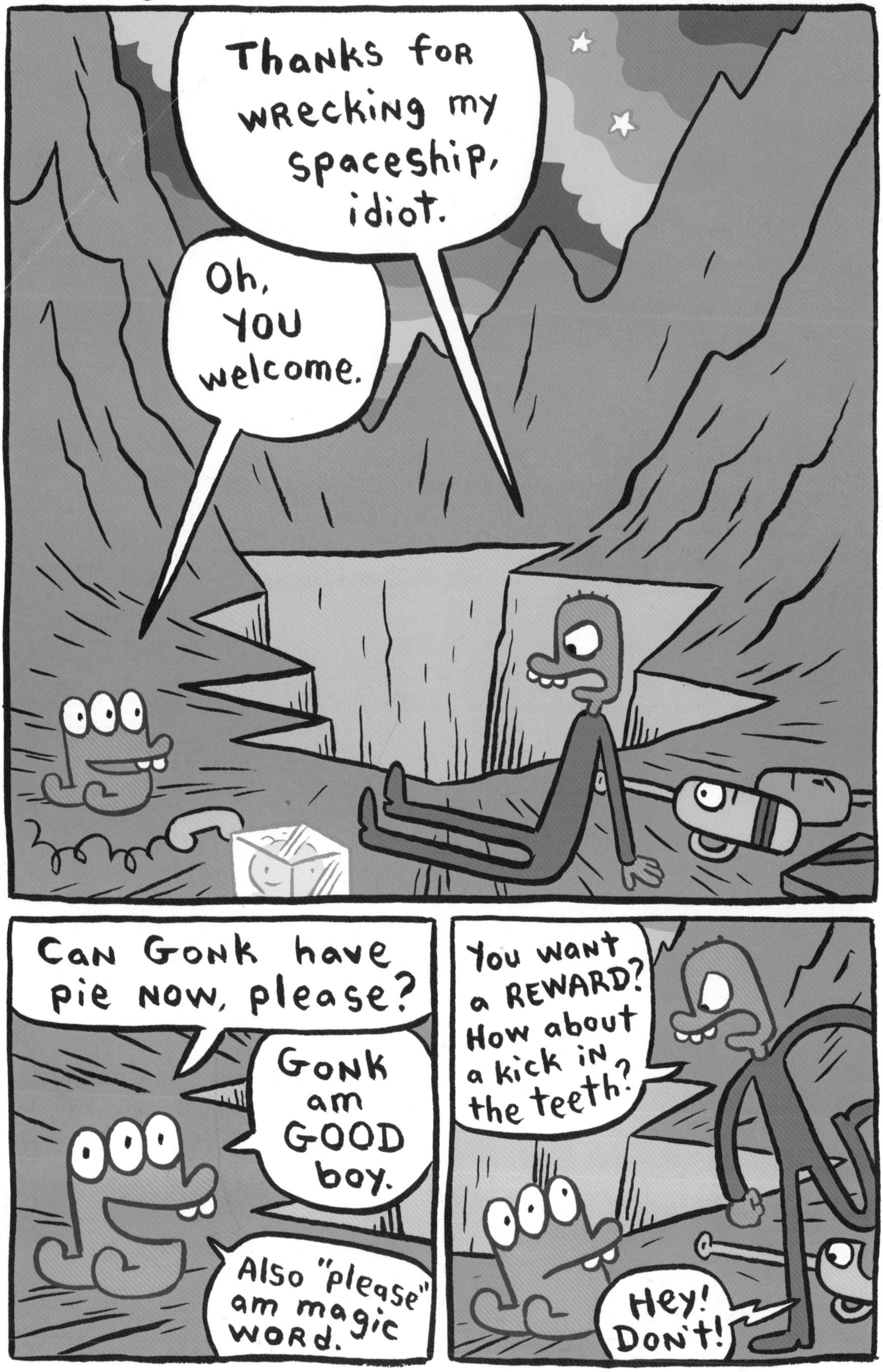
Thanks for wrecking my spaceship, idiot.
Oh, YOU welcome.
Can Gonk have pie now, please?
Gonk am GOOD boy.
Also "please" am magic word.
You want a REWARD? How about a kick in the teeth?
Hey! Don't!

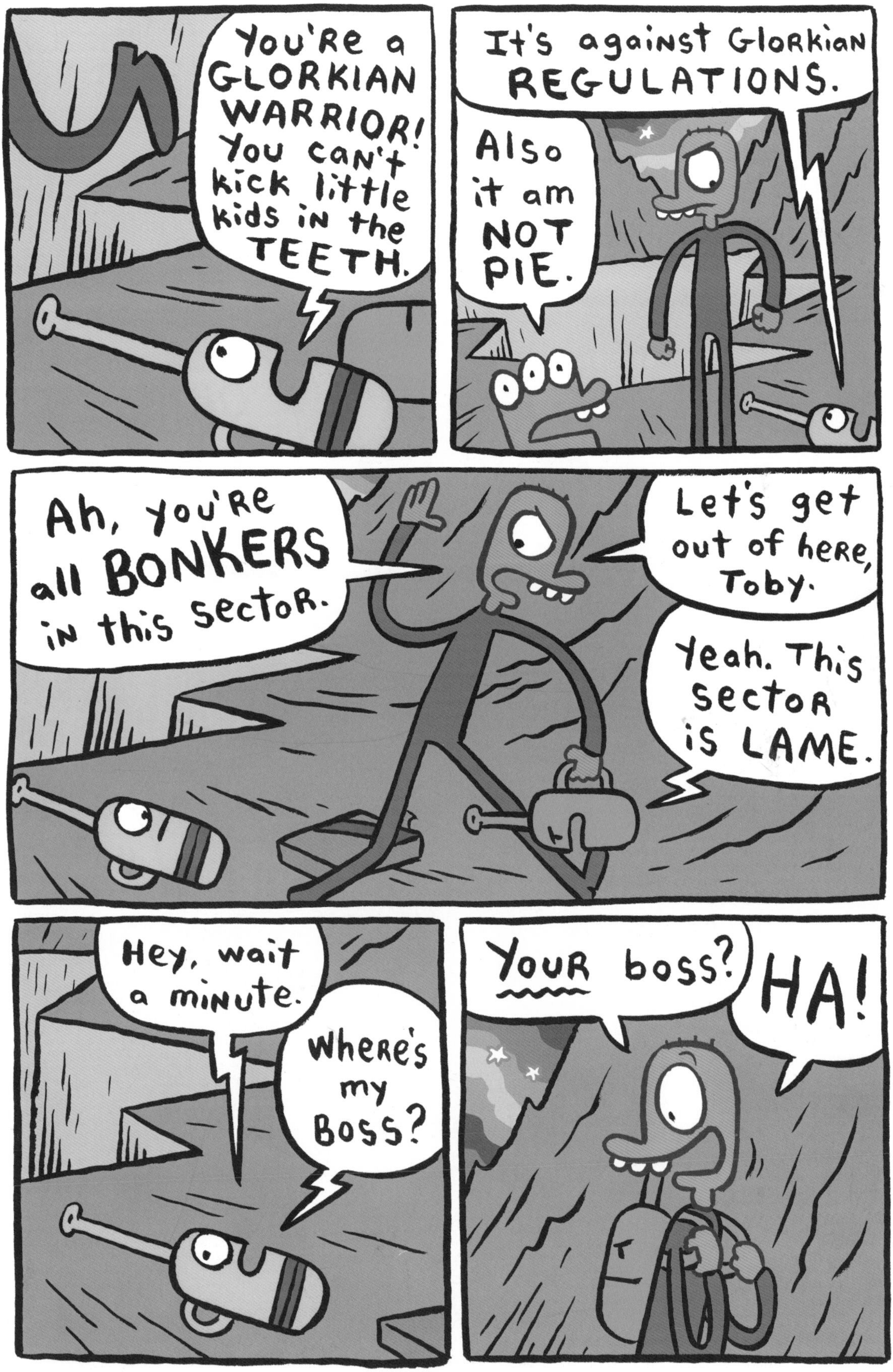
You're a GLORKIAN WARRIOR! You can't kick little kids in the TEETH.
It's against Glorkian REGULATIONS.
Also it am NOT PIE.
Ah, you're all BONKERS in this sector.
Let's get out of here, Toby.
Yeah. This sector is LAME.
Hey, wait a minute.
Where's my BOSS?
YOUR boss?
HA!

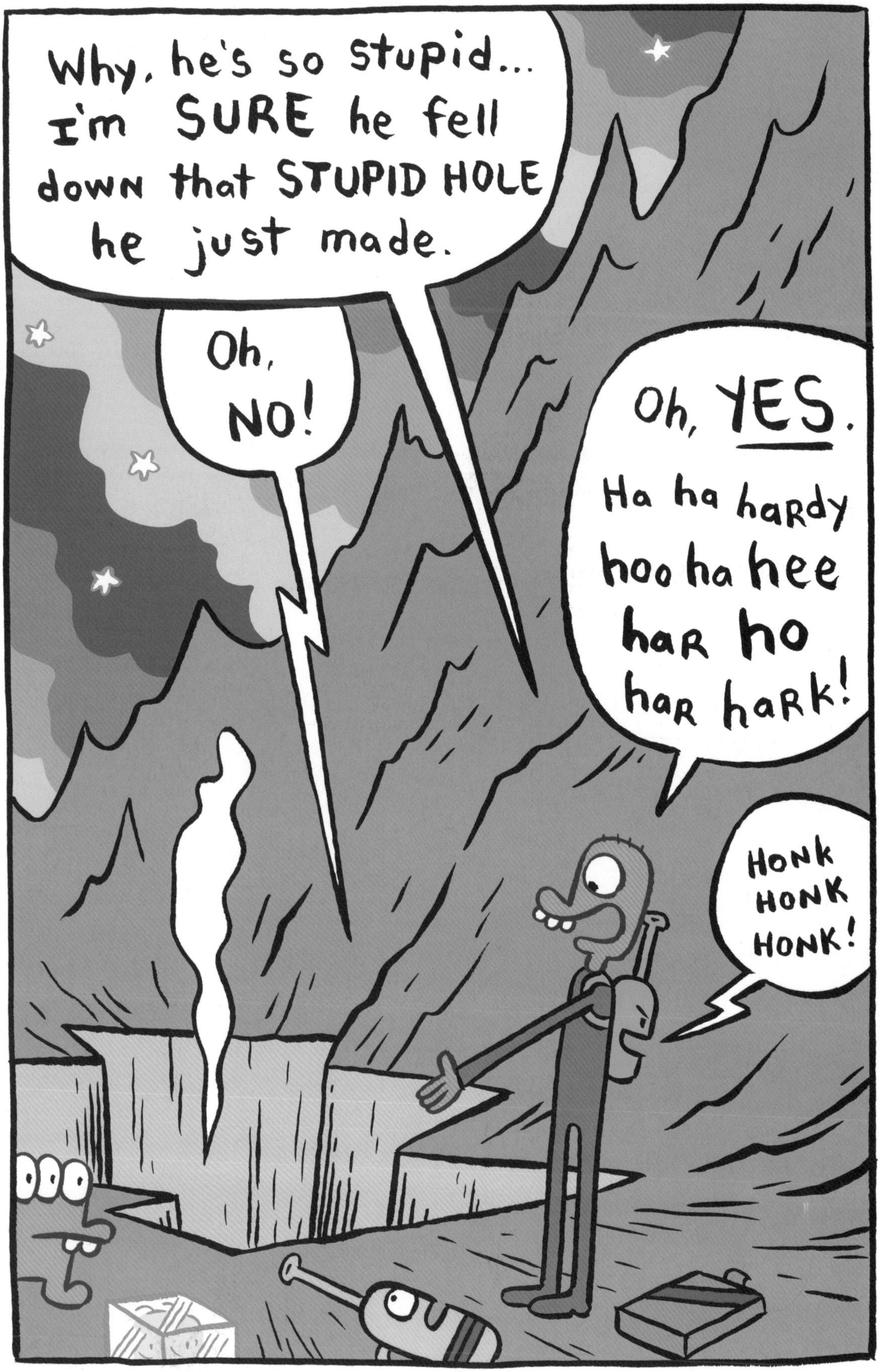
Why, he's so stupid... I'm SURE he fell down that STUPID HOLE he just made.
Oh, NO!
Oh, YES. Ha ha hardy hoo ha hee har ho har hark!
HONK HONK HONK!

CHAPTER FIFTEEN

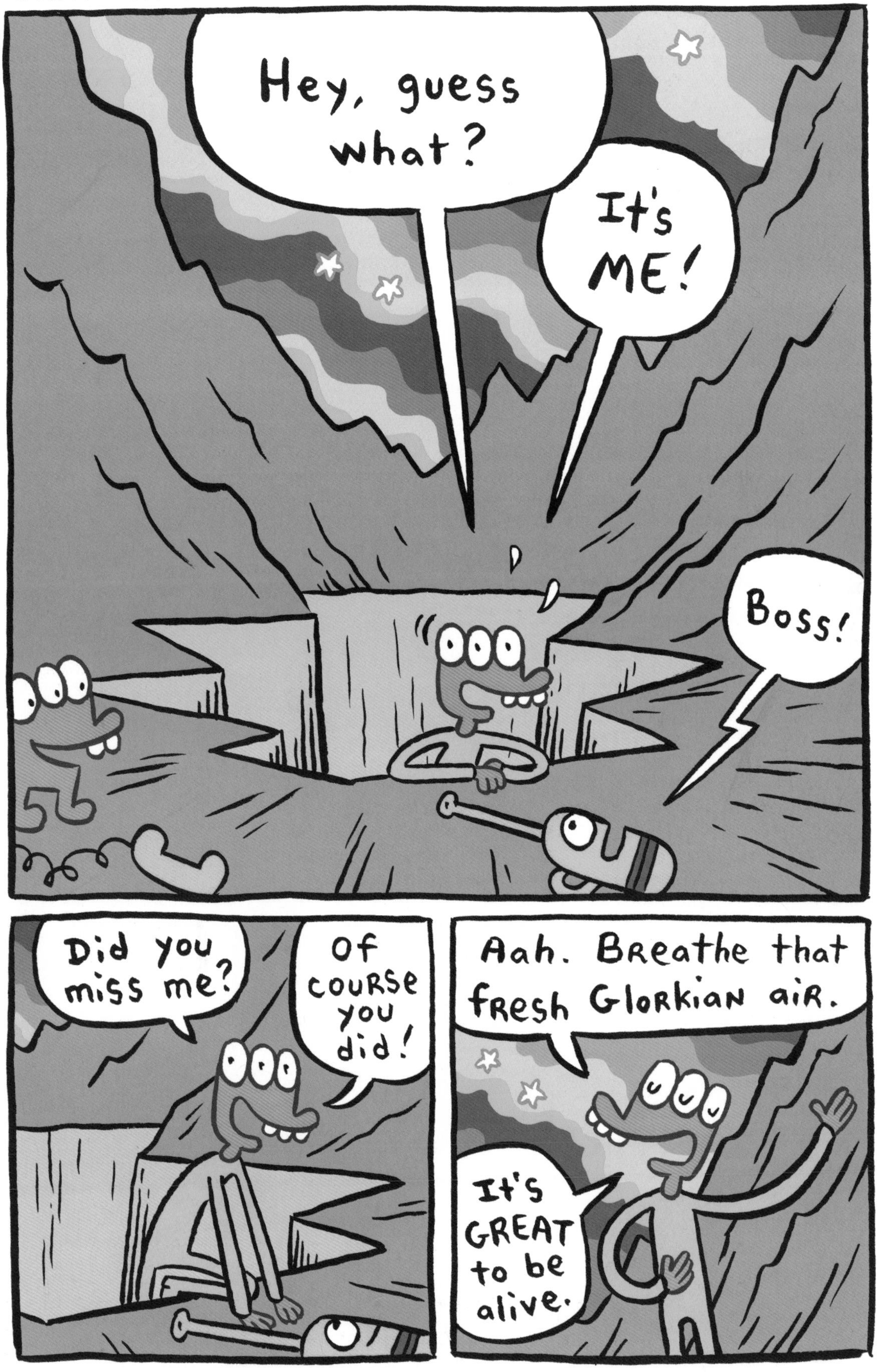

Hey, guess what?
It's ME!
Boss!
Did you miss me?
Of course you did!
Aah. Breathe that fresh Glorkian air.
It's GREAT to be alive.

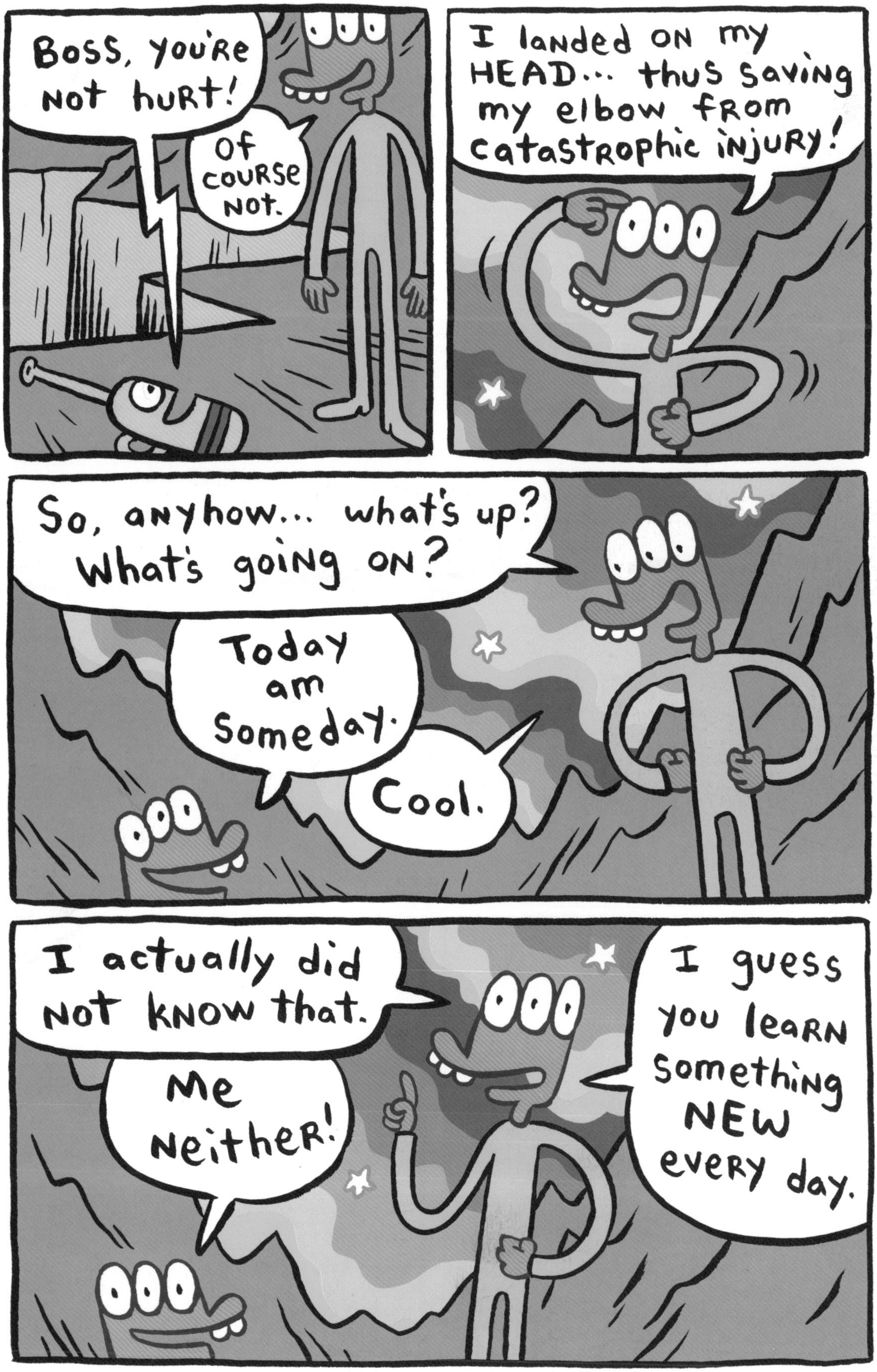

Boss, you're not hurt!
Of course not.
I landed on my HEAD... thus saving my elbow from catastrophic injury!
So, anyhow... what's up? What's going on?
Today am Someday.
Cool.
I actually did not know that.
Me neither!
I guess you learn something NEW every day.

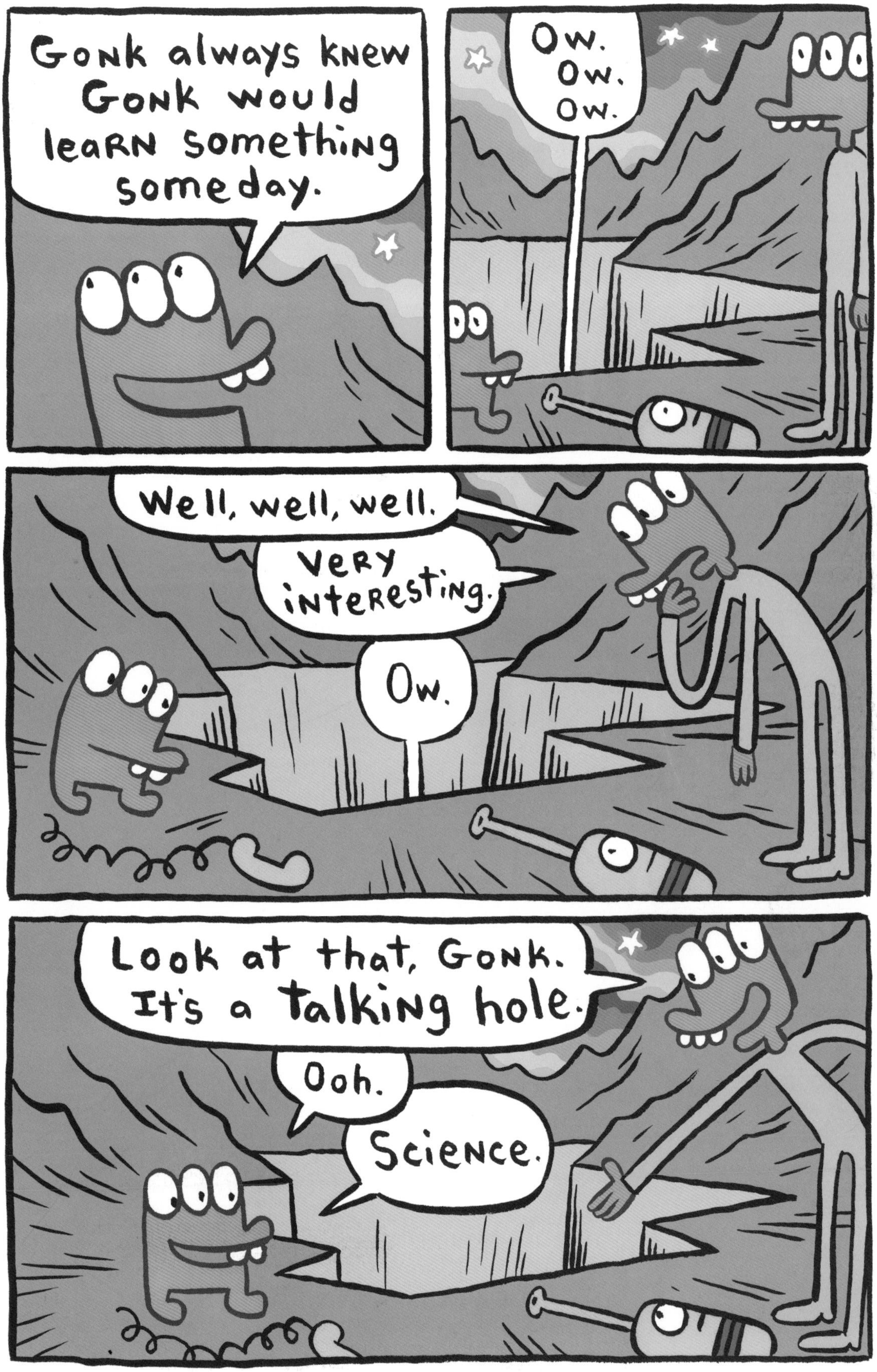
Gonk always knew Gonk would learn something someday.
Ow. Ow. Ow.
Well, well, well.
Very interesting.
Ow.
Look at that, Gonk. It's a talking hole.
Ooh.
Science.

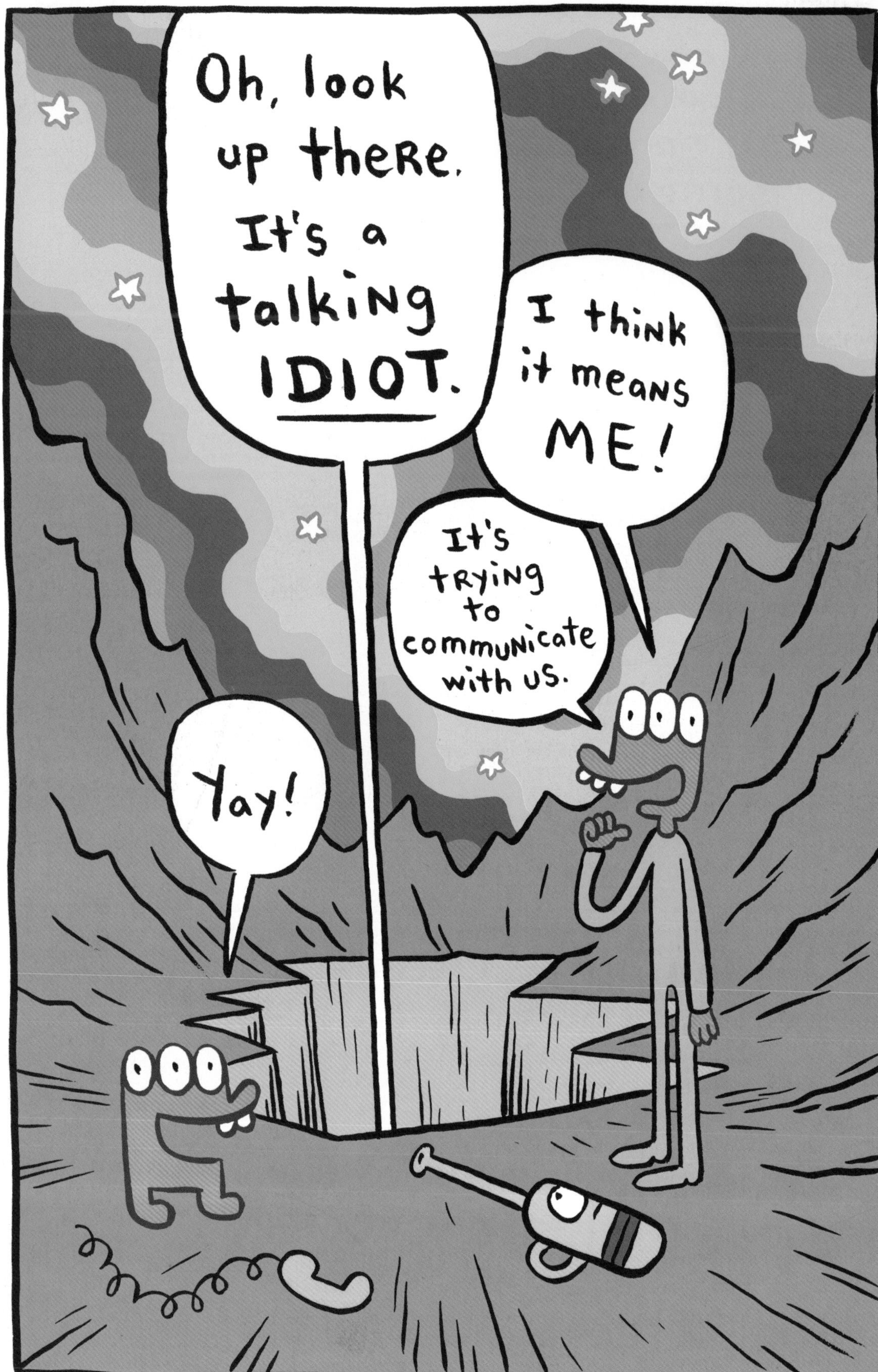
Oh, look up there. It's a talking IDIOT.
I think it means ME!
It's trying to communicate with us.
Yay!

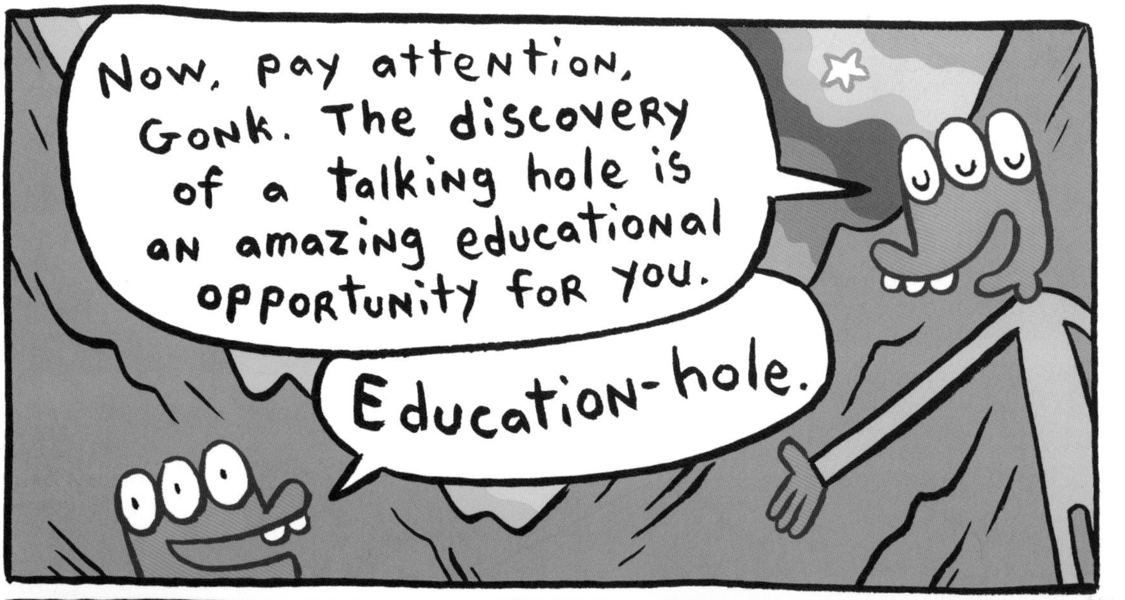
Now, pay attention, Gonk. The discovery of a talking hole is an amazing educational opportunity for you.
Education-hole.

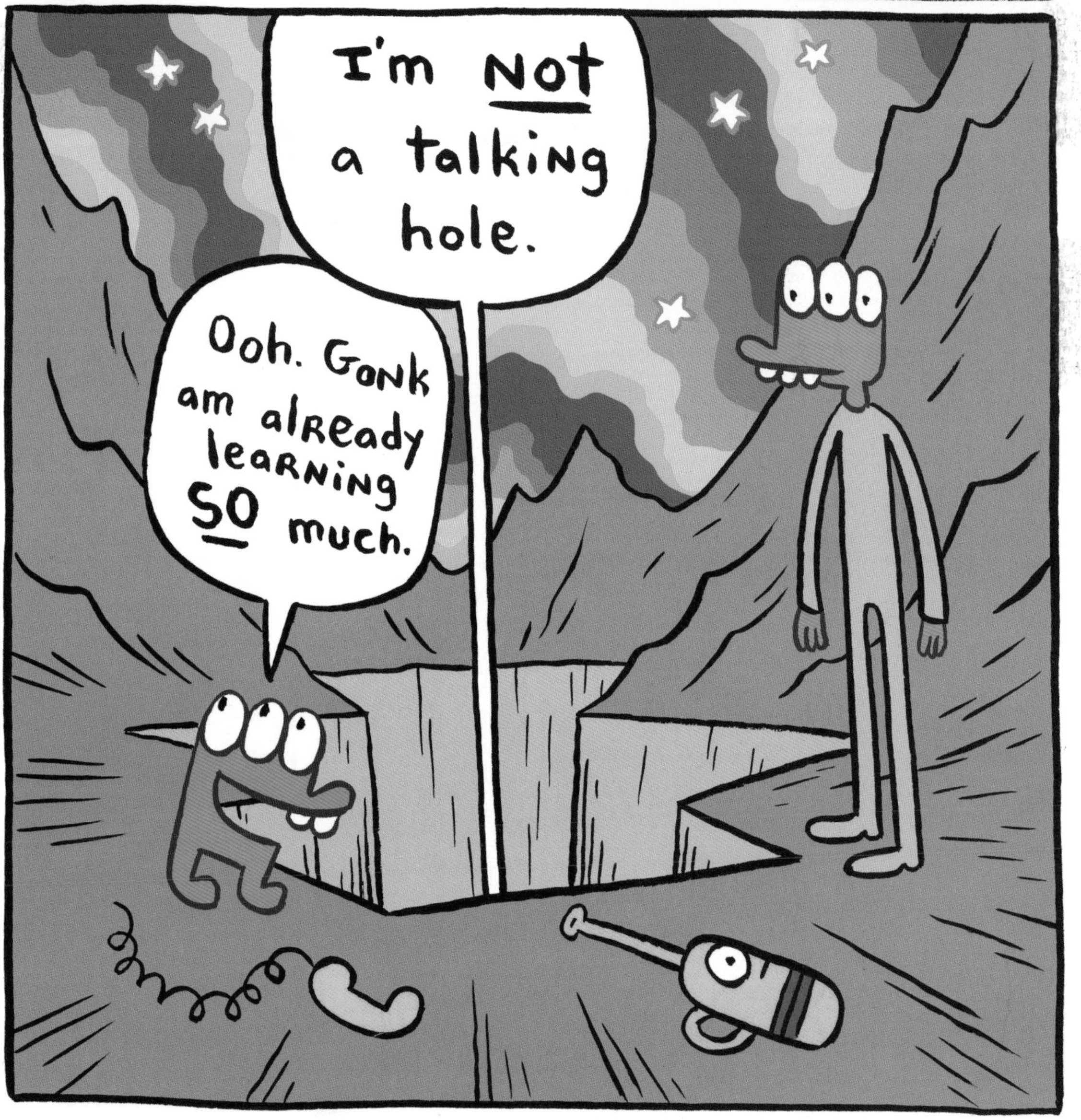
I'm NOT a talking hole.
Ooh. Gonk am already learning SO much.

CHAPTER SIXTEEN

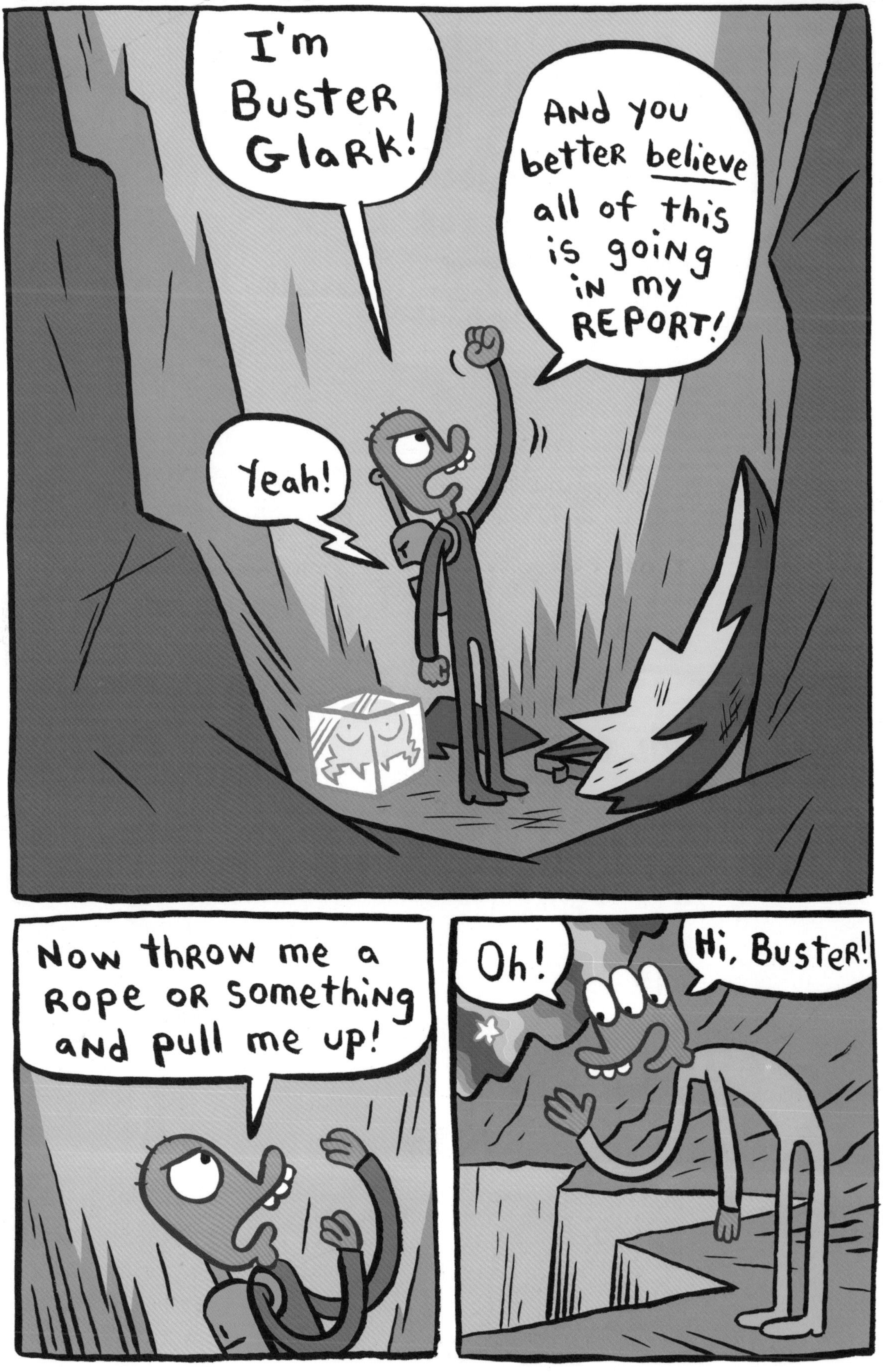
I'm Buster Glark!
And you better believe all of this is going in my REPORT!
Yeah!
Now throw me a rope or something and pull me up!
Oh!
Hi, Buster!

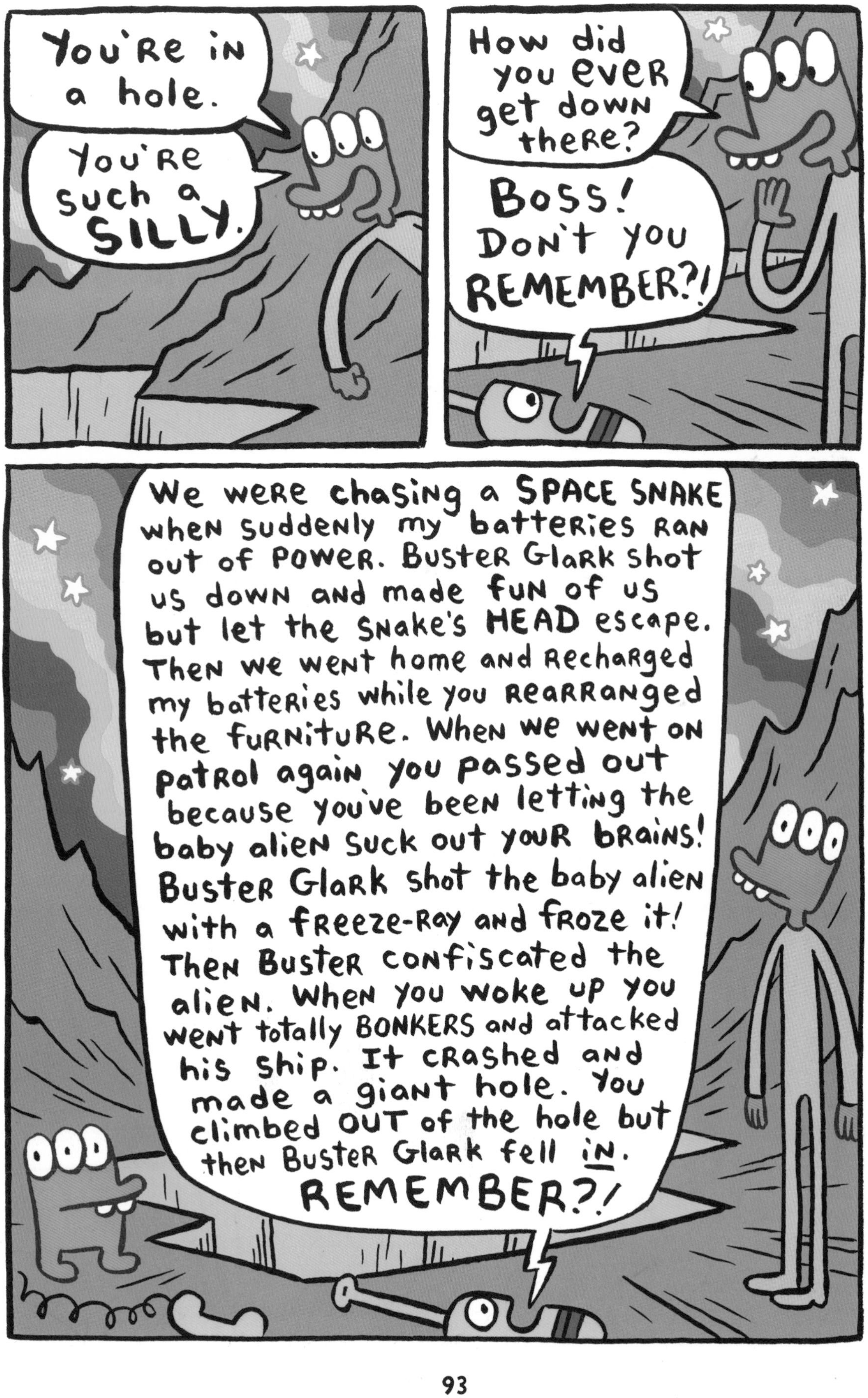
You're in a hole.
You're such a SILLY.
How did you ever get down there?
Boss! Don't you REMEMBER?!
We were chasing a SPACE SNAKE when suddenly my batteries ran out of power. Buster Glark shot us down and made fun of us but let the snake's HEAD escape. Then we went home and recharged my batteries while you rearranged the furniture. When we went on patrol again you passed out because you've been letting the baby alien suck out your brains! Buster Glark shot the baby alien with a freeze-ray and froze it! Then Buster confiscated the alien. When you woke up you went totally BONKERS and attacked his ship. It crashed and made a giant hole. You climbed OUT of the hole but then Buster Glark fell IN. REMEMBER?!

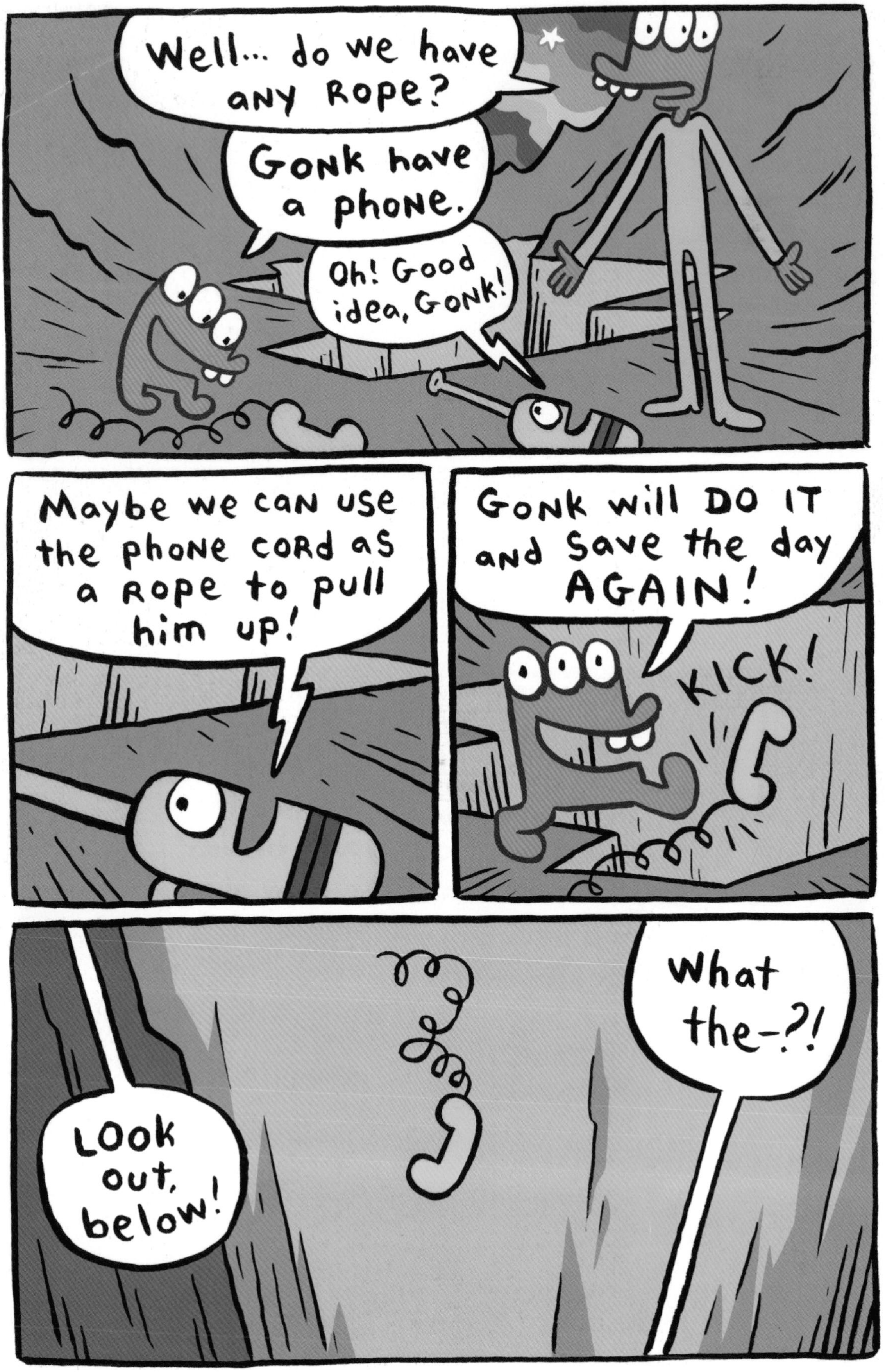
Well... do we have any Rope?
Gonk have a phone.
Oh! Good idea, Gonk!
Maybe we can use the phone cord as a rope to pull him up!
Gonk will DO IT and Save the day AGAIN!
KICK!
What the-?!
LOOK out, below!

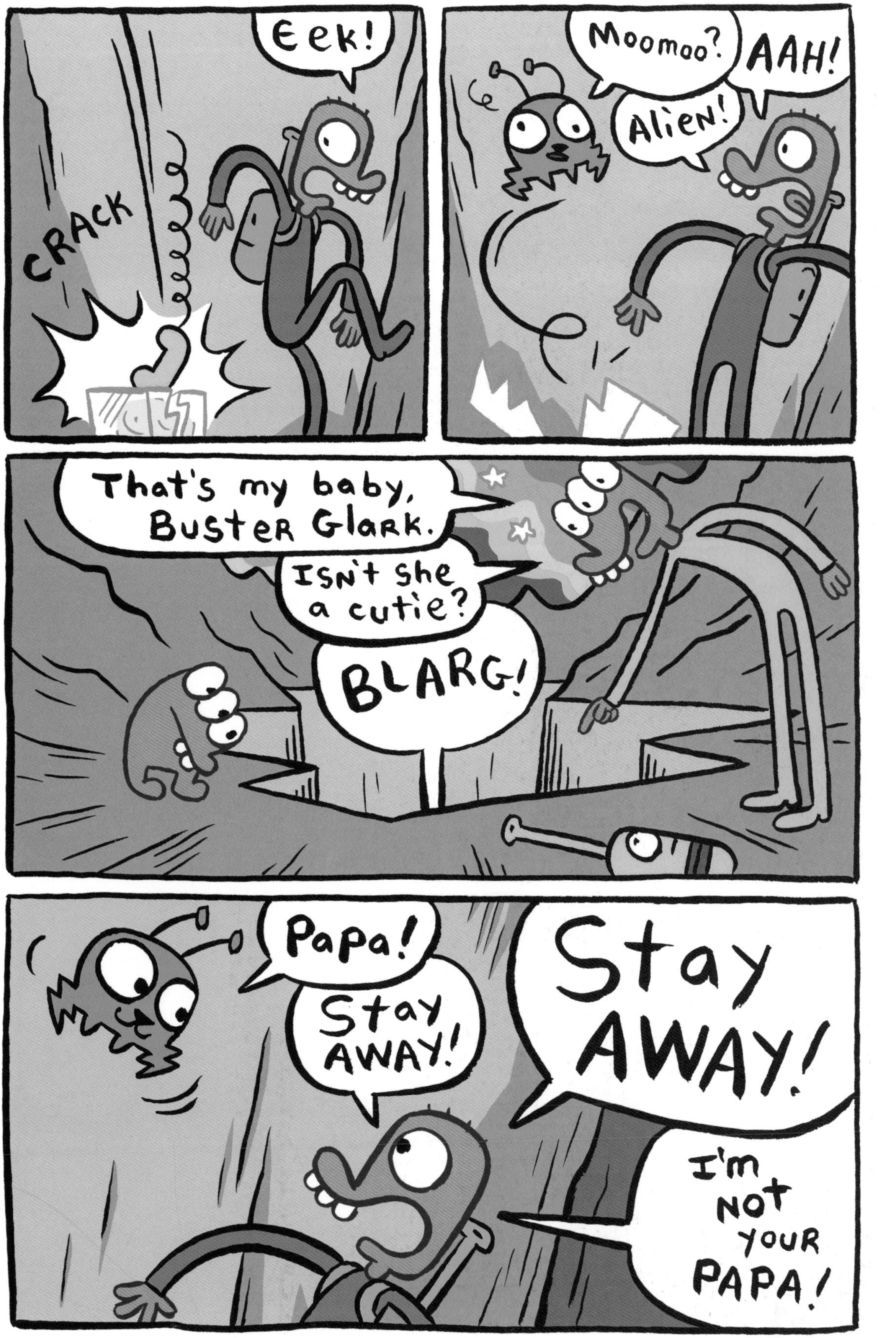
Eek!
CRACK
Moomoo?
AAH!
Alien!
That's my baby, Buster Glark.
Isn't she a cutie?
BLARG!
Papa!
Stay AWAY!
Stay AWAY!
I'm NOT YOUR PAPA!

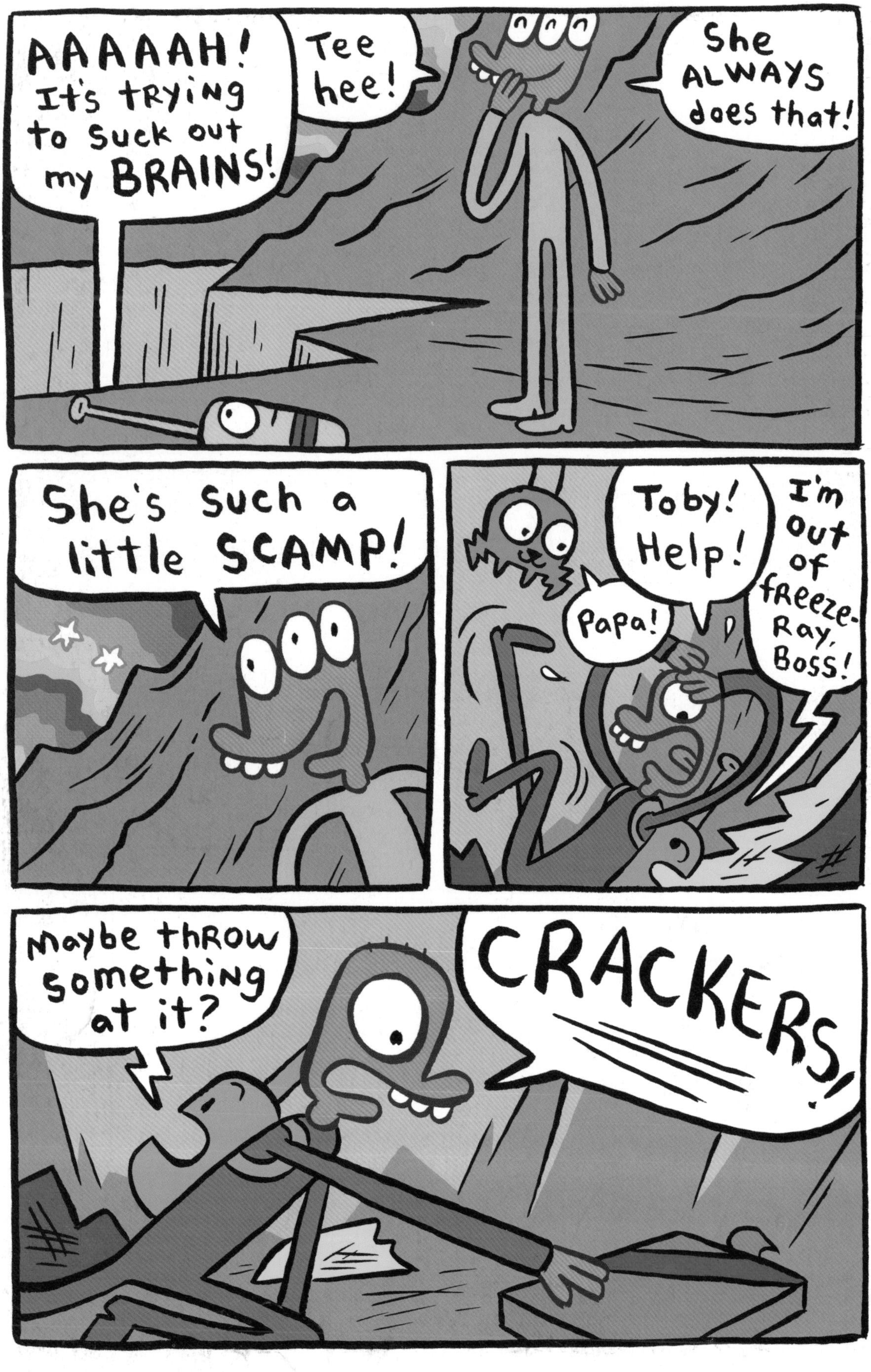
AAAAAH! It's trying to suck out my BRAINS!
Tee hee!
She ALWAYS does that!
She's such a little SCAMP!
Toby! Help!
I'm out of freeze-ray, Boss!
Papa!
Maybe throw something at it?
CRACKERS!

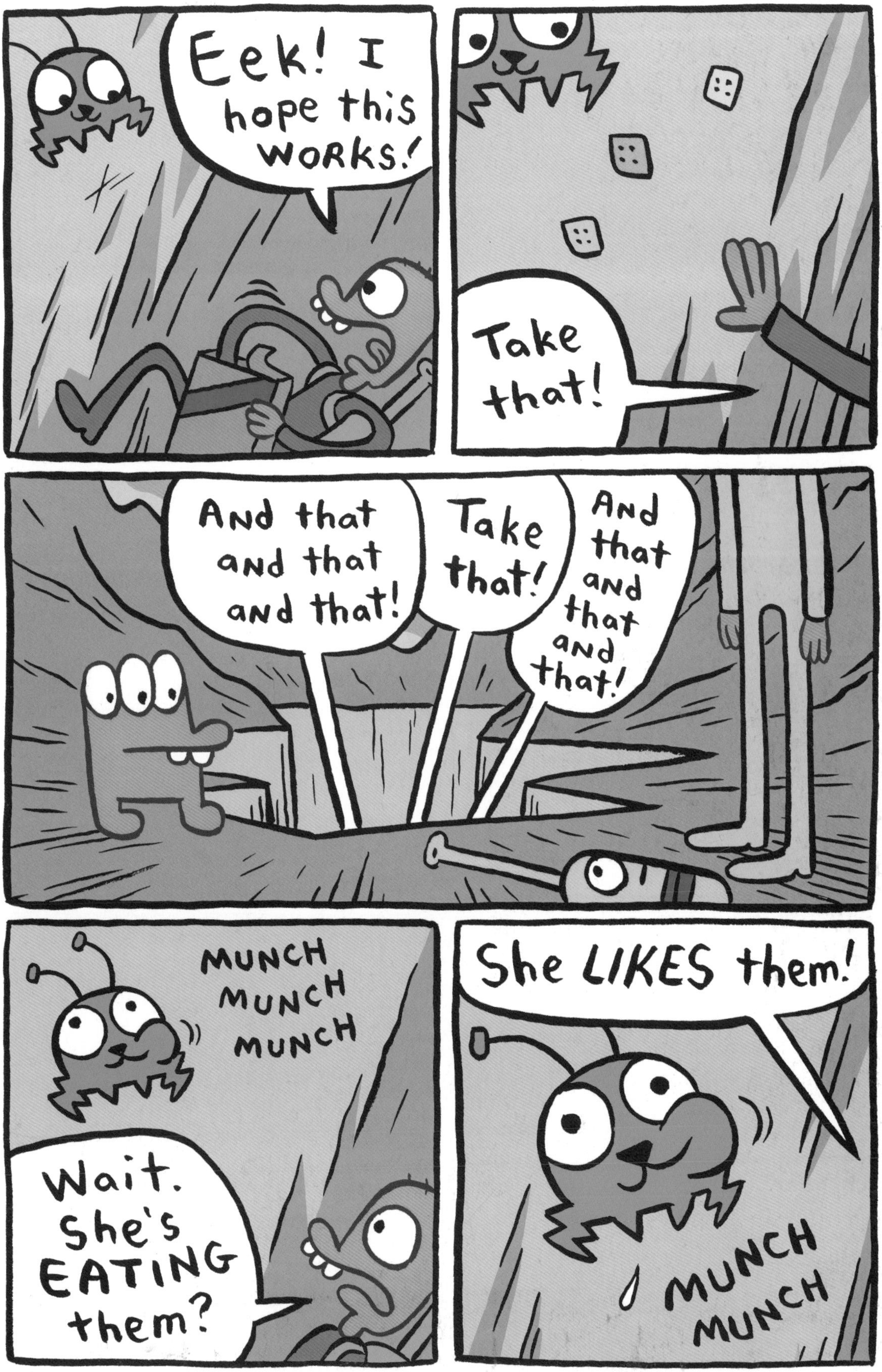

Eek! I hope this WORKS!
Take that!
And that and that and that!
Take that!
And that and that and that!
MUNCH MUNCH MUNCH
Wait. She's EATING them?
She LIKES them!
MUNCH MUNCH

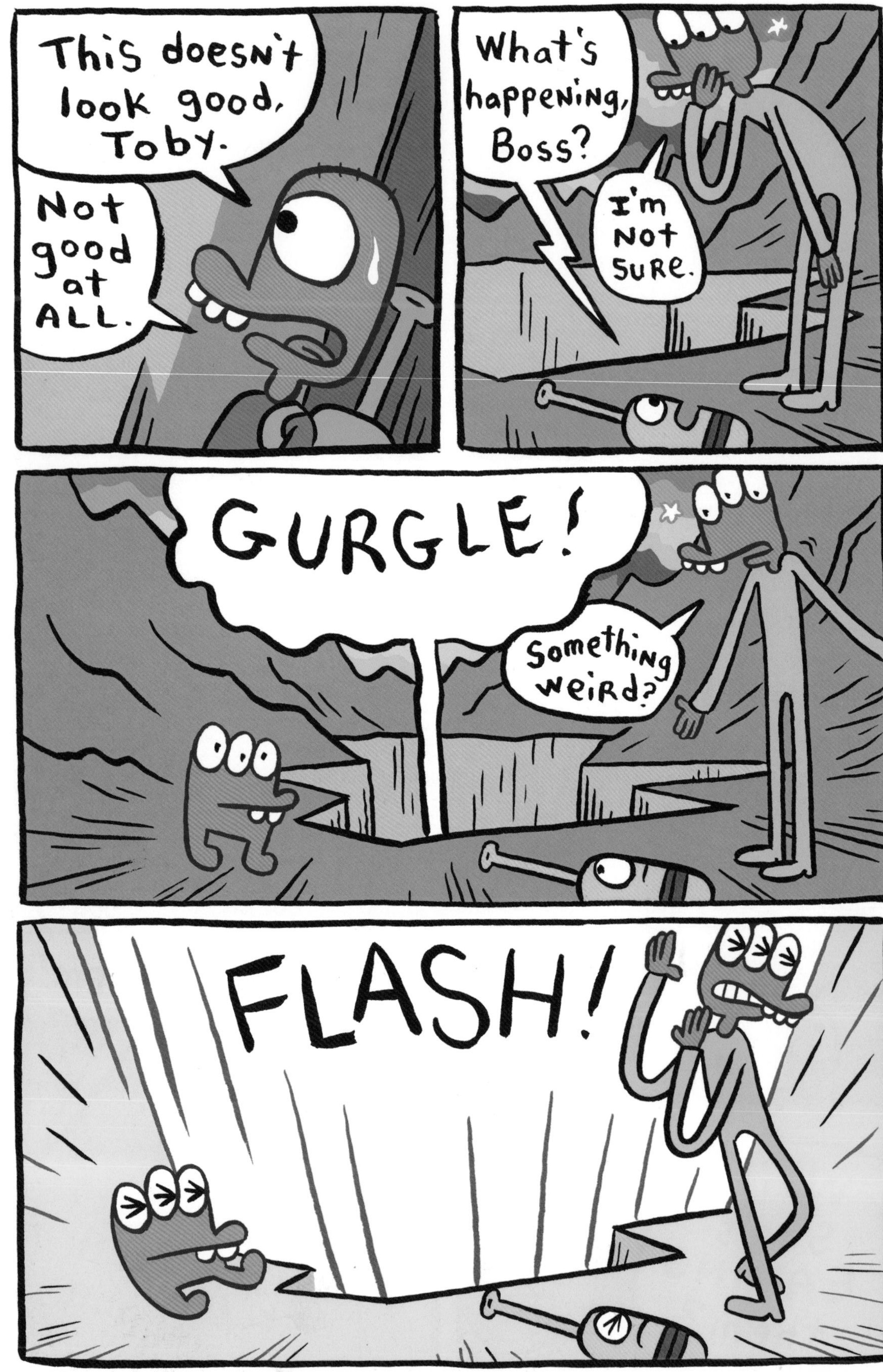
This doesn't look good, Toby.
Not good at ALL.
What's happening, Boss?
I'm not sure.
GURGLE!
Something weird?
FLASH!

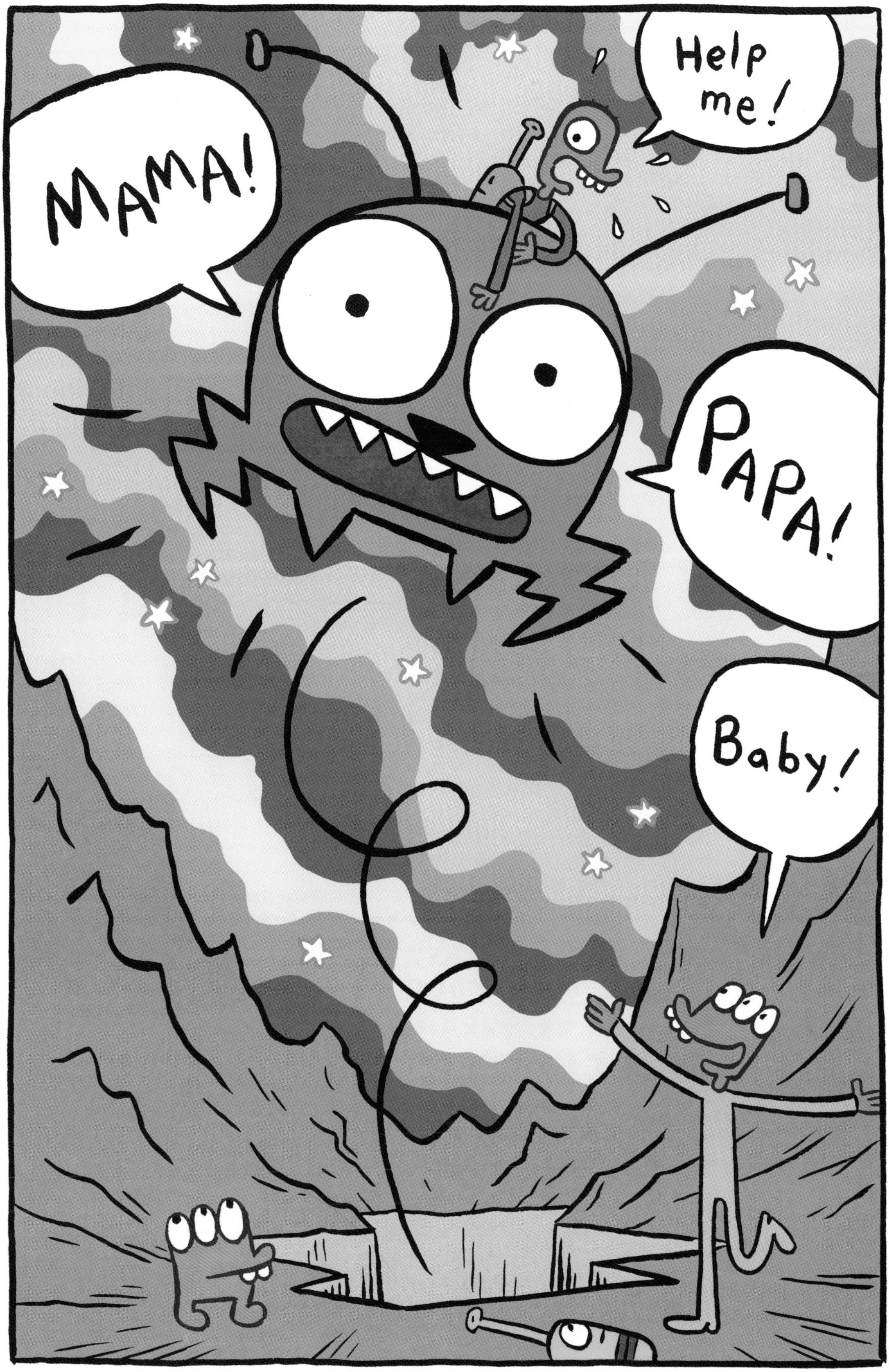
MAMA!
Help me!
PAPA!
Baby!

CHAPTER SEVENTEEN

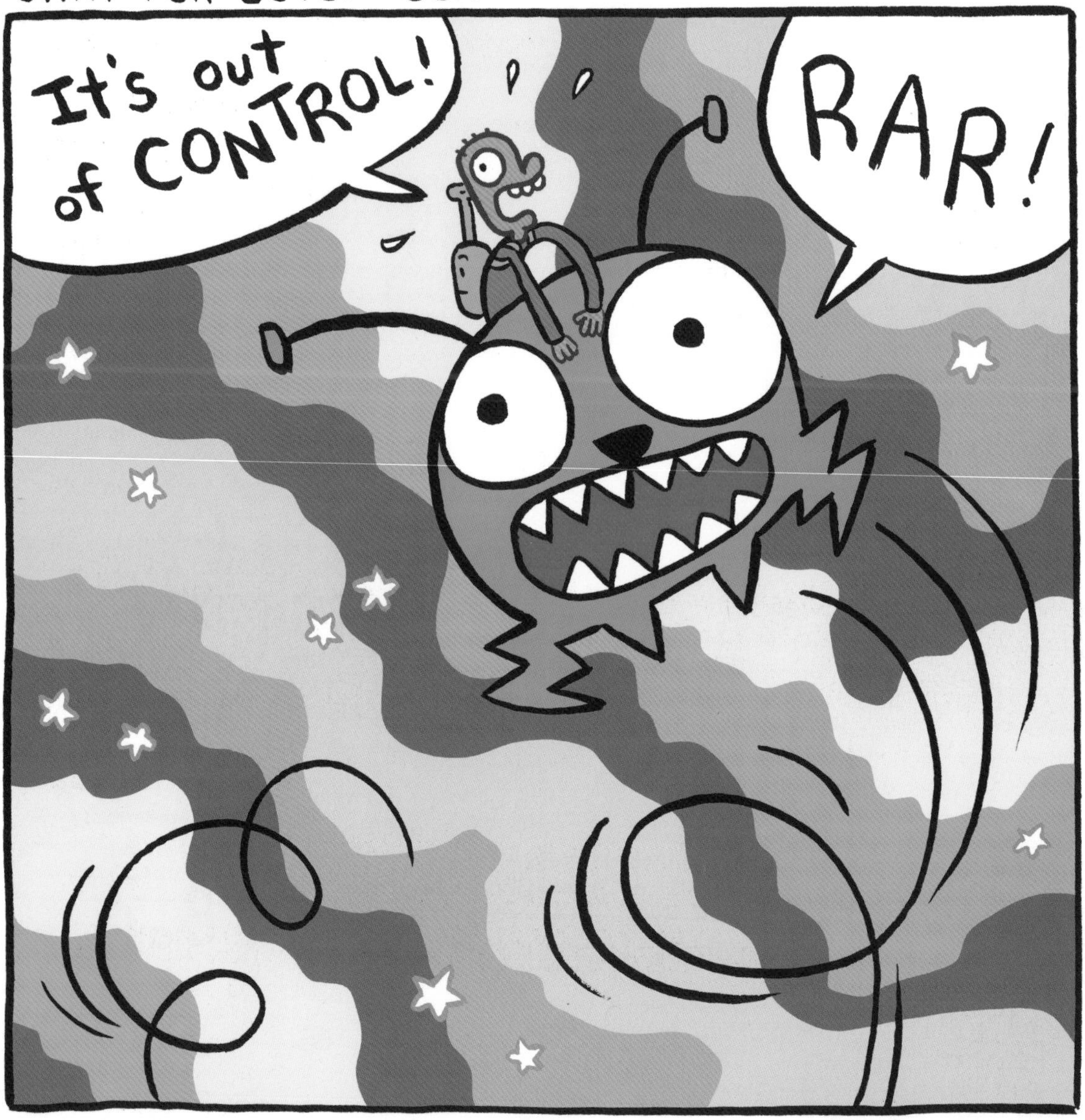
It's out of CONTROL!
RAR!

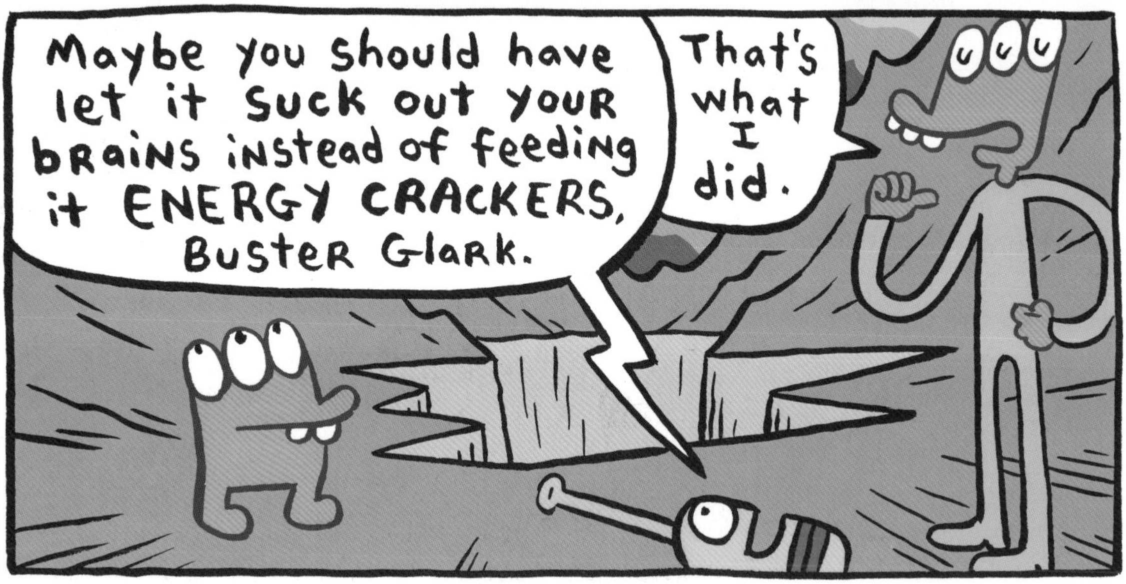
Maybe you should have let it suck out your brains instead of feeding it ENERGY CRACKERS, Buster Glark.
That's what I did.

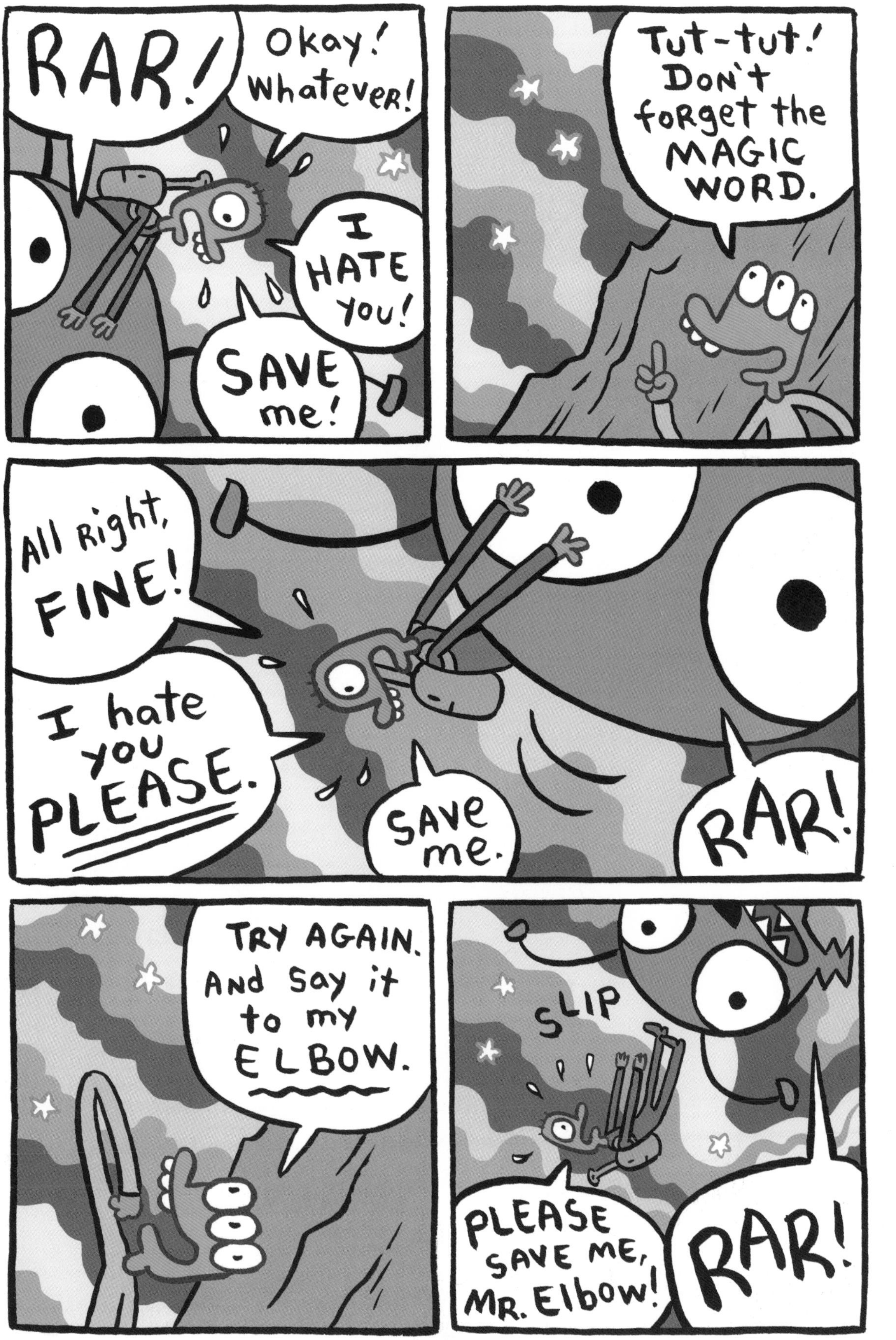
RAR!
Okay! Whatever!
I HATE you!
SAVE me!
Tut-tut! Don't forget the MAGIC WORD.
All Right, FINE!
I hate you PLEASE.
SAVE me.
RAR!
TRY AGAIN. And say it to my ELBOW.
SLIP
PLEASE SAVE ME, MR. Elbow!
RAR!

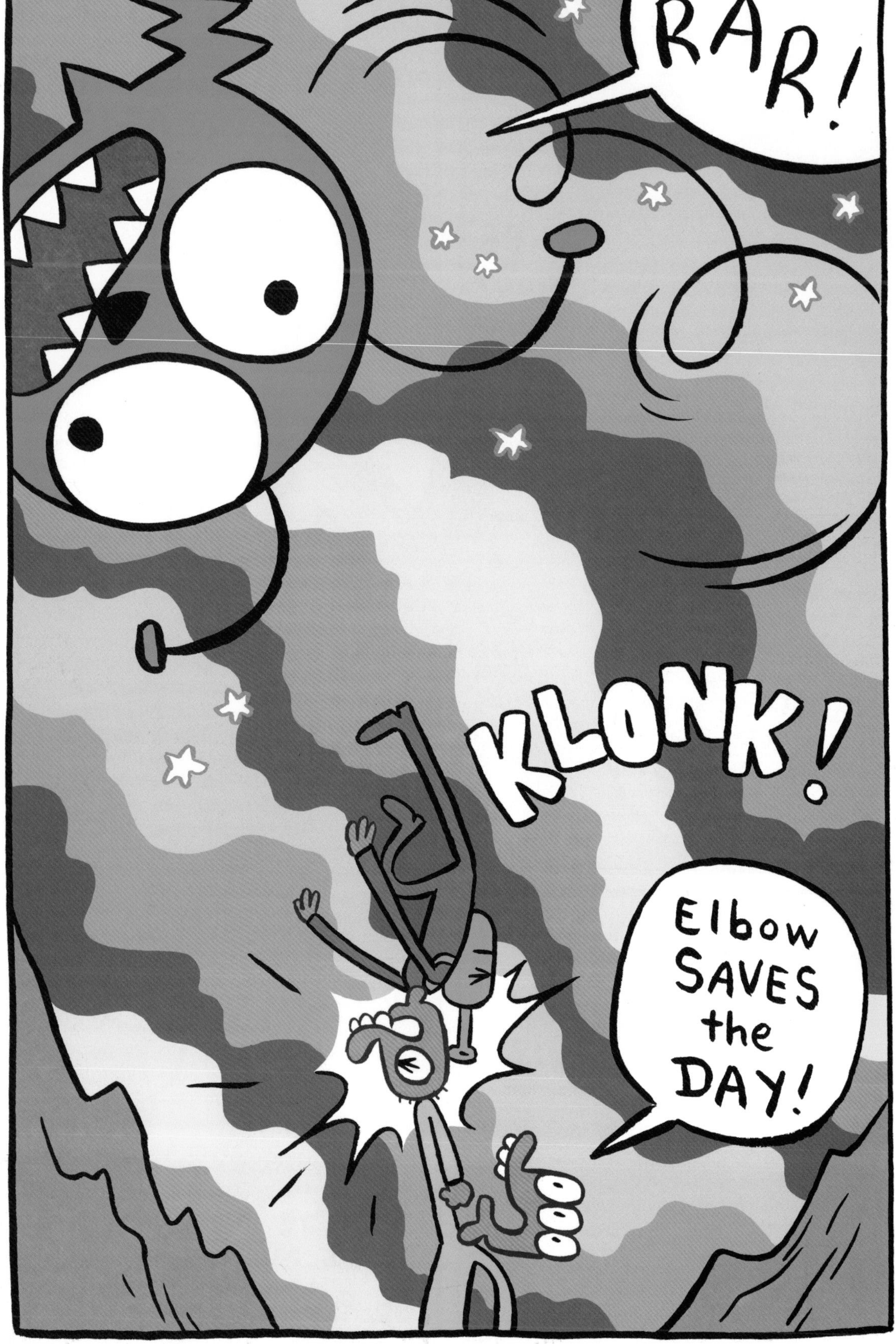
RAR!
KLONK!
Elbow SAVES the DAY!

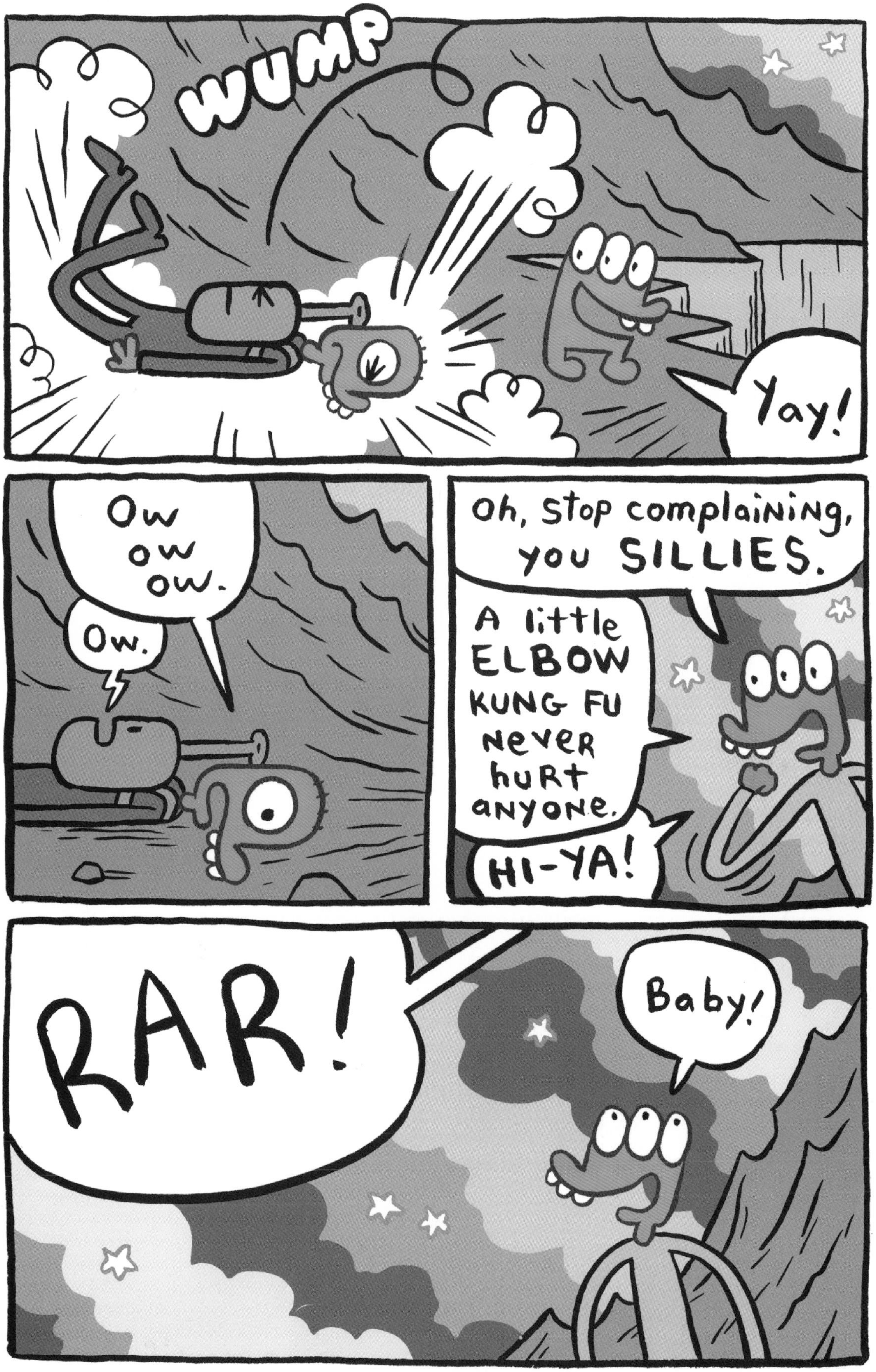
WUMP
Yay!
Ow ow ow.
Ow.
Oh, stop complaining, you SILLIES.
A little ELBOW KUNG FU never hurt anyone.
HI-YA!
RAR!
Baby!

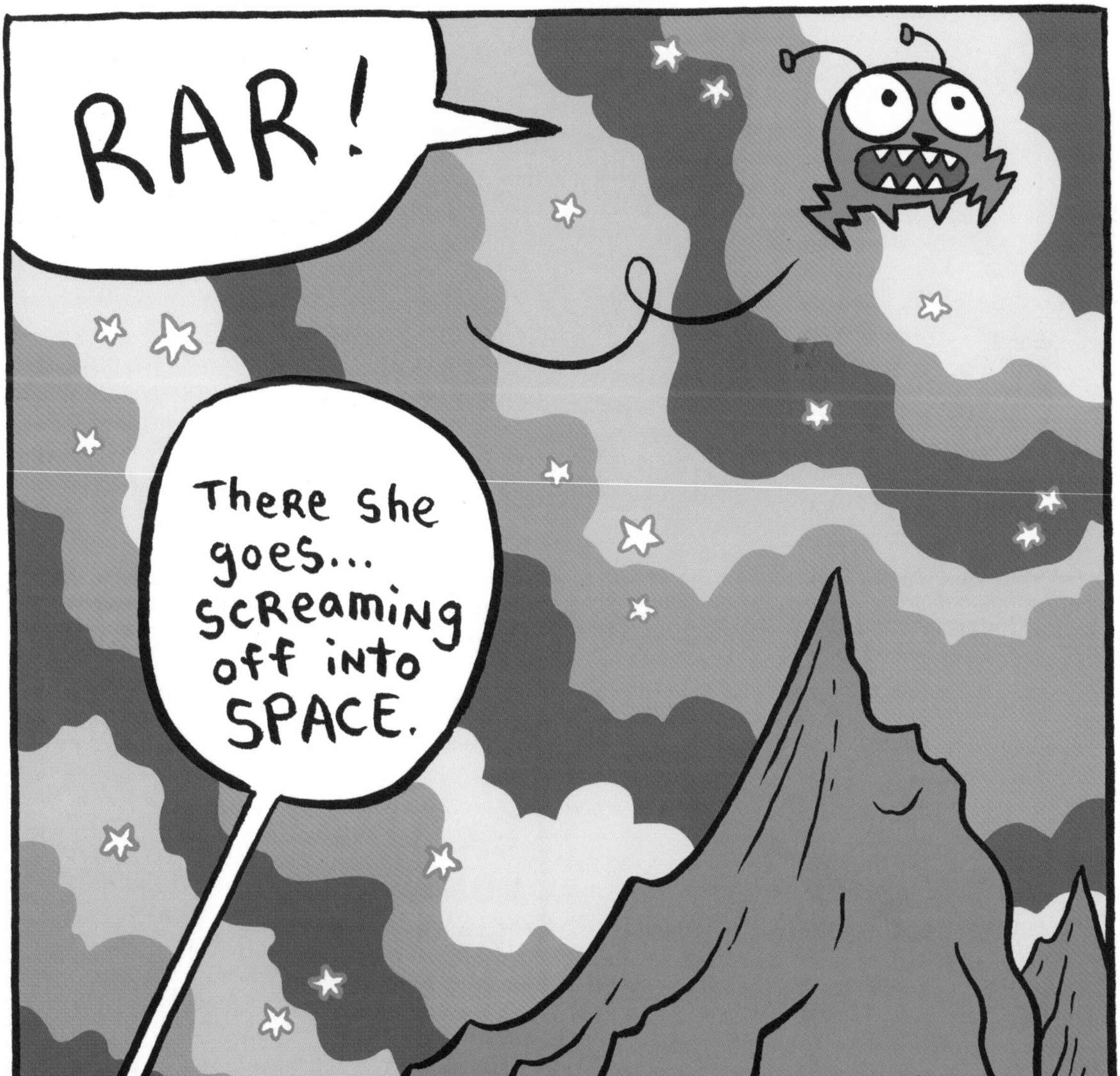
RAR!
There she goes... screaming off into SPACE.

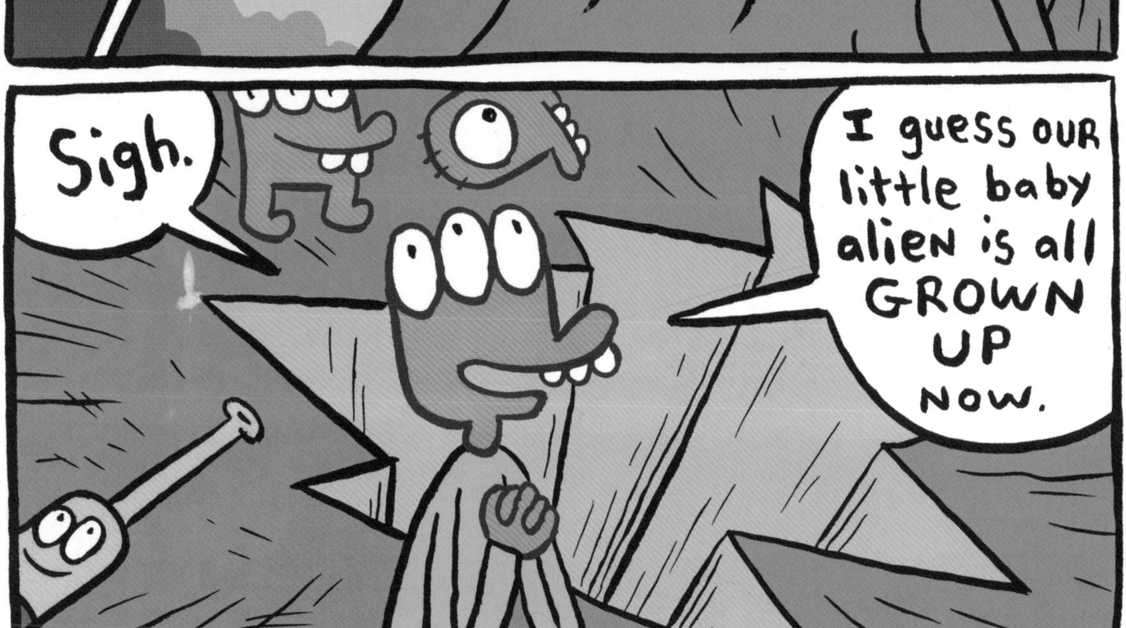
Sigh.
I guess our little baby alien is all GROWN UP now.

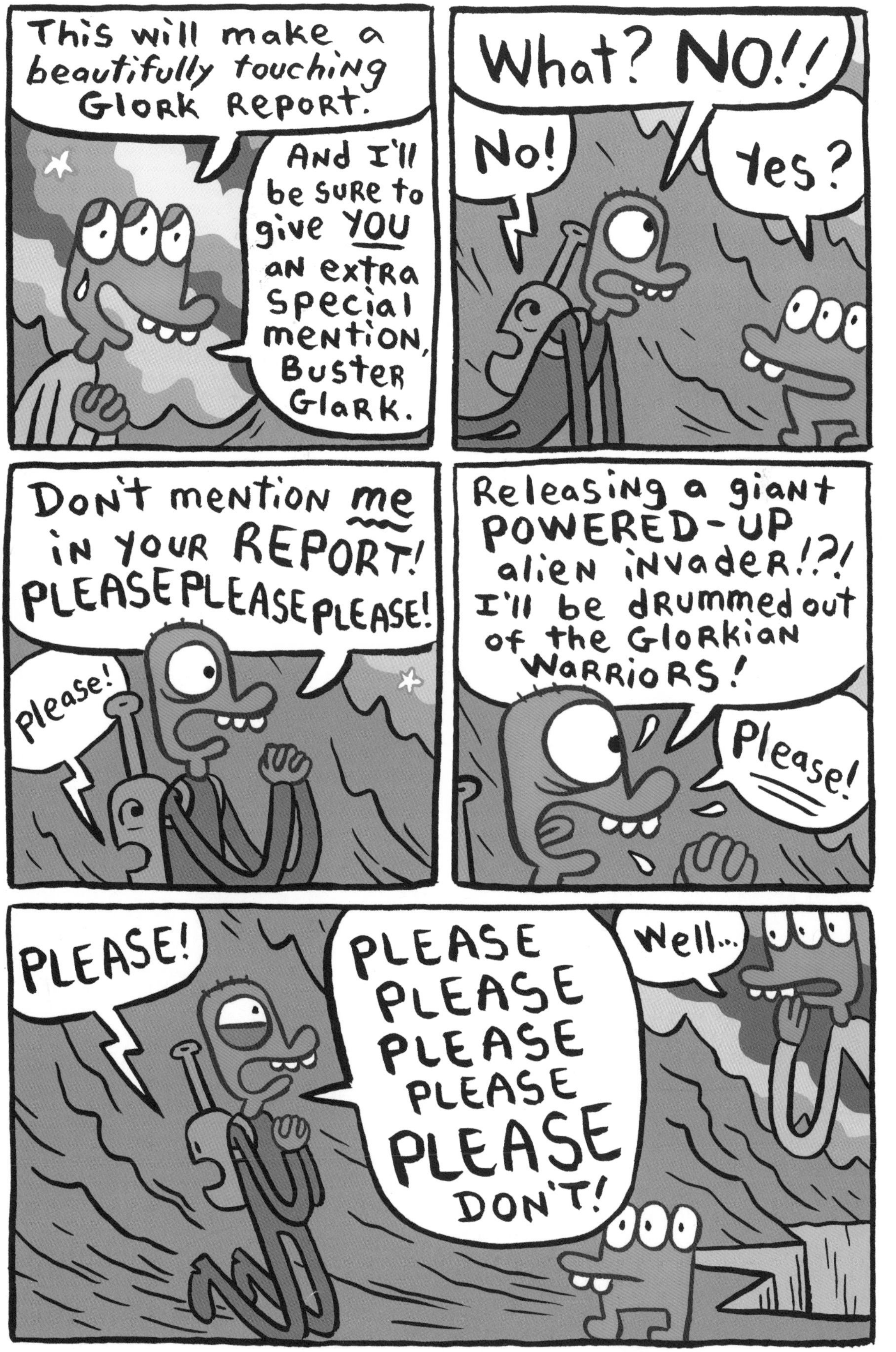
This will make a beautifully touching Glork Report.
And I'll be sure to give YOU an extra special mention, Buster Glark.
What? NO!!
No!
Yes?
Don't mention me in your REPORT! PLEASEPLEASEPLEASE!
Please!
Releasing a giant POWERED-UP alien invader!?! I'll be drummed out of the Glorkian Warriors!
Please!
PLEASE!
PLEASE PLEASE PLEASE PLEASE PLEASE DON'T!
Well...

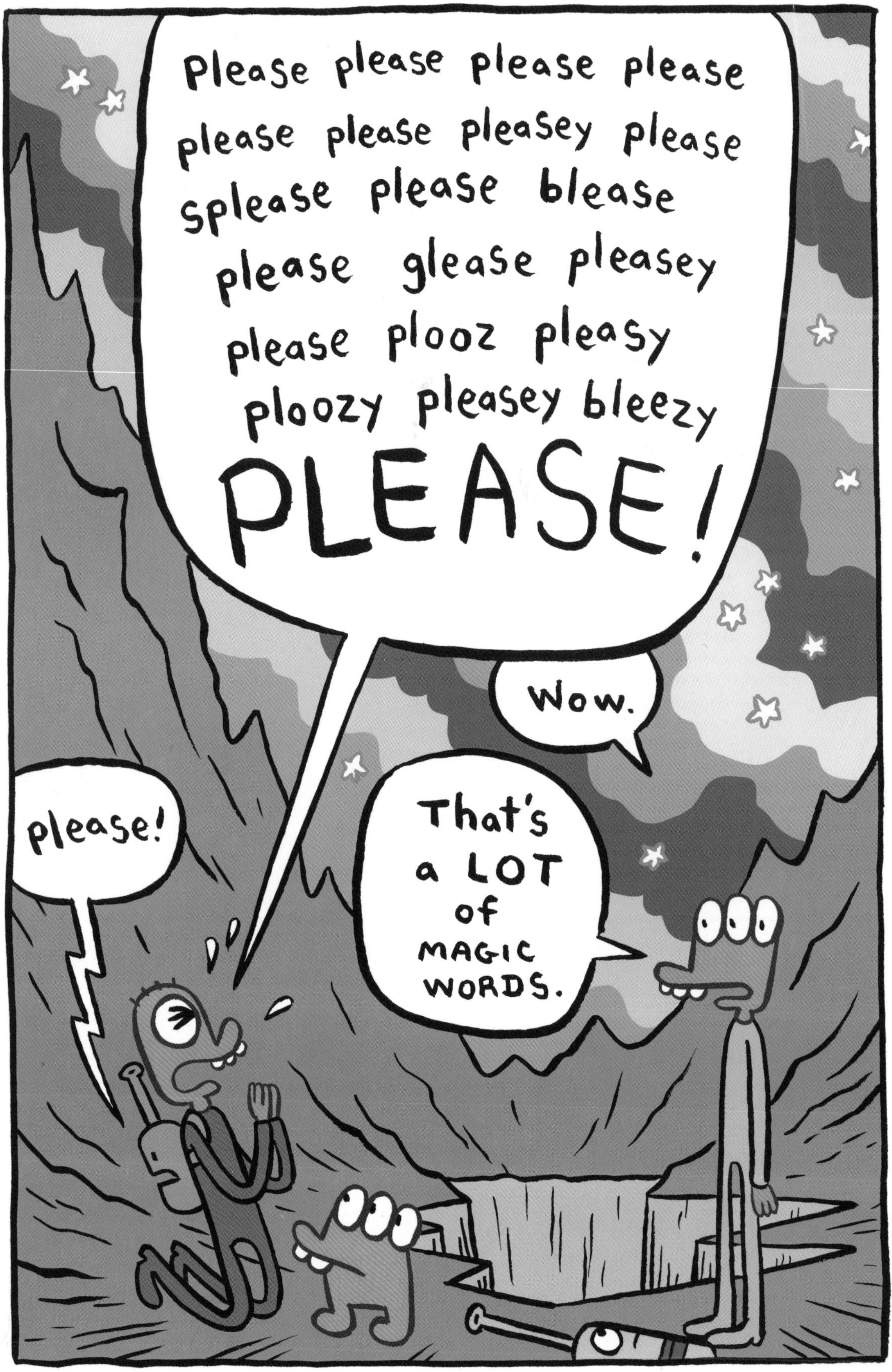
Please please please please please please pleasey please splease please blease please glease pleasey please plooz pleasy ploozy pleasey bleezy PLEASE!
please!
Wow.
That's a LOT of MAGIC WORDS.

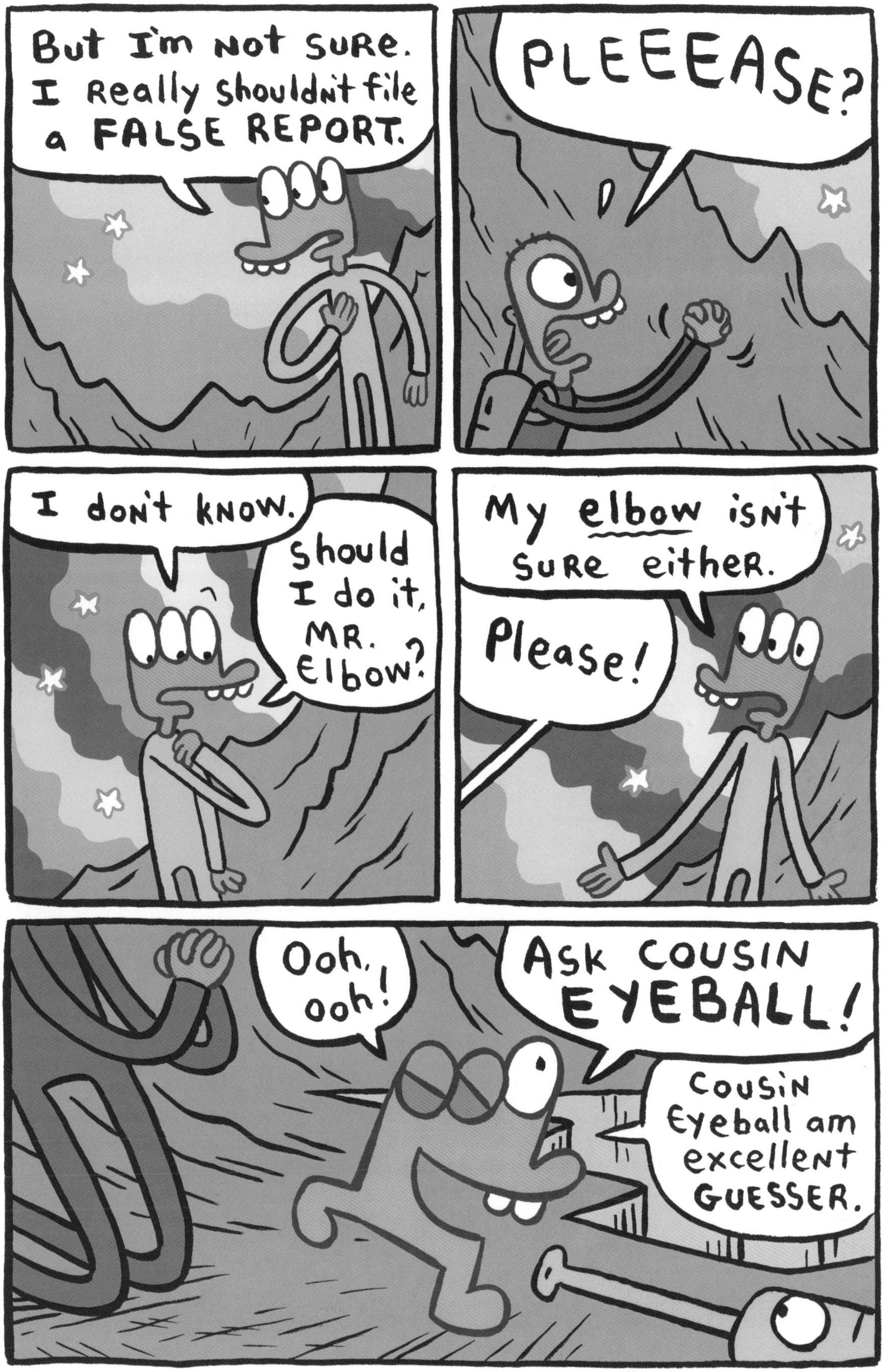
But I'm not sure. I really shouldn't file a FALSE REPORT.
PLEEEASE?
I don't know.
Should I do it, MR. Elbow?
My elbow isn't sure either.
Please!
Ooh, ooh!
ASK COUSIN EYEBALL!
Cousin Eyeball am excellent GUESSER.

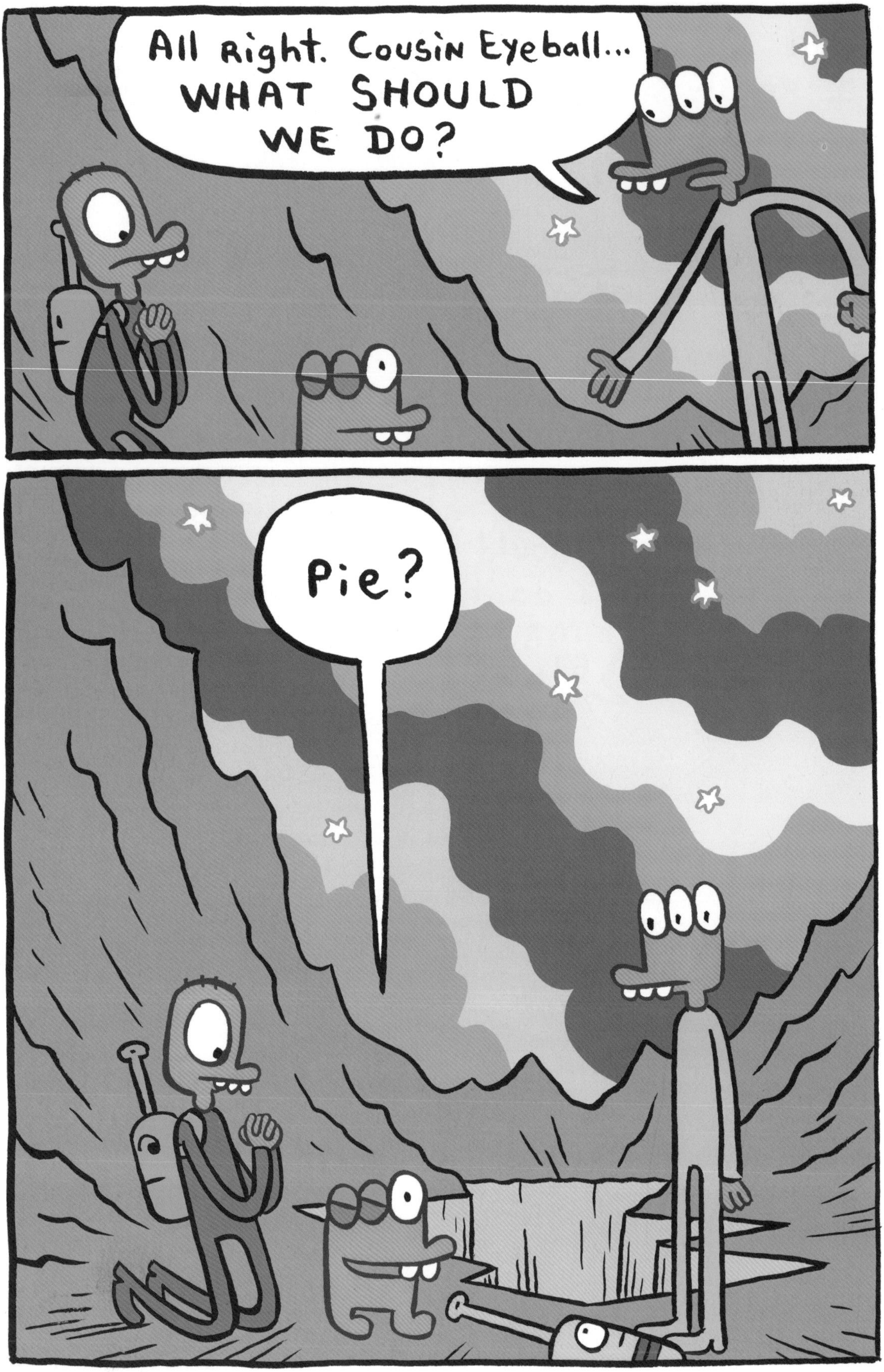
All right. Cousin Eyeball... WHAT SHOULD WE DO?
Pie?

CHAPTER EIGHTEEN

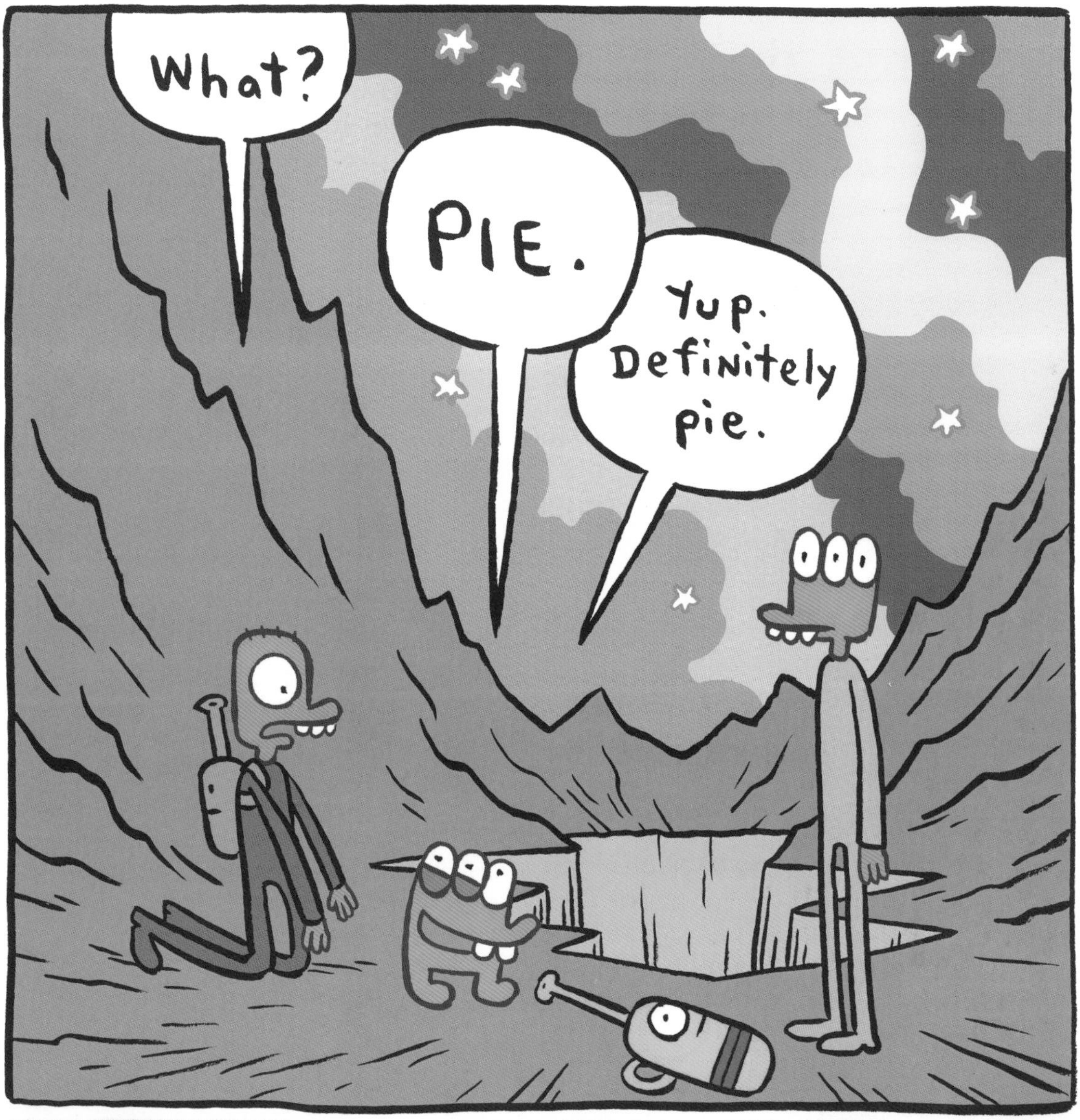
What?
PIE.
Yup. Definitely pie.

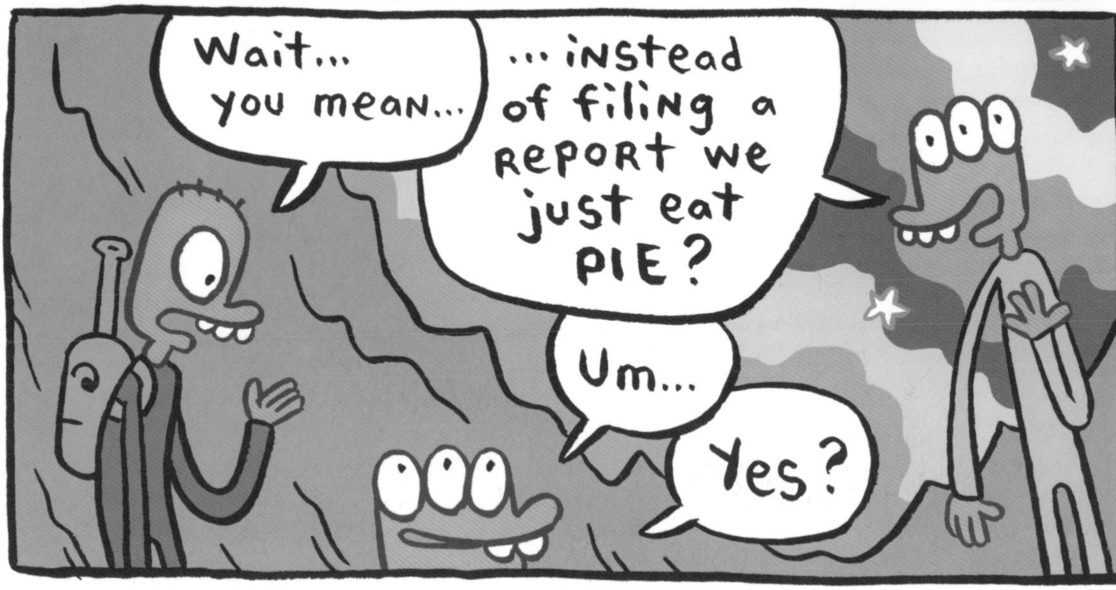
Wait... you mean...
...instead of filing a report we just eat PIE?
Um...
Yes?

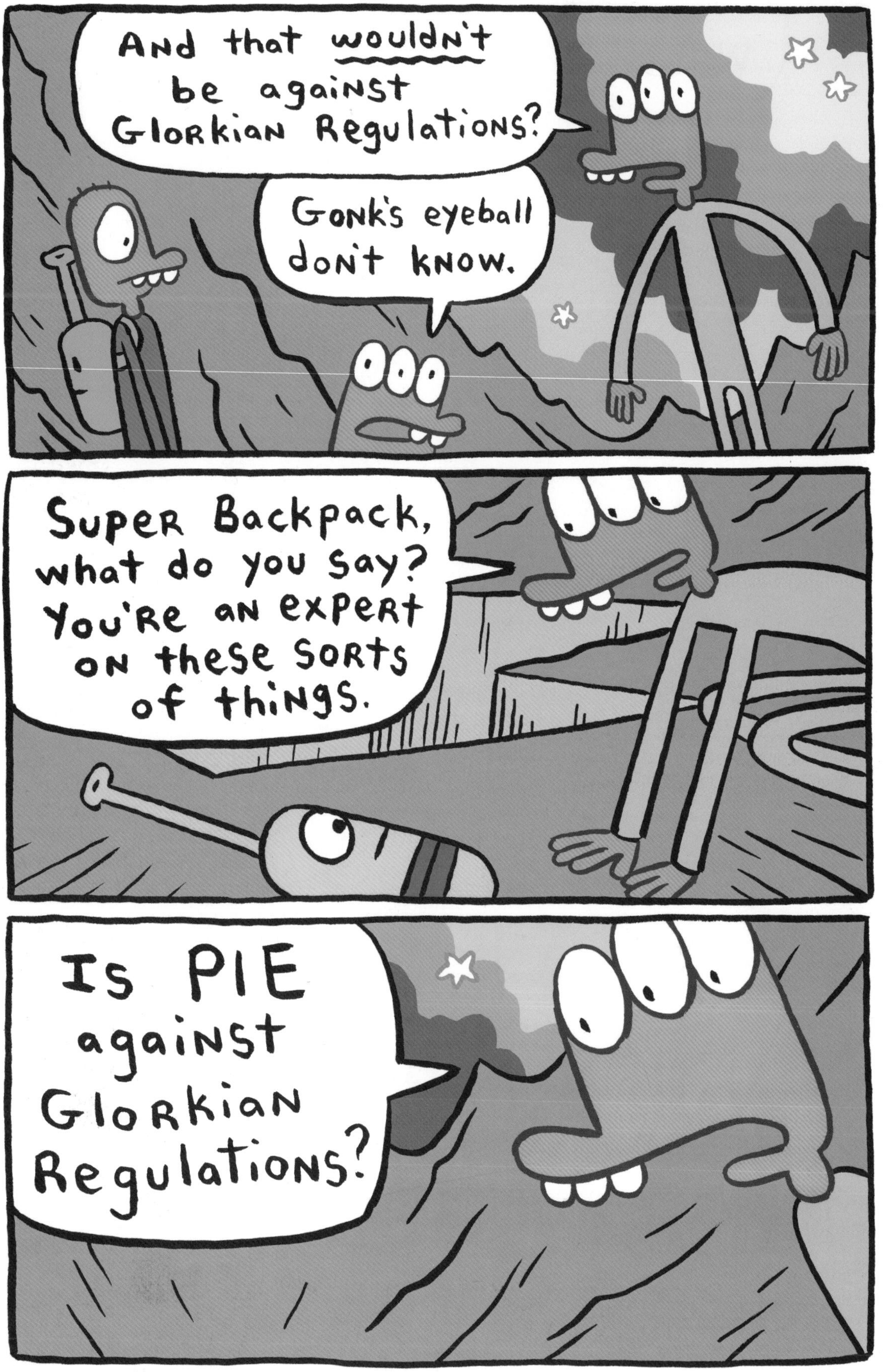
And that wouldn't be against Glorkian Regulations?
Gonk's eyeball don't know.
Super Backpack, what do you say? You're an expert on these sorts of things.
Is PIE against Glorkian Regulations?

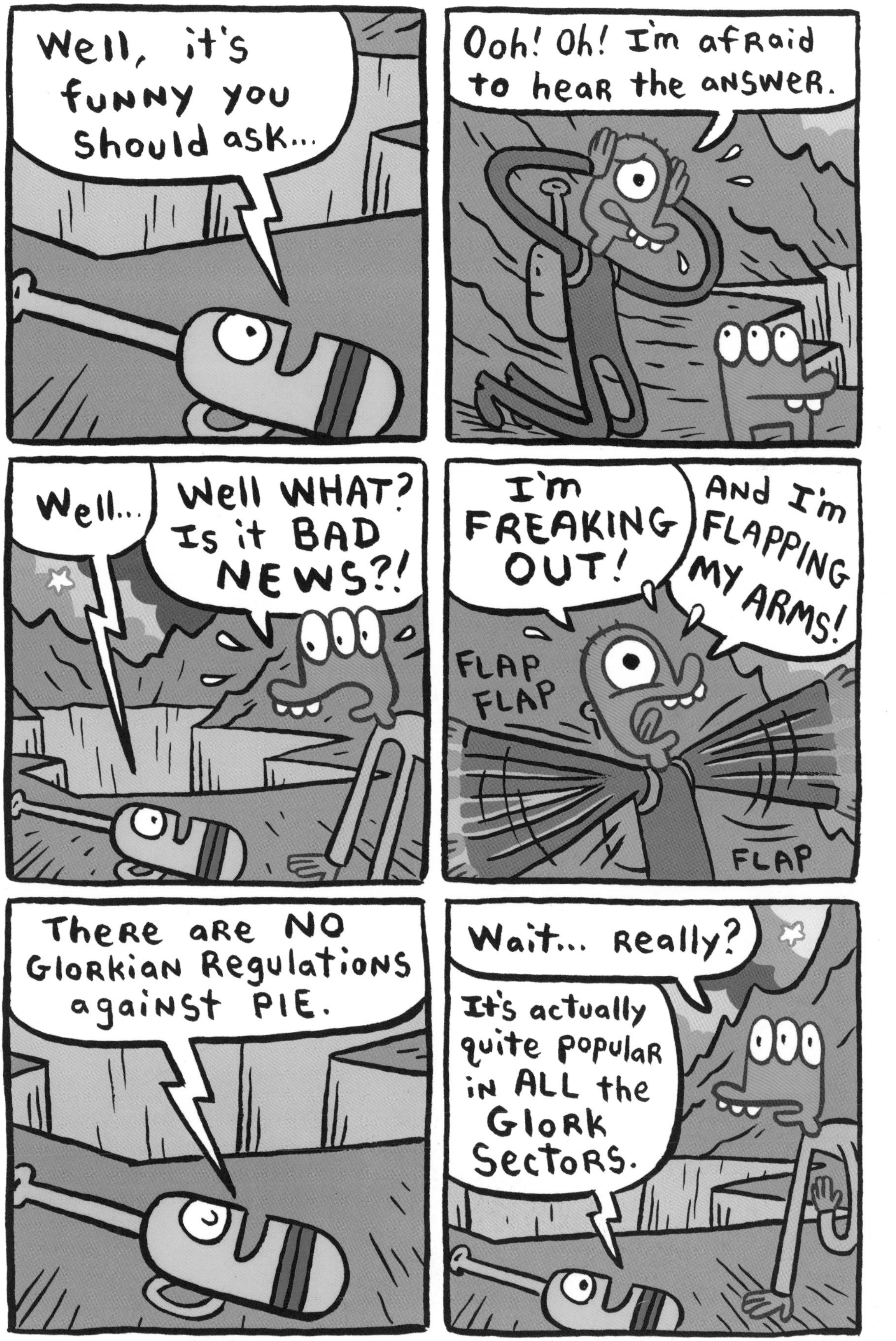
Well, it's funny you should ask...
Ooh! Oh! I'm afraid to hear the answer.
Well...
Well WHAT? Is it BAD NEWS?!
I'm FREAKING OUT!
AND I'm FLAPPING MY ARMS!
FLAP FLAP
FLAP
There are NO Glorkian Regulations against PIE.
Wait... Really?
It's actually quite popular in ALL the Glork Sectors.

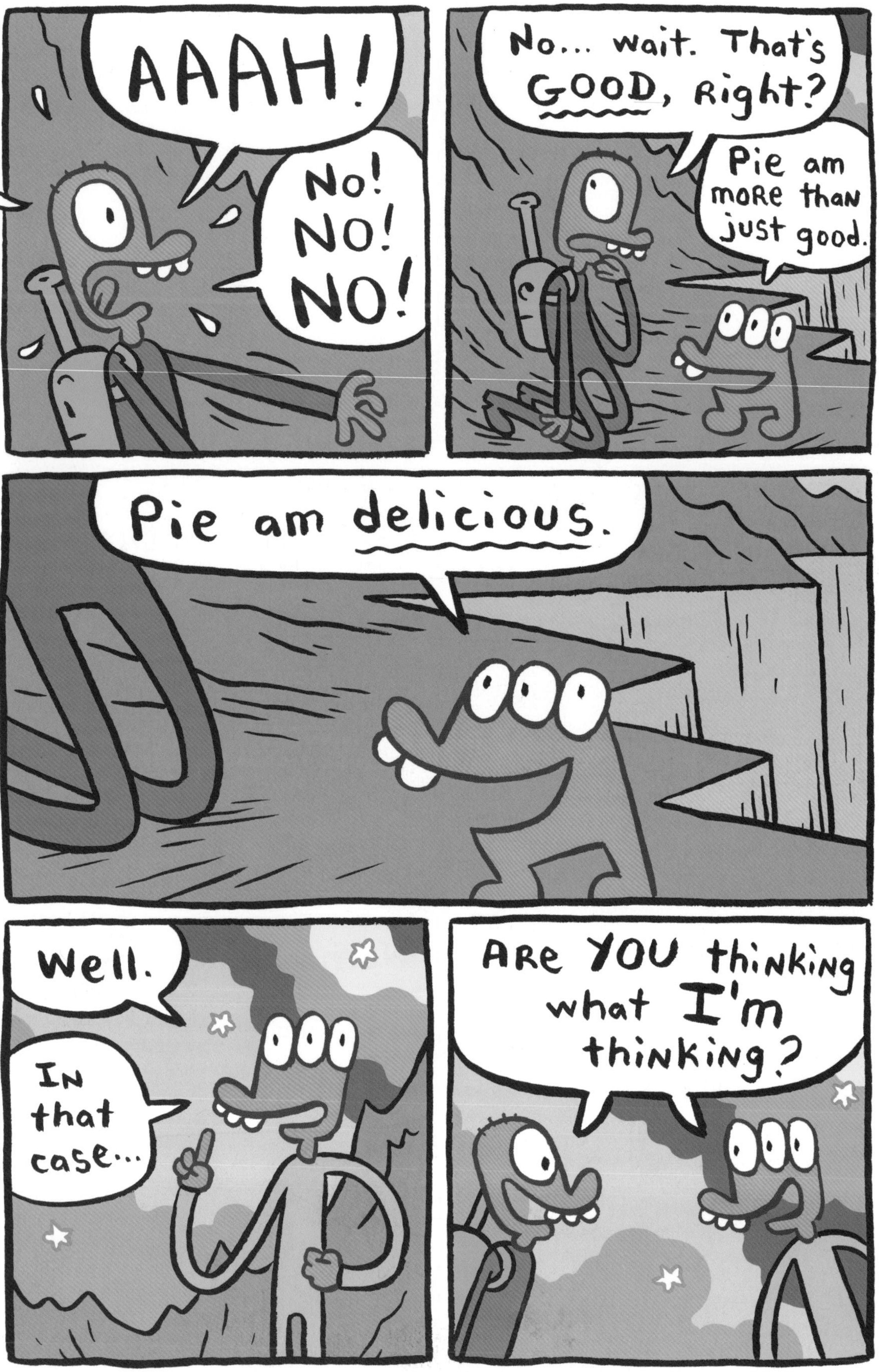
AAAH!
No! NO! NO!
No... wait. That's GOOD, Right?
Pie am more than just good.
Pie am delicious.
Well.
In that case...
ARe YOU thinking what I'm thinking?

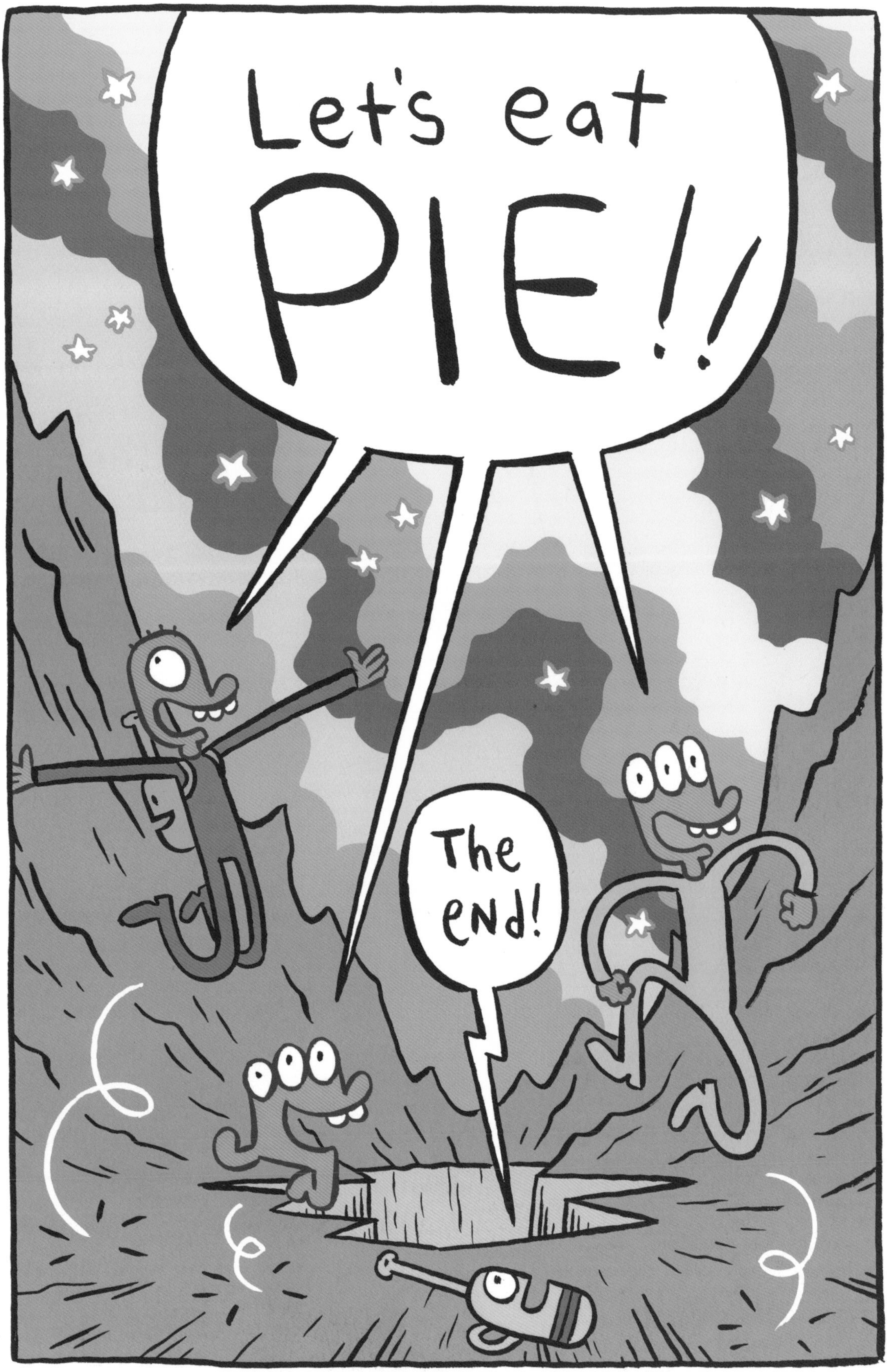
Let's eat PIE!!
The end!

EPILOGUE

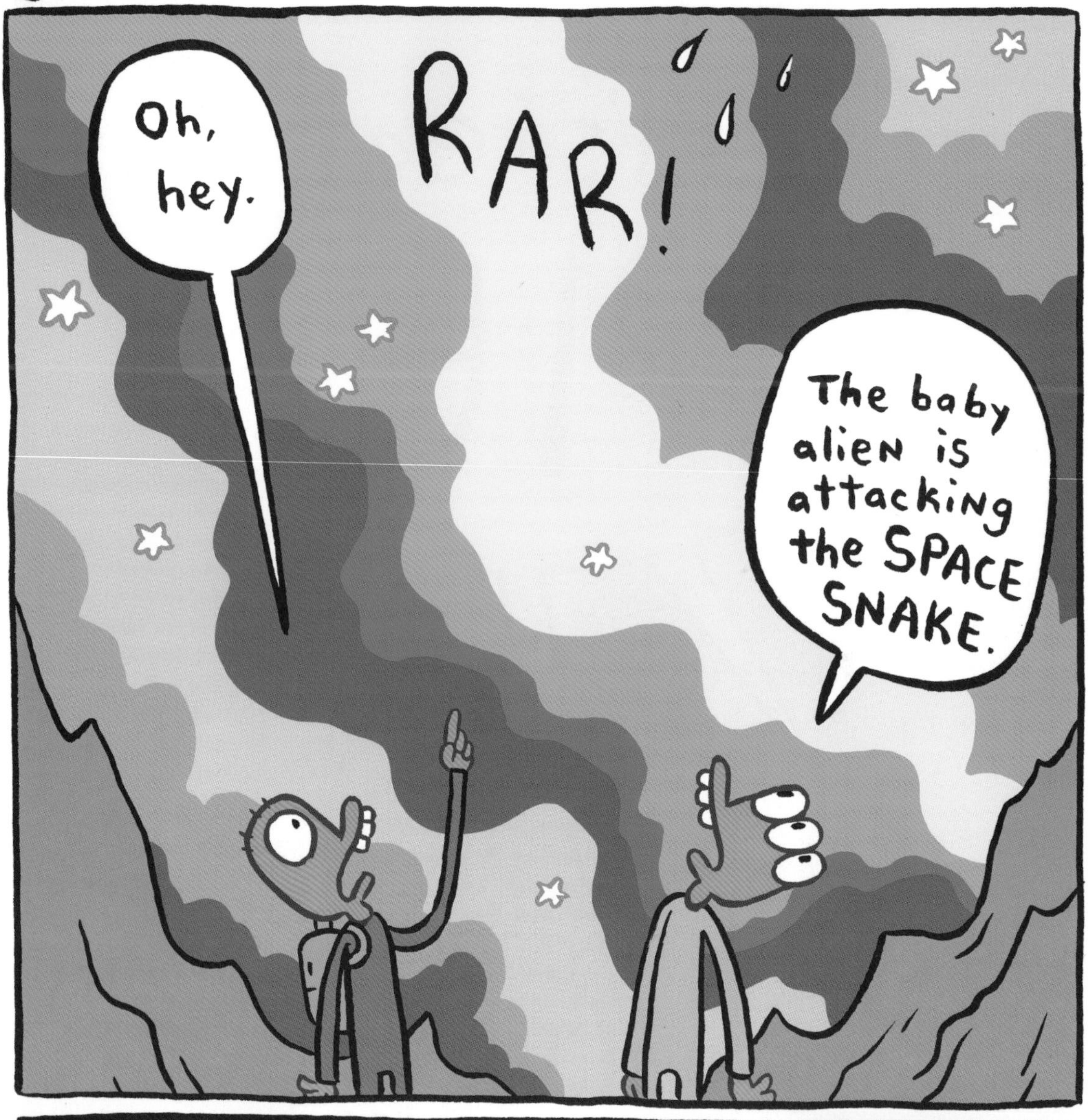
Oh, hey.
RAR!
The baby alien is attacking the SPACE SNAKE.

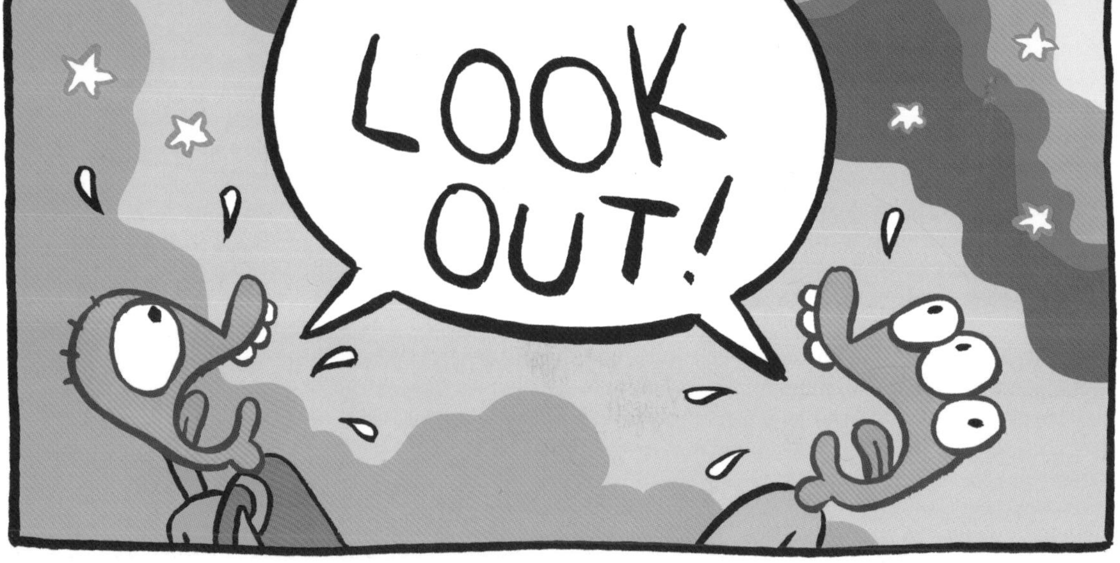
LOOK OUT!

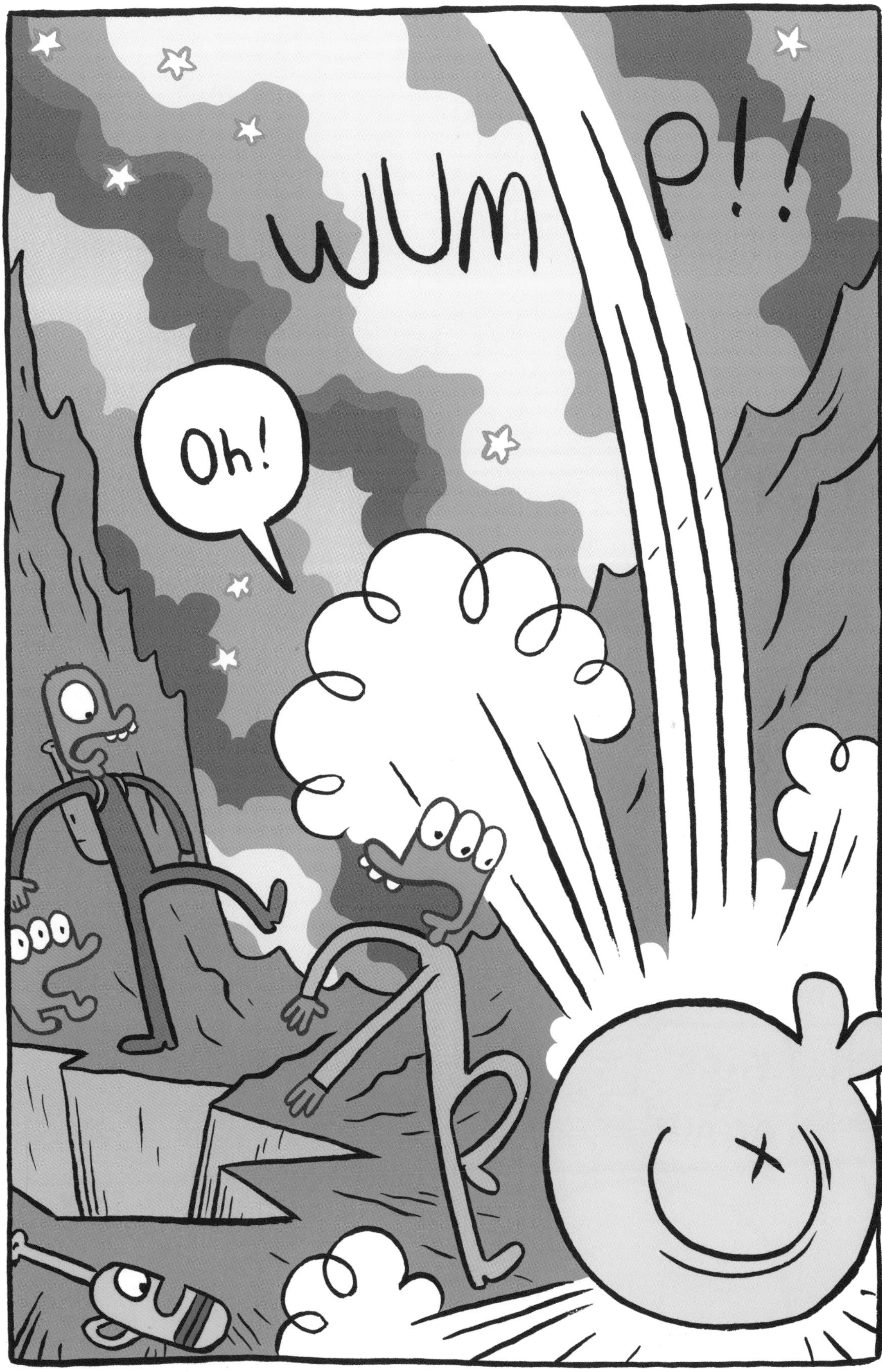
WUMP!!
Oh!

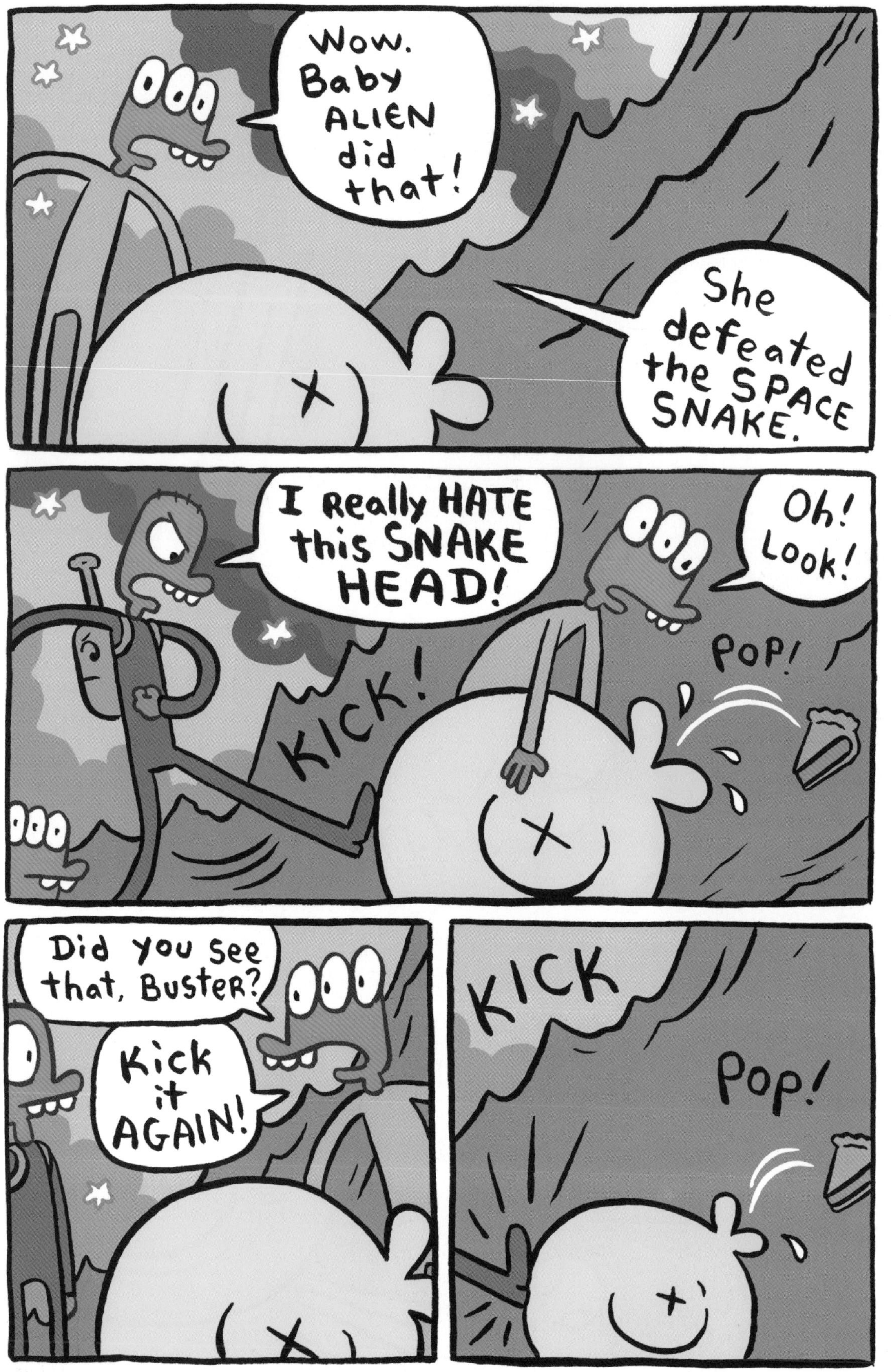
Wow. Baby ALIEN did that!
She defeated the SPACE SNAKE.
I Really HATE this SNAKE HEAD!
Oh! Look!
KICK!
POP!
Did you see that, Buster?
Kick it AGAIN!
KICK
Pop!

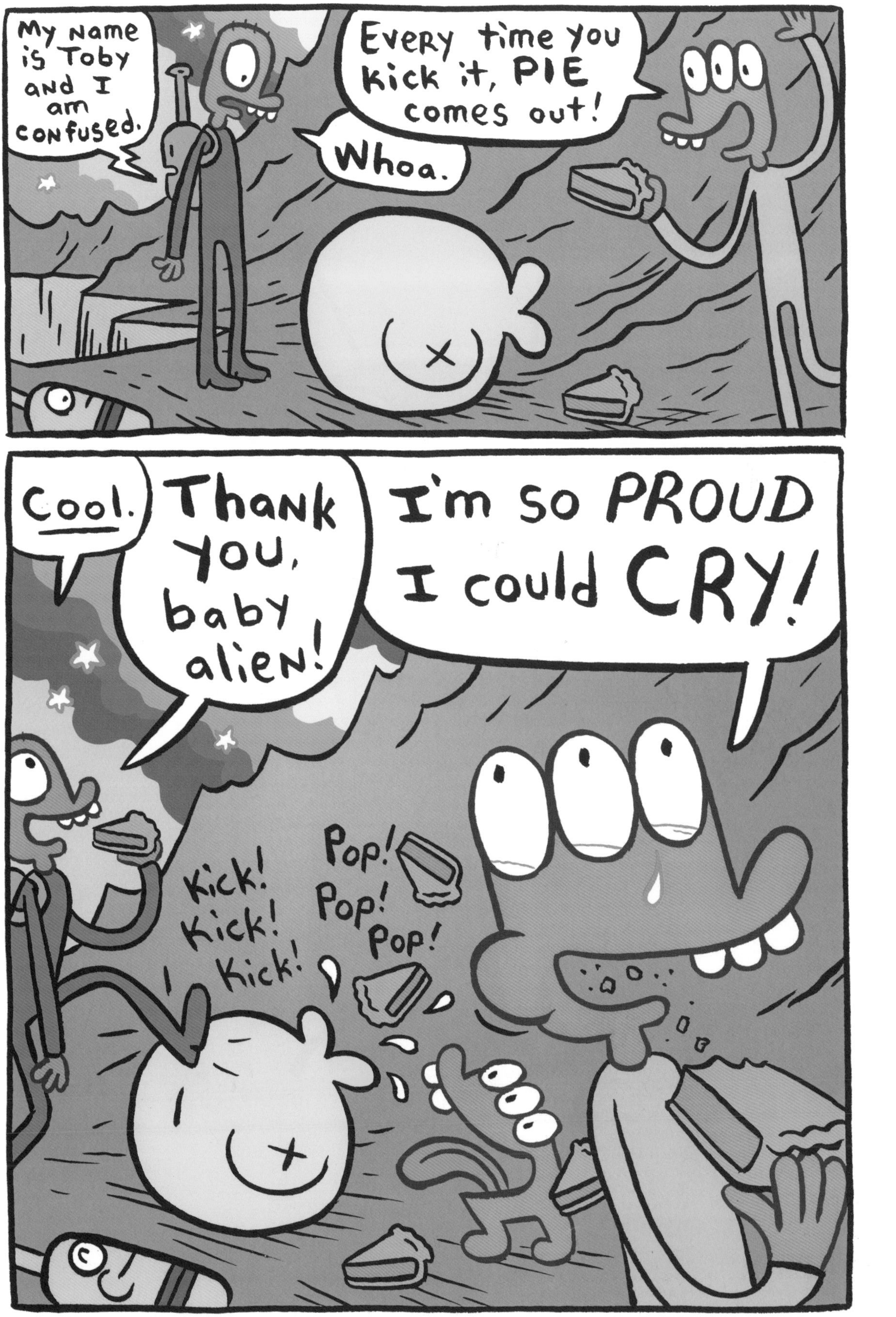
My name is Toby and I am confused.
Every time you kick it, PIE comes out!
Whoa.
Cool.
Thank you, baby alien!
I'm so PROUD I could CRY!
Kick! Kick! Kick!
Pop! Pop! Pop!

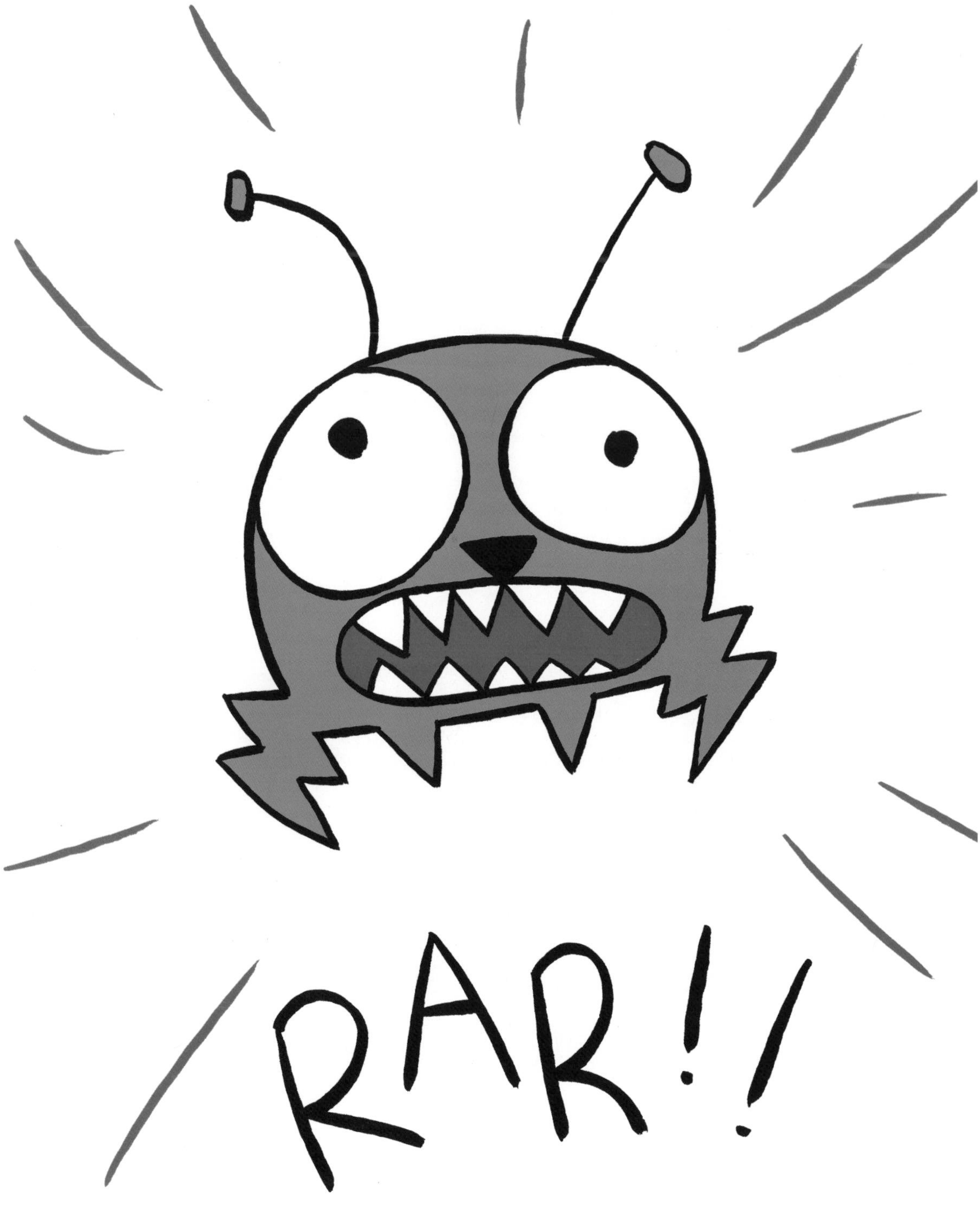
RAR!!

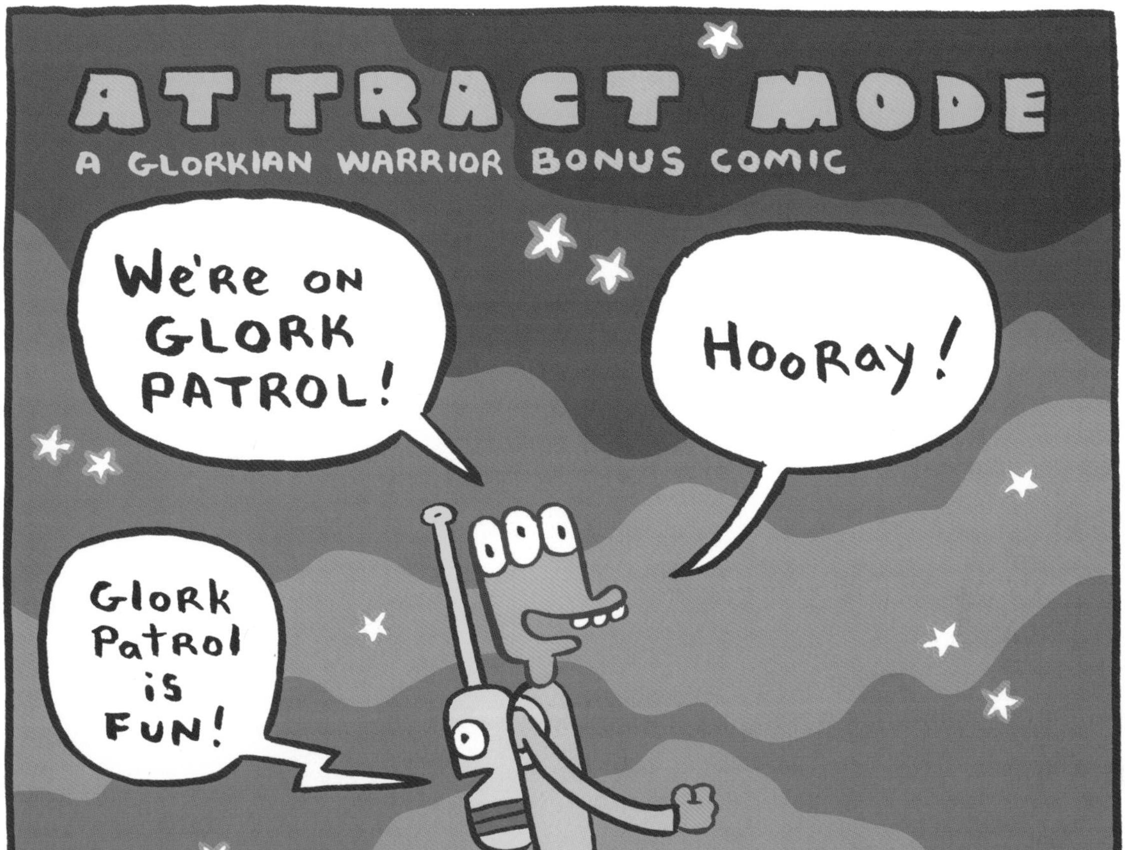
ATTRACT MODE
A GLORKIAN WARRIOR BONUS COMIC
We're on GLORK PATROL!
HooRay!
Glork Patrol is FUN!

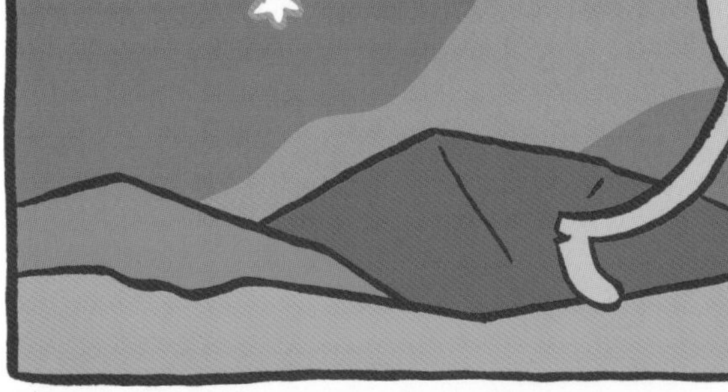
bloop

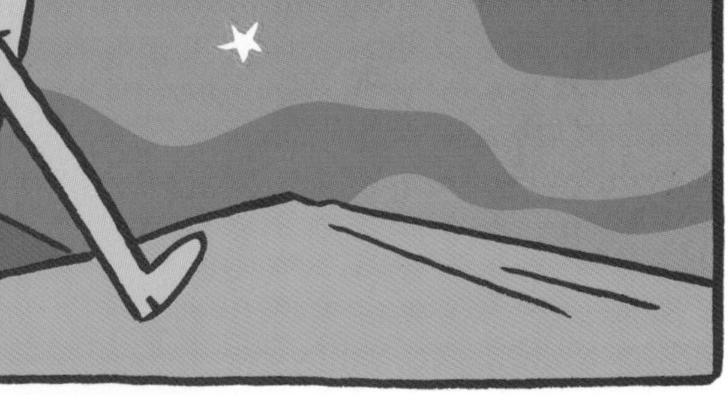
Hey! What the bloop was that!?!

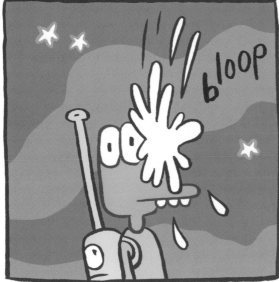

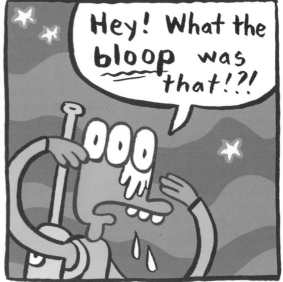

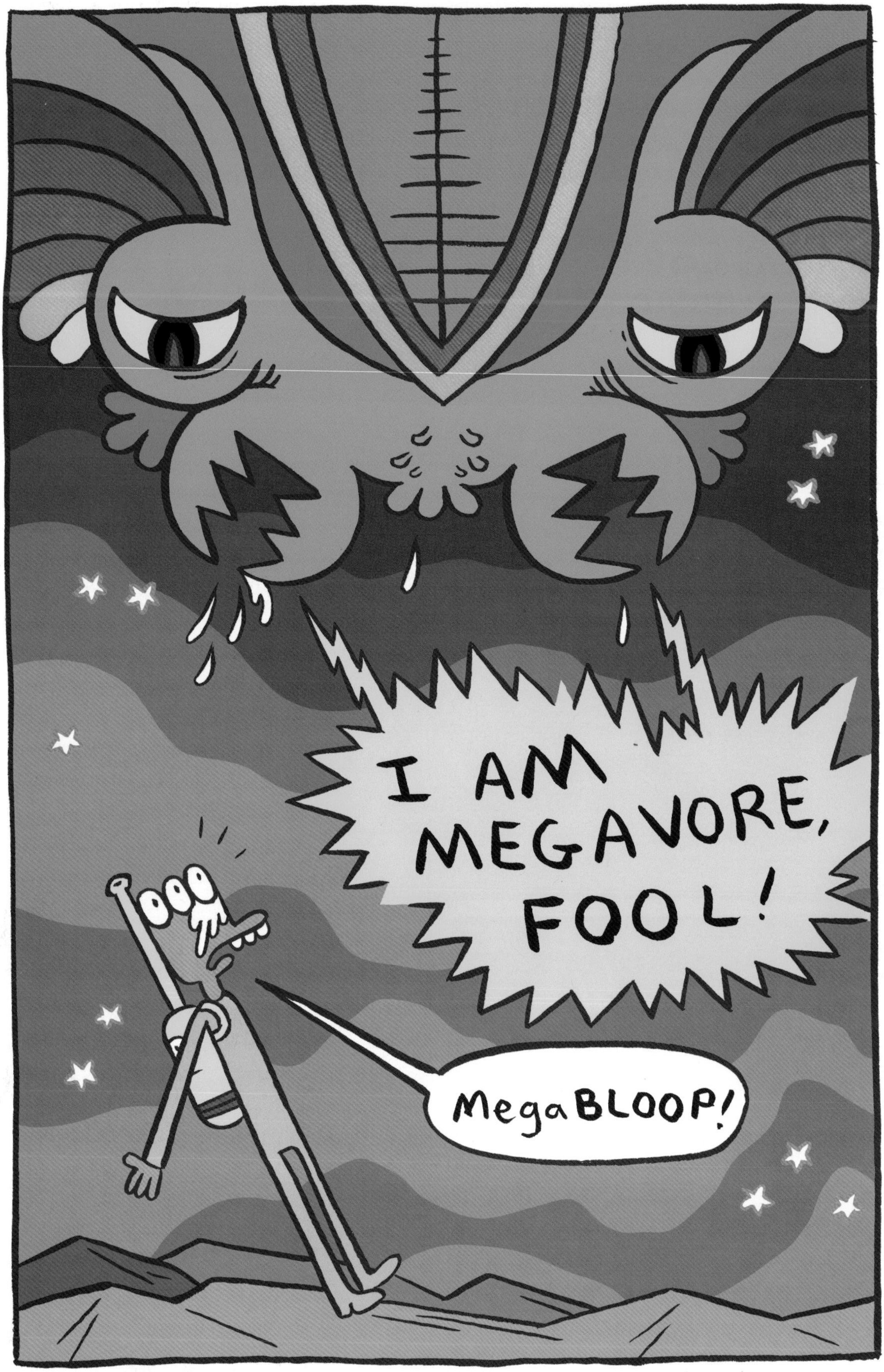
I AM MEGAVORE, FOOL!
MegaBLOOP!

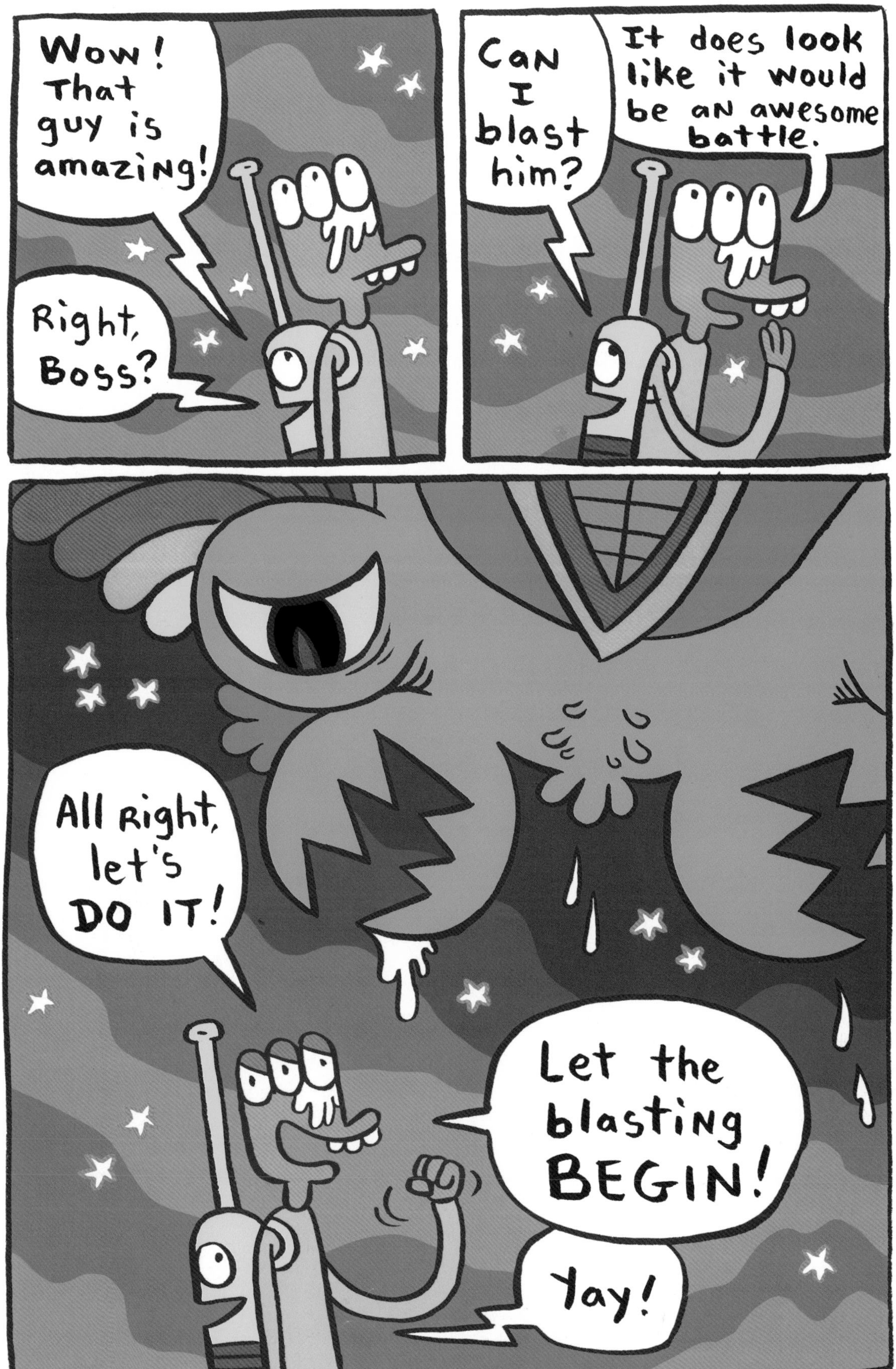

Wow! That guy is amazing!
Right, Boss?
Can I blast him?
It does look like it would be an awesome battle.
All right, let's DO IT!
Let the blasting BEGIN!
Yay!

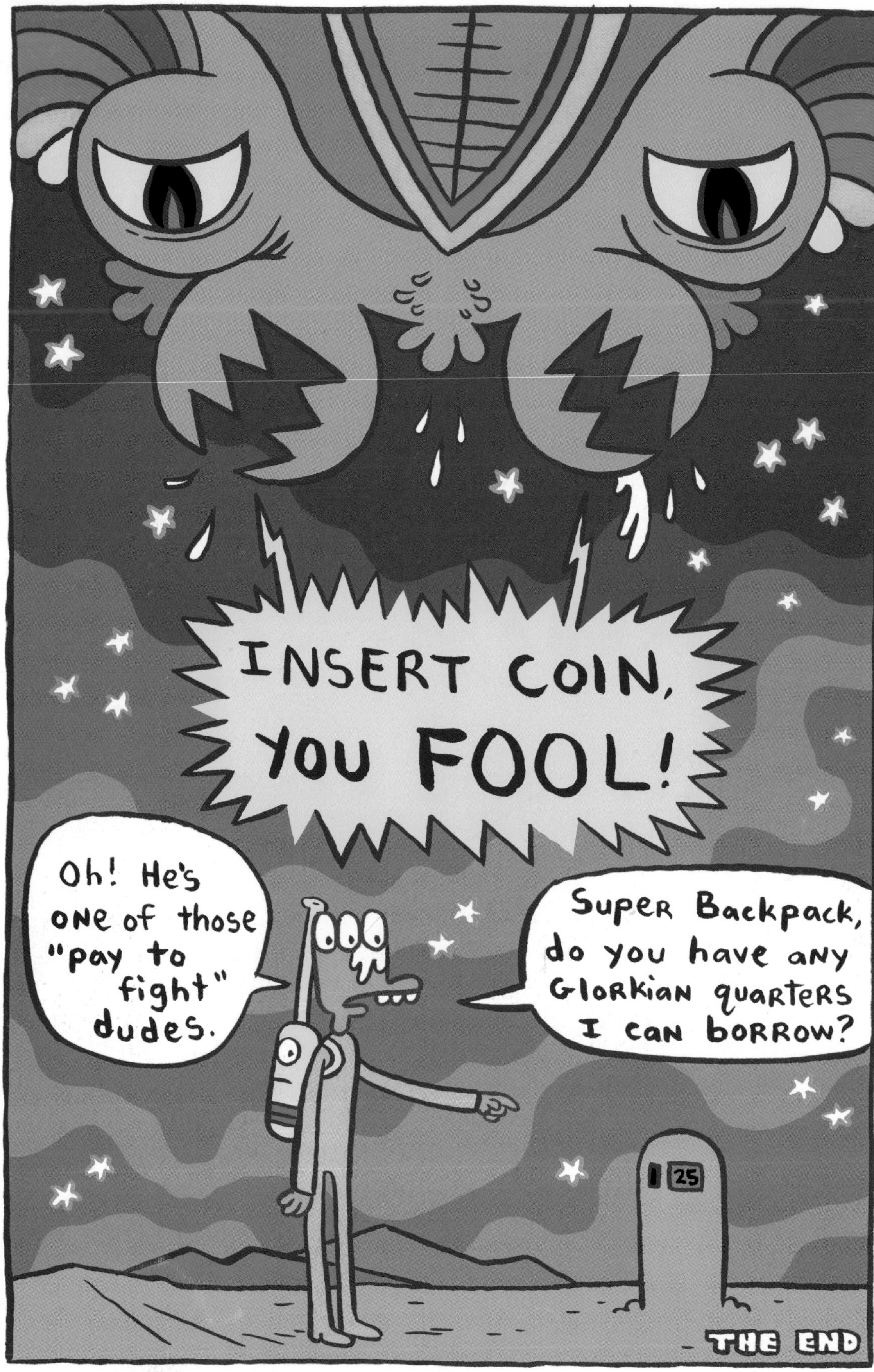
INSERT COIN, YOU FOOL!
Oh! He's one of those "pay to fight" dudes.
Super Backpack, do you have any Glorkian quarters I can borrow?
25
THE END

AN AMAZING WATER STAIN THAT LOOKS EXACTLY LIKE THE REAL GLORKIAN WARRIOR, SORT OF.

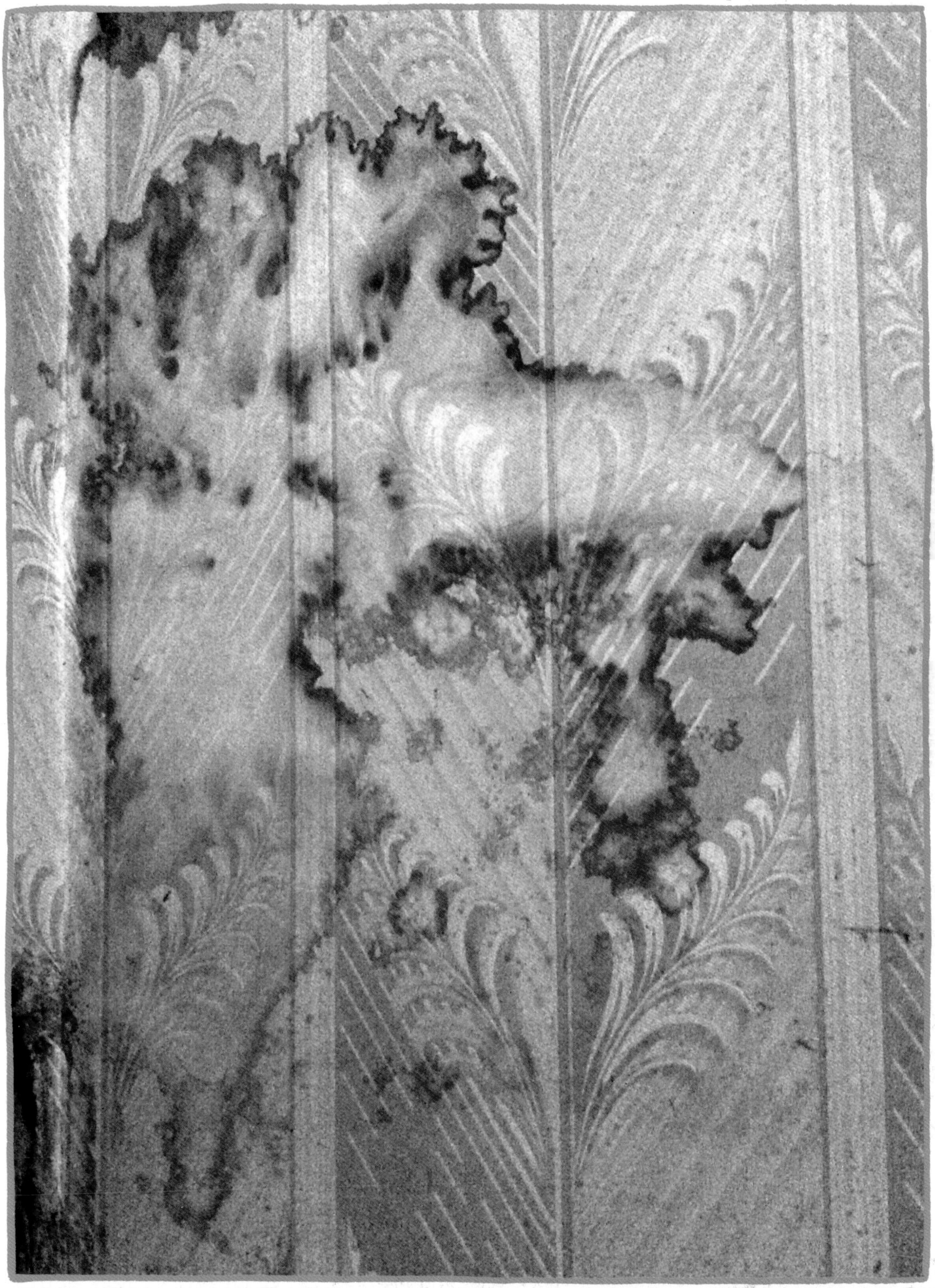

SEE THE EYES? SEE THE TEETH? ISN'T IT AMAZING?! THIS IMAGE MIRACULOUSLY APPEARED ON THE WALLPAPER IN THE HOME OF THE AUTHOR'S MOTHER.

THE AUTHOR:

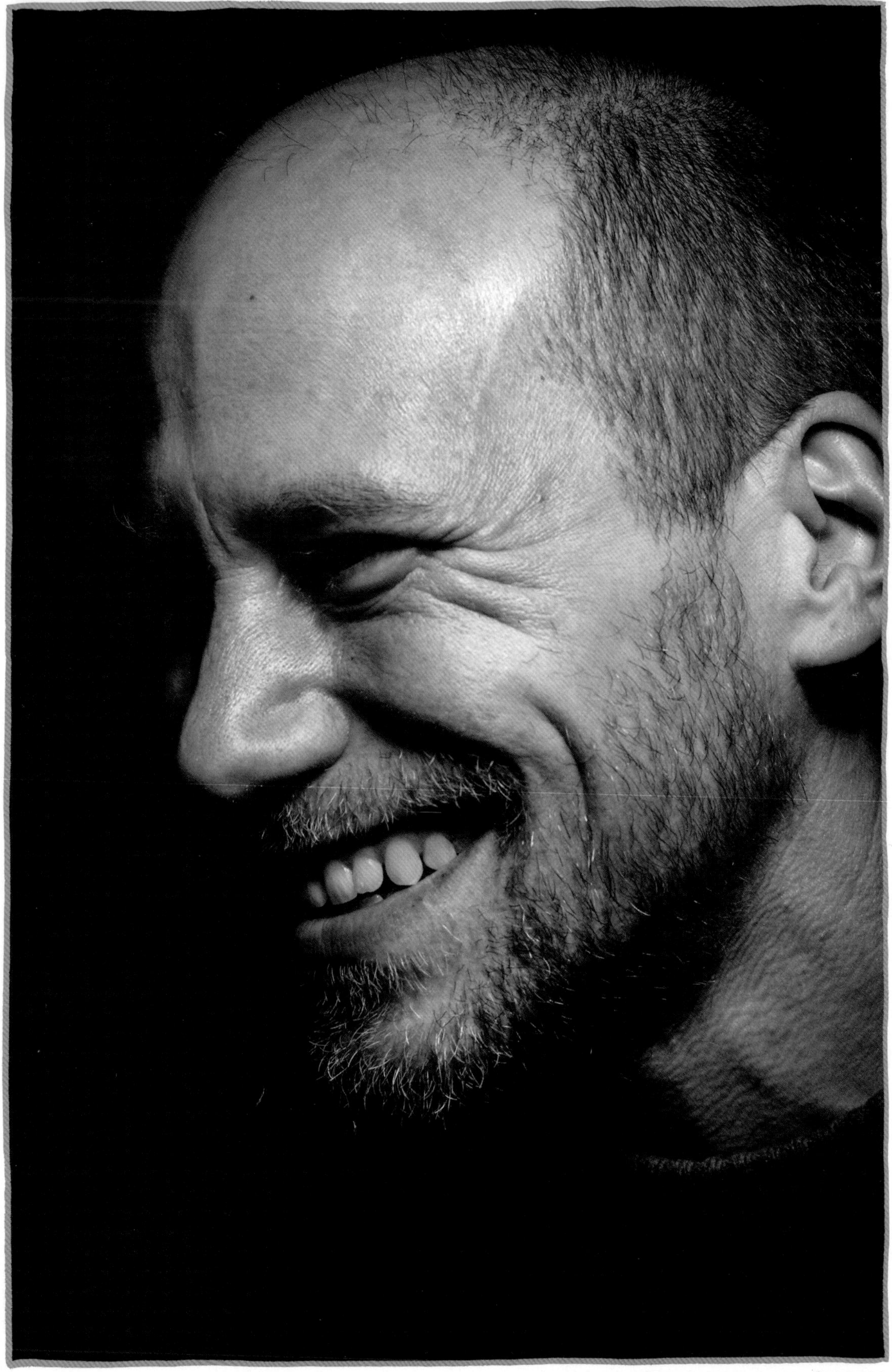

PHOTO BY SAM SIMON